A WARRIOR'S WORD

I drained my wine, staring at her. "What do you ask of me?"

"That you guard Ellyn. That you take her away and see her safe until her day comes. That you be her champion and her guardian, for Chaldor's sake. Hide her in the Highlands—wherever—and see her safe until she gains her power. She'll know what to do then."

"Why me? The gods know, Ellyn has little enough liking for me."

"Or you for her, eh?" Ryadne essayed a wan smile. "But you were Andur's choice, and mine, for we trust none so much as you. Shall you accept, Gailard?"

I felt fate settle on me then, heavier than any armor, heavier than any sword's blow. I felt wary and reluctant, but I could not say her nay: I had given Andur my word. I said, "As you command, my lady."

ANGUS WELLS

THE GUARDIAN

BANTAM BOOKS

New York Toronto London Sydney Auckland

THE GUARDIAN
A Bantam Spectra Book / October 1998

SPECTRA and the portrayal of a boxed "s" are trademarks of Bantam Books,
a division of Bantam Doubleday Dell Publishing Group, Inc.

ISBN 0-553-57789-1
Published simultaneously in the United States and Canada

Bantam Books are published by Bantam Books, a division of Bantam
Doubleday Dell Publishing Group, Inc. Its trademark, consisting of the
words "Bantam Books" and the portrayal of a rooster, is Registered in US
Patent and Trademark Office and in other countries. Marca Registrada.
Bantam Books, 1540 Broadway, New York, New York 10036.

PRINTED IN THE UNITED STATES OF AMERICA
OPM   10   9   8   7   6   5   4   3   2

For Maggie Mann,
who knows all the reasons why

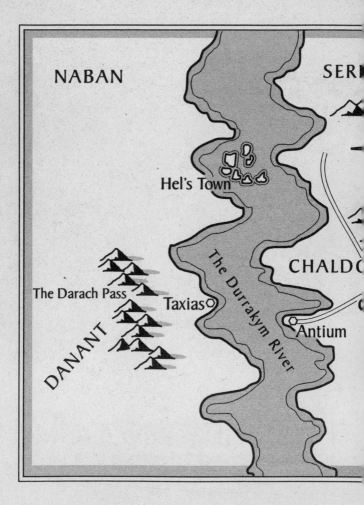

THE STYGE

Shara's Broch

THE BARRENS

(Dur)

THE HIGHLANDS

(Devyn)

Cu-na'Lhair

(Agador)

ym The Geffen Pass

(Arran)

(Quan)

N
W   E
S

═══ The Great Roads

THE BRIGHT KINGDOM

PROLOGUE

My name is Gailard, and I am a soldier. No matter what folk name me now, I consider myself nothing more.

I was born into the Devyn, which is one of the five clans dwelling in the Highlands that border the Bright Kingdom of Chaldor and, be the times and politics right, consider themselves subjects of Chaldor—or not, largely as the mood takes them. Clan folk are of independent mind, and swear their allegiance first to their chieftain, and only after to the king. Or now to the queen . . . But that takes my tale ahead of itself, so:

The Highlands encircle Chaldor's inland boundaries like a stern girdle around the well-fed belly of some fat merchant. Chaldor is rich in farmland, the Highlands bleak and barren—all lonely moors and hills that become mountains as they reach the vastness of the Styge or the bleak coasts of the great southern sea. The living there is hard-won and breeds a hard people, none more so than my father, who was chieftain of the Devyn. And I, had my father had his wish, his successor, save I'd not obey him.

He'd have wed me to Rytha, who was daughter of the Agador's chieftain, and thus blood-bonded our clans that we, together, be greater than any other. But I did not love Rytha, nor much like her, and so I took my sword and my

shield and ran away, which prompted my father to pro-
nounce me outlawed and forbidden to return ever again to
the land of the Devyn. Nor did it much endear me to the
Agador, and most surely not to Rytha. But, for all it pained
me to leave behind the high hills of my youth, I did not then
much care. I was young and headstrong, and I knew that
great adventures lay ahead. So I went west to Chaldor and
found employment in the army of Andur, who was then
king, even though he was no older than I.

There were no few Highlanders in Chaldor's army—
warriors of the Agador and the Quan and the Arran, of the
Dur and my own Devyn—and did the lowlanders name us
mercenaries, and sometimes look down on us as savages,
still we swore our allegiance to the Bright Kingdom and
gave our blood to Andur's cause. And got back the king's respect, and more besides: I learned to read and write in Chaldor; and how to fight in ordered ranks, where thousands
massed on bloody battlefields (though it was always we
Highlanders who led the charge); and how to conduct myself in the chambers of the civilized folk of Chorym, which
was the king's city; and how to use a knife and fork, and
suchlike niceties.

I rose through the ranks of Andur's army until I found
myself commander of five hundred and known to the king.
Indeed, I pride myself that we became friends, and I sat
sometimes at Andur's right hand, and joined him on the
practice ground with wooden swords, and drank with him in
taverns. I spoke with his wife, Ryadne, who was, like me,
from the Highlands, albeit of the Dur, for whom we Devyn
bore little love. Indeed, we'd a saying: "Proud as a Dur," for
they boast themselves magicians (though of nowhere near
so much power as the Vachyn) and claim small sorceries,
which we Devyn eschew. But I liked Ryadne. She was very
lovely and, I thought, honest, and surely Andur loved her
more than anyone save, perhaps, his daughter, Ellyn.

Now Ellyn—who is so large a part of this tale—was different as trout to salmon. She was but a child then, promis-

ing her mother's beauty but none of her mother's wisdom or calm. Perhaps I am unfair—she was, after all, only a girl—but she seemed to me arrogant and willful, selfish in her desires and petulant of temper. I did not like her, but she was the apple of her father's eye, and so I tolerated her displays of childish anger and avoided her as I could.

He was a great king, Andur, and wise beyond his years, and had he lived, I think this world of ours should have known peace sooner. But peace is often hard-wrought, and won only with shed blood, and Andur was not granted the time to see all his dreams made real. Even so, it was he began the construction of the Great Roads that now link the Highlands to the low, and spread compass-pointed across the kingdom. He forged alliances with the clans and brought peace to the kingdom, so that Chaldor shone like some bright jewel, and all enjoyed its bounty. It was a different world then, and unlike Andur I could not see it in its entirety. I lacked his vision, but I loved him fiercer than any brother born of blood—surely far better than my own brother, whose name was Eryk.

It was Andur first told me of the Vachyn sorcerers, of the threat he perceived in their machinations, and I hated them then for his loathing of their wiles. Now I hate them for what they are, and what they'd do, and they are proscribed in Chaldor.

I met them first in Danant, embodied in the form of Nestor, who was, for want of a better title, *counselor* to Danant's ruler, Talan Kedassian, though I and others who thought as I did, believed that Talan had sold his soul to the Vachyn.

Danant stood across the Durrakym from Chaldor, and for long years had vied for the lucrative river trade. Andur was content to take his share and no more; and did the Great Roads afford the kingdom better trade, then even so they were built to benefit all the populace, not to swell the king's coffers. Talan, on the other hand, was greedy and looked to own it all, to which end he emptied his coffers that he might employ a Vachyn sorcerer, and thus bought Nestor's loyalty—if the Vachyn have loyalty to any save their own dark ends—and began the war.

Pirate boats came first, swift river raiders that preyed on Chaldor's craft, and falsely vaunted Chaldor's flag as they assaulted the vessels of Naban and Serian so that both those kingdoms sent embassies of protest to Chorym, which was Andur's capital. Andur explained as best he might, but trade was lost to Danant, where Talan avowed his innocence and Nestor wove his dark magicks that the ambassadors went away convinced of Chaldor's guilt, and the Chaldor ports stood empty of commerce, so that Andur must sustain them from inland. Messages of protest were sent to Danant, and ambassadors, and the messages were ignored and the ambassadors insulted and sent home answerless, so that Chaldor stood alone, and open to Nestor's next fell move.

Direct attacks began, the river raiders assaulting the Chaldor shore, burning villages and towns, slaughtering folk and animals, venturing inland to destroy crops and vineyards. It was, Andur told me, as bad as the ancient days when the Sea Kings came upriver to pillage and rape. It was more than Andur could bear, and he determined to teach Talan the error of his ways. He did not seek war, but all the avenues of peace were explored and found empty of hope, and so Andur must make a terrible decision.

We formed a great army then, and called up all our rivercraft and sailed across the Durrakym to invade Danant.

Which was, had we only known it, exactly what Nestor had planned. We fell neatly and all willing into his trap, and there begins my story.

CHAPTER ONE

Our shield wall broke under the magefire of the Vachyn sorcerer. It was a clear, bright day, the sky a cloudless blue—a day better suited to lounging beneath the shade of the olive trees, conversation oiled with wine, than to bloody battle—and I remember that swallows darted overhead and that my hauberk stank of sweat. Beads of perspiration ran down my face into my eyes, but still I saw the bolts strike from out of that pristine sky: silent lightning that set shields to glowing as if touched by furnace heat, spearheads flaring like lofted torches. I remember the awful dread that filled us, like those sour dreams that sometimes come in the slow, dark hours of the night, all nebulous and filled with guilts and unnamed terrors. Men shouted in alarm, or wept, and shed their weapons in panic, crying out that they held snakes and lizards and suchlike, or screamed that they were burned and flung away their weapons to slap at invisible flames. I fought to hold my own ebbing confidence and shouted that my men hold their place, for all I heard my father's voice condemning me, and saw his accusing face in the magefire that danced about my sword and shield. Tears joined the sweat on my face then, and I wanted nothing more than to turn and run. But I ground my teeth and told myself this was no more than hedge-wizardry, all illusion, though that did little to help.

Then Talan sent in his chariots and his cavalry to break our line.

That was, I believe, the precise moment in time that we lost the war. We were flung back in disarray, the battle no longer the shifting of disciplined forces but a thing of individual combats, of simple survival.

The heavy chariots struck through our line, javelins and arrows flying. The cavalry slashed at us with their curved horse-swords, and then the hoplites came with spears and axes and blades. All was confusion then, and I could not rally my men; only shout curses that they did not stand and fight, but ran in terror. I saw the beginning of Chaldor's demise then, there on the plain before the Darach Pass.

I limped away from that bloody field leaning on a spear. I bore other wounds, but the worst was where a Danant halberdier had swung his blade against my knee and laid me low. I'd have died had a man whose name I did not know not flung himself screaming against the point and granted me the chance to put my sword into the halberdier's belly. That gave me some small satisfaction, but when I clambered to my feet and saw the carnage all around, I knew the day was lost, and our best—our only—hope was retreat. I picked up the fallen halberd and used it for a staff as I sought Andur's gonfalon.

That brave pennant stood where the fighting was thickest, and I saw my chosen king at the brunt. What few were left of the Royal Guard fought with him, but they were hard-pressed, and Talan concentrated his forces there. I began to limp toward him even as the horns belled retreat.

It was hard going, that, back across the plain with Danant's chariots harrying our flanks and the bowmen sending shafts like rain from out of a sky that now faded into dusk. I barely noticed that the magefire had ceased, but I saw that the swallows were replaced with bats, and that flights of carrion birds forgot their homeward journey and settled instead upon the surrounding trees, anticipatory.

The sun went down behind the Darach Pass, shining briefly off the polished armor massed there, and the moon rose dispassionate. Stars twinkled, distinct as the cries of the wounded and the dying. I heard dogs howl, not so loud as the men, and for a little while the battle ceased.

Horns sounded on both sides, Talan's army regrouping, massing for the attack that would surely come at dawn and sweep us away—save we march clear and find the Durrakym; our own summoning Chaldor's bloodily depleted force to Andur.

I found what few were left of my men and went to my king. Fires were lit, and by their light I guessed our army was lessened by perhaps half its number. It was a sorry defeat, and I ordered the remnant of my five hundred to eat and rest as I sought Andur.

He sat beside a guttering fire that threw stark shadows across his dented armor. A bandage sat stained about his head, and he drew a whetstone down the blade of his great sword. He looked up as I approached.

"Greetings, Gailard. You're hurt?" There was concern in his voice and in his eyes, which was characteristic of that brave man.

I shrugged and said, "A trifle."

He beckoned me closer, indicating that I sit, and I slid down my borrowed spear as he waved for an attendant to bring us food and drink.

"How many of your Highlanders survive?"

"Perhaps a hundred hale," I said. "As many again hurt."

"Ah, yes." Andur sighed. "You took the brunt, you Highlanders."

I said, "Were it not for the Vachyn sorcerer, we'd have fared better. But . . ."

"I know." Andur took the flask the attendant brought and filled our cups himself. "Should I have hired a Vachyn?"

"No!" I cried. "There's no honor in such stratagems."

"But victories are there," Andur said, his tone dour. "The gods know, Talan's won this day—and likely tomorrow."

"We can rally," I argued, forgetting all my convictions that the war was lost. "A night's rest . . . We can fight again tomorrow."

Andur drank. At his feet a platter of bread and cold meat went unnoticed as my own. "Tomorrow," he said, "those magicks shall come against us again, and all Talan's army with them. They outnumbered us from the start, but now they overwhelm us by—what?—perhaps five times our number. We cannot fight them, my friend—we can only run from them."

The megrims of the Vachyn were gone now and I felt my blood course hot. It was not the way of us Highlanders to run, but to charge into battle no matter the odds. I said as much.

And Andur gave me back, "You can barely walk, Gailard. How can you attack?"

"The gods shall aid me," I said. "And a healer can tend me tonight."

"We've not so many healers left alive," Andur said, "and I think the gods have forsaken us this day. I'd not see more slaughter than I must. So—no, what we shall do is this."

He set out his plan. I argued, but he motioned me to silence. He was my king and so I listened, for all I liked it not at all.

"If not tonight," he said, "then come the sun's rising the magicks and the fighting shall again commence. We've too many hurt, and too long a journey to the river. Should Talan and his god-cursed Vachyn slay us all on this plain, then Chaldor's scant defense must surely fall. Talan shall come unopposed across the Durrakym and march on Chorym . . ."

The drink he'd poured me was strong and likely fueled my anger at our defeat. Surely it fueled my words: "Chorym's strong enough to withstand siege. Let Talan come against those walls and find his comeuppance there."

"Oh, Gailard," Andur said, "had I only your plain courage I'd have fewer problems to consider."

I felt for a moment insulted, but on his face I saw grave concerns, and so I held my tongue and waited for him to speak again. And when he did I could only listen, confused and somewhat frightened by his words.

"Does Talan cross the river—which he likely shall— then he'll march direct to Chorym. He'll siege the city with more than catapults and towers and miners; he'll have the Vachyn sorcerer send magicks against the walls. And does Chorym fall, then Chaldor's lost her heart. And what, meanwhile, of the countryside? Think you Talan shall leave the little towns and villages alone? No! He'll impose his rule over all—and how shall Ryadne accept that?"

I shook my head. I had learned somewhat of politics during my sojourn in Chaldor, but I still saw war as an affair of swords and shields, of honor, of courage and individual bravery. I suppose I was old-fashioned; I suppose I should have learned better from that day's events.

"She could not," Andur said, "and so should have no choice but to submit."

I frowned. I could not imagine Ryadne submitting to Talan.

Andur laughed, all mournful. "I'll tell you what Talan will do," he said. "He'll cross the Durrakym and march on Chorym. He'll siege the city and lay waste the land. He'll offer to take Ryadne in marriage—end the war and unite Chaldor and Danant as one kingdom."

"She'd not accept," I said. "Never! And what of you?"

He said, "There must be a rear guard to cover this retreat, and I shall lead it. So . . ."

I interrupted him, king or not. "No! Give me the rear guard."

He set a hand on my knee and squeezed. It was a gentle touch, but still I jerked and ground my teeth at the pain.

"I'd not insult you, Gailard, but you cannot stand

unaided, so how can you lead a rear guard? No, I shall do that, and you shall—are you willing—hold a greater duty."

I could not imagine a greater duty. I looked past our fires to where those of the Danant army glowed like scattered embers across the mouth of the Darach Pass. I remember that the night was hot and still, the sky all filled with careless stars and that indifferent moon, heavy with the scent of olives and smoke. I thought that I had believed I'd not see another day, and then believed I must likely die the next. That I accepted: I was a soldier, and it was my chosen duty to die on my king's command.

I said, "What greater duty?"

"I'd see the hurt go safe across the river," Andur answered me, "and find what safety they can in Chorym—or wherever else they choose to go. I'd see you take them across, and then leave them . . ."

"Leave them?" I could scarce comprehend that I was assigned to ferrying wounded men over the Durrakym, let alone leave them there. I was suddenly aware that the night was filled up with more creakings and squealings than wounded men make. I looked about and saw wagons moving, and heard the snickering of horses and mules, and the cries of the wagoneers. I looked at Andur and realized that he had this all planned.

"Listen, eh?" He filled our cups again; I wondered if I grew drunk. "I'll hold Talan's army as long as I can—to give you time to get the hurt away. There are wagons . . ."

I said, bitterly, "I see that."

He said, "The gods know, Gailard, that if you were not hurt I'd keep you with me. I know I could ask for no braver man—but you *are* hurt, and so you'll take the wounded back over the river. The gods willing our boats shall still be there, and I shall buy you enough time. Which is the easy part of what I'd ask."

I gasped, for that seemed the harder part. I said, "And defend Antium?" Antium was the port of our departure. It was our mightiest port, and one of the Great Roads ran from there directly to Chorym. Should Talan take possession of Antium, he'd have a direct path to the heart of Chaldor.

"No." Andur shook his head. "Leave Antium. May the gods forgive me, but I'd ask that you take the hurt to Chorym without delay. Go to the city and speak with Ryadne. Listen to her, eh? Heed what she says, and obey her as you would me."

That was a hard thing to ask of me. I respected his queen, but still she was of the Dur, and I sensed some element of magic in this. And the gods knew, I'd had enough of magic these days. I asked why.

Andur glanced at the sky, at the fires of the Danant army, as if he feared invisible ears. "I'd not say it plain here," he said, and reached out to clasp my hand. "Ryadne shall explain it as I cannot, but it's to do with Ellyn."

"Ellyn?" At mention of that unpleasant child I reared back, almost breaking Andur's grip, but he held my hand tight.

"Only see her safe, eh?" He took my other hand and stared fervently into my eyes. "I'd put her life into your keeping, Gailard. Be her guardian, for my sake and Chaldor's. For the world's!"

I stared at him and said, "What do you mean?"

He looked about, his gaze shifting to the fires that burned around the pass, where Talan camped with his Vachyn sorcerer, and answered, "I'd not tell you here, where magical ears might hear. Only go directly to Chorym, and Ryadne shall explain."

It was a long night, all filled up with the cursing and whimpering of hurt men as we struggled eastward to the river. Mounted archers attacked us from both sides, and wounded as we were, we could put up only a poor defense. More fell along that sorry road, and we with no time to honor them, so that we must leave them where they fell and mutter our prayers as we continued along our grim way. I voiced a plea to the gods that Andur survive and find us at the riverside, but if the gods heard me they did not acknowledge my entreaty, for I heard later that Andur fell as the sun rose on the second day and Talan ordered his full force in pursuit.

Even so, that rear guard bought us the time we needed to reach the river. I saw it a little after noonday, shining bright and broad under the hot sun, our boats tossing on the current. The few men we had left with the vessels raised a shout as we approached, then fell silent as they saw how few we were, and how badly hurt. The commander—a younger man than I, whose name was Kerid—approached me and asked how the battle went. I heard trepidation in his voice that got no better as I told him.

"Lost," I said. "Our king fights a rearguard action, and we must get these men across the river."

"What of Andur and the rest?" Kerid demanded. "Shall we abandon them?"

"No," I said. "Only get these hurt folk across, and leave two boats for the others."

"Two?" Kerid's eyes grew wide. "Only two?"

"That shall be enough."

Kerid nodded, realization settling grim upon his face, and shouted orders that gangplanks be placed and our retreating army be seen safe aboard.

"I shall stay," he declared, "until Andur comes. Or Talan forces me to sail."

I decided I liked him. I said, "And I with you."

He ducked his head and left me on the dockside as he saw to the embarkation. I found a bollard and settled on it like some ancient bird weary of flying. My knee hurt abominably, as if a fire were lit under the cap to send flames coursing up my thigh and down the bones of my leg. I thought to strip off my breeks and examine the wound, then thought better of it. The other cuts I'd taken did not hurt so much, but still flies gathered about me so that I grew irritable of their interest and swatted them away. I slew fewer than I had of the Danant men.

In a while the boats took off the wounded, all save a hundred I held back to defend the exodus. It was by then dusk. We ate what little food we had left, and drained our waterskins and wine flasks. We waited as the moon rose over the river and stars filled up the wide sky. Then men began to straggle in—the sad remnants of our infantry first, followed by what was left of our cavalry, all telling the same tale.

We were beaten and Andur was slain, his head mounted on Talan's chariot; the Danant army came close behind. I questioned sufficient men that I could no longer cling to any remnant of hope. Their eyes were dull and their voices bereft of optimism. They wanted only to go home, to escape. I consulted with Kerid and we saw the last stragglers on board, loosed the mooring lines, and turned the prows of the two boats east.

It was some small time after midnight then, and as we quit the anchorage Talan's advance guard came up. I must admit that I enjoyed a certain vengeful satisfaction as I watched them halt on the farside of the conflagration I'd ordered.

The town was called Taxias, and it burned well, guarding our backs from Talan's men. I did not then feel any pity for the inhabitants whose homes and livelihoods I'd torched. Indeed, had I been able, I'd have danced as I watched the place burn. Whatever pity I felt came later; then, I only laughed and clapped Kerid on the shoulder, telling him we paid them back in some small measure for the slaying of our noble king.

"Perhaps," he said, his face somber. "But shall they not do the same when they cross the river after us?"

I opened my mouth to tell him that we'd meet them on the bank and throw them back, but then I remembered the geas Andur had laid on me, and that I must leave Antium to its own defense as I went on to Chorym. I bit back my hearty words and frowned. Kerid seemed a brave man and I

wondered what he'd make of me, did he know I must run for
Chorym's walls to seek Ryadne's advice. Or did I go to take
her orders? I did not know; nor could until I spoke with her.

Kerid waited on my reply, then ducked as the night split
apart in a thunderous explosion of brilliant light. It was as if
some great torch were lit—so hot it rent the world, so bright
it dimmed the moon and stars, sparks tumbling from the ef-
fulgence to sizzle on the water and scorch our rigging.

Kerid shouted, "Magefire!" and I knew that Talan had
come with his Vachyn sorcerer, and stood beyond burning
Taxias to fling dread power against us. I thought also—and
congratulated myself on it—that had I not set the town afire,
the sorcerer should easier find us and destroy us. But as it
was he could not properly see us—only fling his magicks
blindly through the blaze.

Even so, it was a perilous crossing, and Kerid must set
men to hauling buckets from the river to douse the fires that
started. I could only curse and pray that we reach the farther
bank unscathed. I saw the second boat hit by that weirdling
fire, and it was as if vast fingers of white flame reached
down from the heavens to condemn the vessel, light coursing over masts and deck, running swift and oily over the rigging, so that for horribly long moments the craft was lit
stark, outlined against the river and the night. Then it
burned, as does a ball of dust tossed into a fire: in the instant
of a heartbeat. The vessel was there and lit, and then gone—
and across the Durrakym drifted a cloud of ash that stank of
burning. I heard men scream then, and saw lesser fires dot
the river. None lasted long, but sank, which was likely a
merciful release. I wondered why such powerful magic had
not been used before; perhaps Talan had forbidden it, that he
might claim a military victory, or there were limitations on
the Vachyn's power that I did not understand.

I knew fear then, for I am no riverman and feel no great
love for water, save to slake my thirst or cleanse my body. I
am, at best, a poor swimmer, and hurt as I was, and dressed
in full battle armor, I should surely sink and drown. I

thought then to strip off my armor, then thought better of that, too. How should it look, did I land on Chaldor's shore armorless? I'd not have men name me a coward. So I gritted my teeth and clutched a rope that I not fall down with the ship's rolling, and watched the sky light up. I heard men shouting in terror and limped to the inner rail, from whence I shouted down that they remain calm and that our captain should see us safe ashore. I put into my voice a conviction I did not feel, and when I returned to Kerid's side he grinned at me, though his expression held scant humor.

"Brave words," he said. "The gods grant I live up to them."

"Can you?" I asked, as another thunderclap divided the troubled night and fire roiled above our stern.

He spat to what I think is called leeward and shrugged. "I've no more wish to pay Ardan my coin than you, my friend; I'll do my best."

I nodded and asked, "Shall they pursue us across the river?"

"No doubt in time," he answered, "but not soon." Then he chuckled with genuine amusement. "We think alike. Before you ordered the town burned, I took it upon myself to see their boats torched. So Talan must find himself some more vessels before he can raise a fleet to chase us or bring his army over."

"How long?" I asked.

He shrugged. "Six or seven days, I'd guess. Is Talan's army large as you say, then he shall need a great many boats. I'd reckon a seven day at worst, two at most."

"What chance of halting them on the water?"

"Little chance," Kerid said dourly. "Talan built a pirate fleet, and we've too few such craft to compete with those."

I frowned, not understanding this nautical talk.

"River war is not so different from land war," Kerid explained. "There's light and heavy—like cavalry and infantry. Talan shall need big, heavy boats to transport his troops, and they must be protected—just as you'd use cavalry to protect your infantry. The pirate craft will protect the transports, and we've too few to oppose them." He sighed and added, "Andur never saw fit to commission such a fleet."

I asked why he could not use this craft we sailed on, and he told me, "This is a merchantman, my friend. She's fit to haul cargo or men, but as a warboat she's too cumbersome."

My frown grew darker. "We cannot halt them?"

Kerid barked a sour laugh. "Not now; nor ever easily. But we can try, and I shall! Listen—do you only organize the landward army, I'll do what I can on the river. And the gods be with us both."

He caught my eyes and I saw that he was fervent in his conviction. I felt no doubt but that he would fight Talan as best he could, even to his death. And then a terrible guilt that I might not be able to satisfy the promise he sought, for Andur had set that geas on me and I must journey on. I did not know what Ryadne might ask of me, only that I could not renege on that. I wondered if I lost my honor as I took Kerid's hand and said, "I shall do all I can."

"And I." He smiled. "Between us, Gailard, we'll defeat Talan."

"The gods willing," I agreed, feeling like a traitor.

We found harbor as the sun topped the horizon. The sky was very bright, as if the gods scoured away the clouds that they might better observe our maneuvers. Gulls mewed at our arrival, and all along the wharves I saw the glitter of light on armor, shields, and spearheads. There seemed not a single empty space, but all filled up with waiting men.

Kerid said, "I'll see you safe ashore, then take my boat away. What I can do to halt Talan, I shall. You'll hold Antium?"

"He'll not enter easily," I dissembled.

I fumbled my way down the narrow ladder to the deck and limped to the outflung gangplank. A sailor helped me down that swaying platform, and when I thanked him said, "The gods be with you. Guard our land, eh?"

I turned to answer him, but he was already gone.

I had hoped to slip away, to pass unnoticed back to Chorym, but as I stepped onto the flags of Antium's dockside, I found all that was left of Chaldor's army facing me. Shields and spears rose in salute, and I looked back at Kerid's boat, thinking that some greater commander had been aboard. But only damaged men came after me, and I realized that this salute was for me alone. I felt my heart sink as it dawned on me that all these men looked to me for orders, whilst I must obey my dead king and leave them.

Then Haldur, whom I knew and had drunk with, stepped forward to innocently augment my guilt.

"The king passed word, my friend; you lead us now. What shall we do?"

I limped to where a wagon stood and rested my weight against its side. River mist coiled thick about the wharf, and the risen sun glittered on it like fire on water. At least the magefire had ceased now, but that likely meant only that Talan gathered his army for invasion. I looked Haldur in the eyes and gathered up my courage.

"Andur commanded me to Chorym, to Ryadne's side."

Haldur hesitated a moment in his reply, then gave me back, "Then go to Chorym, but first order our defense here. The gods know," he gestured at my leg, "but you're sore hurt, and Chorym shall need a strong commander."

I felt a great weight settle on me then, and had some inkling of what Andur must have suffered as he ordered men to their deaths—the terrible weight of trust and loyalty. Almost, I told Haldur to flee, to take his men and all the others and run, but that should have branded me coward. And so I grunted and heaved my paining body atop the wagon. I looked about and saw that our army was not so much now. I thought that only a thousand or so manned Antium's shoreline.

"The hurt are gone," Haldur advised me. "We who remain are all hale." He grinned. "And mostly Highlanders. We can hold them!"

I set a hand upon his shoulder lest I fall down—my knee hurt abominably—and slumped onto the wagon's seat. "Talan's a Vachyn sorcerer in his employ," I said. "You know what the mage did to us. You saw that boat burn?"

Haldur shook his head. "I saw lightning, no more." His grin faded. "What do you say, Gailard?"

My belly rumbled, and my mouth was dry as a soldier's purse. I felt a weariness settle on me, and wished for nothing more than a mug of ale and a soft bed, to sleep and forget all this. I cursed myself and scrubbed hands through my hair, feeling them all ashy from the relicts of the burned boat.

"Andur told me to go to Chorym," I said slowly. "I . . ."

"I know that," Haldur interrupted. "But what of Antium? What of our defense?"

"He told me to leave Antium." I spat; my mouth seemed filled with ashes. "I must go to Ryadne—on Andur's command."

He made a sound that might have been a protest, and I saw confusion in his bloodshot eyes then, and perhaps disapproval. I was very weary, and in more than a little pain, so perhaps I spoke sharper than I should. "I tell you what Andur said to me, Haldur; no more, nor any less. Talan comes against us with many times our number—and a Vachyn sorcerer! And I must go to Ryadne."

"So you'll not command us?"

I shook my head.

Haldur climbed off the wagon and stared up at me. "So you go to Chorym? I'd thought you made of stronger stuff, Gailard. Did those Vachyn magicks invade your soul?"

In other circumstances I'd have challenged him for that. He was, like me, of Devyn blood, and knew what he said. But I had no more stomach for this argument. I wanted only to be gone from his accusing gaze, from the waiting men.

Some amongst them were of my own five hundred. "I have my orders. Now find me a sound horse and put me on it."

He nodded and turned swiftly about, marched briskly away. I sat atop the wagon as he bellowed orders, and saw all those expectant faces turn toward me, and the disbelief there as word spread. I wished then that the sorcerer's magicks had taken me, and came close to cursing Andur for this geas.

Then Haldur brought a horse and I clambered awkwardly from the wagon, aware that none moved to help me mount. I stripped off my battle armor and let it clatter to the cobbles of the wharf. I kept only my sword and shield. I took the reins and could not lift my damaged leg to the stirrup, so that the horse skittered and began to prance nervously.

"Shall you help me?"

It hurt to ask that, but less than the look in Haldur's eyes as he motioned men forward to heave me astride.

I set my buttocks in the saddle and took up the reins. Then said, "I'd not have it this way, Haldur."

"Nor I," he answered. "I'd not thought to see you run away."

"Andur commanded me," I said, and before he could reply, or I voice some lamer excuse, urged the horse forward and rode away from Antium.

CHAPTER TWO

Chorym stood atop a hill that rose like a great dais above the fertile plain. Good farmland, fed by streams and patch-worked like a vast quilt with olive groves and vineyards, fields of wheat and barley, orchards, and green meadows where sheep and goats and cattle grazed. The four Great Roads ran from the city, die-straight to the compass points until they reached the distant horizon where hills soared like misty shadows toward the wide sky. And in all that lovely landscape, Chorym was the jewel: a city of white walls and colored tiles, of ocher roofs, and doors and shutters stained blue and green. A city of gardens and wide avenues lined with trees, a city of stone and wood and fountains, of plazas and taverns and eating houses: a pleasant place to live. But still defensive; about the foot of the hill ran a high, thick wall surmounted by watchtowers, inset with the four huge gates that opened onto the four Great Roads. The commercial districts there—the warehouses and trading posts, stables and barracks—and then higher, another, lesser wall, and more rising up the hill, so that all was concentric circles spinning upward to the citadel.

That was a great limestone edifice, entered by a single gate, and built by Chaldor's first rulers. Its walls were sheer curtains rising to wide ramparts that contained an inner city, the monarch's palace within.

Ellyn walked those ramparts with her mother.

This high, a breeze disturbed the summer's heat, ruffling her long red hair and cooling eyes and cheeks grown hot with weeping. She had anticipated her father's death—Ryadne had scryed it in a recent dream—but to anticipate was not the same as *knowing*, and Ellyn had clung to the forlorn hope that somehow her mother was wrong, that her father would ride back victorious from his war.

Then the messenger had come—the first sad remnant of a broken army, followed by others in no better shape—and all with stories of the war and how badly it had gone. Now there could no longer be any doubt or hope, only miserable knowledge and its denial. Ellyn had wept then, and cursed the gods for their infidelity, and her father for deserting her. And Ryadne had taken her aside, away from solicitous courtiers and servants, and—brutally, in Ellyn's view—advised her daughter that fate's wheel turned as it would, and ground men down, and that Ellyn must be brave and put aside her grief in face of the worse things that would surely come against Chaldor. Ellyn had damned her mother for an uncaring bitch (feeling guilty even as she screamed the imprecations) and demanded to know what could be worse than Andur's death, the defeat of Chaldor's army.

Ryadne had told her: that Talan would come across the Durrakym with his Vachyn sorcerer and all his army and besiege Chorym. That he would likely waste the land, and demand Ryadne's hand in marriage. That he might lay legitimate claim to all the Bright Kingdom.

"And shall you accept?" Ellyn had snarled, angry in her grief, not sure with whom and therefore snapping like a hurt dog. "Shall you take him to your bed and be queen of Chaldor and Danant, both?"

"No," Ryadne had answered. "I shall not. So he will

surround us and have his sorcerer send magicks against us, and eventually Chorym's walls shall fall and we shall be overcome."

Her mother's voice had been so grim, her face so dour, that Ellyn had caught her breath and asked, "What shall you do?"

"Die before I accept Talan."

Ellyn's anger had gone then, like a fog scoured away by a fierce wind, and she had stared aghast at her mother. "What?"

"Better the land survives than I," Ryadne said. "Better that Chorym stands and the Bright Kingdom have hope still."

"What hope?" Ellyn asked. "My father is dead and you speak of dying. What hope then?"

"You," Ryadne answered, and had taken Ellyn's hands, and looked long and hard into her eyes. "You are Chaldor's hope."

"I?" Ellyn could scarce believe the intensity of her mother's gaze, or what Ryadne said. She had felt more afraid then, as if all the gods joined to blight her life. She wanted to run away, to find her bed and huddle beneath the sheets until the world was changed back to what she knew and trusted. Yet she knew she could not do that—only listen to her mother, whose words she did not want to hear.

"Am I dead," Ryadne had told her, "then Talan will seek you for his bride. He'll lay much ceremony on it—speak of healing wounds, of unity. Tell Chaldor that he seeks only peace and your welfare . . ."

"I'll not!" Ellyn had snatched her hands away, horrified. "I'll not, and he couldn't . . ." A horrid consideration. "Could he?"

"Yes." Ryadne had nodded solemnly. "You're fifteen years now. In one more you can be legally wed."

"And do I refuse?" Ellyn had drawn herself up, pain and anger lending her a semblance of regal maturity. "What can he do then?"

She had felt her dignity evaporate as Ryadne said, "Tell the world that he takes you for his ward, to protect you. Then have his god-cursed Vachyn sorcerer bespell you so that you agree to wed him."

"I'll die first," Ellyn declared.

And Ryadne answered, "You cannot; you must not. Chaldor needs you."

"Chaldor needs *you*!" Ellyn wailed, fists balled in protestation of unfair fate. She crossed the chamber to escape her mother's gaze and stared from a window at the rose gardens below. She felt afraid and miserable, and very alone.

"Listen!" From behind her she had heard her mother speak again. Ryadne's voice was soft and firm at the same time. "This is not easy for me. I love you . . ."

"Then flee with me!" Ellyn had turned from the window. "We'll go to the Highlanders, to Grandfather's clan. He'll protect us." She crossed the room to stand before her wan-faced mother.

"I cannot," Ryadne sighed. "I am queen now, and Chorym shall need a figurehead when the Danant army comes. I cannot desert my people."

"But you'd have me quit them!" Ellyn snapped.

"I'd not have us both fall to Talan," Ryadne said grimly. "Chaldor must have some hope, and you are it. None must know you've gone until you are far enough away that you're safe. And to that end, I must stay."

"No!"

"We do what we must," Ryadne said, "and ask the gods that they grant us understanding of the hard choices they offer us."

"You offer me no choice at all," Ellyn said as Ryadne took her hands again and drew her close.

"You must not fall into Talan's clutches," Ryadne explained. "You must go away from Chorym before he comes. Your father and I agreed this before . . ." Her voice faltered and tears sparkled in her eyes. "Before he was slain."

"Which you've scryed?" Ellyn faced her mother. "Your magic's told you this?"

"Somewhat of it." Ryadne nodded. "But my magic is only a little thing—I can sometimes dream and see the future . . ."

"And did you dream my father's death?" Ellyn barked.

"Yes." Ryadne's voice was hollow.

"And still let him go?" Ellyn's voice was filled with accusation. "Let him go to his death?"

"I had no other choice; nor he. We could—*can!*—only react to what Talan brings against us, and fight him as best we can. Do you survive, there's a chance."

Ellyn had ceased her pacing at that. Had stopped and stared at her mother, who sat studying her face as if she sought answers there, or confirmations.

"How?"

"By escaping," Ryadne had said. "By living. You must go away—survive—and find your own power."

Ellyn had stared at her mother then, more confused than ever. "My own power? What power?"

"It will come," Ryadne promised her. "You've the blood, and I've scryed somewhat of your future. So . . ."

"What future?" Ellyn had screamed. "I've no *power*! I've nothing, save a mother who'd send me away and a father who's slain."

She had fallen to her knees then, weeping copiously, and Ryadne had gone to her and put comforting arms around her and said, "I cannot tell you what it is, or shall be, for you must find that out for yourself. Do I tell you, then I . . . disrupt what might be. But you must go from Chorym, and to that end there are . . ."

"Plans laid." Ellyn sobbed against her mother's breast. "I know that, but what plans? Shall I go out and hide in hedgerows? Shall I wander like some vagabond? What do you say?"

"You shall be protected," Ryadne told her. "Andur and I chose a guardian for you. Gailard . . ."

"That Devyn hire-sword?" Ellyn lurched back from her mother's embrace. "A Highlander mercenary?"

"He's a good man," Ryadne said, "who loved your father, and would give his life for Chaldor."

"But he lived!" Ellyn wailed. "I've heard the stories. He was in the vanguard and *lived*! He should have died with my father. But he *lived*. He led the retreat!"

"Because Andur pledged him to it," Ryadne said. "Because your father trusted none other so much as Gailard, and set a geas on him—that he come here and protect you."

"Him?" Ellyn had snuffled, outraged. "A stinking, hairy Highlander?"

Almost, Ryadne seemed to laugh. "I think he's no more respect for you than you've for him, but there it is. There's no other way, believe me."

Now Ellyn walked the ramparts with her mother and watched the bedraggled remnants of Chaldor's army straggle home, broken and defeated. She wondered if she might recognize Gailard amongst them. She remembered that he was a handsome man—in an ugly kind of way, with his long hair and beard, his Highlander ways—and that he seemed always ill at ease amongst her parent's courtiers, as if he knew he belonged elsewhere, outside, where the wind blew free. She remembered that he had danced with her, embarrassed, but nonetheless light on his feet. She remembered that once he had let her hold his sword, which was very heavy, and snatched her hand away when she tried to stroke the cutting edge. Beyond that, she remembered only a smell of leather and sweat and the oil the soldiers wiped on their blades.

"Is he there?"

"Not yet." Ryadne drew her mourning veil tighter about her hair and set her hands on the sun-warmed stone of the wall, staring down at the streets below, the opened gates beyond, the sorry, limping men who came home to . . . yet another defeat? Some heroic resistance that could lead only to a worse fate?

"He does not exactly hurry to my defense."

Ryadne sighed and turned from her observation to face her daughter. They stood between two watchtowers, alone and unheard, save for the crows that vaunted the ramparts like dark omens borne on the wind. "Perhaps," the queen said as calmly as she could, "he stayed. Perhaps he's hurt."

"He should be dead beside my father."

"And what good would that do?"

"I do not understand this." Ellyn fisted her hands and drove them hard against her hips. "My father is dead and you speak of dying. You tell me I've some great destiny ahead, but will not tell me what. You tell me I must run away in care of some clansman hire-sword, but where shall he take me? Where shall we go?"

"Oh, child." Ryadne hugged her daughter close, stroking the lustrous red hair, finding brief comfort in that touch. "If I could tell you that, I should—but I do not know. I cannot. Perhaps it's better than none know, for fear Talan's Vachyn sorcerer winkle it out."

She took her daughter's face in her hands, cradling the teared cheeks. "Things move in this world of ours, beyond my comprehension, and all I know is that you must go away with Gailard. Trust him! And in time you'll find that power you own and yourself know what to do. The gods forgive me, but I can tell you no better than that."

"Poor advice, Mother." Ellyn drew back, breaking Ryadne's heart. "You consign me to some unknown fate in care of a Devyn hire-sword. What if he rapes me? Or sells me off to some Naban trader? What if he . . ."

Ryadne raised a hand to silence her daughter. "He'd not: he's a man of honor, Gailard."

"That he forsakes his clan to hire out his blade?"

"You know that story. And you know he swore allegiance to Andur, to Chaldor."

"And left my father to die!"

"Do we let him tell that tale?" Ryadne asked. The gods knew, but it was hard to own the scrying talent; to see somewhat of the future, but all misty, like segments of some dream dispersed with the sun's rising. Knowing she must put together the bits and the pieces to create some whole, and even then not sure it was the right thing, save there was the conviction, the horrid *certainty* that lurks behind on waking like a remembered smell.

"Have I any other choice?"

Ryadne steeled herself before she said, "Yes. You can die, or become Talan's ward—marry him. Or you can—" Oh, the gods grant she said it aright, that Ellyn understand and accept—"do as I ask; as your father would have it."

Ellyn said, "You leave me little choice."

"No," Ryadne allowed, "save to deny your blood and forsake Chaldor."

That hurt: her and Ellyn, both. She saw the pain in her daughter's eyes and felt it in her own heart. She thought then that wearing armor as she was, wearing a sword and a battle-knife, it should be easier to take out those blades and slay her daughter and herself. That should be the easier course, but she could not take it, for love of Andur and her daughter and Chaldor, all mingled in a desperate lack of options. Ellyn *must* live—else all her dreams were false, and all Andur had sought and hoped for lost. And Chaldor doomed.

"So I must," Ellyn said slowly, hurt in her eyes and voice, "do as you ask."

Ryadne said, "Yes." And wondered how many times a heart could break.

CHAPTER THREE

I saw the city readied for siege. Soldiers watched from the walls, and catapults were loaded in place. Horsemen in the royal livery supervised the flood of farmers and shepherds and cattleherds who came in seeking refuge, and I knew that word had arrived of our defeat and that Ryadne prepared for a long war. I wondered if her Dur magic had scryed the outcome.

I vaguely recognized the youthful captain who hailed me as if I were some great commander, and thought that I did not like him much. He was, did my memory serve me right, of noble Chaldorean stock, without much liking for outlanders such as I. He wore polished armor and all his trappings were clean and bright; his horse was groomed and fresh and well fed. My own mount was bedraggled and weary as I, who smelled of sweat and longed for nothing more than a bath and bed after the ride from the coast. I thought I recalled disparaging comments about Highlanders, but he was polite enough now, halting his mount to advise me that Ryadne waited on my arrival. I grunted acceptance and followed him into the city.

I was very weary, and at first paid no attention to the looks I got, the sidelong glances and pointing fingers, but as we climbed the avenue toward the palace I heard snippets of the talk.

I head my name spoken, and the titles "mercenary" and "Highlander" and "coward" (which no man says to my face), and snatches that suggested I was held responsible for the loss of Antium, and even for the defeat and Andur's death. I looked about and saw faces turn quickly from my gaze. I turned to the captain and asked him what rumors spread.

He averted his eyes, his smooth cheeks reddening, and I must press him to tell me. "Folk say you fled the battle, leaving Andur behind. They say you fled Antium, leaving the town to Talan."

I spat and asked him, "Do you believe that?"

He hesitated a moment before he shook his head.

"And what does the queen believe?"

He frowned. "It is not my place to interpret the queen's thoughts."

I murmured. "No," and looked to where the towers of the palace shone in the afternoon sun. Andur's banner fluttered there, alongside the great flag of Chaldor, and I saw the bright sparks of light the sun struck from spearheads and polished helms, glittering shields. I paused, turning to look back down the avenue to where remnants of our army trudged in. Those helms were dented and dark, and all the spearheads were brown with old blood. I shrugged and went to my fate.

I felt out of place in the palace. I was dirty and bandaged and bloodstained; I could smell myself and it was not a pleasant odor. All around me were folk in pristine silks and linens. Their footgear was not dusty from the road, nor their hair in need of washing. Their perfumes scented the air and they glanced at me as if I were some upstart contaminating their privileged domain. I supposed it indication of urgency that my escort did not suggest I first bathe and find myself clean uniform prior to my audience with Ryadne, but instead brought me directly to those sanctums where first I'd met Andur and shouted at the guards to announce my arrival. The guards stared at me curiously, but the doors were swung ceremoniously open and I stepped through into a chamber all filled with sunlight, so that I was awhile blinded and could not clearly make out the shapes before me. I do not like to be blinded. Too often I've seen shields polished for that purpose and then lofted to dazzle opponents.

I heard a voice I knew say, "Welcome, Gailard—sorry welcome that it be," and dropped awkwardly to my knee. As protocol demanded, I had left my sword and other weapons outside.

"My queen."

"Am I, truly?"

I ducked my head.

"My blood is Dur," she said, "and yours Devyn." She left a question dangling in the hot air that smelled of roses and women.

I squinted into the glare and said, "Yet we both serve Chaldor, no?"

Ryadne laughed as if my answer pleased her and said, "Get up, man."

I stood and she beckoned me, ignoring the curious glances of her attendants as she led me to a second chamber where blinds were drawn and I could see her clear. She was lovely as I remembered. Her hair was that shade the oak leaves attain in autumn, brown and copper mingled, and it fell in a great spill of curls about an oval face that seemed all bright eyes and wide mouth. If she wore cosmetics I could not discern them, nor much jewelry other than a silver necklace and two rings. Her gown was blue and flowed over the contours of her body as does a river over the shoreline. She crossed to a table on which stood a decanter of Naban work and two crystal goblets that she filled with pale red wine. She handed one to me.

"You look thirsty."

I was; I drank deep.

"Was it bad?'

I nodded. "You've heard?"

"Yes." In the chamber's dimmed light I saw pain course her eyes, like fish glimpsed fleeting beneath a stream's surface. "Word came. And I scryed it . . ."

I had for a while forgotten her Dur magic, which must have shown on my face, for she said forlornly, "I cannot help my talent, Gailard. I was born with it."

I looked at her and asked bluntly, "Did you know, how could you let him go?"

She met my accusing gaze and answered, "I could not stop him. I can foresee some little part of the future, but not the whole. Only the . . . possibilities. And events moved too swift. Talan's Vachyn hireling owns far stronger magic than mine, and planned all this better than we imagined." She turned away, crossing the chamber to a window that transformed her to a shape of light and shadow, her hair a glowing corona. "My husband had no choice but to defend the kingdom, even to his death. He was caught in the Vachyn's web—the gods know, we are all caught in those strands— and could do naught else."

Her hands rested on the sill and I saw her shoulders tense, her body shudder. I saw then what a terrible thing her talent was. To foresee somewhat of the future and know what it likely holds, but still be bound by humankind's desires and ambitions, unable to divert that juggernaut. I was glad I had no such talent. I said, "I am sorry."

She turned from the window then and faced me again, smiling. It was such a smile as folk show when they'd hold back tears. "I *felt* his death," she said, and the tears came. The goblet fell from her hand and shattered to spill wine across the marbled floor. Her tears were brighter: they shone on her tanned cheeks like sparkling jewels. I did not think then, but crossed the distance between us and took her hands.

"I loved him, too," I said. "I'd have stayed with him, had he not commanded I return to you."

She said, "I know," and, all unqueenly, dragged the sleeve of her gown across her face and blew her nose into the cuff. Then she made a sound midway betwixt a sigh and a laugh and said, "And that shall be no easy duty, do you agree to it."

Briefly, I thought of Ellyn. But I said, "Command me," and began to kneel.

"Gailard, no!" She took my shoulders and halted my descent. "The gods know, but you've been hurt, so I've only one command for now—that you do not kneel to me. Do you agree?"

I ducked my head. I was grateful for that alleviance.

"But I shall ask more painful duties," she said.

"Name them."

She smiled wanly and glanced at the remnants of the shattered goblet, then found another. She took it and mine and refilled them both, then motioned that we sit.

"You need a bath," she said. And when I flushed and began to mouth apologies, waved a dismissive hand and said, "Later, eh? I grew up in the Highlands, like you. I was not always a queen, and I'm used to the smell of honest men." She shook her head, her expression that of someone who recalls easier times. Then: "Andur charged you with a duty, no?"

"Yes."

"Chorym's defense shall not be easy. Talan's sorcerer shall bring magic against us, and so many of our men are slain . . ."

I dared to interrupt. "Even so, the walls are strong, and you've brave men behind them. And you've the gift of magic."

"Not like the Vachyn," she replied. "Theirs is all bellicose—the gods know, you've seen it!—whilst mine is for the scrying, the foretelling. And I've seen . . ."

She paused, her eyes a moment haunted. I quoted her a

saying of the Devyn: "When all you can do is die, then die as well as you can."

"I shall; I've scryed that, too." She smiled and I saw the skull beneath her skin, the ghost that inhabits all our flesh. She raised a hand, stilling my protest. "No, do not seek to dissuade me, Gailard. What's written is written, and it's the only course I can take—save to give Talan what he wants, which I'll never do."

"Surely," I asked, "there's another way?"

"No." She shook her head. "Not for me. But for Ellyn—and for Chaldor—yes. Andur told you what we'd ask, no?"

"He spoke only of a duty that he said you'd explain." I rubbed absently at my hurting knee. "He feared the Vachyn might somehow learn his intent."

"Andur was ever cautious," she murmured sadly, then squared her shoulders and set her goblet aside, her hands entwined as she faced me. "Ellyn must not fall into Talan's clutches, lest he gain some supposedly legitimate claim to the throne. She must go away from Chorym—to some haven where he'll not find her—and live safe until she comes into her own power."

I frowned at that. "What power?"

"She's magic in her, my daughter," Ryadne said. "Not recognized yet, for it's not developed. But when she comes into her own, I suspect her power shall be great—perhaps enough, even, to challenge the Vachyn. But until then, she's vulnerable and needs protection."

"Then take her away," I said. "You and she flee Chorym under the protection of the Palace Guard."

"I cannot." Ryadne shook her head. "I am Andur's queen, and I've a duty to Chaldor—I must stay."

I understood that; she was an honorable woman. I drained my wine, staring at her. "What do you ask of me?"

"That you guard Ellyn. That you take her away and see her safe until her day comes. That you be her champion and her guardian, for Chaldor's sake. Hide her in the Highlands—

wherever—and see her safe until she gains her power. She'll know what to do then."

I swallowed, scratching at an itch. "Why me? The gods know, Ellyn has little enough liking for me."

"Or you for her, eh?" Ryadne essayed a wan smile. "But you were Andur's choice, and mine, for we trust none so much as you. Shall you accept, Gailard?"

I felt fate settle on me then, heavier than any armor, heavier than any sword's blow. I felt wary and reluctant, but I could not say her nay; I had given Andur my word. I said, "As you command, my lady."

That day I was tended by the palace healers and bathed in such a tub as I'd not seen before, all marble and gold, with attendants who'd have soaped me and scrubbed me like a pampered child had I not shouted them away, and even then lurked with towels like fowlers ready to cast their nets. I was, like it or not, perfumed, my wet hair dried and combed and oiled. I felt clumsy and embarrassed, and was thankful when the ritual ended and I was at last allowed to dress. Not in my own familiar clothes, but garments sent by Ryadne— a shirt of fine linen, breeches of soft leather, boots that fit like gloves, a surcoat such as courtiers wear. I slapped away the hands that would have fastened my belt and demanded my sword. I was told it had gone to the palace armories to be polished and edged, and was then escorted to the chamber where Ryadne awaited me with her daughter.

I did not look forward to this audience. Ryadne had explained to me what she'd have me do, and somewhat of it to Ellyn. But Ellyn was a willful and headstrong child, given to tempers and accustomed to the granting of her wishes. Her realm was one of soft beds and servants; granted whims. I doubted she'd take easily to life on the road.

I found them, mother and daughter, seated at a table on which stood food and wine. I had not eaten since that morning, and at sight of the sumptuous fare my stomach rumbled. Ellyn frowned disapprovingly; Ryadne laughed and gestured that I sit.

"Your knee's mended?" she asked.

"It heals apace, thank you."

There were no servants present, and the queen asked that her daughter pour the wine, inviting me to avail myself of the food. I did, the while studying Ellyn. She was a coltish version of her mother, and I saw that one day she would be a great beauty. Her hair was that same shade of coppery brown, her eyes—for all their indignance—large and lustrous. Her mouth—despite its sullen set—was generous and better suited to a smile than the scowl she wore. She was tall, gangly, and a little clumsy—when wine spilled on the damask cloth covering the table, I saw her lips shape a curse—but in a few years she'd come into her own and, I thought, find her mother's grace. For now, however, she was all disgruntlement and angry curiosity, as if she wondered why so lowly a creature as I was invited to dine with royalty.

I knew that Ryadne had explained the outline of our future relationship, but I had forgotten the rumors I'd heard—until she spoke.

She set a goblet that sparkled in the candlelight before me and looked me in the eye and said, "They say you deserted my father."

"Ellyn." Ryadne's voice was sharp.

"That you left him to die."

"Ellyn!"

"That you fled Antium, leaving the town to Talan."

"Enough!"

Even I started at that tone. Ellyn's mouth, readied to continue the diatribe, snapped shut. She glanced at her mother, glared at me, then set her angry gaze firmly on her plate.

"Gailard did not desert Andur," Ryadne said. "He was wounded, and your father charged him with a duty that he dispensed with honor."

Ellyn shook her head, tendrils of long hair falling from the coiffure she wore. "They say he's a coward," she muttered.

"Never to my face," I said, my own anger growing now. "Nor would I have left Andur, had he not commanded me."

Ryadne made a slight gesture with her right hand, indicating that I hold silent, and looked at her daughter. "Think you I'd welcome a man who left your father to die? Think you I'd entertain him?"

The girl had the grace to look at me then, albeit briefly, and mumble, "My apologies."

I nodded my acceptance. I could not like her, nor believe that she would agree to what her mother planned. And did she, I thought, it should be an arduous journey.

Which seemed to be one thing we had in common, for Ellyn set to arguing with her mother, disputing the need for her departure and my guardianship as if she pleaded for her life. I suppose that in a way she did, for what Ryadne proposed must take this brat from all she knew into unknown dangers. Almost, I felt sorry for her, even as my irritation mounted. I was entrusted with her life—yet as she argued, it was Ryadne she addressed, as if I were beneath notice. I watched her pretty face grow red, a pout forming.

"You'd have me flee," she said sullenly. "Go away with this hire-sword. But to where? Shall we flee to the clans, and they hand me back to Talan? Naban and Serian shall not risk war with Danant by taking me in, so where shall I be safe? Shall we go south to the Great Sea, to find the Sea Kings? Or perhaps run to the Styge and live as hermits?"

Ryadne sighed, rising to stand behind her daughter, hands on the girl's shoulders. "Child, when you come into your power, you'll understand this better—but I cannot say where you should go, I only know that you *must*."

"So you ask me to creep away like some night-come thief? You'd ask me to sneak off like some . . . some Devyn horse-stealer?"

That was enough. Heir or no, I had listened long

enough to this irritating child. I said: "The gods know, girl, I'd sooner face Talan's sorcerer than ride away with you—I think that should be an easier task."

Ellyn gasped, her face expressing outrage. I think Ryadne smiled, but I could not be sure, for the night aged and the candles burned down and shadows clouded all our faces.

Then Ellyn said, "How dare you?"

"Easily," I replied. "I've listened long enough to your carping, and were you my child I'd set you across my knee and teach you a sound-earned lesson."

I thought she might fling her wine at me for that, and wondered a moment how I might react, but Ryadne intervened. She moved from behind Ellyn's chair to stand between us, like an adjur settling disputes at the Moot. She put a hand on my shoulder and one on Ellyn's.

"Hear me," she said, "both of you," and waited until we each nodded our agreement. "This shall not be easy for either of you. But I've scryed this—and thus I *know* it is the only way. Easy or hard, can you understand that it must be so? Else Chaldor and all Andur looked to build is lost to Talan."

Ellyn said, "You ask too much of me, Mother."

I did not like to agree with her, but I could only nod.

Ryadne said, "The gods ask much of us all. Understand that were it otherwise—had the gods allowed—I'd see it different. But it cannot be so. Do you fail in this, then Chaldor's lost and Danant shall hold sway, and perhaps all our world fall down. You do not like one another, but I ask you this as queen and mother and seer."

I had not known a woman with fingers so strong: they dug into my shoulder with such force as made me wince. I ducked my head and said, "I've given you my promise already, no?"

Ryadne said, "Yes; and I thank you for that, Gailard."

I wondered if she drove her hand so hard against Ellyn, but the child nodded and grunted irritable acceptance.

The pressure eased and Ryadne loosed her grip. "Then go sleep. Gailard, you'll pass the night here. Take your ease for a day, and then leave at the next dawning. Tell me only what you'll need for the journey, and I'll see it readied. *Do not tell me where you go!* Only you shall know that, and Ellyn in time."

I felt a terrible dread at that, and a great admiration for this brave woman who would defend her husband's city even to her own death. I wondered if Ellyn understood as I watched her rise and quit the room, not meeting my eyes.

"She's qualities," Ryadne told me, "for all her temper."

"Perhaps I'll see them," I said. "Someday."

The queen took my hands again. "I told you it was hard duty."

Her smile made it worthwhile.

That night I spent in a bed so soft I could not sleep. I was accustomed to hard barracks' beds, or the ground, or to sleeping in the saddle. I tossed and turned on that downy, perfumed mattress and listened to the complaints of cocks brought into the city, and the lowing of troubled cattle, the bleating of wondering sheep. I watched the sun rise from a window that looked out over the old town and saw the streets below all filled with frightened folk come to Chorym in search of refuge I knew they'd not find. They'd know fear, and deprivation; they'd know the magicks of the Vachyn sorcerer, and the terror of catapults hurling balefire. The song of arrows and the clatter of javelins.

I felt sorry for them. It was easier for me: I was a soldier. I had sworn my blade to Andur, and therefore to Ryadne—and through them to Ellyn—so I could accept the duty that the king and queen had set upon me. I might not like it—certainly I did not look forward with any joy to that journey I must take with the grumbling Ellyn—but these folk had no sworn duty. They were only citizens and farmers, traders and merchants: plain, honest folk who looked only to till their fields or tend their flocks or sell their wares.

Not fight and starve and suffer the bolts of a Vachyn sorcerer and the terrors of siege.

I dressed and went to find my breakfast, which I ate alone. I assumed Ryadne was with Ellyn, likely locked in further dispute, and melancholy settled on me. I had lost my sworn liege and now must desert his queen while she faced the horrors of siege, and most likely her own death. I was unsure where I should take Ellyn. I knew nothing of the coastal lands, and wondered if the Sea Kings would welcome us or take us prisoner. I could not go to my own clan, nor be certain of the Dur's welcome. Naban and Serian would likely seize Ellyn as a pawn to hold against either Chaldor or Danant, and to reach the Styge we must traverse the Barrens. Worse, Ryadne had spoken of Ellyn's talent burgeoning, and whilst I'd accept that magic if it were used on Chaldor's behalf, I could not imagine the child using it well. It seemed to me that we must become outlaws, and when—as I was sure he eventually would—Talan learned of Ellyn's flight, he'd send hunters after us. I wondered what hunters a Vachyn sorcerer might create with his conjuries.

By the time I finished eating I was in dour mood, so I went to find the armories.

My sword was cleaned of old blood and polished and given such an edge as it had not known since the war began. I was offered a splendid scabbard that I rejected in favor of my own old, worn sheath. We should be traveling incognito, I thought, and I'd not draw attention to us with any overly fine trappings.

I said as much to Ryadne when she found me, and she agreed, kitting me in plain but sturdy gear—a shirt or two of stout linen; good leathern breeches and durable boots; a tunic of cloth and metal sewn together and lined with silk so that arrows might be easier withdrawn; undergarments; and a good, warm cloak. She offered me the pick of the palace stables, and I selected a bay mare. She was deep of chest and long in the leg, and she'd the look of a runner—speed and stamina combined.

"Ellyn will want her favorite," Ryadne advised me, indicating a second mare whose coat was so white as to shine.

The horse was sound, but also very noticeable; I recognized her immediately. I shook my head and told the queen, "Favorite or no, she must ride another—this beauty's too well known."

"She'll argue," Ryadne said.

I looked at her. She smiled and said, "Choose her another then, Gailard."

I picked out a dark chestnut mare the same size as my own.

"What else shall you need?" Ryadne asked.

"A horse bow," I told her, "and a stock of arrows; provisions; coin; bedrolls." I thought of the season. The summer aged and likely by the time we got to wherever we were going the nights would grow cold. "A tent. No! *Two* tents." I could not imagine sharing a single bivouac with Ellyn.

"You'll want a packhorse?" Ryadne asked.

I shook my head. "We'll travel light. What we can't carry between us we'll forage, or buy." I began to feel better. This was akin to planning a campaign and I felt on firmer ground. "And Ellyn must dress plain. No fancy trappings; no jewels or finery. She must not be recognized as your daughter."

"No," Ryadne agreed, and set a hand on my forearm. "Thank you for this, Gailard. I know it is not easy for you, and you've my everlasting gratitude."

I sought fine words in response and could fine none, so I only shrugged and smiled and said, "You're my sworn liege now, my queen."

There was a sadness in her eyes as she answered, "Yet Ellyn's mother still. Guard her well, eh?"

"My word on it," I said. "And my life."

So it was that we quit Chorym in that hour before the sun's rising, when the air hangs still and grey, seemingly undecided between the relinquishment of night and acceptance of the new day. Ellyn rode the chestnut I'd chosen, dressed in boots and breeches, shirt and tunic, her cloak wrapped about her. Her hair was shorn as I'd advised, tucked beneath a peaked leather cap into which she'd set a defiant feather.

This last indignity she'd protested fiercer even than the rest. "I give up my home," she'd cried, "and leave my mother to her fate. I must dress like some . . . some vagabond. I am told I cannot ride my own horse—and now you'd have me shorn. It's too much!"

She had turned to Ryadne for support—and found none, for we had agreed this final measure. She'd not easily pass for a boy, surely not on close inspection, but she looked less like a princess than what our masquerade demanded—a wandering hire-sword's surly offspring.

Ryadne—cloaked and hooded that none recognize her—accompanied us to the East Gate. Our farewells had been said within the confines of the palace, and when we reached the gate she only ducked her head and raised a hand, then turned her horse away and left us to wait for the opening.

I did not see her again.

I felt a great sadness, and a curious excitement. I am no sorcerer—no seer or mage—but I sensed that I rode out toward some great adventure, and must I find it in company with the sullen girl who fidgeted irritably alongside me, then still it was as the gods willed. I only hoped Andur had been wrong when he told me the gods had forsaken us.

The dawn-bells tolled and the gate was opened; we rode through. I heeled my mare to a trot, glancing back at Ellyn. She scowled ferociously, but she came with me, and we took the East Road to whatever fate awaited us.

CHAPTER FOUR

Talan Kedassian, Lord of Danant, stood admiring his reflection as servants buckled on his golden armor. He made, he thought, a splendid figure, impressive and suitably military, as befit the conqueror of Chaldor—which soon enough, he had no doubt, he would be. He savored the title as he savored his own image: the Lord of Danant and Conqueror of Chaldor. Or perhaps, more modestly, the Lord of Danant and Chaldor. The armor was contoured to his slender frame, a snarling lion's head embossed upon the breastplate and reproduced in smaller size upon the greaves and pauldrons. In the light that shone through the cabin's window, the bejeweled eyes glinted ferociously. Talan beamed as his sword was belted around his waist, the jewels in the hilt matching the rubies that shaped the lions' eyes.

He nodded approvingly, then shook his head as his helmet was lifted. He was too handsome, he decided, to hide his features beneath the casque, and opted to carry the helm; that would be more suitable. After all, he came ashore as conqueror, and there could not be any threat left in Antium—Nestor's Vachyn magic and the blades of the advance guard had surely seen to that. So he tucked the helmet beneath his left arm and turned about, admiring himself from all angles, then bowed mockingly to the head floating pickled in a glass jar.

"Think you I look well, Andur?"

The head offered no answer. The skin was very pale, like that of a drowned man, and the yellow hair and beard floated like tendrils of riverweed. The eyes that stared blindly back at Talan began to grow milky, spilling out cloudy streamers of ichor where the little fish Nestor had set in the jar nibbled. Talan chuckled. Andur of Chaldor had made a grave mistake when he invaded Danant.

"I am ready." He waved the anxious servants away. "Nestor, do you accompany me?"

Across the luxurious cabin, the Vachyn sorcerer ducked his head, folding long-nailed hands into the cuffs of his robe. "As you wish, my lord."

Talan smiled. The gods knew that Nestor cost him sacks of gold—but all worthwhile for the power of his magicks. Talan adjusted his expression to one of stern resolve, checked his image a last time, and strode to the opened door.

Trumpets blew a clarion as he came on deck, and his personal guard—all armored in lesser versions of his own splendor—raised their spears and shouted his name. On the dockside, soldiers clattered swords and spears against shields, and for a while Talan basked in the accolades.

"Hail, Talan the Conqueror!"

"Hail, the Lord of the River!"

"Hail, the Destroyer of Chaldor!"

"Hail, Talan!"

He paused at the gangplank, then raised a hand, bidding them be silent. His officers had assured him the town was emptied of defenders, so he felt safe. And Nestor was at his back. The Chaldorean army had fled wounded to the east, doubtless to mass behind the walls of Chorym, and what resistance had been left behind was slain. He could smell the sweet odor of the bodies burning in the torched houses, and beyond the harbor could see the palls of smoke rising into the morning air. He smiled and spoke.

"Well done, my faithful soldiers. You have fought bravely, and I thank you. Now we shall go on to Chorym and raze that enemy city, and the land's plunder shall be yours."

That promise was met with a great shout of approval, a further clattering of blades on shields. Talan smiled wider and strode manfully down the gangplank to the fire-glazed cobbles of the wharf.

Nestor followed him, and Talan could not resist whispering: "It *is* safe, no?"

The Vachyn sorcerer answered, "None shall harm you here; my word on it."

"Good." Talan struck a posture and shouted for his chariot to be brought ashore, then turned to his generals. "Have we left any decent accommodation standing?"

Egor Dival, who owned twice his liege's years, said bluntly, "No. What the Vachyn's magic didn't burn, the defenders did."

Talan frowned. "Then where do I sleep this night? Where shall I find my breakfast?"

Dival wiped a hand through a greying beard that was stained with recent blood and said, "Tonight, in your pavilion. Now? Why, I suppose you might go back on board and eat there, or here with us."

"Here?" Talan gestured at the wreckage of Antium. Now that he saw it closer, he could see that little was left standing other than smoking hulks ready to topple under the weight of their own smoldering and charred timbers. "What's left here?"

"Little enough," Dival said. "My advice is that we see the army ashore and move inland. Make camp beyond this place."

"But I'm hungry," Talan complained.

"Then eat on the ship," Dival returned.

Talan's frown grew darker. "I'll eat with my loyal men," he declared. "I owe them that, at least."

On the dockside, where Nestor's magefire had scoured the cobbles and men had died, tables were set up, chairs around them. Linen cloths were spread, platters of silver and gold, goblets of cut glass, ornate cutlery. Decanters of wine were brought from the ships, and great plates of meat and eggs, bread, cheeses and fruits. Talan ate with Nestor seated on his right, Egor Dival to his left. The men who had fought the battle—the ordinary soldiers—were gifted with ale, and small measures of bread and meat. And were those measures insufficient to fill their hungry bellies, then they must forage through the ruins of Antium for what they could find; the commanders ate well. And before them, on a small table, stood the jar containing Andur's head.

"How do you do that?" Talan stabbed a fork in the direction of the little fishes gnawing at the dead face. "How can they survive in there?"

Nestor smiled and stroked his black beard. "Magic, my lord."

"But he's pickled. And no living thing can survive in that liquid."

"Perhaps," Nestor said, "they are not alive. Indeed, perhaps they are only illusion. Or can live—thanks to my magic—in such liquid as must kill all else."

"So are they dead or alive?" Dival asked through a mouthful of roasted meat and scrambled eggs.

Nestor shrugged.

"Can you," Talan asked, "defy death?"

"I am a Vachyn sorcerer," Nestor answered. "And life and death are not so much different—perhaps only alternate aspects of existence."

"Dead's dead," Dival grunted. "There's surely a large difference."

"Is there?" Nestor turned his saturnine face to the grizzled general. "Shall I show you?"

Dival scowled and shook his head.

The wind had turned as the day aged, and the debris of

Antium blew across the harbor, the air gone grey with the detritus. Dival swilled rich wine around his mouth and spat onto the cobbles.

Talan laughed. "Does the taste of victory offend you, Egor?"

"No, my lord." Dival shook his head again. "But there are better places to eat."

"Where?" Talan spread his splendidly armored arms. "We sit in a vanquished town, ready to conquer the land beyond . . . where better to take our breakfast?"

"In Chorym," Dival answered.

Talan's smile faded; his face grew dark. "We shall take Chorym," he said. "We shall confront the walls, and does Ryadne deny us, then we'll siege the city and tear it down around her." He turned to the Vachyn sorcerer. "Eh, Nestor?"

The Vachyn smiled. "Magic shall bring her to heel."

"And I'll have her for my bride?"

Nestor said, "Yes, my lord," and cast a sly glance at Dival. "Can might of arms not give you what you want, then my magicks shall."

Talan nodded approvingly, then beckoned a servant to wipe his armor where falling ash discolored the gold. He wondered if it stained his hair. Perhaps he should have it washed again, then thought that that was not seemly in a conqueror. No; better to go dirty into battle. He tossed his cutlery aside and rose, signaling the end of the meal.

"We advance! My chariot?"

Two grooms brought up the prancing horses, both stallions, matched for their jet hides. The chariot was all beaten gold, with jagged daggers jutting from each wheel. It bore nine javelins and a jewel-mounted quiver in which stood seventeen silver-headed arrows and a bow of lacquered jet. Ceremoniously, Talan Kedassian settled his golden helmet on his dark-oiled hair. He latched the cheek pieces and took a spear in his hand, raising it dramatically as Nestor clambered in.

"Onward, to Chorym and victory!"

Ryadne paced the walls of the inner city, wondering how long it should be before Talan's army came.

The day was warm, the sun halfway to its zenith. The sky was a pristine blue, save where the darting shapes of swallows punctuated the azure. High on the walls, she could hear their calling; below, she could hear the lowing of cattle and the muted voices of all the folk looking to her for protection, for safety.

Chorym was readied for siege. All those farmers and vintners and herders who'd come into the city were gathered. There was food aplenty. The walls were manned by the army Gailard had brought back; the catapults were prepared, well armed with missiles and balefire, great buckets of water and of oil set ready. She could do no more. Her scrying magic seemed dimmed now, likely fuddled by the workings of Talan's Vachyn sorcerer. She could not discern the outcome or the time. She only knew it was vital Ellyn be gone, and that Gailard go with her daughter.

Ellyn was Chaldor's only hope, and without Gailard that hope was lost.

Beyond that she could foresee little, save her own death.

She looked at the bright summer sun and blinked away tears.

Then, out of the west, she saw a brightness, a glowing that came along the West Road like approaching fire, and knew it for the glitter of sunlight on polished chariots and shields and spearheads, even before the scouts came back shouting warning that Danant's army came.

She sighed and turned to her last duties.

Kerid held the *Blessing* close to the Chaldor shore, his eyes firm on the river ahead—save for the nervous glances he cast at his lookouts. The water ran shallow here, sandbanks and rocky shoals a constant danger to the unwary, and he would usually have held to midstream. But thrice since

quitting Antium he had encountered Danant's god-cursed
river raiders, and the *Blessing* was sore hurt. Her forrard
mast was down, and catapults had stove holes in her port
side that threatened to ship enough water to sink her should
the weather shift or a high tide run. Worse was the loss of the
Pride, which had gone down at the first encounter with all
hands, or so Kerid assumed; he'd had no chance to try a rescue, but could only run as best he could from the sleek warboats. He wished he commanded one of those craft. The
Blessing, for all her greater size, was no match for those
swift hunters. Indeed, he believed that had they not been
called to the invasion, and thus not had the time to complete
their task, his own vessel would now add its wreckage to the
detritus of the Durrakym's graveyard bed.

Nor had he seen any other Chaldor craft—save for the
smoldering wreck of the *Glory*, and the masts of the *Revela-
tion* jutting from the river—since leaving Gailard on the
shore. He wondered where the other boats had gone. Anchored and waiting for Talan to seize them? Fled south? He
did not know, and could only curse the coward captains
who'd desert the Bright Kingdom in its hour of need. For
himself, he was determined to fulfill his promise to the
Highlander and return to smite Danant on the river as he believed Gailard would strike from the land.

But to achieve that aim he must survive and bring the
Blessing safely north. He could not resist shouting at the
lookouts, asking what they saw ahead.

"Clear water," was the answer. "No sail, no mast."

"Only shoals and sandbanks and eddies this close in,
and few mad enough to risk them."

Kerid turned to the swarthy man who joined him on the
raised steering deck. Nassim was a Bordersman, his mother
of Chaldorean stock, his father from Naban. He was Kerid's
first mate, and no less familiar with the river than his
Chaldor-born captain; in some respects, more familiar.

"I'll not chance the deep river," Kerid grunted, holding

the wheel against a sudden swirl that threatened to spill more water into his flooding hold. "The gods know, she's hurt enough already. How do the repairs go?"

"As well as we can hope." Nassim opened a sodden pouch and extracted a pinch of wet tobacco that he chewed awhile before grimacing and spitting. "We're patched as best we can be, and I've men on the pumps. But we need to put in and find sound wood."

"And have some Danant boat find us?" Kerid shook his head. "No, we'll sail this tub to Hel's Town and sell her for what we can get."

"And then what?" Nassim emptied his mouth over the side, inspected his pouch afresh, and stared sadly at the contents before tucking the pouch back inside his shirt. "What will a damaged cargo vessel like this fetch there?"

"I don't know." Kerid shrugged. "I've never sold a boat before, and you know those pirates better than I."

"Pirates?" Nassim affected a look of outrage. "Some of those pirates are blood kin."

"Then I'll let you handle the sale," Kerid declared.

"And then what?"

"We get a raiding craft and attack every god-cursed Danant boat we find."

"Ha!" Nassim leaned against the rail, staring moodily at the mist swirling across the wide expanse of the Durrakym. "We'll be lucky to reach the islands before we sink. And even do we, think you we'll get enough for this broken sow to buy us a raider?"

Kerid said, "I made a promise."

"And I swore to serve Chaldor," Nassim said. "But what poor navy Andur built is destroyed or fled. What can we do?"

"Any man who wishes to quit my command may go." Kerid stared at his mate. "Shall you?"

"No." Nassim shook his head. "My father told me I was mad to seek service in Chaldor when I could have been a Hel's Town pirate, but still I did. Like you, I gave my word."

Kerid grinned. "Then we'd best pray we reach the islands, eh?"

Nassim opened his mouth to answer, but the forward lookout shouted: "Sail ho!"

"What colors?" Kerid yelled back.

The lookout hesitated. The mist swirled thick. They'd sailed the last two nights and anchored—nervously—by day. Now the sun was but a promise along the horizon and the moon's light lost in the grey of dawn.

Then: "Danant's. And they've seen us!"

Kerid made an abrupt decision. He could take the *Blessing* closer in to the shore and hope the Danant boat went by for fear of foundering on the same sandbanks and shoals as might well destroy his own craft. Or . . .

"What is it?" he bellowed. "A warboat?"

"Larger," came back. "A two-master."

"Ready for battle!" Kerid swung his wheel, bringing the *Blessing* over farther shoreward. "We'll take her!"

"You're mad." But there was a light in Nassim's eyes that matched and met the excitement in Kerid's. "You'll ground us and we'll be a sitting duck."

"Exactly." Kerid held his course. "Tell the men to act dead. And light some smoky fires."

"The gods be with us now," Nassim said, and sprang from the steering deck to convey Kerid's orders.

Kerid swung his wheel, aiming the *Blessing*'s prow at a sandbank. It was not difficult to make the stricken craft wallow, and with her downed mast and holed side, she surely looked dead in the water. And the more so for the fires Nassim lit, that sent ugly streamers of smoke drifting to join the mist.

Kerid ran the bow onto the sandbank, almost stumbling as the boat grounded. *The gods be with me now,* he thought, *for she'll not come off.* He watched the lookouts scurry down the rigging and take their places on the deck. He could not yet see the Danant boat.

Then it came out of the mist: a solid-built two-master, with an arbalest mounted forrard and another aft, Danant's hated pennants fluttering limply. She slowed, coursing in toward the foundered *Blessing*, and sent a shaft from the forward arbalest thudding into the grounded boat's flank.

Kerid cursed and called, low, "Hold steady and we'll take her."

The Danant boat came closer, sending a second shaft hurtling through the *Blessing*'s rigging, then drew alongside. Kerid spat curses and ran to the rail, sword in hand.

"May all the gods damn you! May they damn your parents and your children and send your wives into whoredom!"

He staggered a little, for greater affect, then fell down as arrows whistled through the dawn air. He picked one up from the deck and tucked it between his arm and ribs so that it thrust out as if he were hit, then clambered up again and shouted, "You'll not take my boat!"

Laughter and a fresh volley met his sally, and he slumped to the deck.

He waited as commands drifted across the river and he felt the vibration of the Danant craft striking the *Blessing*'s side. Then grappling irons landed on the thwarts and the Danant men swarmed aboard.

They were met with steel and fury. The first onto the *Blessing* died as Kerid's men rose up and vented their anger on the attackers. Then the *Blessing*'s crew clambered over the thwarts and dropped onto the Danant boat, sweeping across the deck like ravaging pirates. Kerid went with them, leaping from his own steering deck into the rigging of the attacker, swinging down to confront the startled captain.

The Danant man was protected by two sturdy rivermen, each with bucklers on their forearms and wide-bladed swords held ready. Kerid cut the first down with a savage sweep that took the man's legs from under him, and kicked him away. The second blocked his cut and aimed a blow at Kerid's midriff. The Danant captain danced back, shouting, then fell silent as a belaying pin struck him between the eyes, sending him staggering from the wheel to slump against the stern rail. Another pin bounced off the chest of the second riverman and, as he raised his buckler against further airborne attack, Kerid drove his blade into the exposed belly. The Danant man screamed and fell down. Kerid struck him across the back of his neck and swung around to pierce the other. Then he paced across the deck to the captain and drove his sword into the man's chest.

He spun as Nassim came grinning to join him.

"They'd have stuck you like a pig if I hadn't thrown that pin."

Kerid frowned and said, "Perhaps, but I think I'd have taken them. Even so, thank you."

Nassim bowed, still grinning. "A favor owed;" and they both went down onto the lower deck to finish the fight.

It was soon won. Taken by surprise, the Danant men were swiftly defeated. None lived, and their bodies were tossed overboard. Fish rose to eat them, and from the shoreline and the sandbanks riparine mammals came to feast. The sun rose higher, waking birds that came winging in search of such bounty. Kerid beamed as he shouted for his crew to bring their gear over from the *Blessing*—and Chaldor's colors, which he had set in place where the Danant pennants had hung.

He checked the boat and knew it was sound. It would fetch a better price than his abandoned vessel.

"Set sail! We go to Hel's Town."

He paused as he saw his mate staring in naked amazement at the river. "What is it?"

"By all the gods!" Nassim pointed at the water. "That I've never seen before."

"What?" Kerid asked.

"Look." His mate angled a finger at the V-shapes of disturbed water that came toward the boat. "Rats joining a sinking ship."

"We're not sinking," Kerid returned. "We're sailing on to glory, and to revenge Chaldor."

Nassim stared at him awhile, then smiled. "By the gods, I think perhaps you're right."

CHAPTER FIVE

Ellyn rode in sulky silence, or perhaps a contemplative mood; I could not tell for sure. Her mouth was a grim line and she spoke to me not at all. I tried awhile to make conversation, but I am not very good at that and soon gave up. I could not, truly, blame her. After all, she was but fifteen years of age and cast adrift in a world torn by war. Her father was slain and she knew her mother would likely die ere long. Did she not know for sure, then surely she must guess that we should soon be hunted; and she was accustomed to the luxuries of the palace, not the road. I was pleased to see that she was a good horsewoman, and considerably less pleased with her first display of arrogant temper.

I had set a brisk pace, and Chorym lay a good few leagues behind us by the time the sun approached its zenith. We traveled the Great East Road that pierced the hills ringing Chaldor's heart through a pass known as the Geffyn, but we should not reach that boundary for at least another day. The road was crowded with folk going in to the hoped-for sanctuary of the city, and we must often turn our mounts off the paved way onto the grass beside as herds of lowing cattle or flocks of bleating sheep blocked our path. There were numerous wagons, groups of riders, and more folk afoot. I pitied them all for what they faced, knowing their hopes were faint, and prayed none recognize Ellyn. I thought they would not, save on close inspection, for with her shorn hair and boyish gear, she looked, at least on brief examination, like some gangly, sulking youth.

We came to the first way station as the sun climbed past its midpoint, and Ellyn spoke for the first time. "I know this place; they set a good table."

That was true; I had eaten there. I said, "We ride on."

She gave me as haughty a look as any fifteen-year-old can manage and said, "I'm hungry," as if that settled all argument.

"We've food." I patted saddlebags. "We'll eat beside the road."

"I'm *hungry*," she repeated obstinately. "And I'd wash."

"We'll find a stream," I said.

She gaped at me, then reined in her horse—and when I did not halt, heeled the beast back alongside mine. "I said"—her eyes narrowed in anger—"that I am hungry, and that I'd stop here awhile."

"We cannot always have what we want," I returned. "You say you know this place? Then likely they'll know you as Ellyn, daughter of Andur and Ryadne."

She said, "Of course they know me."

"And therefore would likely tell any hunters Talan sends out that you passed this way."

"But they'd not know to where." Her brows furrowed into a scowl. "By all the gods, do *you* know where we're going?"

"Not yet." I shook my head. "But I'd not leave any trail."

"You're afraid?"

I nodded. "Do you understand nothing? If Talan cannot have your mother, then he'll have you—that he might claim Chaldor by marriage-right. That or slay you, and to that end he'll seek us. Likely with the aid of his Vachyn sorcerer, who *does* frighten me. By the gods, girl, would you halt at every way station? As well remain in Chorym."

"I wish I had," she snapped.

"Save your mother commanded otherwise, and made me your guardian. Therefore, you will obey me."

"A Highlander hire-sword?" She favored me with a sly glance. "I'll not!"

I saw her intention even as she gathered up her reins. I brought my mare a little closer and reached across to seize the chestnut's bridle. Ellyn struck at me and I turned my head, hauling my own mount's reins over so that she danced aside, drawing the other animal with her. Ellyn mouthed a curse worthy of any soldier and sawed her reins, trying to break my grip. Almost, I was yanked from the saddle, but I kept my hold and fought the chestnut to a standstill. Curious folk watched us from the road.

Then, my hand still firm on the bridle, I said, "Do you continue this, I'll take you off that horse and set you across my knee and deliver you the drubbing you deserve."

I was angry. In the names of all the gods, did she not understand the gravity of our situation? Was she truly so willful as to jeopardize her own escape with childish tantrums? I suppose my ire must have shown on my face and echoed in my tone, for she paled and stared at me a moment out of wide eyes.

"You'd lay hands on me?" Her voice was harsh with disbelief, then rose shrill. "You'd threaten Chaldor's heir?"

"Quiet!" I was aware of the traffic flowing by us, the looks we got. "Be silent, damn you!"

Ellyn snarled and bristled like some cat cornered by a dog, and slammed her heels against the chestnut's ribs so that the horse plunged forward. I let go my hold before I was dragged from my saddle and heeled the mare after the princess. I swung my reins over, driving across Ellyn's path, blocking her moves so that she was herded at a gallop past the way station.

Finally, she slowed the chestnut. Traffic was eased now and the road mostly ours, though we still gathered catcalls and looks. I shouted something about headstrong boys who'd taste ale before their time, and led her off the road, onto a pasture where the air smelled sweet with dung, for all no animals remained. A little way farther there was a small copse of alders growing beside a stream, and I brought us to the water.

"We can eat now."

I held her horse until she dismounted, then walked both animals awhile as she paced the streamside and stood staring at the sun-dappled water with her hands fisted on her hips, her shoulders hunched in irritation. I could hear her muttering furiously. I let her wait, taking my time as I brought the horses to the stream and let them drink, then hobbled them and left them to graze. I opened my saddlebags and fetched out provisions. I was, I must admit, hungry myself, but I was a soldier and accustomed to an empty belly. I took out cold meat and bread and offered her a share. She stared at the food and turned away, so I stretched on the grass and began to eat. Ryadne had thought to include wine, for which I was most grateful—I felt in need of drink—and settled myself comfortably with one eye on the princess.

I had thought she might make a run for her horse, but instead she came back along the stream's bank and hunkered down where I had left her food.

"You would have spanked me?" she asked.

I nodded. "And might yet, do you continue to act like a spoiled child."

"I am Chaldor's heir!" She stared at me, outraged. "I am a princess!"

I laughed, which pleased her not at all. "Here," I told her, gesturing at our bucolic surroundings, "you are not a princess. You are my charge—I am sworn to defend you to my death; to protect and guard you. And I shall do that, even does it offend you."

She chewed the meat and spat a piece of gristle into the stream, where small fishes rose to nibble. I tossed her the wineskin.

"This is not easy," she said.

"No." I watched as she drank.

"I am not used to this."

I said again, "No, but these are strange times and we must adapt to them if we are to survive."

She looked at me then and asked, "Shall we?"

"Whilst I live," I said, "no harm shall come you."

"And Chorym; my mother?" Her pretty face grew troubled. "Chaldor?"

I felt suddenly awkward. "Did Ryadne . . . your mother . . . not explain?"

Ellyn nodded. "But I'd hear it from you."

"Why?" I asked.

"Because you're a soldier. Because my mother trusts you—as did my father."

Her voice had grown small, and when I looked at her, I saw tears slowly traverse her cheeks. Bereft of her arrogance, her haughtiness, she seemed very young. I said, "Talan brings all the might of Danant against us. He defeated us—thanks to his Vachyn sorcerer—on the plain before the Darach Pass. He slew your father and is bent on conquering the Bright Kingdom. He'll land his army and bring it against Chorym, and I think the city shall fall."

I might have put it softer, smoother, but such tact is not the Devyn way, and in my clan we believe that a child is best taught the hard lessons early. Also, I'd no wish that Ellyn perceive this journey of ours as some casual pleasure trip, an outing on which she might behave as she chose. I had sooner she know and accept the reality early, that our journeying be easier.

Even so, I regretted the flood of tears my words elicited.

"And Mother shall die, no?"

"She'll not wed Talan," I said.

"Mother said he'd have her; or me."

"He'll have neither."

She swung her head to face me. Her eyes were red now,

her cheeks all silvery with tears. "Because Mother will die before he can?"

I nodded.

"And me?"

"Not while I live," I said.

Ellyn's laughter came strange and shrill. Both horses started at the sound.

"Why not? You don't even like me."

"I gave my word," I said. "Andur was my sworn liege lord, and I gave my word to Ryadne."

"And so you'd die for me?"

"For you and Chaldor."

"But you're a mercenary. You're a Devyn clansman. A . . ."

"Hire-sword?" I finished for her. "Yes; I am. But I hired my blade to Andur, and swore then to defend Chaldor—and I do not break my word, Ellyn."

"Even though it might cost you your life? Even though Talan shall hunt us? And you might win great wealth by handing me to him?"

"You don't understand."

"I'm trying to."

"Then know this: Yes, I could give you to Talan and ride away with sacks of gold, or find some high office in his army. But then I should be less than I expect myself to be. Do I break my word, I am nothing."

"You'd be alive and free."

Now I laughed. "I am alive and free now, no?"

"Hardly free." She tapped her chest. "You've me to think of."

"There's that," I allowed.

She stared at me awhile, then slowly, almost shyly, smiled. "No easy duty, eh?"

I shook my head.

"I'll do my best," she promised.

"Good," I said. "So, eat and we'll be on our way."

We finished our simple meal in silence then mounted our horses and continued along the Great Road.

The way stretched out before us, straight as an arrow to the slash in the hills that was the Geffyn Pass. There was little traffic now, and the majority of the farms we passed were tenanted, the meadows filled with cattle and sheep, folk working in the fields. To the east, the sky darkened, the great disk of the moon we Devyn name the Huntsman suspended like some indifferent eye above the blue line of the hills. Lights began to show in distant buildings, and Ellyn began to speak of finding lodgings for the night.

She was in a foul humor. The previous night we had slept beside the road, our tents sheltered by tall beech trees, a stream nearby. I had built a fire and roasted meat, we had fresh water and wine to drink, and I had thought it as fine a bivouac as any I'd known. But I suppose that Ellyn was accustomed to the luxury of royal hunting trips—all canopied pavilions and soft beds set up by servants, such food as the palace cooks prepared. Her earlier gentleness had evaporated, and she had complained then and since, until I grew weary of her carping and rode in grim silence with her complaints battering my tired ears. There was a way station ahead, at the entrance to the pass, and she spoke of spending the night there. I had no more intention of halting there than any other place she might be recognized, and told her so.

She looked at me sidelong then, her eyes hooded, her mouth a line thinned by disgruntlement. By, I supposed, the lack of those comforts she knew.

Like a vicious dog sensing weakness, she pounced. "How shall I be recognized?" She snatched off her feathered cap, ducking her shorn head at me, slapping the cap against her boyish tunic. "I am near bald—thanks to you! And I am dressed like some . . . some . . ."

"Mercenary's child?" I supplied.

"Yes, like some hire-sword's offspring! Who'd know me now, like this?"

"There's your face," I said, "and your manner."

"What manner?"

I could not help grinning. "You do not behave like some 'hire-sword's offspring,' but rather like an arrogant princess."

"You've known princesses, eh?"

Whatever faults she had—and the gods knew, I could name them in abundance—her wits were not slow. I shook my head. "Only you." And added, "Which is quite enough for me."

I could not tell if she laughed, but surely she turned her face away and studied the road awhile.

I looked ahead. The sun lost its battle with the night now and the way grew dark. The pass rose before us like a sword's cut in the stone of the hills. Lights twinkled where the way station stood and the road was walled in by the surrounding stone. It occurred to me that Ellyn need only cry out and men would likely come to investigate the disturbance, allowing her to spin whatever yarn came to mind, and doubtless not to my good. I reined in and dismounted.

"Why are you stopping?"

"She's lame."

My bay turned her head at that, as if questioning my lie, but Ellyn halted and came back to where I waited.

"How so? She was sound a moment since."

I said, "Look," and when Ellyn leaned from her saddle, I grabbed her and dragged her free. She opened her mouth to scream, but I clapped a hand over the sound and flung her down. I'd cord ready in my hand and looped it swift over her wrists; then gagged her. Her eyes bulged in fear and fury, and I said, "I intend you no harm, but neither shall you give us away."

Then I lifted her astride her saddle and lashed her ankles to the stirrups, mounted my bay again, and took up the chestnut's reins.

Thus did I bring Chaldor's heir, the princess Ellyn, up into the Geffyn Pass, past the way station, like some olden-time captive carried off by my Highlander ancestors.

The pass climbed, lined along its top by pines, to its egress, where it fed out onto a great swath of woodland. This was an area mostly given over to forestry and hunting. What pastures there were were located within the great spread of forest that stretched out like some moon-washed sea to the far horizons. Beyond lay the high moors and mountains of the clans, but those should take us long days to reach, and now it was deepening night. I deemed it safe to remove Ellyn's gag and set her free.

She kicked me in the chest when I loosed her bonds and sprang from her horse to pummel fists against my chest and face, accompanied by as foul a flood of curses as any I'd heard.

I fended her off until her anger was spent and she stood gasping, her face flushed in the moonlight.

"I'll have you hanged! By the gods, no! I'll have you stretched and drawn through the streets and then quartered! I'll have you . . ."

"You must live to do all that," I said. "You must become the queen first."

"I shall." She glowered at me. "I shall become queen and condemn you to the most horrible death I can imagine."

"Worse than Talan would deliver me? Worse than his Vachyn sorcerer might imagine?"

"Yes!" she shrieked. Then, "Why did you tie me?"

"Because you'd have run to that way station, no?"

"Yes," she said again, but in a softer tone.

"And perhaps given Talan's hunters a sign."

She nodded—a brief lowering of her head, reluctant—and rubbed at her wrists.

"Little more chance of that. Now shall we make camp and sleep?"

I found a place where a game trail suggested water, which I found within a ring of trees. A brook babbled its way by grassy banks, through a tiny meadow overseen by oaks and ash and hazel, and I told Ellyn we might safely halt. I stripped the horses of their gear and rubbed them down, then hobbled them and found wood for a fire. I set meat over the flames and erected a single tent—I'd no need of canvas, but would sleep under the stars. I felt my home-land close, as if the Highlands called to me, and I was not at all sure how I felt about returning. Ellyn did not speak to me further.

We ate, and drank a little wine; cleansed ourselves in the stream and settled to sleep. The night was warm, and did the buzzing of the insects worry Ellyn, their sound was to me a soporific that swiftly lulled me into slumber.

Soldier's instinct woke me.

I did not know why I woke, nor think on how my sword came to be in my hand. I only rolled clear of my blanket as moonlight glinted on steel and thrust my blade into the belly of the man who would have slain me as I slept. He screamed like the stuck pig he was and pulled himself off my point as I rose and swung at his throat.

I cut his neck halfway through. He stopped screaming and fell down to sully the brook with his blood. I heard a footstep behind me and turned in time to parry a blow di-rected at my back. I deflected the sword and stepped in close as my attacker was swung off-balance. I drove a knee into his groin and, as he doubled over, smashed my pommel against his temple. Metal clanged on metal and, as the fel-low grunted, I saw that he wore a half helm, and also a breastplate that was dented and rusting. I struck again and he pitched onto his face. I reversed my blade and stabbed it into his back, into the gap between the breastplate and the wide leather belt he wore. I felt his spine snap, but if he screamed I did not hear him, for I was already spinning, my sword outthrust to divert the spear that came toward me.

I did hear Ellyn scream, and saw two more half armored figures dragging her from the tent. I danced aside, letting the spear slide by me as I dropped my left arm to trap the haft. The spearman grunted and pulled back. He looked sur-prised as I took a hold on his weapon and stabbed him in the throat. My blade emerged all bloody from behind his head and he stared at me with wide, disbelieving eyes. I twisted my blade as I withdrew, and sprang away as a great jet of blood gouted from his sundered windpipe. He made an odd whistling sound and fell down onto his knees. I kicked him aside and ran toward the tent.

The chestnut and the bay were shrilling. I heard Ellyn screaming, but I could not see her. Then I heard hoofbeats and a last cry, abruptly ended as if a blow stunned the princess. I cursed and sheathed my sword. I snatched out my knife and hacked the hobble free of the bay mare's forelegs, sheathed that blade, and swung astride. It had been some time since I'd ridden bareback, but I'd not lost the knack. I wrapped my legs about the mare and clutched a handful of mane, turned her toward the sounds I'd heard and slammed my heels hard into her ribs.

It was a wild ride, that—all full of fear and guilt and self-recrimination. Why had I not considered the threat of bandits? The gods knew, Chaldor had been at war long enough that the borderlands were unpoliced by Andur's soldiery. What if bandits took the princess? Should I return to Chorym to advise Ryadne I'd lost her daughter so soon? I yelled at the mare, urging her to greater speed. And saw ahead, through the trees, the two riders, one slowed by the precious burden he carried across his saddle. They made for the road. I drew my sword and slapped the mare's flank.

She responded willingly, closing the distance between us and my quarry. Even so, the kidnappers reached the road and turned their horses east at full gallop. I did not think they were Highlanders, but more likely ex-soldiers, deserters or only common brigands, who'd have some stronghold in the forest. I wondered how many more might wait within that stronghold, and knew that I must rescue Ellyn before the two men reached safety.

Hooves rang loud on the paving of the road, and the moon lit my way clear. The road was wide enough here that two wagons might pass abreast, but ahead it curved around an outcrop of rock and for a while I lost sight of them. I turned my horse wide around the outcrop, which was as well, for as I rounded the jut of stone a rider charged me.

My instincts had suspected a possible ambush, but even so my attention was focused on Ellyn, and I had to some extent assumed the bandits too cowardly to stand and fight. This one, however, owned some measure of courage and was his attack not entirely unexpected, still it threatened to unseat me. His horse—a shaggy black—came charging from the shadow of the outcrop, directly at me. I saw that he wore a breastplate and greaves, a dented pot surmounting his head. He swung a flail: three long chains attached to the wooden pole, each ending in a spiked ball. The flail is a weapon both clumsy and powerful. It can inflict terrible damage, and requires little skill to use, but save the wielder be both strong and dexterous it is awkward, each swing leaving space for counterattack. This man *was* strong, and dexterous—and adept with the weapon. As I swung my mare away, fearing she be ridden down and I tossed to the ground, he adjusted the angle of his swing away from my head toward my horse's. I tugged on her mane and she shrieked a protest, but the savage spiked balls cut only air, not yielding flesh. I hacked my sword at the black's muzzle. I am Devyn—I do not care for the harming of animals— but I was also a soldier, and knew that any horse cut across the muzzle will turn away. The black screamed and began to buck.

The bandit shouted a curse and struggled long enough to bring his hurt animal under control that I was able to swing my mare around and raise my blade. He stood up in his stirrups, his right arm turning in great circles as he increased the momentum of the flail. I saw that he was a big man, taller than me, black-bearded and shaggy as his mount. He brought the flail around in a sweeping arc that would have shattered my skull had I not ducked. I felt the wind of the chains' passage ruffle my hair and swung my sword at his ribs. I could not hurt him there, not through the metal of his armor, but he was knocked a little off-balance, and the flail lost its momentum. He cursed some more and rose again in his stirrups, and I heeled my bay alongside his black and thrust my sword into his armpit. He shouted in pain, blood brighter than the rust on his breastplate pouring over the metal. I stabbed again, this time at his face, and he lurched back. I forced my mare closer, crowding the black horse, not allowing the brigand time to recover.

It is not easy to use a sword from the back of an unaccoutred horse—stirrups afford a solid platform from which to direct the swing, and reins grant precise control—but I drove a blow at his head and saw his eyes widen and glaze as my edge struck his helm. He shook his head and I cut at his arm, which was unprotected save for a leathern shirt, and opened a wide wound there. The flail dropped from his hand and I saw fear in his eyes. He began to saw his reins, seeking to turn the black and run, but I gave him no chance. I drew back my sword arm and rammed the point into his mouth. He bit the blade and teeth shattered as I twisted the steel. He spat blood and fought his horse around, seeking now only to flee. I struck him across the back of his neck, and then across his thigh, and his back arched. I struck again, pitching him from his saddle, and the black horse shrilled and ran northward. The brigand's left foot was caught in the stirrup and he bounced over the pavestones of the road, screaming.

I brought my bay around and heeled her after Ellyn. She was nervous from the fight and the smell of spilled blood, but she ran, overtaking the black, and I blessed her for her willingness.

The road ahead stood straight and empty in the moon's light, and the forest stretched out to either side all shadowy and ominous. I began to fear the remaining kidnapper had found refuge amongst the trees. I slowed the mare to a fast canter, my head turning from side to side, scanning the timber for some inward-leading trail. None showed and I increased my pace, but still there was no sign of another rider. I began to feel dreadfully afraid.

After a while I halted, listening to the night. The black horse, still dragging its ragged burden, walked toward me. Blood dripped from its muzzle where I'd cut the hapless beast, and it kicked irritably at the brigand. I dismounted and caught the reins; I loosed the black's harness and set it free. I left the bandit where he lay and remounted. I could not believe the last brigand had got so far ahead, and so I rode back the way I'd come, asking that the gods send me some sign, that they lead me to Ellyn.

I rode slow now, moving from one side of the road to the other, seeking sign: hoofprints in the edging grass, broken branches, droppings—anything that might show me where the bandit had taken my charge.

I blessed the Huntsman moon for its light when I saw the hank of hair caught on the thorns of a bramble thicket. Was the last kidnapper's horse shaggy as the black, then that tuft had come from its hide. I slid off the bay and studied the ground. Hoofprints led into the timber, and when I looked closer, I saw where the brambles were displaced; deeper in, a broken twig. I hesitated a moment, wondering if I should ride into the forest or go afoot.

There was no clear trail here, nor had the dead man's horse sought this ingress, and so I decided the last kidnapper was not making for any stronghold but only seeking refuge. I chose to approach on foot.

I left the bay mare and pushed through the thicket. Beyond, the way opened a little, looming trees dappling the sward with harlequin patterns of light and shadow. I saw the indentations of hooves and smelled the odor of horse dung. I trod carefully, wondering if the bandit owned a bow, if I might feel the sudden thud of an arrow in my chest or back. I decided not. Surely they'd have used arrows against me before, did they possess such weapons. Even so, I went wary, and horribly afraid that Ellyn was gone beyond my rescuing.

Then I heard the soft whicker of a horse cut off by a muffling hand. I halted, listening, sniffing the night air. It was cool now; I could not be sure it was horse sweat I smelled, but there was surely something drifting on the listless breeze, coming from my right.

I leaned my back against the bole of an oak that stood on the edge of a grassy clearing. Hoofprints showed in the light that filtered through the overlapping branches, the grass crushed down in a line that went off to the east. I scanned the edge of the clearing and saw that the tracks went up to a stand of ferns and disappeared into the undergrowth. I trod slowly around the oak and circled the clearing. I did not enter where the tracks went in but to the north, easing gently through the encircling ferns. I heard the horse whicker again, softly, and made my way toward the sound.

Beyond the ferns the ground fell away into a shallow, grassy bowl. A spring rose there, from amongst mossy stones, feeding a tiny stream. Ellyn lay beside the water. Her hands and feet were bound, and a strip of dirty cloth gagged her mouth. A roan horse stood drinking, and beyond the animal stood the last brigand. He held a sword in his right hand and a long knife in his left. Like his dead companions, he wore a breastplate and helmet; greaves protected his lower legs, and on each forearm he wore a vambrace. He stared around, head cocked for sound of my approach. He seemed frightened, and I supposed he had heard the sounds of dying coming from the road.

I went carefully along the lip of the bowl until I reached a point where I stood between him and Ellyn. Then I charged.

The bandit turned at my approach, sword and knife rising in defense. I smashed them both aside and cannoned into him, knocking us both to the ground. I rose the swifter and drove my blade into his throat. I rested all my weight on the weapon, pinning him to the sward, and set my feet on his wrists as he twisted and kicked. In a while a rattling sound came from his gaping mouth and he ceased his movements. I pulled my sword free and went to Ellyn.

Her eyes were huge, and when I cut the gag from her mouth she spat and rolled away from me as if she were afraid. I loosed her wrists and ankles and she crawled to the spring, gulping up water, splashing it vigorously over her face.

"Are you harmed?" I asked. "Did he touch you?"

She shook her head, sucking in great lungfuls of air. I reached toward her and she started back, staring at me as if I were some monster. I left her and went to the bandit's horse, soothing the nervous animal. When I turned away, Ellyn was on her feet. She looked at the dead brigand and then at me.

"The others?"

"Dead."

"You slew them?"

I nodded.

"How many were there?"

"Five."

"But you were asleep."

I said, "I woke in time."

"We should have spent the night in the way station."

"I explained that to you." I stared at her, irritation stirring. I had saved her—either her life or her virginity—yet she seemed critical. "And even had we, this forest spreads wide and they'd have likely found us sooner or later."

She lowered her head awhile. Then: "Shall we bury him? Them?"

"No." I glanced at the dead brigand. "The beasts and birds will see to them."

"We should," she said. "Even them . . . that the gods . . ."

"Do the gods want their souls," I said, "then they'll take them. We've not the time to waste."

She folded her arms across her chest and lowered her head. It came to me that she'd not seen a man die before, and that she was a child cast adrift from all she knew—aware that her mother should soon die, her father already slain, and she become an orphan. I remembered the first time I'd seen death, and the first time I killed a man. I would have gone to her and put my arms around her, but I thought that was not what she wanted. I said, "Are you ready, you can ride this horse and we'll . . ."

"Go back?" She looked up, her eyes wide and blank. "To our camp, where the bodies are?"

"Where else?" I asked. "Your own horse is there, and all our gear."

She said, "To the way station! Then back to Chorym."

"No," I said, gentle as I could, "that's not a possibility. We must go on—as your mother asked."

"And if I refuse?"

"Then I must bind you again, and take you; but I'll not renege my promise."

"You would, no? You'd tie me up like he did." She glanced quickly at the dead man. "You'd treat me like he did."

"Not like that," I said. "But yes, must I."

She looked at me; her eyes were forlorn. "I've no say in this, have I? I'm just some *thing*, some *package*."

"You're Chaldor's heir," I said. "Your mother's daughter, and I must see you safe."

"No matter what I want?"

I shook my head.

She began to weep then. She fell to her knees and pressed her hands to her face. I went to her and knelt before her. I touched her shoulder and murmured soft words, such as I'd use to gentle a horse or a dog—I knew none others. She looked up at me and suddenly flung her arms about me. I held her, feeling her body shudder, hearing her sobs. I wondered if this was what it was like to have a child. I stroked her short hair, voicing platitudes, and she clung to me as if I were a rock and she some boatless riverman lost in a storm.

Then, abruptly, she shook off my grip and pushed away,

rubbing at her tear-stained face. I left her, and walked the dead brigand's horse over. I picked her up and set her on the saddle. She did not struggle or argue; she was listless as a sack.

I led the horses out of the woods back to the road. My bay waited for me and I mounted her, and took Ellyn back to our camp. Those insects that inhabit the night were already on the bodies. I deemed it best we not linger. I thought Ellyn should not like it, and I also thought that perhaps the brigands' fellows—had they companions—might come searching. So I stowed our gear as the princess slumped silent beside the stream, then thought that the three dead men there must have owned animals.

I found them tethered a little way off. They were not very good horses, but they'd make for trade. I also searched the dead men, which afforded me little save a few coins; I supposed they were not very successful bandits. Neither their weapons nor their armor were worth the taking.

"You plunder the dead?"

I looked up from a corpse and shrugged. I was a soldier; I was accustomed to plundering the dead. They'd no more use for what they had owned in life; nor these deserved it. I thought this child had lessons to learn.

I said, "We've now four horses we can sell."

"My mother gave you coin."

"Aplenty," I agreed. "And useful, do we truly need it. But the Bright Kingdom ends here. Folk hereafter trade in kind, and only fat merchants carry gold coin. We're not merchants, but a hire-sword and his brat; better that we trade horses than pay in Chorym's gold."

"And how explain the horses?" she demanded.

I could not help but chuckle at her innocence. "The truth," I said. "That we were attacked by brigands, slew them, and took their animals."

She said, "You're a Devyn savage."

I said, "Yes, if you will. But also your guardian. Now

mount that pretty chestnut and we'll be on our way. Do you
behave yourself, we'll even stop for breakfast."

She climbed obediently astride her horse. She seemed
too shocked, too numbed, to argue more. I mounted my bay
and took up the ropes I'd set on the bandits' animals. And we
rode toward the dawn.

CHAPTER SIX

Ellyn said nothing. There seemed nothing to say, for all she felt like screaming. It was as if she were trapped inside a nightmare, powerless in the hands of the unkind fate that carried her away from all she knew, all that was familiar, to a world of violence and bloody death. Gailard's dispatch of the bandits had been so abrupt, so mercilessly efficient, it took her breath away, and in a way she admired him for his soldierly skills. In another, however, it changed him in her eyes, rendering him suddenly dangerous, like some great wildcat that was untamed and deadly for all its lazy purring. She stared morosely at his back, telling herself that he was the guardian chosen by her father and her mother, and therefore to be trusted. But she had seen his face as he struck, and there was nothing tame in that. She clenched her teeth, quelling the sigh that threatened to erupt into weeping. Her country was at war, and she Chaldor's heir—she must be strong, and she must go with Gailard. That was her geas.

She blinked back tears, conjuring images of the palace, of happier times. Or trying, for mostly she found herself remembering the statuary and the tapestries, the mosaics that depicted battles, glorious victories, and Chaldor's enemies kneeling in obeisance. None showed the blood that flowed, nor did the fallen bear such expressions as the man she had seen killed. The gods knew, but she wanted so badly to go home, and knew she could not. She must go on with this . . . What was he, savage or champion? Her father had trusted him, named him friend, and her mother clearly believed her daughter safe in the guardian's hands. But Ellyn was not so sure. She relived those recent moments—the shock of the bandits' approach, her outrage giving way to naked terror, the desperate flight and the horrid threats, Gailard's arrival and its bloody aftermath. Surely her father would have offered the last brigand honorable quarter, certainly he would not have looted the dead. Yet after, Gailard had been gentle, and she had clung to him gratefully, aware of his solid body, his strength. In those brief moments he had seemed no savage, but kind as her father, as caring. Then she had grown conscious of the blood-smell, the stench of the dead man's death-opened bowels, and pushed away. And then Gailard had picked her up and set her astride the dead man's horse as if she were a possession, his prize.

She felt anger stir. He had no right to handle her like that. She might be his charge, but she was still a princess of Chaldor, heir to Chorym's throne, and deserving of far greater respect. But she could do nothing. She was, she thought, as helpless in his hands as she had been in the bandits', and did he treat her gentler, still he had threatened to strike her and lash her to her mount. And that sop he'd thrown her—"do you behave yourself, we'll even stop for breakfast." How dare he patronize her so! She ground her teeth as ire mounted, replacing despondency. When she came into her own power she would repay these insults. Were she crowned, she'd repay him; did she find her talent, she'd lash him with magic.

But when would that be? Her mother had assured her she owned the magical talent, but Ellyn could find no sign of it. The far-seeing of the Dur was, Ryadne had explained, a whimsical thing, stronger in some than in others, and never truly reliable. She did not think, she had told her daughter, that Ellyn owned that kind of magic, for it became apparent as a girl became a woman, and her first bleedings had brought no evidence. However, Ryadne had assured her, the talent *was* in her, likely closer to those powers the Vachyn wielded, and consequently later to develop. She recalled the conversation, before her world was turned upside down.

A warm summer breeze had swept swallows about Chorym's battlements, soft as a caress, gentle as the ordered fields that spread about the city. The war had seemed far away then, and Ryadne had as yet kept her grim foreknowledge of Andur's death to herself—Ellyn anticipated her father's triumphant return, and wondered why her mother seemed so withdrawn, so intense.

"I have spoken of this with those who own some little knowledge," Ryadne had said, "and read what little there is to read on the subject. But only the Vachyn truly know, and I cannot speak with them."

"Perhaps I have no talent," Ellyn had suggested. "Perhaps the blood of Chaldor dilutes the Dur gift."

"No." Ryadne had shaken her head. "I sense it in you, like a smoldering fire."

"Then when shall it kindle?"

Ryadne shrugged at that, her brow creased in puzzled frown. "I know not. Perhaps it shall manifest itself suddenly; pehaps you must be taught to use it."

"By whom?" Ellyn had felt an odd chill then, as if some cold wind from the future blew back to touch her with ominous promise.

"I cannot say." Ryadne shrugged again. "Not the Vachyn." Then, almost too soft for Ellyn to hear, "But I pray you do learn. I pray you learn in time."

"Perhaps when Father comes home," Ellyn said. "Perhaps he'll know."

"Perhaps," Ryadne allowed, and changed the subject.

Now Ellyn longed for the talent, and wondered if her mother had been wrong. She had willed it to the fore when the bandits came, seeking to send fire, thunderous blasts to sweep them from their horses, but nothing had happened.

She exhaled irritably, thinking that if only she commanded magic, she would scourge Gailard for his impertinence, force him to his knees before her, his head bowed in due respect.

Then she felt guilt stir. After all, he *had* saved her from rape and slavery and likely death, all those things the brigand had promised. And he was, she must admit, a brave and skillful warrior who risked his life on her behalf. Indeed, were he only dressed suitably—in good armor, her colors— he would make a most admirable champion. He was, she thought, a handsome man—in a rough way. But were his long hair trimmed, and that Highlander beard . . . She shook her head, dismissing such thoughts even as she felt her cheeks grow warm. The gods knew, the last thing she needed now was to form some childish liking for the man. She was Chaldor's heir, she reminded herself, representative of the high bloodline of the Bright Kingdom, and he no more than she had named him—a Devyn savage.

But still, she could not help but notice his broad shoulders, his straight back, the easy way he sat his horse. Perhaps she would not, even were she able, punish him, but only demand an apology. And meanwhile, she could do nothing but follow him and obey him, for the alternative was to return and he would not allow that. With which thought her anger flared anew, so that when he turned in his saddle and smiled at her, she scowled in reply.

Though she noticed for the first time how white his teeth were and how warm his smile.

CHAPTER SEVEN

I rode wary, studying the road before us and the surrounding trees, my head turning from side to side, listening for any sounds other than the steady clatter of our horses' hooves. Ellyn rode in silence, seemingly lost in her own thoughts, and I was grateful for that, no matter the cause. Likely the bandits had been some solitary group, but I could not help fearing that they were part of some larger gathering of outlaws that might, in time, miss their felonious brethren and come seeking them. Were that the case, we'd have little chance. The forest was a lonely place, and in these troubled times there were no patrols or caravans abroad to offer us shelter. Indeed, save things had greatly changed since last I traveled these parts, there was no major habitation until the woods ended and the Highlands began. There, where also the Great Road terminated, was a town of sorts, a meeting place for merchants and peddlers where Highlanders would come in to trade with the foresters and the caravans come out from the Bright Kingdom's heartland. It was my reluctant intention to halt there, for before I ventured back into my homeland, I'd glean news of events—who allied with whom, which clans fought. It was a chancy undertaking—there might well be folk who knew me and would carry

word back to my father—but I could think of no other
course save to go blind into the Highlands.

I mused on all this even as I watched the forest, and the
moon faded into a dull grey sky that slowly brightened
as dawn came knocking. Birds began to sing, and from
amongst the trees came the sounds of wakened animals. A
plump rabbit crossed our path, halted a moment to stare at
us, then lolloped away. A stag came out from the timber,
antlers high as he tested the air. He caught our scent and
belled a warning that brought a harem of seven does trotting
swift across the road. Then the first rays of the sun lofted
above the trees and I felt the promise of warmth. The grey
faded like a curtain drawn back to reveal the pristine blue
behind, and a sudden breeze skirled through the leaves, setting them all to rustling in harmony with the swelling birdsong. I could not help smiling, for a new day dawned and we
had survived ambush and kidnap, and it seemed that perhaps the gods favored us now.

From ahead, I heard the sound of water tumbling over
rocks, and in a while we came to a bridge that spanned a
fast-flowing river. It was an arch of dark blue stone, walled
on either side and supported by three buttresses, rising
above the old ford. I decided to halt and make us some
breakfast.

We went down to the water's edge and I built a small
fire. Ellyn knelt, vigorously bathing her face and hands, as if
she'd wash away the blood I'd spilled. I set a pot to boiling
and brought food from our supplies, and soon had a decent
enough meal readying.

Ellyn returned from her ablutions and settled on the
shingled bench beside the fire. She stared moodily at the
flames, ignoring me, then took up a pebble and flung it.
Abruptly, she turned toward me and began to speak.

"Shall it all be like that, like last night?"

I shrugged, not knowing the answer she wanted to hear.

"Shall there be more killing?"

"Likely. These are . . . troubled times. What law your father imposed is gone."

"With his death?"

"With the war. That took the soldiers away, so the outlands grow more lawless than ever."

"Soldiers kept the law?"

"Who else? Andur's men patrolled these roads and made them safe."

"Men like you?"

I shrugged again. "I suppose so."

"But what if . . ." She hesitated, frowning. "What if *Highlanders* came a-raiding?"

"Men like me would fight them."

"Even your own kin?"

"Yes. I swore allegiance to Andur, to Chaldor. So even were it my own kin I'd fight them."

"Because you gave your word?"

"Yes."

She stared at me, and her eyes seemed to penetrate me, looking deep inside me, as if she plumbed the depths of my soul and judged me. She seemed in that moment no spoiled child but ageless and timeless as the stone that flanked the river. I felt a sudden need to explain.

"I am outcast from my clan—by my father's word. I have no family, no kin. I return to the Highlands on pain of death. Andur gave me a home, a place . . . respect . . . and I swore to serve him. I serve him now."

"By going back to the Highlands?"

I grinned, though I felt not much amused, and took a stick from the fire. "What do you know of the Highlands? Of the lands beyond Chaldor's valley?"

She shrugged. "Not much."

"Look." I blew the flames from the stick and turned around, using a smooth boulder for parchment. "This is the Durrakym, this Chaldor." I marked the river and ringed the valley in smoking charcoal. "We are here; beyond are the Highlands, then the Styge here. We ride north, into the lands of the clans." I marked the boundaries.

The lines I drew were tenuous as the real boundaries between the clans, and the lands of my own were perilously close to where we headed, but beyond lay the Barrens, and I thought that if we could only reach that wasteland we must surely be safe until that day Ryadne had promised dawned.

Ellyn said, "Why not seek my grandfather? Surely he'd offer us sanctuary with the Dur."

"Which Talan would doubtless guess, and send hunters." I shook my head. "It's as I've told you—best we leave no trail at all."

"Then where do we go?"

"To the end of the road. There's a town there; it's called Cu-na'Lhair. It's a barter town, where folk trade."

"I thought," she said, "that we were avoiding inhabited places."

"We were," I replied, "but we shall need food by then. I'd not take the time to hunt, so we shall need to replenish our supplies and buy ourselves winter gear."

She looked a question at me and I could not help but chuckle.

"Did you think this was some summer outing? The summer ages and the Highlands are cold, and who knows where we shall be when the snows come."

"The war might be ended by then."

"Yes." I nodded, my laughter abruptly quelled. "By Talan, who'll then have all the time he needs to seek you out."

Almost, I regretted my harsh words as I saw her pretty face blanch, her lips tighten. "Then we are truly fugitives," she said, and her voice was forlorn.

I nodded again.

"But you'd chance this—what was it . . . Cu-na'Lhair? What if I'm recognized there? What if you're recognized?"

"Likely your face is not known there," I said. "And mine hasn't been seen in a long time, so perhaps I can escape unknown. Anyway, we shall need supplies, so we must take the chance."

"But after . . ." She studied my charcoal map. "We must still enter the Highlands."

"All well," I said, "we'll cross them unnoticed."

"To where?"

"The Barrens, if we must."

She swallowed noisily. "There are savages in the Barrens, no? And worse things in the Styge?"

I said, "I don't know. I've never been there."

"But you've heard the stories."

"Yes, but I can't think of any safer place."

"You're my guardian," she said, and I could not decide whether she spoke in confidence or accusation, for she turned away then and left me to pour our tea and set out our breakfast.

The forest ended on a wide, rocky ridge, the timber breaking against the foot like some vast dendroid sea. What few trees had succeeded in gaining a hold on the slope seemed like tidal pools, green against the grey-blue of the stone. The rimrock was bare, and from its long hogback we looked out across a grassy valley that stretched northward to the foothills of the Highlands. They shone all misty in the morning light, patterned with sunshine and cloud like a patchwork quilt, and I wondered if I caught the scent of heather on the wind. I suppose not, that it was only memory tricking my senses, but I could not help a pang of nostalgia. I halted and looked awhile, then brought my gaze down to the center of the valley, where Cu-na'Lhair stood.

The road continued on down the ridge's farther side and ended at the town, which stood beside a broad river that ran away north and east into the hazy distance. It was larger than I remembered, walled with native stone and wood from the forest, its single gate opening on the road and a short jetty thrusting a little way into the river. Smoke rose lazy in the morning air and I could see folk moving about the gate, boats moored along the jetty. I glanced at Ellyn, but before I could warn her to maintain her disguise, she tugged her feathered cap lower on her forehead and assumed a belligerent expression. I thought that she would do and wondered about myself. I had gained height and weight since I left this land, and my beard was thickened, patched in places with grey. I might go unrecognized; or not, but Cu-na'Lhair was traditionally peaceful, and I trusted the sheriff and his men still kept discipline within the walls. Was I recognized, then I thought any threat must come after we left—and I could think of nowhere else to go. So I heeled my bay onto the downslope, Ellyn following.

I waved her alongside and said, "We shall be questioned here, and likely about the war. Do you stay silent. Please?"

"You ask me with a pretty *please*? No orders?" She stared at me, as if she could not believe I requested her silence.

I said, "Yes, I *ask* you. Please."

She smiled a little and ducked her head in agreement.

We crossed the stone bridge that led to the gate and halted in the shadow of the great portal as armed men blocked our way. There were five of them, bearing swords and bucklers, javelins in their hands. Their leader faced me, seeming neither hostile or friendly, but mostly curious. I thought he did not know me, and surely I did not know him.

"Hail, strangers. Where are you from?" His eyes scanned us with professional interest.

"Chaldor," I said.

"Few have come from the Bright Kingdom these past weeks." He moved a little aside, studying our mounts and our captured horses. I saw that his men shifted to either side, where they might take us from our saddles with four swift throws. "What news of the war?"

"Poor news," I replied. "You know that Andur took his army across the Durrakym?"

He nodded. "And took that bastard Talan's head, I hope."

"No." I shook my head. "Andur's slain, and Talan comes across the river."

"To Chorym?" His eyes were a very bright blue and they widened as he spoke. "How fares the queen?"

"She readies for siege."

"Chorym must be a hard place to take."

"Surely; but Talan employs a Vachyn sorcerer."

He mouthed a foul curse. "May all the gods damn the Vachyn."

I said, fervently, "Amen to that."

"And what brings you here? You've a soldierly look about you. Why are you not on Chorym's walls?"

"I lost my hire when Andur died. I took a wound"—I patted my knee—"and I've no wish to face Vachyn magic again." That at least was the truth. "So I took my pay and rode away."

"To come home? You're a Highlander, no?"

I shrugged. "A hire-sword now. Are there clansmen here?"

"Some." He accepted my dissembling, which was not so unusual in this town, and turned his attention to Ellyn. "And who's this?"

"My son," I lied. "He's never seen the Highlands."

"And these horses?"

"Bandits attacked us and I slew them. I'd trade their horses for food and winter gear."

He grunted as if this were no unusual announcement. "The forest's thick with brigands these days. Enter and be welcome."

I smiled my thanks. "Can you recommend an inn? And a trustworthy horse dealer?"

"The Lonely Traveler. It's five streets down and left-ward; ask there for directions to Jerym Connach. He'll give you a fair price."

I thanked him and he stood aside, waving us through.

As we rode slowly up the wide street Ellyn asked me, "Should you not have given him small coin for that information?"

I grinned. "That's not the way here. Besides, he likely receives some stipend from the inn and the horse dealer both. But thank you for staying silent."

She offered no response to that, but stared about, her eyes wide under the peak of her cap. I supposed she had never seen a town built all from wood before. Chorym and those few towns that dotted the Bright Kingdom's valley were all of stone and brick and tile, with wood an ornamentation. Cu-na'Lhair—save for its walls—was only timber. The street was, given the summer's heat, hard-packed earth, flanked to either side by pavements of planed wood polished by myriad feet, the buildings that rose two and three stories high were solid timber, with balconies on the upper floors and shutters and doors of ornately carved wood, all painted with bright colors depicting flowers and animals and birds. Folk milled about us, on horseback and in carts and afoot. They wore mostly the breeches and skirts and shirts of Highlanders, with the patterned cloaks that denoted their clans folded and pinned over their shoulders. The men were all armed, swords at their waists and shields slung on their backs, and most of the women carried daggers on their belts. No few stout staffs were tipped with metal, and it came to me that in Chorym only soldiers bore weapons and that it must seem strange to Ellyn to see every passerby armed in some way. I watched her carefully, afraid that she give herself away in some manner. But she did not, and we found the Lonely Traveler without incident.

It was a tall, wide building, the first and second levels both balconied, with its broadest front facing the street and a timbered wall containing a yard behind. I dismounted and tethered the horses to the hitching rail and with Ellyn, all wide-eyed and agog, on my heels, went inside.

The room was the full width of the building across, and almost as deep. The floor was of polished planks that gleamed despite the scouring of the boots that crossed it. Against one wall stood a stone hearth where a fire burned and the carcass of a pig turned slowly on a spit rotated by a child half Ellyn's age. On the farther side was a long counter behind which stood racked barrels and shelves of wine bottles, gleaming glasses and sturdier clay mugs. Numerous tables, chairs, and benches made the navigation of the floor a labyrinth, and the place was loud with laughter and hearty conversation. Servingwomen in flounced skirts and low-cut blouses traversed the maze with practiced ease and ready smiles, trays of ale mugs and bottles of wine carried aloft past the clutching hands and ribald comments. The air smelled of roasting pork and woodsmoke, alcohol and sweat and tobacco. I noticed Ellyn frown, her nostrils pinching, and nudged her, whispering.

"You're a hire-sword's son, remember? You've been in such places before—you're at home here."

She grunted and hitched up her belt, affecting an expression midway between a scowl and a smile, and came with me to the counter.

A man wide as he was tall stood there, busily wiping his hands on a once-clean apron. He was bald, but the lower part of his face was decorated with a luxuriant red beard, and from amongst its many hairs came a gleaming smile.

"Well met, strangers!" His voice was deep as his beard. "What'll it be?"

"A mug of your best ale," I said, "and a cup for the boy. After that, a room, and stabling for our animals."

He pulled a tankard for me and filled a half measure for Ellyn, named me prices and advised me that we might have a chamber on the upper floor. Food would be paid for as we took it.

I gave him coin and asked, "Do you know Jerym Connach, the horse dealer?"

"I do," he said solemnly, then beamed again. "He's my brother. You've animals to trade?"

I told him my story and he commiserated with me on

the dangers of the road in such troubled times, then asked about the war. When I told him, he said, echoing the gateman: "The gods' curse on Talan of Danant and all the Vachyn, and their blessings on the queen. But it's not likely those whoreson bastards'll bother us, eh? Now, as for those horses, why don't you stable them with me—I'll give you a special price—and I'll send word to Jerym that he take a look."

I thanked him and drank my ale. It was good, that dark yellow hue that comes only from Highland hops. I drained the mug and called for a second. Then I heard Ellyn coughing, and turned to see her spluttering over her cup. It had not occurred to me that she was not used to ale, and I cursed myself for that lack of forethought.

"The lad's something of a fever," I said, and complimented myself on my quick thinking: I thought that if Ellyn remained in the room it should enhance our chances of passing unnoticed. "But a night's sleep in a decent bed shall cure him."

Ellyn wiped her mouth and favored me with a glare. "It's that I'm not used to such fine ale," she muttered throatily. "It's weaker stuff in the Bright Kingdom."

Our landlord chuckled. "The lad's got it right there, friend. Poor, prissy ale they brew down there. Not like our good, strong stuff. But you're familiar with it, no? What are you, a Highlander come home? I didn't get your name, by the way. Mine's Jach."

Almost, I told him my true name, but in the nick remembered and so said, "Gavin, and the lad's Elward."

Jach beamed some more and asked if I'd have a fire in our chamber for "Elward's" sake—which should cost a little extra. I told him no, but I'd see our horses safely stabled, and likely take dinner in our room.

"The lad's not much accustomed to the road," I said, "nor to bandits. He grew up in the south."

"The south, eh?" Jach nodded his bald head as if that explained all. "Soft there, no?"

I said, "Yes," and trod on Ellyn's foot as I saw her about to argue.

She gasped and spilled her cup over my boot. "My pardon, Father. But this *is* strong ale."

"No matter, you'll get used to it." I smiled and shook my foot. "Such ale, and the Highlands, shall make a man of you, eh?"

She smiled, as does a cat about to pounce on a cowering mouse. I swiftly drained my mug and asked that we stable our horses and find our chamber.

"And a bath?" Ellyn said gruffly. "Hot water?"

"That shall be extra," Jach said.

I passed him another coin and roughly took Ellyn's elbow. I thought that no one had much noticed us as I led her out and took the horses around the inn to the yard.

"A bath? Hot water? This is not Chorym. Folk live harder here."

"But I've a fever, no?" She raised her cap to mop her brow. "I *need* a bath. The gods know, but you need one, too. You stink like . . . like . . . some . . ."

"Traveler too long on the road?" I asked.

"Yes!" she snarled.

I chuckled. "It shall not be in some marbled tub with servants to soap you and dry you: it shall be a tub brought to our room. Which we share."

"In which case," she answered with a terrible dignity, "you shall leave me to it and wait elsewhere until I am done."

"Leave me the water, eh?" I asked.

We saw the horses stabled and found our chamber. It was comfortable enough for me; small and mean for Ellyn. There was a high window that opened onto the balcony, and a worn rug on the wooden floor; hooks were fixed to the walls, and a washstand stood beside the single bed.

"Where," Ellyn asked, "shall you sleep?"

I looked at the bed and knew it should not be there. I pointed at the floor.

"You must hang a curtain," she said. "Have Jach arrange it."

"By the gods," I said, "you're supposed to be my *son*. I can't ask for a curtain."

"Then use that." Imperiously, she gestured at our gear, our folded tents. "I'll not sleep unless you do."

I thought a moment to argue—the gods knew, I felt no desire for her; I did not even like her much—but then I thought that she was a child on the verge of womanhood, and must likely feel afraid to occupy this room with a man of my years. Indeed, with any man. Somehow, it was different to the open road, as if the accoutrements of civilization imposed a different consciousness.

"I'll do it," I promised, "but only after the water's delivered, lest they suspect."

"But before I bathe," she said. "You'll not watch me bathe."

I agreed. I waited for the tub to be hauled in and filled with hot water. Then I strung cords and hung the tents around the tub. I went out onto the balcony and watched the world go by as she bathed.

By the time I got the tub, the water was cold.

I took down the makeshift curtain—servants would come to remove the tub—and suggested to Ellyn that she eat in the room. She stared at me as if I were mad and shook her head.

"You'd have me twiddle my thumbs here while you gallivant?"

"Hardly that," I said. "I must trade those horses and find out what I can of events in the Highlands."

"Then I'll come with you," she declared firmly.

I sighed. The room was latched only from the inside, and even did I secure the door, she might still escape via the balcony, or set up such a fuss as must surely render us suspicious. "Very well," I allowed, "but only on condition you draw no attention to us. Keep your mouth shut and play the part of my son, eh?"

She promptly settled her cap on her head and hooked her thumbs in her belt, squaring her shoulders and assuming a slouch I supposed she considered manly.

"As you command, *Father*."

I sighed again and quit the chamber.

We went down to the common room and found a table in a shadowy corner. A servingwoman came to take our order and soon we were settled to platters of roast pork and steaming vegetables, mugs of ale at our elbows. Inevitably, because we were last come from the Bright Kingdom, folk came asking questions. I answered past mouthfuls of food, grateful that Ellyn kept her mouth shut.

Then Jach came to us with a man who looked his twin and we settled to trading. Jerym had already examined our horses, and offered to buy both the chestnut and the bay at prices greatly in advance of what he'd offer for the brigands' mounts. I refused that offer and settled on a reasonable sum for the others, save the soundest, which I thought to use for a packhorse. It was sufficient that we might purchase what supplies I thought we'd need without touching Ryadne's gift. Jerym and I spat on our palms and clenched the deal; he gave me a small sack of coin and Jach celebrated our agreement with glasses of that liquor we brew in the Highlands, which is called brose. I was disappointed that Ellyn did not choke on it.

Our meal and business concluded, I took Ellyn out into the streets of Cu-na'Lhair to find us winter clothing.

Jach had recommended an emporium, and there I bought us sturdy sheepskin jerkins and heavy cloaks; gloves and fur-lined boots; two whole cowhides to floor our tents, and sufficient dried and cured and salted food to see us through several weeks. And then Ellyn surprised me again.

"Do you not think it time I had a sword?" she asked mildly, adding, after, a casual "Father."

I gulped, taken aback. What new game was this? The merchant beamed, sensing more business, and before I had chance to argue, swept out an arm to indicate the weaponry on display.

"Indeed the lad should have a blade," he declared. "And a decent shield. But light, eh? He's but a stripling yet, so nothing too heavy. Look . . ."

Ellyn was already examining the blades.

I said, "You're young yet."

The merchant said, "Old enough to wear a blade."

Ellyn said, "Think of those bandits, Father."

From the look in her eyes I knew I was defeated, and so I said, "I'll choose it, and the shield."

She agreed to that and I selected a light blade; a smaller version of my own sword, with a basket hilt and breaker-rings, double-edged with a fuller most of its length. For a shield I chose her a small buckler, leather on wood, with embossed metal plates at the center and around the edge. I also chose the scabbard and the belt.

And as we returned to the Lonely Traveler, laden with our purchases, I asked her why she wanted a sword.

"We go the gods alone know where," she answered, "but surely into danger. What if you are hurt? Or slain? Shall I be then left all alone, without the means to defend myself?"

There was sense in that, but even so I could not imagine this pampered princess wielding a sword. "You were disturbed," I said, "when I slew those brigands."

"Yes, I was." She nodded solemnly. "But I also saw that it was necessary. And might be again. In which case, I'd defend myself."

"What do you know of bladework?" I asked her.

"Very little," she said cheerfully, "but you shall teach me."

And so, it seemed, the matter was decided. I wondered who led our expedition now. Surely there was more to this girl than I'd first thought, and I found myself respecting her more.

"It's not easy," I told her. "A sword gets heavy after a while, nor less the shield. And striking a man is harder still."

"You do it easily enough," she returned from around the bundles she carried. "I've seen you."

"I'm old," I said, "and stronger than you. And I've carried a blade since I was . . ."

I broke off the sentence, but she finished it for me: "Younger than me?"

I nodded. "Yes."

"So you will teach me?"

"I will," I said, "but not here. Only when we're on the road again."

"And when shall that be?"

"Soon," I said. "There's no point lingering here."

"But I like this place," she gave me back. "Can we not stay awhile?"

I said, "No."

And when we reached the Lonely Traveler, I knew that I was right.

We stowed our gear and found the common room again. Ellyn would have worn her new-bought sword, but I managed to persuade her against that. It was by now dusk, and the inn was filling up. I recognized clan colors in the room, amongst them those of the Devyn. A side of beef was turning on the spit, and I bought us ale as we waited for the meat to be carved. Ellyn demanded that I buy her a measure of brose, which she favored over the ale, and for want of peace I agreed, finding us as secluded a table as was possible in the crowded room.

I sipped my ale and Ellyn sipped her brose. Then two men rose and came toward us. Both wore the Devyn colors, and I knew them both from long ago. One was Athol, the other Rurrid; they were both cohorts of my brother.

They halted before us and Athol said, "You are Gailard, no?"

I shook my head. "My name is Gavin."

"No." Rurrid stared hard at me. "You're Gailard the Exile. Colum banished you, and you return to the Highlands on pain of death."

From the corner of my eye I saw Ellyn tense. I prayed she not speak, but dared not indicate that need to her. I stared back at Rurrid and said, "You mistake me, friend. I am Gavin, out of Chaldor."

"You ran to Chaldor," Athol said, "when your father exiled you, and Eryk would pay us well to bring you home."

"Eryk?" I could not hide my surprise. "Is Colum no longer clan chief?"

"Colum died," he answered. "Now Eryk leads the Devyn."

I was startled. I had not heard of my father's death, nor known that my brother took his place. I suppose that I had assumed my father would live forever. I shrugged and said, "You mistake me for this other fellow."

Then Ellyn spoke. "Who are these men, Father? Do they speak of Gailard, the great warrior?"

Rurrid glanced at her and dismissed her. Athol said, "Who are you, boy?"

"Why," she answered gruffly, "I am Elward, Gavin's son."

"He's not Gavin," Rurrid declared, "he's Gailard." He was, I recalled, ever obstinate as some dog guarding a prized bone.

Ellyn looked at him from under her cap. "Should I not know my own father? He's Gavin, I tell you. Do I have it right, then this Gailard fought the Danant and, after, went away and has not been seen since."

Athol frowned as if almost convinced by her display of innocence, but Rurrid stared at her and said, "There's something odd about you, boy."

He reached toward her. I set a hand on my sword and drew the blade a little way clear of the scabbard.

"Do you lay hand on my son, I'll slay you." I raised my voice a little, enough that the folk around us—already interested in our dispute—should hear. "What are you? Some fancier of boys?"

Rurrid blushed and snatched back his hand. "You lie," he shouted. "I've no truck with boys."

Ellyn said, loud, "Protect me, Father!"

Both clansmen touched their swords now, and I thought I might have to fight them, but then Jach appeared. He held a cudgel, and with him came two sheriff's men, armed with swords.

"What is this?" our landlord asked. "I'll have no fighting in my inn."

Rurrid said, "He's Gailard of the Devyn, and forbidden the Highlands."

Jach said, "This is Cu-na'Lhair, friend, not the Highlands. And do you draw that blade farther, I'll crack your skull."

The sheriff's men already had their blades out. Rurrid and Athol looked at them and sheathed their half-drawn weapons. Rurrid said, "We'll find you later, Gailard."

I said, again, "Gavin."

"No matter the names," Jach declared. "You two are not welcome here. Go!"

They went and Jach turned to me. "I know not what that was about, but I think it best you also depart. By day's break, eh?"

CHAPTER EIGHT

Light ringed Chorym in an obscene halo. By night it was the glow of myriad fires, by day the glint of sunshine on polished shields and helmets and spearheads. But always light, and the sounds of siegement—the clatter of weapons and the rattle of chariots, the whickering of impatient horses, the shouting of Talan's soldiers, and the thudding of axes and hammers and adzes as the siege machinery was built. Towers mounted on wheeled platforms rose ever higher, dwarfing the metal-decked battering rams; catapults took shape, arbalests and trebuchets, mangonels; and pickaxes and mallets hammered against outlying buildings, reducing them to such rubble as might be flung against the walls. Fences and hedges were stripped to construct protective barriers for the Danant archers. And all the while, drums beat a sullen rhythm even as trumpets sounded strident challenge.

Ryadne watched from the outer wall of her city. She stared at the gaily colored pavilions, at the banners fluttering there. At the comings and goings of her attackers. Sometimes she caught sight of Talan, circuiting the walls in his splendid golden chariot, magnificently armored. Sometimes he flourished a bejeweled spear, at others the jar that held her husband's head. But he never ventured within bowshot; he was too careful.

Thrice, the queen had allowed her commanders to per-suade her to send out skirmishers, in what had proven vain hope of slaying Danant's king. And three times the mounted raiders had been slaughtered. Her finest archers watched the golden chariot with narrowed eyes, shafts nocked ready, but Talan stayed always out of range. Ryadne hated him as she had not known she could hate a man, and nightly prayed that the gods send him a fever or toss him from his chariot, or some camp whore infect him with the rotting sickness. But still, each morning, he presented himself—safely distanced— and hailed her.

"Shall you surrender now, or suffer my wrath? Better now, eh? Your city and all its folk shall suffer else. Surren-der now, Ryadne, and I'll let your people live."

She doubted that. Already Danant stripped the land. What few animals had been left on the farms were slaugh-tered, the farms burned; cavalry trampled down the harvest and foot soldiers hacked away the vineyards and the or-chards. Beyond that horrid ring of light stood a great swath of wanton destruction. And every so often the Danant men found Chaldor folk and brought them before the walls and slew them—or nailed them to crossed wood, or set them to roasting over slow fires—so that their screaming pierced the days and the nights. Ryadne gave orders that her bowmen put merciful shafts in any they could reach, save they could not and so the screaming went on and on.

The gods knew, but she hated Talan—and scryed his victory.

Albeit that was only a dim scrying, she still felt certain he must prevail. She exercised all those disciplines taught her by the Dur wisewomen, meditating and consuming such herbal potions as augmented the talent, but still her scrying was a misty, undecided thing. It was as if Talan's Vachyn sorcerer clouded her vision, weakened her ability. She could no longer sense Ellyn or Gailard, as if that aetheric plane she traversed in dreams had become fogged by the Vachyn's more powerful magicks, and she could only pray they lived.

She had recognized the Vachyn on sight. That fading
part of her that still commanded the talent knew him like an
aching in her bones, the smell of rain on the air. He was the
black-robed one, his face aquiline, sallow as diseased flesh,
framed with an oily spill of long black hair. Often he stood
alone, staring at the walls, and then it was as if he stared at
Ryadne and knew her as she knew him.

She wondered when he would send his magic against
her city, and felt a terrible dread.

It would be easy enough to die—she felt no fear of that
journey—indeed, she thought suicide preferable to this awful waiting, but she must concern herself with her people,
Andur's people, and seek their survival above her own
wishes.

And all the time the drums beat and the trumpets
sounded and tortured folk screamed and the preparations
for siege went on until she feared she might go mad and
open the gates only to end it all.

She put on a smile and turned to her escort.

"Does Talan intend to attack us, or bore us to death with
this display? The gods know, but he wearies me with his
prancing—so I'll leave him to it. Should he cease his strut-
ting and do anything constructive, you'll send me word,
eh?"

Her captains laughed, voicing their agreement, and
watched their queen depart.

"She's brave," one said.

"But only a woman," said another. "And a Dur, besides."

"Our queen, and worthy of Andur's throne," said a
third.

"Even so, I wish Andur was with us."

There was no answer save that admission, and the captains turned to study the forces massed against them.

Ryadne found her chambers and allowed her women to remove the light armor she wore, agreed that a bath be drawn.

Her chambers smelled of roses and a multitude of other scents: it seemed incongruous. Roses and perfumes when beyond the walls there was the porcine odor of burning flesh? Were these the Highlands, she thought, and these fluttering women the sisters of her Dur homeland, they'd be girded for battle, ready behind their men with knives and billhooks to gut any attacker. But this was Chorym, the heart of the Bright Kingdom, and these were court women—more used to wielding a needle than a knife. She stifled a sigh that might have become a sob and allowed them to undress her, lead her to the scented bath.

Rose petals floated on the steaming water and reminded her of blood, but she said nothing, only sank beneath the surface and closed her eyes as she thought of Ellyn.

Where was her daughter now? Had Gailard taken the child to her grandfather or back to his own Devyn? She had not, deliberately, asked where he would go—for fear the Vachyn plumb that knowledge and find Ellyn; she could only hope they were both safe. She had only the single certainty: that Ellyn was the key to victory, Chaldor's hope. She did not know how or why, save that Ellyn shared her blood and thus owned the talent. She closed her eyes and endeavored to scry her daughter's whereabouts, her welfare.

But all she saw was Nestor's face, as if it rose from the steam and the rose petals to mock her. She mouthed a silent curse and called for drink.

"Wine?" a waiting woman asked.

"No." Ryadne shook her head. "Bring me a glass of brose. Bring me a *mug* of brose."

The woman looked shocked and Ryadne splashed water, drenching her, then felt immediately sorry.

"Forgive me, please. I've much on my mind and I forget my manners."

"No matter, my lady." The woman wiped nervous hands down her soaking dress. "These are difficult times, and you've much to concern you."

Ryadne began to laugh and could not stop.

"Why not now?" Talan slammed his goblet hard against the table's top. "Why not attack now?"

Egor Dival sighed and ran a hand across his balding pate. "We face a great city," he said slowly, as if speaking to a recalcitrant child. "A strong-walled city with all its forces there."

"Ours are greater," Talan snapped. "We've more men."

"Indeed." Dival wiped his sweaty palm against his shirt. "But we face *walls*, and therefore need siege machinery. Until we've the towers and catapults, we cannot attack. It would be pointless. Better to wait—the gods know, we've all this land to support us and they've only what they've stored. We can starve them out, and lose few men."

"And how long shall that take?" Talan demanded.

Dival shrugged. "A year?"

"I'll not wait so long." Talan swung his head toward Nestor. "Can you not bring down the walls?"

The Vachyn sorcerer smiled. "In time, yes."

"In what time? How long?"

"I cannot say," Nestor replied. "I've yet to test their strength. It might well be as Egor says, a year."

Talan drank, staring at the sorcerer from across the brim of the goblet. "I hired you with sacks of gold," he said. "And now you tell me you can do no more than my own army? Is my coin all wasted?"

Calm, dark eyes met his angry glare. "I gave you Andur," Nestor said, gesturing at the jar that stood obscene between them, "and drove Chaldor's forces from your land. I'll give you Chorym, are you a little patient. But do you want the city *now*, then you must hire more of my kind. Say, five more—and the walls shall fall to our command."

"Five?" Talan's stare lost its heat. "The gods know, but you alone cost me enough. I cannot afford five of you Vachyn."

"Then you must be content with me." Nestor shrugged.

"I'll fulfill my contract. Chorym shall be yours—but you must be patient."

"For a year?" Talan scowled.

Dival said, "War's not all swift victories, my lord, it's often boring."

Talan grunted irritably, "I do not enjoy boredom. I want this city now, and I want Ryadne for my bride. Her or her daughter, eh?"

"Ellyn's but a child." Dival's ruddy face expressed disgust. "She's what, fifteen?"

"Old enough," Nestor murmured.

"For you Vachyn, perhaps." Dival studied the sorcerer with undisguised contempt. "But to me she's a child."

"Child or no," Talan said, "I'll wed her, can I not have her mother. I'll lay my claim on this land however I can, and do any dispute my right . . ." He stared at his companions.

Nestor ducked his head. "Your wish is my command."

Dival frowned, but said, "I obey my king."

"Then win me this city," Talan said. "Give me Chorym and all Chaldor. Give me Ryadne or her daughter."

Nestor smiled; Egor Dival rose and went to inspect his troops.

When he was gone and they were left alone, Nestor said, "Your general fights old battles, Talan. He'd keep you waiting for this victory."

"You agreed with him." Talan drank more wine. "You agreed it might well be a year."

"I'd not . . . upset . . . your general." The Vachyn smiled slyly. "At least, not too much. Better that allies trust one another, no? Egor does not trust my magic. He'd sooner rely on his towers and catapults; his men."

"Damn what Egor wants," Talan growled. He poured more wine.

"And yet he's your general," the Vachyn murmured, "and commands the loyalty of your army."

"Yes, *my* army. Not his."

Nestor shrugged. "You are, undoubtedly, the king. But such power is a subtle thing, no? It is, I always think, akin to a tripod—dependent on three legs. One is your *right* to rule—and that is undisputed."

Talan nodded sagely, wondering where the Vachyn's conversation led him.

"Another," Nestor said, "is the support of your people."

"I've that," Talan declared. He poured another cup of wine. "The people love me, and do I conquer Chaldor and control the Durrakym, they'll love me better for the wealth that brings."

"Absolutely," Nestor agreed. "But the third leg is the army. Do you lack the support of the army, then you've no strength; the tripod collapses."

"You say that Egor would betray me?" Talon frowned, frightened by the notion. "That he'd take the army from me?"

"No, no." Nestor shook his head, his hands moving in placatory gestures. "I say only that he doubts your methods. He'd fight this war as he's always fought wars—in the old, time-honored ways. He does not approve of my presence, nor what I bring to your side."

"Shall I dismiss him then?" Talan asked. "Have him assassinated?"

"No!" Nestor waved an urgent negative. "That would lead only to trouble. We need him, for the common soldiery trust him. They'll follow him."

"They'll follow me!" Talan cried. "I can lead the army. I *do* lead the army."

"You *command* the army," Nestor said. "You are too important to lead it into battle—better leave that task to such as Egor."

"I don't understand." Talan's handsome brow furrowed as he frowned. "What do you say?"

"That we need Egor Dival for now," Nestor answered. "And that you must be a little while patient. Let him build his machinery. Indeed, let it pound Chorym's walls awhile— say a month?—and then I'll use my magic and give you the city. Then, when we've no more need of Egor, it should be as well to dispose of him."

Kerid had never seen Hel's Town before. He'd heard the stories—every riverman had; the place was a legend—but his voyaging had not yet brought him so far north, and the first sight of so fabulous a location prompted him to gape as his captured boat drew closer.

The Durrakym stood at its broadest span here, the banks lost in the sunlit distances of midmorning, but the islands that comprised Hel's Town dominated the channel like some great toll post, which in a way it was. Little traffic worked the river without paying dues to the inhabitants of the islands.

There were seven, wide craggy outcrops linked by arching bridges and floating walkways, their slopes all covered with fantastical structures that glittered bright as a jester's coat. Wharves and jetties thrust into the river like the legs of some unimaginable insect. Boats bobbed on the current: fat-bellied traders out of Naban, Serian's sleek galleys, fishing boats, and the low, lean river raiders. No few flew Danant's pennants, and at least three boasted Chaldor's colors. Kerid supposed they had fled north when Talan invaded, and was torn between cursing their captains for cowards and thanking the gods that he might claim them.

"That might be difficult," Nassim told him when he expressed the thought. "Hel's Town gives allegiance to none save Mother Hel, and she's a law unto herself."

Kerid nodded, recalling what he knew of the place.

Some claimed it was founded by the Sea Kings, in ages long past, when those legendary rovers sailed upriver; others that it was, and had always been, a pirate stronghold. What was certain was that the islands occupied a kind of aquatic no-man's-land. Chaldor's borders, like Danant's, ended to the south; those of Naban and Serian began to the north. Between lay unclaimed wasteland, with Hel's Town at its waterborne center. It had never been conquered: it was easier to leave it be, a place where all might meet on neutral ground.

"What's she like?" Kerid asked.

Nassim shrugged. "I've not met her. My father did—though I suppose he likely met her mother. You know of the succession?"

Kerid grunted an affirmative. Hel's Town was always ruled by a woman descended from the original Mother, whose palace occupied the highest hill on the island at the center of the cluster. He squinted into the brightness, seeing gold flash, and brilliant lapis lazuli, and guessed that must be the palace.

"We'll be taken there," Nassim opined, "when you tell them why you've come."

"But they'll trade us warboats?" Kerid thought of those three Chaldor flags. He'd lay claim to those boats and barter them for raiders.

"Likely," Nassim allowed, "but it shall only be by permission of the Mother."

"I'll persuade her," Kerid declared.

Nassim grunted and cut himself a wad of tobacco as their captured craft eased gently to anchor.

This close it was easy to see why none chose to invade. Beyond the jetties the dockside ended on a high machiolated wall, surmounted with arbalests and mangonels, the gateway protected by a barbican. Not even Chorym was so well defended, and as Kerid brought his boat in armed men waited to greet the newcomers while others watched from the walls. Two of the heavy throwing machines were trained on the boat.

Kerid sprang to the dockside and flourished an elaborate bow.

"Greetings, friends. I am Kerid of Chaldor, and I seek sanctuary and trade."

A man in fish-plate mail faced him. He carried a long sword; the rest bore spears that were angled toward Kerid and his men. "That's a Danant boat, Kerid of Chaldor."

"Indeed it is." Kerid beamed. "We captured her."

"And the crew?"

"Dead."

The officer sniffed. "Your war is nothing to do with us."

"Nor would I bring it here," Kerid said. "Only put up awhile and talk trade."

"Your enemies say the same." The officer pointed toward the Danant flags. "Shall you hold peace with them in Hel's Town?"

"Have I a choice?"

"Of course. You can obey our laws, or not." The officer chuckled and swung his sword to indicate ten cages hung from the walls. Each one contained a naked man. "Five from Chaldor, five from Danant. They brought their troubles here, and thus suffer the Mother's judgment."

"What did they do?" Kerid asked.

"A tavern brawl," the officer replied casually. "They looked to continue your war. Now they'll rot—an example to others."

"We'll give you no trouble," Kerid declared. "My word on it. We'd only trade this boat for a better. This, and the other Chaldor craft."

"That," the officer said, "shall be decided by the Mother. Come with me."

"And my crew?" Kerid asked.

"Have the freedom of Hel's Town. But unarmed. And do any cause trouble . . ." Again, the sword indicated the cages.

Kerid nodded and ordered Nassim to keep the men in check. He gestured that the officer lead on, and the man smiled grimly and told him to remove his weapons. Reluctantly, Kerid obeyed, then he followed the officer into the barbican.

Beyond that, a tunnel through the deep wall, and then a steep flight of walled stairs led up to an avenue that ran like a gulley between the close-packed buildings. Narrow alleys intersected the climbing path, and Kerid thought there was not a hand's span of open ground anywhere in Hel's Town. He climbed dutifully, legs grown long accustomed to a boat's deck aching, and the air—after the open river—was thick with the mingled odors of densely packed humanity, food, and, he realized after a while, the multitude of cats he saw inhabiting the gutters and window ledges and balconies. He was grateful when the avenue gave way to a thin plateau, across which rose white walls; behind, the gold and brilliant blue he'd seen from the river.

The officer approached a gateway of polished wood and banded brass, and dropped a heavy golden knocker. The gate opened, words were exchanged, and Kerid was ushered through to find himself in a bailey where roses grew and fountains played, shedding rainbows over harlequin flagstones of marble and jet. The air was rich with the flowers' scent, and small birds darted, singing shrilly. The officer was no longer with him, and he was now escorted by two tall men he guessed from their color to be of Nabanese stock. They wore white surcoats that could not quite conceal the mail shirts beneath, and each wore a sheathed blade. They did not speak, only beckoned him to follow and took him across the courtyard to an arched doorway, where he was given into the charge of two others dressed in scarlet slashed across with black and silver.

Past the arch lay a vast chamber floored with pale blue stone that seemed to ripple in the light entering from the high windows. Kerid had the impression that he walked through water, augmented by the murals decorating the walls: all river scenes of boats and fabulous fishes, waving weeds and merfolk. He saw that people watched him, and that they wore flowing robes in a multitude of colors that added to the submarine impressions, as if they were merfolk, drifting on the currents of the chamber. Eventually he was halted before a door of beaten gold that opened to admit him to a smaller chamber, plainly set, with wooden floors like a ship's deck, and round windows that spilled light over the throne at the center.

It was a simple throne of old black wood that looked as if it had been dredged from the river after long ages underwater. Kerid was unsure whether the patterns he saw were carved, or merely the results of long immersion. He did not care—could not—for his gaze was fixed in awe on the woman who sat there.

He had assumed Mother Hel to be some crone, aged and wrinkled and ugly. But he saw a girl, golden-haired and laughing, and lovely as any woman he'd seen, playing with a black kitten. He halted, confused and bowed.

"Mother Hel?"

The girl set the kitten aside, and laughed as it fought its way back up her gown to curl in her lap. "I am she. Who are you?" She tickled the kitten as she spoke, playing slender fingers in its mouth, laughing as it bit her.

"Kerid of Chaldor," he said.

"Yes, of course. I had word."

He could not imagine how, but as he looked at her he saw old wisdom in her grey eyes. "I'd ask your favor."

"Do you come to Hel's Town, then you must. Tell me what you want here."

"I took a Danant boat, and I'd trade it—and all its cargo—for a warboat."

"To pursue your struggle with Danant?"

Kerid nodded. "Also, there are at least three Chaldor vessels at anchor. I am commander of Chaldor's navy, and I'd claim them for further trade."

"You'd *claim* them?" Steel entered the youthful voice. "What comes to Hel's Town is mine."

Kerid swallowed his instinctive protest, acted the diplomat. "I'd *ask* that you consider my request."

"Better; much better. But why should I help you? You bring a boat here, and it is mine—such is our law. I might give it back to you; or not. But Talan of Danant hires himself a Vachyn sorcerer—and do I offend the Vachyn . . ." She let the sentence tail off, glancing around the room, where heads bowed in mute agreement.

"Talan hires one Vachyn," Kerid agreed, "but has not yet won his war. He's yet to take Chorym; and the clans, as yet, take no part."

"Shall they?" Mother Hel asked. "Or shall they stand apart and let Chorym fall?"

"That should be a hard thing," Kerid said, unsure where this conversation went. "The city shall be hard to take, and there's . . ."

The girl raised an imperious hand, halting his words. "There's a beaten army crawling home. Andur is dead, and his greatest commander fled."

"What?"

"You did not know? Then let me tell you. Gailard quit Antium and left the town to Talan. He went to Chorym and has not been seen since."

"Then he's behind the walls," Kerid said, "organizing the defense."

"He's not been seen. In Chaldor," Mother Hel announced, "folk say that Gailard is a coward who ran from battle."

"No!"

"You dispute me?"

Kerid bit back his instinctive response. "I find it hard to believe Gailard is a coward. I knew the man, and thought him brave. But be it so, there must be a reason. And even is there not, and he has run, I shall not."

"But drag Hel's Town into your war? Against Vachyn magicks?"

"Not that—only what you've always done: trade. Take that boat I captured and give me a warboat. Are you agreeable, then acknowledge that I've some right to those other Chaldor boats, and give me more warboats in return."

"To continue your fight against Talan?"

Kerid nodded.

"And shall I risk bringing Vachyn magic against Hel's Town?"

"Are you afraid of Vachyn magic?"

Now Mother Hel nodded. "Anyone who says they are not is a fool."

"Talan's but the one sorcerer," Kerid said, "and I doubt he can afford more."

"Even so."

"Think on it," Kerid asked. "Does Talan conquer Chaldor, where shall he turn next? Here? Should he own both shores—Danant's and Chaldor's—then he owns the southward river. Might he not—and remember, with the wealth of two lands, he'll own much—hire more Vachyn and look northward? Might he not employ more Vachyn and turn against you?" He thought fast, seeking to persuade her. "And if not you, then Naban and Serian. I think he'd own all the Durrakym—and you'd be in his way. How should you stand then?"

"There's that, yes." Mother Hel stroked the kitten in her lap. Then picked the little cat up and tossed it aside; it squealed piteously as it hit the floor. "I must think on this. And you shall help me. Come."

Kerid frowned as she rose from her ancient throne. "I don't understand."

"You shall," she promised, beckoning that he follow her.

CHAPTER NINE

We finished our meal with Jach's watchful eyes on us, and the sheriff's men lingering to ensure our departure. I settled our account, and our landlord had the grace to blush beneath his beard and offer an apology of a kind.

"I can't afford trouble," he explained, "and are you who they say . . ."

His shrug was eloquent. I asked, "Are there many Devyn in Cu-na'Lhair?"

"A good few."

"And Eryk is truly clan chief now?"

Jach nodded. Ellyn fidgeted at my side and I motioned her to be still; there was information I'd have before we departed, and little time to glean it. "What happened to the old chief?"

I think that Jach guessed my identity by now, but the rules that allowed Cu-na'Lhair to exist and prosper denied him open declaration or profit therefrom. I thanked the gods for those rules and could only pray he did not recognize Ellyn. He said, "Colum? He fell off his horse and cracked his skull. Before he died, he named Eryk his successor." He sighed, scrubbing busily at a pot, averting his eyes. "Eryk wed Rytha of the Agador, and announced a bounty on Gailard's head."

I endeavored to conceal my discomfort.

Jach looked up from his scrubbing and I wondered if I saw pity in his eye. "I've heard it said," he murmured, "that it was Rytha persuaded Eryk to set the bounty. It would seem that Gailard deserted Rytha, and she'd have her revenge for that slight. Were I you, my friend, I'd not risk the Highlands but go back to Chaldor. I think you should be safer there."

I nodded. "See our animals saddled, eh? We'll go now."

"As you wish."

I turned away, beckoning Ellyn after me. She was in a most curious mood. I could not decide whether she was exhilarated by our clandestine departure, or infuriated that she must leave her comfortable bed and take again to the road. She seemed to dart between the two, like a swallow plucking insects from the summer air. She sought at first to argue.

"So fat Jach has thrown us out, but why can we not find another inn?"

"Because," I told her, "Rurrid and Athol will be seeking every Devyn clansman they can find, and likely Agador, too, telling them I'm here."

"So? Is this not Cu-na'Lhair? What can they do here?"

"Here, little enough. But have they the time, then they can mount an ambush—meet us on the road and bring us to my brother."

I packed my saddlebags as I spoke, and noticed that even as she argued, she did the same.

"Is your brother so terrible?"

"There's little love between us; and our father *did* banish me."

"So perhaps your brother will forgive you."

I laughed. "You heard what they said, no? That Eryk would pay them well to bring me home. And Jach confirmed that."

"Perhaps because he'd see you again—reconcile your differences."

"I doubt that." My laughter grew bitter. "I think that Eryk would sooner take my head."

"Your own brother?"

"And our father's son. Eryk's little pity in him, nor much fondness for me."

"Because of this woman?"

"Rytha? My father betrothed me to her that he might forge alliance between the Devyn and the Agador, but I never loved her."

"Was she not pretty?"

"She was beautiful. Eryk always wanted her, but I was the elder son."

"So why did you not wed her?"

"I didn't like her."

"Even though she was pretty?"

"Even though. She had a temper, and such pride as I've never seen—not even in princesses."

Ellyn snorted then, muttering something about Highlanders and their ways as she buckled on her new sword. I finished our packing and ushered her out of the room. I must admit that I, too, was reluctant to depart these comfortable quarters, but I'd have us abroad and running before Rurrid and Athol got chance to raise a hunt.

"Listen," I said, "We cannot risk encounter with either the Devyn or the Agador, so we must ride hard now, and live awhile off the land and what we carry with us."

"The Dur are to the north," she said.

"I know. And does Talan take Chorym, he'll look for us there. Better that we avoid everyone."

"Can we?"

I drew a deep breath and let it out slowly, staring at the moon-silvered rooftops across the street. It should be hard to cross the Highlands unnoticed, and harder still to find sanctuary. I knew only that we must run like hunted animals. I said, "Trust me."

Ellyn snorted again.

So it was we left the Lonely Traveler as the waning moon rose overhead. I loaded our horses and disturbed a drowsy gateman, who opened the gates so that we might ride out into the streets of Cu-na'Lhair, and then through the city gates into the hills beyond.

They shone bright under the moon, patchworked by drifting cloud and silvery light. Gorse and heather scented the air, and I saw owls winging silently in search of prey. I wondered if they were omens of death or wisdom, and hoped we had escaped unnoticed; but then all my hopes were dashed.

We rounded a curve where a shoulder of moorland thrust out to block the view ahead and past it found Rurrid and Athol waiting for us. They sat their horses at the center of the trail, both with drawn swords. A score or so clansmen wearing the colors of the Devyn and the Agador waited to either side. Some held strung bows, and I knew we had no chance to run.

I tried to bluff them. "What is this?" I cried, feigning outrage. "Do you pursue this foolish argument?"

"You are Gailard," Rurrid said, "and we shall bring you to Eryk."

"I am *Gavin*!"

Rurrid laughed. "And I am the peddler's dog."

Athol said, "Are we right, then Eryk shall reward us well. Are we wrong, then we'll apologize, and you shall enjoy Devyn hospitality for a while. But Eryk shall know, eh?"

From my side, a little way behind, I heard Ellyn ask, "Do we fight?" And heard the scrape of her sword loosened.

"No!" I prayed she not be so foolish. "There are too many of them."

"Even for the mighty Gailard?"

"Yes; and too many to run from. They'll shoot us down."

"Then we go with them?"

"We've no choice."

"Perhaps you are a coward."

That hurt, and I turned to face her. "Were I alone, I'd meet them sword to sword, and damn the consequences. But I'm not, and I gave my word to see you safe."

"Into your brother's hands?"

"He's no reason to harm you. Perhaps he'll let you go, and should he recognize you I'll parley with him—ask that he send you to the Dur."

"And you?"

"Me?" I shrugged, unable to stifle a bitter chuckle. "Why, Eryk shall likely have my skull for a wine cup."

"So?" Rurrid interrupted our whispered conversation. "Do you come willing, or do you come dead?"

I raised my hands. "Willing."

They took away our weapons and bound our wrists to the saddle horns, our ankles to the stirrups. We rode out the night and halted at dawn to eat and rest awhile. Ellyn and I were kept bound, our escort ever watchful, so that I grew fearful they'd know Ellyn for the girl she was. I thought that some were not happy with this duty and its probable outcome, but none would speak to us, save when needful, and I perceived no chance of escape. At least we were fed. I supposed that Rurrid and Athol would deliver me healthy to Eryk, that he might sport with me the longer. I wondered what fate Ellyn might suffer when—inevitably—her true sex was discovered. Or worse, her true identity: my brother was ever a devious little worm, and I would not put it past him to hand her to Talan.

I chafed at my bonds as we rode on through the morning, and through those next few days. I felt I had betrayed Andur's trust. I should have devised a better plan, not just run, but could think of nothing else I might have done. By the time we reached Eryk's camp, my wrists were bloody.

The summer had aged by now and the clans drifted along the paths of the seasonal horse-hunt; come winter they'd return home to see out the snows from behind warm walls, but for now they lived under canvas, trailing the herds of shaggy Highland horses. I thought that Rurrid and Athol would take us east, but they continued northward, toward the Dur lands.

Eryk's camp was set on a high stretch of moorland, above a wide blue-black tarn all ringed with heather and pines. Salmon splashed in the streams that fed the tarn, and eagles circled overhead. The heather spread in shades of blue and grey, burnished with the golden luxuriance of the gorse that shifted under the stirring breeze. I felt a thrill as I saw the encampment: all clan colors and drifting smoke from the cookfires, horses penned by the water, dogs running and barking to greet us in, faces aged by the passed years coming to stare at us. I thought that in other circumstances I'd have felt joy.

Now all I felt was fear, and a great wonder at the size of the camp and its location.

I knew on the instant which was Eryk's tent: I had seen nothing like it since last I looked on Danant's pavilions. It bore the headman's emblem, but it was larger than our father's, encircled by embossed poles decorated with horsehair and skulls—some animal, others human—and the shields of those who had pledged to him about the bases. Our father, I thought, had never been so grandiose.

But Eryk was not much like Colum. Folk had always said that I bore my father's looks, and said little about Eryk save that he'd a temper. Now I saw a man I barely recognized—except for those remembered hawkish eyes— emerge. He was shorter than I, and gone to fat. There was yet muscle beneath his bulgings, but I was startled at the change in him. A beard disguised the swelling of his cheeks and the jowls beneath, but little could conceal the gut that hung above his belt, or the thickness of the thighs that stretched his breeks so tight. I thought that he must need a sturdy horse to carry his newfound weight, which was not only of his body but also in the adornments he wore. His shirt was surmounted with a breastplate of hammered silver that matched the trappings of his swordbelt and the fanciful stitchings of his boots. The hilts of his sword and dagger were both chased with silver wire, and rings glittered on his fingers, jewels in his ears. He looked to me more like some Nabanese emissary than a Highlander. And I discerned a waddle in his walk that almost prompted laughter—were I not so afraid of the look in his eyes, which was that of a raptor surveying its prey.

Ellyn said, "By the gods, is that popinjay your brother?"

I said, "Quiet! Leave me to talk, eh?"

Eryk waited between the poles that formed the entrance to his splendid tent. Then: "Well met, Gailard."

He motioned at our escort and we were cut loose, dragged from our horses, and forced to our knees before him.

"And who is your companion?"

"No boy, despite the gear."

I knew that voice, despite the years. It was sultry as ever, like the hot summer sun on the skin. But I barely recognized the woman who emerged behind my brother. The Rytha I had known was slender as a spring doe, with eyes to match and hair wild and free as the wind. She was never a pleasant woman, but she had been beautiful. This was a different creature. Like Eryk, she was thickened, those big, soft eyes ringed now with rolls of fat, her lips no longer sensuous but only fleshy. Her hair was bound up and wrapped in a mesh of silver set with little jewels, and those parts of her legs that showed beneath her skirt were pudgy as her beringed fingers.

"He says," Rurrid declared, "that the lad's his son."

Rytha chuckled and elbowed Eryk aside—so that I wondered who ruled this tent, this clan—and plucked Ellyn's cap from her head. Then she stooped, cupping Ellyn's chin to force her face upward.

"A lad? His son?" She laughed. "This is a girl, you fool. Who is she, Gailard?"

I debated awhile whether to tell the truth or not. The decision was made for me by my charge.

"I am Ellyn of Chaldor!" she shouted furiously. "I am daughter to Andur and Ryadne, and do you harm me—or my guardian—my mother will send armies against you. And my grandfather will bring his clan to war."

Rytha laughed and slapped Ellyn. I doubted she had ever been slapped before, for her face went pale and her eyes grew wide, her mouth gaping in outraged surprise.

Rytha said, "Speak when I allow you, girl, else I'll have you flogged," then smiled at me. "Shall I add my welcome to your brother's, Gailard? It is *very* good to see you again."

I heard the menace in her voice, saw it in her eyes. I looked past her to Eryk.

"The girl's no part in this. Let her go—put her on her horse and send her to the Dur, eh? Treat me as you will, but let her go."

Eryk laughed, and looked to Rytha. "What say you, wife?"

"That you've your brother, as you've dreamed," Rytha said. "And we've a pawn in this child."

"How so?" Eryk frowned. "My brother, yes; I understand. But her?"

Rytha sighed. "Why do you think he's here? He runs from Talan of Danant like the coward he is, and brings us Chaldor's heir in tow. What price shall Talan set on her? Or Mattich—he'd likely pay well for his daughter's child. Either way, we've a powerful pawn."

Eryk smiled, nodding. Rytha prompted him further. "Think on it. We've already the Devyn and the Agador by marriage-bond. Do we hold Mattich's granddaughter, then we can force the Dur to fealty. And surely Talan must reward us greatly, do we give him Andur's daughter."

I said, "You bitch!" and she kicked me low in the belly.

For so fat a woman she was quick and strong, and I found myself curled upon the ground, fighting the desire to vomit.

From that undignified position I heard them talking.

Eryk said, "We might upset the clans. The gods know, but some still favor Chaldor."

"And when Talan seizes Chorym, and Danant owns all Chaldor?"

"There's that, yes. But what if he does not?"

"He's a Vachyn sorcerer, no? How can he lose? Ryadne shall soon be dead, or forced into marriage with him. What price then on her daughter?"

"I don't know."

"The highest! Talan will pay well for her; and Mattich will likely swear allegiance to save her life. How can we lose?"

I began, almost, to pity my brother—married to this monster.

"Listen, send messengers now to both Mattich and Talan. Tell them we've Ellyn in our charge—for sale to the highest bidder."

Eryk chuckled. "I did well to marry you."

"Yes. Now do as I say."

"And them?"

"Put them in a guarded tent." She bent toward me and I saw chins wobbling. "Shall you enjoy her company, Gailard? Shall you enjoy it better than mine? Do you like them young, eh?"

I opened my mouth to answer, but she kicked me again and took my breath away, so that I could only curl against the pain and feel myself hauled off like some butchered carcass even as I heard Ellyn screaming.

At least we were not bound. There was no need, for we were placed in a tent ringed by armed men. It had some furs on the floor and an empty fire pit at the center. I doubted the fire should be lit and wondered why Eryk did not kill me on the spot. I supposed he planned some longer vengeance.

"Are you all right?"

I found my head was cradled in Ellyn's lap and that her hands wandered nervously over my hair. I said, "I'll recover."

"She kicked you hard."

I grunted and forced myself to sit up. My belly protested, but Ellyn's arm supported me, and I was surprised by her concern. "I've taken worse," I said.

"You must have disappointed her greatly, that she hates you so. Did she love you very much?"

"I think she loved the notion of marriage to the Devyn's headman better—the idea that she rule two clans." I chuckled sourly. "Now she's her wish, eh?"

"Was she always so fat?"

"No." I shook my head. "She was slender. As I told you, she was pretty."

"But you still refused to marry her."

I nodded, wondering why Ellyn seemed so pleased with that rejection.

"So what shall we do now?"

I shrugged. "Nothing. There's nothing we can do."

"There must be something," Ellyn removed her arm and shifted a little way away across the furs, as if embarrassed by those moments of intimacy. "We can wait until nightfall and escape. Take back our horses and run . . ."

"We're too well guarded," I said. "And they'd hunt us down."

"We might reach my grandfather. We're close to his territory, no?"

I nodded, my initial curiosity at the location of this camp reignited. The Devyn had never come so close to the Dur lands in my time, but even so I could not believe we had any chance of reaching Mattich. I said, "How close we are is of no account when so many men surround us." I snorted bitter laughter. "Ryadne said you own the magical talent— shall you use that to free us?"

Ellyn pouted. "Perhaps I shall," she answered indignantly.

At dusk we were taken from our tent and brought to Eryk and Rytha. They sat on fur-swathed chairs before the fire. Rurrid and Athol sat in honor beside, and Ellyn and I were pushed unceremoniously to the ground. Eryk gnawed on a steak of venison, tossing the remnant to me as if I were a cringing dog. I spat on it.

Rytha laughed. "Husband, husband, not so unkind, eh? Would you not have him strong for what he must face? Better feed him well, that he last the longer. And the princess, that she not lose her worth to us."

I felt a sourness in my belly at that, but still I took the plate that was brought me and ate. I was even given a mug of ale.

"What do you plan?" I asked.

Eryk looked to Rytha as if he required her permission to speak. Then: "Why, brother, it is our decree that you shall be stripped naked and dragged through all our camp; then you shall be flogged, and when your bones are bared you shall be hung on a tree to await the crows."

I set my plate down and rose. Men drew blades around me. I said, "I claim right of combat!"

"You?" Eryk laughed. "A clansman might claim right of combat, but you are not a clansman. Our father stripped you of that when he banished you. You are nothing, brother, save some wandering hire-sword who has no rights save to die in pain." His belly wobbled as he chuckled. "Oh, I shall enjoy that—watching the crows and the ravens come down to eat your eyes, strip the bloody flesh from off your bones."

"You are a coward," I cried, "afraid to face me in honest combat."

"I am chieftain of the Devyn and the Agador," he replied, "and I need not soil my blade with such filth as you."

"You are afraid of me," I said, louder. "I name you coward."

That was such insult as would have prompted any Highlander to draw his blade and accept—save my brother. I saw some heads nod agreement, but none spoke up on my behalf. I wondered what malaise possessed the Devyn that none came to my defense. Yes, I was banished on pain of death, but that death should be swift, not flogging and the tree—and even a banished exile had the right to combat. It was as if Eryk and Rytha held the clan in horrid thrall. I stared at my brother, hating him.

But it was Rytha who spoke. "It shall be a slow death, Gailard. The lash shall hurt, but the birds will be worse. And as they pluck away your flesh, you will know that your little friend aids our purpose."

I glanced sidelong at Ellyn. She sat pale-faced and—for once—silent. "Don't harm her," I asked.

"Oh, we'll not harm her," Rytha mocked, "at least, not too much, for she's too valuable. The gods know, Talan will surely pay well for her; but before him, Mattich." I had forgotten how strident her laugh could be. "Do you not understand? We go to war, Gailard. We ride against the Dur, and even though we'd doubtless conquer them, now we likely shall not need to fight—we'll offer them a trade instead. Ellyn's life for oaths of fealty, eh? And does Mattich doubt us, we shall send him *pieces* of his daughter's child until some finger, or some toe—perhaps an ear—persuades him."

I choked on bile as I heard Ellyn gasp. "And what of Talan, then?" I demanded. "Shall he accept a butchered bride?"

"Do you think he'll care?" Rytha gave me back. "He wants legitimate claim to Chaldor's throne, and can he not have Ryadne, then he'll take Ellyn—in whatever form. Better a handless wife than no throne."

In that moment it crossed my mind that I might close the distance between us and kill her with my hands. Perhaps

even slay Eryk, too. But then Ellyn would be alone, and if
one of them lived, she would surely suffer. Besides, men
stood with spears and swords, and some with bows that they
nocked and pointed at me as they guessed what passed
through my mind. I chose to live and cling to such hope as I
could not truly believe in. I settled and cursed them. "The
gods damn you both, and all who follow you."

"Many shall," Eryk said, "for we'll command the Dur
soon, and then all three clans will ride against the Quan and
the Arran, and we shall own all the Highlands. And we shall
cede treaties with Talan and rule here, and our kingdom
shall be greater than Chaldor ever was, and folk shall sing
the praises of King Eryk and Queen Rytha."

He clambered from his padded chair and raised his
arms, and the guard that ringed us lifted up their spears and
swords and beat their shields in accolade, and I felt all hope
die. I thought that I had failed Andur, failed Ryadne, delivered Ellyn to mutilation and—perhaps worst of all—to Talan. I had betrayed my king, his queen, and my charge as
guardian. I was close to weeping then, filled with chagrin
and hatred.

Then I heard Ellyn ask, "When shall this foul execution
take place?"

"Tomorrow," Eryk said, "at dawn, when the crows are
hungry."

We were taken back to our tent and flung inside. As the
flaps closed I saw a ring of steel placed around the lodge. A
dozen men at least, and far more beyond, ready to halt us
and slay us. And dogs to bark, and we without weapons or
horses. I could see no hope at all.

"What shall we do?" Ellyn asked me.

I could not help laughing as I answered, "Die. Me, at
least. And you be traded like some Serian whore."

"I'm no whore," she whispered.

I crossed the tent to crouch beside her. Her face was
very pale and she chewed on a thumb. I placed a hand upon
her shoulder and felt her body trembling beneath my touch.

I thought that she would pull away and vent her anger on me, but she did not; instead, she curled against me, as if I might still protect her. I felt a terrible guilt that I had brought her to this. "Listen," I said, "do as they ask. Go willing and avoid their wrath."

"Would they really do that? Would they butcher me?"

"I think they might, but also that they'd sooner not. I think that such savagery would offend too many. Why do you not write Mattich a letter—I think they'd allow you that. At least, play their game and, as best you can, keep in their good graces."

"So they can sell me to Talan?"

"That's surely better than . . ." I shrugged.

"And you?" She turned eyes that I now saw were filled with tears toward my face. "What of you?"

"What they promised."

"No!" She flung her arms around me, holding close against me. "I could not bear that."

"I thought," I said, "that you did not care so much for me."

She buried her face in my chest. "You're my guardian, Gailard. What shall I do if they slay you?"

"Live on," I said, confused by this sudden display of emotion. "Does it come to it, marry Talan."

"No! Never!"

"And some night, put a knife in his heart."

"I could do that. But . . ." She looked up at me all tearful. "There must be some other way."

"What?" I asked. I felt resigned to my fate, and wanted only to give her comfort, but could not think of how, or what more I could say. "Only do as I ask, eh?"

Ellyn shook her head and curled on the furs.

I curled apart from her and contemplated my impending death.

CHAPTER TEN

Their negotiations completed, Kerid rose from Mother Hel's bed and splashed cold water on his face and chest. He felt weary, and pleased with himself, and turned to smile at the woman lounging carelessly against the crumpled pillows. Sunlight from the high windows lit her blond hair and her answering smile was the beam of a satiated cat. She beckoned him and he went to her, settling beside her on the bed.

"So, we are agreed?"

Long nails traced a path down his chest, and Kerid nodded. "The Danant boat I captured in exchange for one fully stocked warboat. Those three Chaldor craft in harbor for two more. You drive a hard bargain, Mother."

Mother Hel laughed. "And others, remember, do you return my tithe. It seems fair to me. After all, I risk Danant's wrath for this."

"Talan would not dare attack you." Kerid shifted as her hand scratched lower. "Save he first conquer Chaldor, and have I those warboats . . ."

"You'll become a great river pirate and defeat him."

Kerid wondered if she mocked him. It was hard to tell, and hard to concentrate as her hand continued its investigation. He nodded again, and said, "I'll pay your tithe and trade you every ship I take that does not sink, and soon I'll have a navy that shall defeat Talan on the river."

"And does Chorym fall? Does Talan claim the throne?"

"Then still I shall fight him."

"You're brave."

Kerid shrugged modestly. "I do only my duty, Mother."

"And well." She drew him closer. "Now shall we seal our bargain?"

Kerid sighed, torn between the desire to inspect the warboats and what he felt for this demanding woman. *Best please her,* he thought, *for she rules Hel's Town, and without her agreement I can achieve nothing.* Besides, it was a pleasant way to negotiate.

In a while, Mother Hel rose and pulled on a robe of saffron silk, indicated a luxurious dressing gown that prompted Kerid to wonder how many such negotiations she had conducted, and tugged a bell cord.

"We shall take breakfast, and then I'll come with you to the harbor. We'll take a guard."

"A guard, why?" Kerid belted the dressing gown, feeling oddly foolish.

Mother Hel laughed. "Why, think on it, my love. You've your crew and three others; with them, three other captains. But only three warboats. You've more men than you need, and surely too many captains. Do you think they'll calmly agree to your choosing who mans your boats?"

"Andur . . ." Kerid began.

"Is dead," Mother Hel interrupted. "His army is defeated and, by all accounts, his greatest commander is fled. Talan brings all his might and a Vachyn sorcerer against Chorym, which shall likely fall. There are already Chaldor men here who look to join my pirates. Why, one of your captains has already offered his services."

"I'll slay him," Kerid snarled. "By the gods, I'll hang him as a traitor."

"No!" Mother Hel lost her smile, her lovely face

suddenly stern. "Here, you do not make such decisions; those are my province."

Kerid opened his mouth to argue, but then thought better of it. "Forgive me," he asked, "I forget myself."

"Yes; do not do it again." The smile returned. "I'd not lose you so soon."

There was such threat implicit in her sentence as prompted Kerid to remember the men hanging in the baskets. He bowed. "As you wish, Mother."

"Exactly."

There was a tapping at the door then, and Mother Hel motioned with careless imperiousness that Kerid open it. He obeyed, hiding his embarrassment behind a smile.

Breakfast was brought in by liveried servants, silver platters redolent of eggs and kidneys, warm bread, fruit and cheeses set down. Kerid filled two cups with tea and brought them to the bed where Mother Hel still reclined.

"We shall take my carriage," she declared, "and I shall explain the situation to your fellows."

Kerid nodded, smiling his agreement.

It was close on noon before Mother Hel had bathed and dressed, and then awhile longer before a two-wheeled cart was brought to the palace gates. Kerid was startled to see the vehicle was hauled not by horses, but six burly men.

"Where could I stable horses on these islands?" Mother Hel asked. "I use convicted men instead. Drawing a carriage is easier than manning a galley's oars, no?"

"Yes," Kerid said, wondering at this strange and apparently omnipotent woman.

Around them formed an escort of some fifty men, half-armored, with bucklers and short swords. Scarlet plumes fluttered atop their helmets, and Kerid saw that most wore scars. He thought they looked battle-hardened. Mother Hel clapped her hands and the cart and its entourage started forward.

They reached the harbor and Kerid sprang from the cart, offering a gallant hand to Mother Hel as Nassim came forward. His mate turned aside to spit out a stream of filthy tobacco and effected a deep bow.

"Mother Hel, it is an honor to meet you. I had not expected such a privilege."

Mother Hel beamed, extending a hand that Nassim dutifully kissed.

"This," Kerid said, "is Nassim, my first mate."

"And knows his manners," the Mother returned. "Welcome to Hel's Town, Nassim."

She clapped her hands and a man Kerid had not previously noticed came forward, opening a wooden box to extract numerous documents. He was short and bald, and panting from the journey.

"The Danant vessel *Talan's Pride*," he intoned when he'd caught his breath. "Captured by Kerid of Chaldor, and therefore fair bounty. Of the other Chaldor vessels there are three—a triple-master, a barque, and a brig. The crews number some three hundred and fifty men. I calculate their value at . . ."

He quoted figures Kerid did not understand, only that the promised warboats would take perhaps fifty men apiece, which meant he'd have to leave some two hundred Chaldor men stranded in Hel's Town. He caught Nassim's eyes speculative on him, shifting to Mother Hel. His first mate smiled lasciviously.

"You drove a hard bargain, eh?" he whispered.

Kerid felt his cheeks grow warm. "I did what I had to do."

Nassim chuckled.

"So, shall we inspect your new boats?" asked Mother Hel.

Kerid nodded dutifully and offered his arm as they walked along the wharf.

The warboats sat low in the water, sleek as sharks, each with a single central mast and fifty oarlocks. Rowing benches angled like ribs from the gunwales to the central deck, and at the sterns there were wide rudders controlled by the tillers. To the prow of each boat was a small forrard deck on which was mounted a small arbalest, storage lockers for the metal-tipped shafts beside. They were not deep-water craft, but superbly designed for swift strikes—to run from shoreward cover and hit hard, then run back. Kerid thought they'd serve his purpose well.

He watched as Nassim sprang down onto the first deck.

"Shall you not inspect them?" asked Mother Hel.

"Nassim knows his business," Kerid said, patting her hand. "And I'd sooner stay here with you."

The Mother smiled and waited until Nassim was done.

"They're fine boats," he announced, "but our lads are more used to ropes than oars. I wonder how they'll like sitting on those benches."

"They'll learn," Kerid declared. "And now we've a means of fighting Danant."

"Can we crew them." Nassim opened his pouch, extracting a wad of tobacco, then glanced at Mother Hel and thought better of it.

She said, "You shall. Trust me."

They went along the harbor to where the other Chaldor craft were anchored. Soldiers fell in about them, more than Kerid remembered coming with them, and then others, herding grumbling rivermen from the taverns and whore-houses until a great crowd, augmented by curious onlookers, watched as the three captains appeared.

Kerid was about to speak, but Mother Hel motioned him silent and stepped forward. She was flanked by her guard, six to either side, the rest watchful behind.

"You know who I am." For one so young and seemingly delicate, her voice rang loud, carrying through the noonday air so that it seemed even the squalling gulls fell silent. "I rule here; it is *my* word that decides your fate."

One captain—Julyan was his name, Kerid recalled—stepped a pace forward and offered a curt bow. "Madam, I am captain of the *Justice*, which is a Chaldor vessel. How shall you decide my fate?"

"Do you dispute my right?" Mother Hel's voice was mild; Kerid felt suddenly nervous. "You come running to Hel's Town seeking refuge from your war, asking my protection, and then wonder what right I have?"

Julyan said, "Madam, I do. The *Justice* is mine, and *I* decide her fate."

"And did you buy this vessel? Or did Andur give it you to command?"

Julyan shook his head. "You know I did not buy her, madam, but Andur is dead and Chaldor broken. I claim the craft as my own."

Mother Hel smiled and nodded and raised a hand, and two men stepped forward and plunged their swords into Julyan's belly. He screamed and fell down onto the cobbles.

"Now, who else disputes my right to judge?" asked Mother Hel in the same mild voice as the corpse was kicked into the river.

None answered, and she clapped her hands like a delighted child. "This is my judgment and decree—that all those Chaldor craft come into my domain are forfeit to me, and I give them to Kerid of Chaldor, who in return shall receive warboats, and men to crew them. Those men he cannot take with him shall receive the hospitality of these islands until such time as Kerid can repay his debt and purchase more boats. How say the rest of you?"

The two remaining captains ducked their heads; their crews shouted approval.

Nassim whispered, "Was it a *very* hard bargain?"

Kerid said, "You command one boat. Pick your own crew and mine."

Nassim chuckled and asked, "And the third?"

Kerid studied the two remaining captains. Roburt he knew for a sound riverman; Yvor he knew only a little. But Yvor's craft was battle-marked, the thwarts were scorched by fire and one mast stood splintered: Yvor had fought. So he said, "I'll take Yvor."

And so it was decided. Kerid had three warboats under

his command, and—the gods willing—more to come. He
felt ready to fight.

He turned to Mother Hel and bowed deep. "Thank you,
Mother, I appreciate your judgment."

"You shall show me how much," she returned, and
beckoned him to her cart.

"Select the crews, Nassim," he called back. "I'll see
you . . ."

"No sooner than tomorrow," Mother Hel declared. "Or
perhaps the next day."

Kerid climbed into the cart. He wondered which he'd
sooner do: see the warboats fit and the crews chosen, or
spend another night with Mother Hel. But he had no choice,
and so he decided to enjoy his lack of opportunity. He
turned to the blond woman and smiled.

"I trust, Mother, that you remember I have a war to fight?"

"Indeed, but first some lesser battles, eh?"

Kerid wanted to agree, but he could not speak because
her lips locked tight to his and he was pressed for breath as
the cart rattled back toward the palace.

"Loose!"

A trumpet sounded, and the mangonels and trebuchets
rattled upward. Stones and bundles of tight-wrapped straw
soaked in oil that was lit by the torches of the catapulters
soared into the sky and struck the walls of Chorym—some
over, some under.

Egor Dival assessed the aim and shouted further orders.
The catapults were wound back, reloaded, and fired again.
Showers of stone rained against Chorym's walls; burning
bales struck at the gates. But those gates were doused with
water, and the walls were high and strong. And the miners
digging under them had a long way to go. Egor Dival wondered how long this siege should take, and what part the
Vachyn sorcerer should play. Nor less what part those few
prisoners who remained might take: he did not enjoy this
business of burning and crucifying farmers, but Talan lis-

tened to Nestor, and the Vachyn had advised those horrid executions. Egor Dival's sworn liege lord listened to the Vachyn as if the sorcerer owned the king's mind.

Dival raised his helm and wiped a sleeve across his sweaty brow, then called out further orders and went to find Talan.

"So, how goes the siege?" his king asked him.

Dival shrugged. "As any siege—slowly."

Talan chuckled. "Perhaps quicker than you think. Nestor's a trick or two to come."

Dival grunted and helped himself to wine. "He'll bring down those walls?"

"He works on it now."

Dival did not like to contemplate just how, so he drank his wine and asked, "When shall we know?"

Talan shrugged, "In Nestor's good time, General. And meanwhile, what of the outlands?"

"We hold this valley," Dival explained, unrolling the map that sat between them, pinning it with cups. "This is the heart of Chaldor, and it's all ours. Two thirds of our force is despatched, and holds a ring around the heart just as we ring Chorym. Do the clans rise, they'll find our men waiting for them."

"Shall they rise?" Talan asked.

Dival shrugged inside his armor. "Likely not. It's the time they go hunting horses, and my spies have heard they fight a war of some petty kind. It would seem there's some Devyn lordling who'd conquer his fellows—we might make him our ally."

"Against what promises?" Talan frowned. "I'll not make treaties with Highlander savages."

"They're fine soldiers," Dival said. "The gods know, but Gailard and his clansmen held us long enough at the Darach Pass. Could we win them over . . ."

"Nestor won us that battle," Talan interrupted.

"I'd thought," Dival said stiffly, "that my men played some part in that."

"Of course they did." Talan smiled placatingly. "But it was Nestor who broke them, no?"

Dival poured himself more wine, drank before he replied. "His sorcery had a part, yes. But even so . . ."

"He shall win us Chorym," Talan said. "Do the Highlanders not agree to my terms, we shall destroy them. But it should be easier if they agree to my terms—so look to that, eh?"

He waived a dismissive hand. Egor Dival grunted and set down his unfinished cup. "As my king commands. But meanwhile, what of the Vachyn?"

"I shall let you know," Talan declared.

The king of Danant waited until Dival was gone stamping back to his troops before he quit the pavilion and went to Nestor's black tent. He hesitated outside the sable construction, aware of an unpleasant smell that reminded him of middens and charnel houses. Then, as if he were expected, the Vachyn sorcerer called that he enter.

Inside, the tent was dark and filled with smoke and stench. A brazier burned, its light a flickering alternation of fire and shadow in which Talan wondered if he truly saw pieces of human bodies littering the carpeted floor, and if the coloration of the carpet was a trick of the light or bloody stains. Nestor squatted at the center, before the jar that contained Andur's severed head. He beckoned Talan closer and said, "Listen."

Talan knelt beside the Vachyn, who pointed at the floating head.

"So tell me, Andur, are there no secret ways into your city?"

The walls are strong, and the gates. There are no secret ways.

"No tunnels? No secret passages from which you might escape?"

Why should I need them? My people loved me.

"How shall we attack then?"

You shall find it hard.

Talan watched mesmerized. The head floated in the liquor Nestor had inserted, surrounded by the little fishes that darted hither and yon as if disturbed by such arcane communication. The eyes were all gone now, only sockets remaining, like underwater caves, and the slack jaw did not move, but still he heard the words his hired sorcerer elicited. They came slow, like the speech of dreams, but still clear. He sensed resistance, as if the head that had no right to speak or think, and must surely be dead, was forced to unwilling communication by the Vachyn. He saw a fish emerge from an empty socket and dart between the gaping teeth to appear again from the tunnel of the neck.

"It should go easier if Ryadne surrendered."

She'll not. We agreed.

"Did she surrender, then your people might live. Talan Kedassian would wed her. He'd make her his wife—queen of Chaldor and Danant, both. She could be a great queen."

It seemed to Talan that the floating head voiced silent laughter as it said, *The gods condemn Talan. Ryadne will never wed him. She'll die first.*

"Then he'll wed your daughter. He'll take Ellyn for his bride."

The subtle, silent laughter came again. *Never! Ellyn's gone.*

Talan gasped as he saw Nestor scowl.

"Where?"

I don't know.

"Alone?" Nestor reached toward the brazier, sprinkling some concoction onto the coals that brought a fierce burst of fire, flames reaching high, augmenting the stench with some further foulness that prompted Talan to cough and cover his mouth and nostrils with a sleeve. He wondered how much more of this necromancy he might take before he emptied his belly.

She's a guardian. He'll protect her until she comes into her power.

"Who is her guardian?"

Gailard.

"And her power? What power does she own?"

She's her mother's blood. She's Dur.

"We knew that," Talan said. "Ryadne's father is Mattich of the Dur."

Nestor clamped a hand over his mouth. "Quiet! You do not understand this."

Long and dirty nails dug into Talan's flesh and he cringed, suddenly aware that he was frightened of his hired Vachyn.

"Why should the Dur frighten us?"

They've magic. Ryadne has it, and Ellyn.

"Dur magic is only for the scrying."

But Ellyn's more. She has true power, when she finds it.

"Where shall she find it? Where has Gailard taken her?"

I don't know.

"Who does?"

No one.

"We can put Ryadne to torture. I can set such pain in her as shall loose her tongue."

She doesn't know. Only Gailard knows.

Talan was unsure whether the floating head laughed or wailed. Surely, the fishes grew agitated, darting wildly through the tendrils of hair, the empty sockets, the jaw and throat. Then he started as Nestor rose to his feet and picked up the jar and flung it across the tent. It shattered against a pole, spilling acidic liquor and the fishes and the head in a great flood that washed back and sent Danant's king lurching away for fear of some contamination he had condoned but did not understand.

Nestor said, "Damn you," and kicked the head withershins about the floor.

Then: "We must act fast. Tell Dival to speed his siege."

"And you?" Talan stared wide-eyed at the Vachyn, struggling against the desire to flee the tent. "What shall you do?"

"Give you Chorym," Nestor replied, delivering Andur's battered head a last kick. "Then Ryadne, save she does not die first. Then, all well, Ellyn."

"Have I Ryadne," Talan said nervously, "what does Ellyn matter?"

"Everything!" Nestor shouted. "She's the key, you fool! I *must* find her. Now go!"

Talan stumbled toward the tent's opening. His head felt thick with the fumes, and it seemed that Andur's ephemeral laughter echoed inside his skull.

"Wait!"

Danant's king halted as if paralyzed.

"Tonight, a little before midnight, bring me five of your best men. Strong, eh? And battle-hardened. And five dogs—strong dogs, with good teeth and fierce tempers."

Talan found the courage to ask, "Why?"

"I'll show you," Nestor promised. "Now go."

Talan went, clutching his robe about him, and scurried to his pavilion, where he called for strong wine.

Ryadne woke from a dream in which she stood naked in a howling wind that blew her long hair out behind her head and plucked at her breasts like violating fingers. She stood against a battered oak and the sky above was dark as the night before her eyes, and lightning flashed, illuminating the figures that stood before her, each one calling to her in words she could not comprehend. She saw Andur, and Ellyn, then Gailard, Talan, and a dark-robed figure she knew was the Vachyn sorcerer. Then another: a woman armored, with long black hair and a face she did not recognize, who raised a gleaming sword and beckoned her toward a precipice that fell down into glorious light.

She woke to the hand upon her shoulder and saw one of her women standing, face concerned, above her.

"Something is happening, my queen."

Ryadne dismissed the nocturnal images. "What?"

She could hear, even this far, the thud of Danant's

missiles against her walls, and when she rose and went to the window, she saw the trails of fire the lit projectiles left across the sky.

"I don't know." The woman—by the gods, what was her name?—paced nervously behind the queen. "But your generals would have your attention."

"Ask them to wait a moment while I dress."

Ryadne splashed water on her face and pulled on a gown, then motioned that the waiting woman open the door.

It was not all of her commanders who attended. Only two appeared, but they wore grey faces and hollow eyes, and one bore great burns on his armor, and more on his face.

"They bring magic against us, my queen."

"We expected as much." Ryadne felt her heart flutter. "After all, we face a Vachyn sorcerer."

It was the unmarked one who spoke. "We cannot defeat a Vachyn."

He fell to his knees, and Ryadne saw tears stain his cheeks. She felt his dread then, as if it pervaded her sleeping quarters like some miasmic fog. It seemed to emanate from him like the sour stink of old sweat; and from the windows, as if the night were filled with it, and the moon sent it down; and from the candles that burned in her chamber, filling it with the persuasion to accept defeat. She felt it in herself, coming from her armpits and from between her legs. It was defeat made real, fingers beckoning and unheard voices whispering, *Give in. You cannot win. Give up. Surrender.*

She steeled herself. *I am Ryadne of the Dur,* she told herself. *I am Andur's widow, and I can defeat this.*

She knew she could not, but even so she said, "Tell me what happens," in as firm a tone as she could manage, "and then I shall dress and come to the walls."

"They send fire against us." It was the unmarked, frightened man who spoke.

"We expected that," she said.

"No, this is not what we expected. This is different."

The burned commander set a hand on his companion's

shoulder and said, "They send strange fire against us, my queen. Vachyn fire, I think. And . . . other things."

Ryadne thought an instant on what Gailard had told her of the defeat, the retreat from the Darach Pass, her own dreams.

"Wait, and I'll come with you."

She donned her armor and went with them to the walls. It was akin to walking into a fog of despair. She remembered a time she'd been lost in the Highlands, when a mist had settled in and she could not discern any landmarks. She had known that stream and bogs lay ahead, and ravines, and thought that she must surely die, and it was like that now: all insensate terror and despair.

She could hear the thud of missiles against the walls and see the blazing bundles landing. She could hear men weeping, and the whistle of arrows, and had she not been a mother afraid for her daughter, she would likely have given up. But she could not. Ellyn ran abroad in Gailard's care, and she must live long enough to grant them the chance of survival.

So she steeled herself and dismissed the phantoms, calling for her troops to stand firm and ignore the Vachyn's magic.

Which was very hard to do, for it came in that foggy nightmare form that prompted folk to dwell on ancient fears and dreads, old guilts and shames, embarrassments and unrequited loves, old hatreds and slights. And with it came the thunder of Danant's catapults, the mangonels and trebuchets and heavy arbalests hurling stones and blazing bundles and severed heads. And then the worst: a column of fire that gusted like the breath of legend's dragons against the gates and set them, despite the drenching water, aflame.

Ryadne knew then that Chorym must fall; Talan's Vachyn sorcerer owned too much power. But she'd not give up; she'd hold so long as she could, and hide her daughter's tracks as best she could—for Ellyn and all the world she knew. For which end, when finally the gates broke, there could be only one fate for her.

Nestor gestured at what he'd made. "These shall find Ellyn."

"Marriage with Ryadne would be easier." Talan paced
the confines of the building that had once been a temple,
now given over to Nestor's dark machinations. He found it
difficult to look at the Vachyn sorcerer's creations. "What
are they? How shall they find me Ellyn?"

"Come, look." Nestor set a hand on Talan's shoulder,
propelling him toward the closest of his creations. "You
gave me men and dogs, no? And I have melded them into
one creature. They'll find Ellyn wherever she is."

He touched the creature and it rose snarling from its
bed. Talan sprang back, horrified. The thing wore the outlines of a man, but altered, the body massively muscled and
thick with hair, the eyes sunk red beneath overhanging
craggy brows, the nostrils wide and flaring. The jaw extended so that the lips parted over long yellow fangs. Nestor
gestured and it sank onto its haunches like some obedient
dog. Talan saw that its fingers ended in long claws, and that
its feet were similarly weaponed. It panted noisily, looking
from him to the Vachyn as if it awaited Nestor's order to
attack.

"By the gods, what have you made?" Talan backed
away from the snarling beast.

"The answer to your problem." Nestor chuckled.
"They'll not harm you, only Ellyn and whoever guards her.
Trust me, eh?"

Ellyn lay sleepless and despairing on the cold ground. She
could hear Gailard's steady breathing, and wondered how
he could find slumber's refuge when so awful a fate awaited
him. It seemed as if he were resigned to death, concerned
only for her safety and willing to trade his life to that end.
Almost, she could rage against his fatalism—was tempted
to shake him awake and demand he find them some avenue
of escape—but that would be tantamount to questioning his

courage, and *that* was a commodity she could not deny. So she only stared at his supine form and struggled to hold back her tears, wondering what she could do.

Her mother had promised her she owned the magical talent: she screwed her eyes tight shut and clenched her fists, endeavoring to summon that power.

She would call up magic to spirit them both away, sending thunderbolts raining down on Eryk and Rytha as she went. She'd flay them as they threatened to flay Gailard. She'd . . . Feel nothing, and open her eyes to find the tent night-dark and cold, and Gailard still asleep. She moaned, burgeoning anger ebbing as despair flooded back. There was nothing she could do. She was helpless. She was caught surely as a partridge in some poacher's net, and these Devyn savages would execute Gailard and trade her to Talan.

Tears came again, running silently down her cheeks, unstemmed now that all hope was lost. She reached out a hand to touch Gailard's shoulder, anxious for what small comfort that contact might bring. Then held back. He would need all his strength come the morrow, and the least she could do was allow him a sound night's sleep. Though she could not understand how he could sleep when such an awful fate awaited him.

He was, she thought forlornly, a most unusual man. Then she drew up her knees and curled her arms around her breeches and sat staring at him as the night aged and the day's horrors drew closer.

The gates were broken down and Chorym's walls were jagged and wrecked. Fires burned, ignited by the catapults and magic, and frightened folk filled the streets. Talan's men entered the city, and Ryadne saw her commanders fall. Danant's soldiers raged like some bloody flood tide, slaying at will, careless of whether they put their blades into armored warriors or terrified citizens.

She met Talan on the ramparts. She had a dozen guardsmen around her—all that were left now—and she wore

golden armor that echoed that of her dead husband. To her
left stood a section of broken wall tumbled down like sad,
old dreams onto the conquered ground below.

Talan said, "Lady, only agree that I am the rightful conqueror and I shall marry you and make you great. You shall
be queen of both Chaldor and Danant."

She said, "Will you let my people live?"

"As my subjects," Talan said.

"And these?" Ryadne gestured at her last defenders.

"Do they lay down their blades and swear fealty to me."

One of Ryadne's men said, "I'll not do that."

Another said, "I cannot."

Egor Dival said, "Your city is lost. You fought bravely,
and do you surrender you shall be treated well—my word
on that."

A man said, "Danant's word? Did you treat our people
well?"

And Talan gestured, and archers stepped forward and
put shafts through the guards' armor so that they fell down
around Ryadne like chaff under the sickle even as Dival
shouted, "No!"

"What other choice was there?" Talan asked his general
as Dival fumed and protested. "They'd not surrender, and
I'd have this woman for my bride."

Ryadne said, "You'll not, and I pray that the gods curse
you and damn you."

Then, before any could halt her, she stepped onto the
broken ramparts of her defeated city and flung herself away
and down into the oblivion she hoped might reunite her with
Andur.

CHAPTER ELEVEN

I slept not at all that night; I could not, for fear of the dawn. It was not so much fear of my own fate—I had faced death before—as concern for Ellyn, and the guilt my failure to protect her brought. True, it should be a shameful way to die, but that shame belonged more to Eryk and Rytha than to me, and whilst I knew it should be painful I also believed I could bear it as a Highlander should. What I could not bear was the knowledge that I had failed Andur and Ryadne and Ellyn, and that the latter would become a helpless pawn in Eryk's grandiose (and, I thought, insane) plan. I contemplated prayer, but decided that Andur had been right when he said the gods forsook us and so only lay still awhile, long enough that I heard Ellyn's breathing soften and guessed that she slept, then crept about the tent, checking its fastenings as my mind raced desperately in search of escape. I could find no hope: the tent was secure, and I knew that watchful and armored men waited beyond its confines. And even did I find some way past those watchmen, still we should need to circumvent the camp's dogs, find our horses, and even then flee weaponless and unsupplied to the very clan Eryk intended to conquer.

Ellyn slept restlessly. She tossed and turned and spoke brief fragments of sentences as if she conversed with someone. I heard her say my name, and her parents', and her grandfather's, and it was as if she then received answers, for she'd lie silent awhile, then nod and mumble unintelligible words, and sometimes smile. Finally, she slept, and I envied her that respite as I lay staring into the shadows.

Then, slowly, the shadows departed and I heard the camp awake. Horses nickered and dogs barked; I heard voices, and the crackling sounds of fresh logs and turves set on the morning cookfires. Soon the smells of tea and porridge and charring meat filled the tent. Then the entry flap was unlaced and light flooded in. Rurrid and Athol stood there, flanked by a dozen men. I supposed it was their privilege to escort me to my execution. I hoped I disappointed them when I rose and bade them good day and stepped toward them as if I were not at all afraid.

Ellyn cried out and sprang from her bed to clutch at me.

I said, "Put on a brave face. Don't let them see you weep."

She answered, "How can I not?" and held me tight.

"Live," I whispered to her, stroking her hair, "and do you get the chance, revenge me."

She nodded and gave me back, "I shall, Gailard."

Then Rurrid pricked me in the buttocks with his sword and aped apology. "Forgive me for such interruption, Gailard, but your presence is required at our ceremony."

I turned to face him, ignoring the pain. "Were you a man, Rurrid, I'd challenge you to combat. But you're not, so I only curse you for a coward and a traitor."

His face blanched at that and he raised his blade. I hoped he'd strike and slay me, delivering me an easier death, but Athol stayed his hand. "No, brother, no. We need him alive, eh?"

Rurrid nodded and lowered his sword, turning a leering smile on me. "That's true—alive for the crows. Whilst she"— his gaze swung to Ellyn—"shall be our guest awhile. She's what—fifteen? Old enough to know a man, eh, Gailard? Have you not had her, perhaps I shall make her a woman."

Ellyn spat and shrieked, "I'll die first! I'd sooner lie with dogs than such as you!"

I sprang at Rurrid, and kicked him hard between the legs. He squealed like the pig he was and fell down, and before the others reached me I landed two more hard kicks. I felt ribs snap and shouted my satisfaction even as the sword-hilts thudded against me and I was forced to the ground, pinned under shields, my wrists bound and a loose tether set about my ankles.

Thus was I brought before my brother and his wife, Ellyn dragged—howling furiously—behind. My head spun from the blows, but I enjoyed the sight of Rurrid, who was held upright by two men, his face mightily pale, his legs loose, one hand pressed tight to his breeches and the other clasping his side. I wished I might deliver the same drubbing to Eryk.

But I was bound and my brother sat well guarded, resting back in his fur-swathed chair, a bowl of porridge in his hand. Rytha sat beside him, sipping from a horn cup, her eyes alight with speculation.

"So even now you offend us," Eryk said. "Can you not accept your just fate with good grace?"

"What do you know of grace?" I snarled. "You and your fat wife?"

Rytha started at that, and flung her tea in my face. It was somewhat cooled, and so it did not burn me too much, and I was able to smile and say, "Aye, lady—fat like some sow stuffed for eating." I managed a laugh. "You and my brother deserve one another."

She began to rise, snatching at the dagger on her belt, but Eryk restrained her.

"No, wife, no. Not so swift a death, eh? Better that he suffer as we planned."

Rytha seethed like a scalded cat, but allowed Eryk to re-seat her. He smiled malignantly and beckoned men forward.

"It was to be Rurrid or Athol who dragged you, Gailard, but as you've unmanned Rurrid it shall be Athol's privilege."

He motioned again and men held me fast as Athol smiled and stepped forward, loosening my clothes until they lay scattered about me and I stood naked before all the camp. I caught Ellyn's eyes on me, and saw her pale face grow red. Then the cords holding my wrists were cut and my hands bound before me with a length of strong rope that was lashed to the saddle of a black horse.

Athol mounted and Eryk said, "Three times around the camp. No more, lest he not feel the whip."

Athol laughed and urged the horse forward.

For the first few steps I was able to keep my feet, but then Athol lifted the horse to a swifter pace and the tether on my ankles tripped me so that I fell down and was dragged behind. Thoughtful of my manhood, I contrived to twist onto my back, and watched the camp go by in a blur that became increasingly hazy as hard ground and stones and tussocks struck me. I saw faces. Folk struck at me with sticks, some flung rocks or clods or handfuls of dung; some—not many—merely watched, and I thought I saw pity and shame in their eyes. Then all was a bouncing, pain-filled blur. Athol dragged me through fires, and over the hardest ground he could find, and through the pasture where the two clans' horses grazed, so that I was bespattered with dung and a great pack of dogs chased me, barking and snapping.

The world grew distant then, until cold water doused me and I felt myself hauled upright. I struggled to stand on my own feet, shrugging off the clutching hands, and stared at Eryk from between swollen lids. I could taste blood in my mouth and spat, fearing I should vomit and that be construed as weakness. From the corner of one bloodied eye I saw Ellyn held by two warriors. She was weeping and I saw her mouth moving, but I could not hear what she said, only Eryk's words.

"Now take him to the tree and beat his bones bare."

I was dragged away and tied face forward to a windblown hemlock. Its bark was rough against my face as my arms were stretched out and lashed to two outflung branches. I braced my feet, praying that I owned the strength to stand firm.

Then my head was pulled back and I smelled my brother's breath as he put his face close to mine and held something before my eyes. It was hard to focus, but I recognized what he brandished, stroking it obscenely against my cheek.

"Five strands of plaited bull's hide, Gailard; and its end all sewn with metal pellets. It shall take the flesh off you, brother. It shall lay your ribs bare and spill your blood like a newfound spring. You'll know pain now."

I mumbled, "Damn you," and he laughed.

"Beg me for mercy, and perhaps I'll have you slain quicker."

"Damn you! The gods curse you and your fat wife."

Eryk struck me. It was a weak blow that I barely felt. Those that followed were far harder.

I leaned against the tree and clenched my teeth. I'd not cry out, could I resist it; not give them that satisfaction. But it was hard. The first blow was a knife-cut across my back, the second a bludgeon to my spine, the third a spray of fire over my buttocks. Tears sprang from my eyes and I felt my body jerk and jump involuntarily, twitching to each swing of the whip. I felt warmth trickling down my legs and wondered if it was blood or urine. I closed my eyes—that, at least, was not hard to do—and ground my teeth so hard together I feared they'd break. I believe I whimpered, but I do not think I cried aloud for all I longed to scream. The pain went on until I dimly felt my legs give way, my body slumping so that all my weight was supported by my bound wrists and I feared they might dislocate. And then it went on longer, until I could no longer feel it—only ride away into the red shadows that filled my eyes.

I woke again, gagging on the taste that filled my mouth, choking and gasping as I saw Rytha standing before me. She held a cloth soaked in water and vinegar, which had restored me to my senses. That, of course, was her intent, and

I loathed her for it; I'd sooner have gone away into that red darkness. My body burned as if consumed in fire, and it was very difficult to focus on her smiling face.

"So, you're awake. Good; I'd not have you miss what's to come." She pressed the cloth to my mouth again, forcing me to swallow the bitter mixture. "You bleed well, Gailard, and it's a fine, warm day. The ants will find you soon, and the flies. They'll feast on you, and the crows will come. They'll peck out your eyes before they eat your flesh, and when night falls there'll be dogs and wolves." She smiled horribly. "I hope you live a long time, Gailard. Long enough you know true suffering."

She wiped the cloth across my chest, which burned fiery, and rose. I still hung suspended from my wrists. I found it hard to breathe, but even so I saw Eryk come to stand before me, Athol behind him, and Rurrid, wearing a bandage about his ribs.

"We go now," my brother said, "to conquer the Dur. We shall ride with your little friend at our head, and does Mattich not concede, I shall do as I promised—send her to him in pieces. Think on that as you die, Gailard."

I said, "Our father would curse you for this," but I think it came out in a mumble, for Eryk cocked his head and beamed and said, "What's that, Gailard? Do you beg for mercy?"

I said, "No," but that, also, was a mumble Eryk did not seem to understand, for he laughed and touched my cheek, and licked blood from his fingers and turned away.

I saw Ellyn then. She was very pale, and her hands were bound before her. Two men stood beside her; one had a hand on her shoulder, restraining her. I think she'd have run to me, but she could not, and so only mouthed words I could not hear.

Then Eryk clapped his hands and gestured and they all turned away, leaving me to die.

It was, as Rytha had pointed out, a warm day. The sky was blue and filled with magnificent billows of high, white cloud. I dimly heard the sounds of bees buzzing. I saw birds darting in search of insects. I tried to stand upright, but my legs would not support me. I licked my lips and tasted blood. I tested the ropes that bound me to the tree and knew I was too weak to break the bonds. I knew that I should die, and so I let myself slump, thinking that it were better I choked on my own straining weight than the crows come peck me to death.

I did pray then—to gods I was no longer sure I believed in, and who surely seemed to have deserted Chaldor—and asked them that I might die.

Then I felt a new pain. It seemed unlikely that I could, for my whole body burned. Each breath was a labor, and the tree's bark against my back was agony, but still I felt a fresh intrusion on my suffering. It was as if tiny fingers traversed my broken skin, and I moaned as I knew the ants had come. I craned my head around and saw long trails of scurrying black bodies moving over the tree, running busily back and forth from bark to wounds, carrying tiny pieces of me away. I was barely aware of the flies, for they were a busy cloud around me that fell into the kaleidoscope pattern of my swimming vision, less important than the carrion birds.

Those I saw distantly: black specks that floated beyond the swarming flies, growing larger as they descended. I heard their cawing and then the windrush of their wings. They landed—a flock of twenty or thirty—some in the tree, others on the ground before me, where they paced about, beaks clacking in speculation. I tried to shout, but could find no voice louder than theirs. I tried to kick at them, but my legs were too weak. I whispered a curse and gave myself over to inevitable fate. I felt a bird land on my shoulder. Its claws dug into my flesh; I felt it begin to peck at my back. Another came down from the tree, and I saw its bleak eyes contemplate my face, its beak dart forward.

I felt such pain as I had never known, and knew that I must be plucked apart. I wished it had been the wolves and wild dogs, for that should be a swifter fate. But there were only the black birds. I thought of the Darrach Pass and the horrid feasting there; I would make a poor repast, in comparison. I think I screamed, but I hope it was in anger rather than fear—for all I felt such fear as I'd never known. I had thought to die in battle, honorably; or aged, in bed. But always with honor, and there was none in this.

I felt my scalp tugged as a crow landed on my head, felt its wings rustle my hair as I tossed my head back. I looked into blank yellow eyes that contained no mercy. Then there were more, and I died.

CHAPTER TWELVE

Ellyn rode in a blur of tears that clouded her vision so that it seemed she traveled through fog. She fought the tears, but no matter how hard she blinked or wiped a sleeve across her face they would not stop falling, trickling from her eyes like old memories of shared pain. She gritted her teeth and cursed, but still she could not stop—only remember the horror. Her hands were unfastened now, but her ankles were lashed securely to the stirrups, and the reins were looped about the saddle horn. Her mount was tethered to that in front, which was ridden by the one called Rurrid. She hated him, and when she could, she'd heel her mare aside or slow the horse to cause him discomfort. And he'd gasp, and clutch at his bandaged ribs, and curse her, and make vile promises.

She wondered which of these Highlander savages she hated the most. Eryk, for what he'd ordered done to Gailard, or his fat wife, Rytha, for the scorn she spat? Rurrid for his lewd suggestions, or Athol, for swinging that awful whip against Gailard's body?

She shuddered at the memory. Gailard had been bruised and bloody when finally that awful ride had ended, and she could hardly believe that he'd owned the strength to

stand and face his brother. She had seen executions—her
dead father had explained they were sometimes necessary—but in Chaldor they were done swift, not like . . . She
swallowed, her eyes clouding again. Not so bloody and
vengeful.

And then the whipping . . .

By all the gods, she'd seen her guardian's bones exposed, bloody through the severed flesh, and screamed in
protest—which had gotten her a blow from fat Rytha,
whose eyes were wide with pleasure. And had she not taken
more as she dripped the vinegar-soaked sponge into
Gailard's mouth? And then, as Gailard hung from the tree
and distant flocks of crows cawed announcement of feast
and winged toward the bloody offering, Eryk had announced departure, and Ellyn had been tossed astride the
chestnut horse and they had gone away.

She blinked some semblance of vision back into her
eyes and saw the twinned clans riding out in battle array
around her, and thought on her dreams.

They had been strange, full of promises and threat. She
wondered if her mother's promise of magical talent to come
arrived, or if she only suffered feverish dreamings born of
terror. Was Ryadne right, then there was hope—though she
could not see it, not bound and carried like some captured
slave. But still she prayed, asking that her dreams be true
and the impossible happen.

"Do you slow that god-cursed horse again I'll slit its
throat and drag you behind me." Rurrid turned awkwardly
in his saddle to glare back at her. "And tonight I'll teach you
to be a woman."

Ellyn spat her contempt. "I doubt you could do that,
even had Gailard not unmanned you."

Rurrid slowed his horse awhile and poked a finger
painfully against her breast. "Wait and see, eh?" He grinned
lasciviously. "I'll show you what a real man is."

Ellyn closed her eyes and prayed her dreams were true.

"Sail ho, and it's Danant's flag!"

Kerid stared into the morning's mist. The sun was scarce over the horizon, and the Durrakym was swathed in fog. From the steering deck of the warboat—now renamed simply the *Andur*—he could see little of the river ahead.

"Whereabouts?"

"Starboard a half quarter."

"How big?"

"A three-master. A transport, I think."

Kerid trusted his lookout and put the tiller over, hoping that Nassim and Yvor follow. He had little enough real experience of river war; Andur had never seen fit to pirate his fellow kingdoms.

"Battle station! Quietly!"

No time for grand gestures now. No howling horns, no drums or blaring bugles—better a silent approach through the mist. He glanced back and saw Nassim turn the *Ryadne* into line, Yvor bring the *Ellyn* abreast.

It was the strategy Mother Hel had explained to him as they said their farewells and he quit her luxurious bed: attack when you are not expected, and let stealth be your friend. Take the victim athwarts, but set one boat behind and one afore. And are you close to the shore, let them run. A frightened crew will fight when cornered, so leave them—if you can—some avenue of escape. That way they'll quit the ship rather than fight, and you can bring it back to me.

Kerid chuckled and said softly, "For Chaldor and Mother Hel." Then, louder: "Battle speed. Stand ready!"

The oarsmen leaned into their sweeps and the *Andur* leapt across the river like some hunting dog. The *Ryadne* and the *Ellyn* swung abaft and forrard. Those few men not tending the oars readied their shields and drew their swords; they—the chosen—would be first onto the deck of the Danant boat.

Their prey saw them too late.

They came out of the fog like wolves onto an unsuspecting deer. Kerid shouted, and the arbalest fired a bolt that swept through the Danant vessel's sail and tore away the pennant. Then the *Andur* was alongside and grappling irons lofted. The *Ryadne* hove out of the mist and fired a heavy shaft into the Danant boat's prow. The *Ellyn* hove to astern, loosing a bolt that tore across the steering deck of the larger craft and sent her tillerman screaming shrilly onto the deck below.

Kerid's men swung on board. There were sixty in all on the *Andur*, the same aboard the *Ryadne* and the *Ellyn*. There were likely three hundred on the big Danant vessel, and the attackers athwart and astern would need time to maneuver into position before they might send men aboard. Kerid lashed his tiller and ran across the deck to seize a rope and clamber upward.

He breasted the thwarts and ducked as shafts whistled overhead; he had not anticipated bowmen. He saw men—his own—fall, and charged headlong at the archers.

"For Chaldor and for Andur!"

He slashed his sword across a bow, severing the wood and the face behind, and swung the blade in a scythelike movement that cut strings to left and right. He felt a blade prick his ribs and spun, falling back as his men swarmed across the deck of the Danant craft, driving his attackers away. He saw a man standing undecided between flight and victory above him, and drove his blade upward into the groin before the descending blade made the decision for him. The Danant man screamed and fell down, and Kerid rose with blood running down his side, and looked around.

Fifty at most of his own men left. He'd mourn the dead later; now he wanted only to take this vessel. He swung his blade and shouted for followers, and the Danant sailors were driven back under the sheer ferocity of the attack.

Then Nassim came on board with all his men, and from the stern Yvor sent fighters, and the boat was taken. Those Danant sailors who chose to fight were slain; those who dived overboard and swam for the shore were left to live.

And Kerid laughed.

"By all the gods, we did it, no?" He stood on the steering deck. Blood ran down his side where he'd been stuck, but he ignored that, jubilant in his victory. "We've taken another of Talan's boats, and there'll be more to come. Now let's take this one back to Hel's Town and trade with Mother, and then come back to fight Danant again."

A roar of approval met his suggestion, and they turned about, all save one, setting lines on the crippled Danant boat that they might haul her back to Hel's Town and trade her and her cargo for more warboats.

Nassim lingered awhile.

"Is it Chaldor you fight for, or Mother Hel's bed?"

"Is there so much difference?" Kerid grinned over the heads of the men winding bandages around his wounded side. "The one brings us the other, no?"

"It depends," Nassim said. "I'll sail with you on Chaldor's behalf, but is it the other . . ."

Kerid frowned. "I'll not deny I enjoy her company, but I fight for Chaldor."

"I hope so," Nassim said, and swung down the trailing lines to his own boat.

"This is not . . ." Egor Dival hesitated, seeking in the midst of his disgust to find the right words. "Not how I'd fight this war."

"But this is *my* war," Talan returned, "and you are my sworn general."

"Even so! These . . . *things*?" Dival gestured at the creatures Nestor had made.

They stood, dressed in semblance of human men, but panting like dogs, anxious to be released from the leash of the sorcerer's power. They wore shirts and breeches, and about each waist was a belt containing a sword and a pouch of food. Bits and pieces of the armor they had worn as men hung about their bodies. At close quarters none would believe them human, and Dival felt a great loathing for all they represented.

"You took my soldiers," he protested.

"*Your* soldiers?" Talan exaggerated his expression. "Surely mine. To do with as I want."

"To order into battle, yes." Dival frowned as he ducked his head. "But this?"

"They go to battle," Talan said. "They go to find Ellyn."

Dival studied the five hunters with obvious disapproval. "And do they find her? What then? Shall they bring her back or tear her apart?"

"I'll wed her if I can, but if I cannot, then . . ." Talan shrugged. "Better Chaldor have no heir than some symbol of Andur's line. Would you not agree, my general?"

Dival grunted, turning uncomfortably on his chair. "I'd not thought it would go this way."

"These are modern times," Talan said, "and we use modern methods. Must I use a Vachyn sorcerer, then I shall—and use his methods to conquer."

Dival nodded mournfully. "And when you've Ellyn—alive or dead?"

"I shall own Chaldor beyond dispute." Talan raised a goblet, waiting for a servant to fill the cup. "And none shall argue my dominion. I shall own both sides of the Durrakym and make Danant the greatest kingdom this world has ever known."

"Save you'll owe it to the Vachyn."

Talan shrugged. "Nestor's a hired man. I've paid his price and he works for me."

"And when he's given you what you want?"

"I shall discharge him. He'll go back to the temple."

"Will he?"

"What else?" Talan drank wine. "The Vachyn work for money, no? They hire their magicks to the highest bidder, and when they're done . . ."

"I wonder," Dival said. "Do they go home to that temple of theirs, or do they . . . linger?"

"I've paid Nestor to give me Chaldor." Talan set down his cup, staring at his doubtful general. "Already he's given me Andur's head and Chorym. Now he'll give me Ellyn and dominion over Chaldor. Then he'll go away."

Nestor came into the chamber then. The things he had made panted hotter at sight of him, as if his presence energized them. He smiled and motioned them silent, like a huntsman calming his pack.

"It's arranged." The Vachyn seated himself. "A cart awaits and they can be taken unseen from the city. I'll take the cart myself and let them loose some distance from Chorym. They'll find her." He smiled and gestured for a servant to bring him wine. "My word on it."

"How long shall that take?" Talan asked.

"It depends," Nestor answered, far calmer than his employer, "on where Gailard has taken her."

"The sooner the better," Talan said. "I'd not linger too long here—I'd go back to Danant."

"Of course." Nestor made a placatory gesture. "And I'd return to the Vachyn temple. But it shall take as long as it takes."

Egor Dival snorted and the sorcerer smiled at him.

"My general doubts you," Talan said. "He wonders at your motives."

Nestor's smile grew wider; Egor Dival scowled.

"My motives?" Nestor spread his hands wide, beaming at Dival. "I do what I am hired to do, General. Your king has hired me to win him a war and I am doing so. Do you argue with that?"

Sullenly, Dival shook his head.

"Then we've no dispute." Nestor pushed back his chair, looking at Talan. "Shall I release my hunters?"

Talan nodded, avoiding Egor Dival's angry stare.

The Vachyn went to the chamber's door and beckoned.

The five hunters paced forward. The sorcerer opened the door and went through, his creatures following.

"This will not sit well with most folk," Dival said. "They'll say you league with dark magicks."

"Does it win me Chaldor, I'll not complain." Talan held out his cup that a servant might fill it again. "Does it win me Ellyn, I'll thank Nestor."

Egor Dival sighed and watched the door swing closed.

Nestor took his creatures down through the corridors of Ryadne's conquered palace to the waiting wagon. He saw them safe on board, then climbed astride the seat. He flicked the reins and murmured words to the four restive horses, steering them down through the rubble-filled streets to the East Gate. He passed that portal and drove awhile through ravaged farmlands. It was a mild afternoon, the sky blue and filled with billows of high white cloud. Swallows oblivious of the dramas beneath them darted in pursuit of insects. Nestor drove the wagon a league or so clear of Chorym, then halted.

He climbed from the seat and beckoned his creations down. They ranked about him, eager to hunt. He said, "Find Ellyn," and set them loose.

He stood awhile, watching as they sniffed about, then set out running eastward. He smiled as he watched them disappear. All went well, just as he'd anticipated.

CHAPTER THIRTEEN

Idied.
I went beyond pain into a
terrible darkness, and felt myself fall away, embracing that
promised oblivion. I wanted it to end; I had failed. I had lost
Ellyn to Eryk, who'd use her as he would to further his ends.
I had failed Ryadne's trust and Andur's geas. It had been
better I died in the Darach Pass than come to this, failing all
who set their trust in me. I thought I had lost my honor, and
in despair gave myself to oblivion. I dived into the darkness,
willing that it take me. I thought that this must have been
how it was for the men we lost on the river, coming back
from our defeat at the Darrach Pass—all those who fell into
the Durrakym, weighted by their armor and sinking remorseless into the water.

Then I saw light: a long, wide tunnel of brilliance that
opened—far off—onto a brighter land. Promise hung in
that light, like a lantern calling a wanderer home.

I wondered if the gods called me.

I gave up my body and—I can only describe it as swimming, for all I cannot swim—swam toward the light. I
wanted to go there; I wanted to be free of this agony, and
find peace.

And there I found a light so bright I was forced to
open my hurting eyes, and found them healed and my body

painless, so that I stared into the brightness, and felt gentle hands cleanse my wounds, and saw a woman lave my naked body with tender touches.

It did not occur to me to feel embarrassment. I asked: "Who are you?"

"My name is Shara," she said, "and I shall bring you back to life."

"Then I did die?" I asked. It did not occur to me, then, to wonder how or why she saved me.

She nodded. "Yes."

Her face was solemn and lovely. Hair black as a raven's wing hung about her shoulders and I wondered how I could smell it; it was clean and scented like fresh juniper as it brushed my face. Her eyes were grey, and I thought she was not young. Webworks of age and care set crow's-feet about those calm orbs, and there were lines on her face, about her mouth and cheeks; but they only seemed to me to make her more beautiful. She wore a robe, or armor—I could not tell which, for my vision floated about, and perhaps she was even naked—but she touched my body and my pain ceased. I saw again, clearly, and felt a great confusion.

"Are you a goddess?" I asked her.

She shook her head—which sent tendrils of that long black hair to stroking across my face—and said, "No; far less than that. Better think of me as a penitent seeking to make reparations for old sins."

"Then how," I asked, "can you return me to life?"

"Because I can," she said.

It did not then—as pain ceased and I accepted that, in some manner I could not understand, I lived—occur to me to ask more questions. I did not ask her how she might work my resurrection, or to what end. I only looked down at my body and saw it healed; *felt* it healed.

I said, "Thank you," and she touched my face and said, "Sleep now, and come the morning we'll be on our way."

I slept on her touch.

I woke to a warming fire and the scent of heather. I stretched—wary—and found my body limber, healed of the dragging and the whipping and the crows' attentions. I looked at the sky above me and saw clouds scudding across the blue; I felt a warm wind on my face, and heard it rustling the branches of the tree I'd been hung on. I rose and stretched and paced, examining my body and finding it clear of the scars I'd expected.

I was confused. Was I alive or dead? Was I gone to some benign afterlife or tormented by some succubus? I stared about, recognizing my surroundings and finding them entirely normal. I felt the grass under my feet and the wind on my skin, and realized I was naked.

There was no sign of Shara, but a fire burned and a prosaic kettle steamed. I felt embarrassed now, and confused, and crouched under my execution tree with my hands pressed about my genitals. I wondered what happened; I could not understand it. I had died and a beautiful woman had brought me back to life. I wondered where Ellyn was, and felt fresh guilt; Eryk's camp was gone and I supposed Ellyn gone with them. I could see the detritus of their trail, leading away toward the Dur territory, but I could not see how I might follow. Not naked and afoot—even was I truly alive.

"Shall we eat breakfast and then go on?"

I jumped like a startled hare. I was not used to anyone creeping up on me, but Shara had caught me unawares. I covered myself as best I could and stared at the two fresh trout she held.

I still wondered if I lived, or if this was all some dream.

If the latter, then my dreams contained a remarkable semblance of reality, for the trout sizzled in the pan she set on the fire and I could smell their flesh crisping, feel saliva in my mouth as I realized I was very hungry. She sprinkled them with herbs and dropped leaves into the boiling kettle, then looked at me and smiled.

"Forgive me, I had forgotten." She gestured toward the tree. "You'll want your clothes."

I followed the direction of her eyes and saw my gear set out, neatly folded. Undergarments and shirt, tunic and breeches, my boots, even my sword and shield—all was there, and I pulled them on, too grateful to wonder what magic delivered them.

Shara said, "I am sorry I could not bring you a horse, but that's too large a burden to carry."

"Carry?" I laced my breeks. "You *carried* these from Eryk's camp?"

"Not as you mean it." She shrugged, laughing. "I brought them by other means."

I frowned and her smile faded. "Of course, you are Devyn, no? And you Devyn mistrust magic."

I was no longer so sure I did, but still I asked her, "Who are you? *What* are you?" I felt mightily confused. "Am I alive or dead?"

"Alive," she said. "Can you not feel that, not know it?"

I reexamined my body. I set my hands against the tree and felt its bark. I saw the marks I'd left there, red against the grey. There were still insects making the last of their feasting. I ducked my head. "I feel alive, but I do not understand."

"Eat." She passed me a platter. "Eat and listen, for we must soon be on our way if we're to rescue Ellyn."

Her voice was mellow, but I heard beneath its softness an urgency that matched my own. I nodded and took the plate and set to picking at the fish as she spoke, explaining what she'd done, with me interrupting as I failed to grasp the wonder of her magic. This was such stuff as baffled and befuddled me, and gave me hope and left me wondering, all at the same time.

"Two days you hung on the tree before I understood what I must do," she told me. "I took another five to bring you back to life."

"So I was dead for seven days?"

"I think only five; you clung hard to life, Gailard." She smiled. "You're strong, and your sense of honor supported you. I'd suppose that's why you clung so hard to life—because of that geas."

I shrugged, still anticipating that such a movement must bring me pain, and felt none. It was an odd feeling to have died and been resurrected, as if I could no longer be sure who I was, or who owned my life. I had owed debts before. Men had saved me in battle, but that was a thing of clashing swords and support of comrades—a thing warriors understood—whilst this was . . . I could not tell.

"You accepted Andur's geas," she said, then paused to delicately extract a bone from her mouth, "and Ryadne's wishes. You did your best for Ellyn."

I choked on what I ate. "Poor best with her taken by Eryk."

"We'll catch them up," she said. "My word on that. But . . ."

"But?" I asked.

She sipped tea and looked me in the eyes. "There are things you must accept, or reject. Perhaps things you'll not much like."

"Such as?"

She set her cup aside. "Likely the first is that I am a Vachyn sorcerer."

I reached for my blade and Shara smiled sadly.

"Ah, is that not ever the reaction? Because of what my people have done—would do."

I held the sword above my head. I had not known I rose, only that I stood above her, poised to deliver a cut that should strike her head from her shoulders and cleave her to the waist.

She only went on smiling. "Shall you kill me, then?"

I hesitated, afraid of some trick. "You gave me back my life, so I'm in your debt. But you're a Vachyn?"

"I am. Or was." She nodded, seemingly unperturbed by my threatening stance. I wondered if I *could* kill her. "Do you sheathe that sword and hear me out?"

I could not possibly owe her less, so I nodded and settled to the ground. But I held my blade naked across my legs.

"I was born Vachyn," she said sadly, as if telling an old, regretted story, "and I owned—*own*—much power. What do you know of the Vachyn, Gailard?"

"Not much." I did not shake my head, for that would have taken my eyes from her face and I'd be ready to strike her if I must. "They—you?—inhabit the mountains north and west of Danant. They've a temple there—more, it's said, that none know of—from which they send their sorcerers out on hire. Talan hired one—Nestor—and he delivered Andur to that bastard. Delivered Talan his victory, and likely Chorym."

"Chorym's fallen," she said, "and Ryadne's dead. And Nestor's set hunters on Ellyn's trail, which is also yours."

My hands tensed on my sword's hilt. She said, "I was born into the Vachyn, but I left them when I saw what they'd do."

"Which is?"

"Own the world," she answered. "The Vachyn possess powerful magicks, and they'd use that talent to dominate. They're a small clan, Gailard, but possessed of such magical abilities as make what the Dur know seem nothing. And they're ambitious. The gods know, there cannot be more than a few hundred Vachyn—and the strongest remain in the temple, lending their wills and their powers to those who go out into the world, like Nestor. And . . ."

"You?" I asked.

She shook her head. "No! I left them, and like you was banished. I saw what they'd do and did not like it, so I quit them and went away. I wanted only to be alone; away from the temptations of magic—away from what my folk want."

"Which is?"

"The Vachyn," she said, "would seat councillors with every kingdom and satrapy and empire this world knows. They hire out their talent because the rulers of this world understand only power, and their power is augmented by Vachyn magic. Vachyn sorcerers make men like Talan great; they conquer where honest strength of arms cannot. Would Talan have defeated Andur had it been a test of honest strength?"

I shook my head. "I think we'd have beaten Danant, had Nestor not sent his magicks against us."

"And there are Vachyn sorcerers advising the rulers of Serian and Naban; those lands to the north and south and east and west—to lands you've not heard of. They work their magicks and whisper soft promises of conquest into the ears of willing kings and queens. And deliver those promises with magic, so that the rulers believe they cannot survive without their Vachyn sorcerers. Who all the while are bleeding away their will, so that the kings and queens and emperors and satraps cannot make a decision of their own, but turn to their Vachyn advisers to ask what they should do.

"And does it go on like this, all the world will be ruled by the Vachyn."

"Why did you quit them?" I asked. "When you might have ruled with them?"

"Why did you refuse to marry Rytha," she gave me back, "when you might have been chieftain of the Devyn and the Agador like your brother?"

I shrugged and shook my head, confusion layered on confusion. I thought of Ellyn taken hostage to Mattich's Dur, to be traded off hostage, or in bits and pieces as my brother had threatened.

"I could do naught else."

"Nor I," she said. "And so—like you—I am banished. So let's go find them and upset this plan."

"What plan?" I asked. "How shall Eryk's war with the Dur upset your Vachyn's plans?"

"Because he'll deliver Chaldor's last hope to Nestor," she said. "He'll use her to conquer the Dur, and then raise all the Highland clans in support of Talan of Danant—which shall deliver all the Bright Kingdom to Talan's rule. Save Talan shall not know that it's really Nestor who governs, only that he thinks he owns both shores of the Durrakym and can dictate all passing trade." She shrugged and smiled a wan smile. "But he'll not know that when Nestor whispers in his ear of further conquests, other Vachyn are whispering in Naban and Serian and those other kingdoms, all talking of conquest."

"But that," I said, frowning, "should bring all the world to war—bring it all down into chaos."

Shara nodded. "Which is what the Vachyn would have happen. Who emerges from the ruins, Gailard?"

I stared at her, not knowing the answer, still not entirely sure I trusted her. Perhaps she'd returned me to life for reasons of her own—some subtle Vachyn reason.

"The strong," she said when I did not answer. "The Vachyn! They'll survive; they'll not be part of the fighting, but sit safe and watch men die, until the survivors turn to them in search of peace and salvation—and the Vachyn shall rule all the world, bit by bit."

I thought on what Eryk had told me of his grandiose plans and saw the pattern in what Shara told me. But still . . .

"Why did they let you go?" I asked. "Are their plans what you describe, and their power such, why did they not hold you, or slay you?"

"It's hard to slay a Vachyn," she answered, "but there were more subtle reasons, also. Perhaps it was as it was with you and your father. Why did he not have you slain?"

I shrugged. "I suppose he still felt some kinship, and believed I'd be gone from the Highlands. It must be hard to slay your own blood kin."

"The same for me."

"How so?" I asked.

And she said, "Because my father was leader of the Vachyn, and I suppose that when I renounced his aims and said I'd live solitary he supposed I'd be no threat."

"But you are now, do you take the part you promise."

"Yes." She ducked her head. "But I've lived alone far longer than you can imagine, offering no harm to their plans—only watching. So perhaps they think me no threat. Or perhaps they even think me dead."

"And only now you take a part? Why?"

"Because I cannot deny my magic. It's . . ." She gestured around, at the grass we sat on, at the tree with my blood staining its bark, at the stream. "Can the water stop flowing, or the tree stop growing? No. They must do that, to survive. It's in their making . . ."

"Men might dam that stream," I said. "I could find an ax and chop down that tree; I could dig up the grass."

"But it would come back. Sooner or later, the water would find a way past your dam; the tree would grow again; the grass would sprout after a while." She shook tea leaves into the fire and smiled at me. "Could you lay up your sword? Shall I offer you the chance? Listen, I'll take you away to a land where the Vachyn have no power as yet, and set you down there. There'll be no wars, nor any warriors— only farmers who till the land in peace. You could be a farmer, Gailard; you could grow corn and raise mild-mannered sheep and fat pigs. Shall I do that?"

I shook my head, knowing the truth.

"And it's the same for me." She gathered up our emptied plates and scrubbed them clean like any normal woman. Unthinking, I cleaned our cups and the kettle, stamped out the fire—at which she chuckled and said, "You see? We're not so different? I own magic I can use—for good or ill; you've a sword, and the skill to wield it—for good or ill. We make our choices."

I said: "I pledged my blade to Andur. Now it's pledged to Ellyn."

Shara said, "So help her, and let me."

"Save you seem to know me, while I know you not at all."

"We'll learn along the way."

I said, still wary: "Even so, how can I trust you? A Vachyn you say—but opposed to Vachyn magicks. And come to resurrect me and save Ellyn that she gain her rightful kingdom?"

"That was not my promise—only that I'd *endeavor* to do that. I make you no sure promises. I saved you because I felt . . ." She hesitated, her eyes on mine like . . . Suddenly I remembered Andur's when he laid that geas on me; and Ryadne's as she asked me for my promise. And Ellyn's when Eryk's men had come to take me away. "I felt that you and I stand at a crossroads. I think that's how I knew you: that fate—the gods; whatever—come together here, and you are a part of it. And me, and—*surely*—Ellyn. I cannot explain it better, Gailard—only that Ellyn *must* survive, else the Vachyn shall conquer all the world."

"Ryadne said as much," I murmured, "save not so clear: that Ellyn is Chaldor's only hope."

"And you," she said, looking into my eyes.

"Me?"

She nodded. "I think you've a destiny for the choosing, Gailard, do you accept it. How say you?"

She seemed to be clad in armor that shone in the rising sun. It seemed to blaze golden, as if afire, and a shield was strapped about her shoulders and a sword hung at her waist. Then she was robed in white again, and I stared at her, not properly understanding or entirely trusting her. Even then I wondered at her Vachyn ancestry.

I looked into those marvelous eyes and lowered my head. "You can take us to Eryk's camp?"

She nodded.

"And rescue Ellyn?"

"I believe so. I *hope* so. I shall do all I can, but much shall depend on you."

"And then?"

"We go to my stronghold and teach Ellyn what she must be. When the time comes, we'll bring her back to Chaldor and, all well, defeat Talan and Nestor."

"All well? Only that?"

"I can offer no better," she said. "I believe we can rescue Ellyn, but she needs time to come into her own power— to learn its use. And remember that Nestor's set hunters on your trail."

"These hunters?" I asked, for her expression suggested we did not speak of mortal men. "What are they?"

"Abominations of Vachyn magic," she replied. "Men and dogs melded by Nestor's magic. They're strong and tireless, and will not give up their hunt until they or Nestor are slain."

Instinctively, I looked about at the pristine landscape. There was no sign of threat, only grass and bright-blooming heather, birds singing and a blue sky painted with white clouds in which, if I squinted my eyes, I might see fantastical beasts such as those she spoke of.

"Are they very dangerous?"

"Yes." She nodded solemnly. "They are hard to kill, and remorseless in their pursuit."

"Then how can we escape them?"

She shrugged. "Perhaps we cannot; perhaps we'll need to fight them. But my stronghold is very hard to find. I think we shall be safe there, until we go out again."

I noticed that hesitation again and asked her, "This stronghold of yours, is it so impregnable?"

"It's an old place," she said. "A city from before our time, forgotten now—even by the Vachyn—and thus lost in old legends. I found it by accident, as I wandered seeking solitude. I do not think it allows many entry."

"And does it refuse me entry?" I asked. "And Ellyn?"

"I doubt it shall," she answered. "Surely I hope not; but if it does . . . then we shall find some other place."

"Safe from these hunters? Safe from Nestor's magic?"

She shrugged. "I can only do my best, Gailard. Like you."

I nodded. "But you're confident we can take Ellyn from Eryk's clutches?"

"Yes."

"Then tell me one last thing: how do you know so much of Nestor?"

She looked me squarely in the eyes and answered, "Because he's my brother."

I started, my sword again poised.

She laughed sadly and said, "Are you such friends with Eryk? Must siblings always follow the same path?"

"No." I shook my head, reluctantly lowering my blade. "But Nestor's your *brother*?"

"As Eryk's yours—and as you'd slay Eryk, so I'd slay Nestor."

"Then let's do it."

I gave myself up—to seduction, or promise? I was not sure. Only that this was my final hope, and I could see no other choice. I gave my hand to Shara as we both rose, and she smiled.

She gathered up the cooking gear as I stamped out the last sparks of the fire. I wondered how we might catch up with Eryk—seven days gone now—without horses, and watched as Shara stowed plates and kettle in an entirely prosaic leather satchel that she set on her shoulder. I checked my belt, settling my sword firm in the scabbard, and belted my shield to my back. Then Shara faced me. She was suddenly dressed in that golden armor I'd glimpsed before, and a blade hung on her waist. She reached for my hands, and when I gave them to her, she said, "Trust me, eh?"

And the world shifted around me.

CHAPTER FOURTEEN

Ellyn felt afraid. Indeed, she could barely remember a time when she had not. Since leaving Chorym it seemed her life had become filled up with fear. She could see no way to escape. She was surrounded by the thousands of Eryk's two clans as they rode northward, and even then guarded. Her ankles remained lashed to her stirrups as they moved, and when she was allowed to dismount she was hobbled and constantly watched. The humiliation of bathing and performing her natural functions under the leering gaze of Rurrid and the others was a refinement of her torment. Nor did the nights bring surcease, for then she was fed and ushered unceremoniously to her lonely tent, aware that Rurrid lurked outside. She thought perhaps he only stayed his hand for fear of damaging Eryk's prize. But when the Dur were conquered—she could not imagine her grandfather's clan defeating so great a horde as Eryk led—she thought her value must be diminished and Rurrid have his way. Talan, he assured her, would have no qualms about taking a sullied bride—even did she live so long.

She shuddered at the thought. She had feared Gailard might press himself upon her, but he had acted always the gentleman. Perhaps sometimes roughly, careless of her status and dignity, but now she could not envisage her guardian

performing such acts as Rurrid described. It was as if, day
by day, all vestiges of the civilization she had known were
stripped away to expose the awful reality of her fate.

She could hear the great encampment noisy about her
tent. Torchlight made the leather walls glow, and she
smelled the myriad fires that fed the massed ranks. She
could hear dogs barking and horses nickering, men shouting and women calling to one another. And she was alone.

It came to her that she had not felt so alone with
Gailard. Yes, he had at first frightened her with his blunt
ways, his uncourtly practicality—but he had been a companion. He had defended her, and even comforted her. And
now he was dead, no doubt an eyeless corpse ravaged by the
carrion birds and the wolves and wild dogs. And she was ut-
terly alone, without friends or allies or hope.

Rytha—in her own way as foul as Rurrid—had explained in minute detail what plans she and Eryk hatched.
She had come visiting, telling Ellyn how word would be
sent to Mattich when they reached the Dur lands, informing
him that his granddaughter was held captive and would be
slowly dismembered did the Dur chieftain not surrender
and swear fealty to Eryk and Rytha. Then word would be
sent to Talan Kedassian, offering him the bride he wanted to
ensure his claim to Chaldor's throne in return for military
support and the allegiance of the clans once Eryk was established as paramount chieftain.

Ellyn was not, even now, accustomed to the role of
pawn. Yet she must admit she had become no more than
that: a helpless piece on the gaming board of men's ambition. She wished Gailard was with her—his solid presence
would be a comfort—and then a terrible regret that she had
not treated him better. He had, after all, proven himself her
champion. And he was dead. She clenched her fists and
fought to dismiss the ghastly memory of his last moments,
the last time she had seen him, flayed and bleeding on the
tree with the birds gathering.

Terror and despair mingled and were joined by anger.

She sought to channel all three emotions, just as she had done that last night, before Gailard was executed. The result was the same.

Then, when she had sought to find that power her mother had promised, she had found only confusion: strange dreams of flight and rescue and safety, mumbled words inside her head, most of them unintelligible as any dream's whisperings. Nothing had come of it, and she had despaired of finding that talent Ryadne had vowed she owned.

Nor better now: only dancing lights behind her knuckled eyes, and the celebratory noise of the camp in her ears.

"You weep? I'll make you cry with joy."

She turned toward the opened entry flap, and saw Rurrid there, leering. He set a platter of food and a mug of ale on the floor.

"Touch me and I'll kill you."

It sounded foolish in her own ears. What could she do, were he to press her?

It surely amused him. "Kill me? I think not. I think you'll only submit." He began to laugh.

Ellyn felt the anger grow—refuge of a kind—and stiffened her courage that she might face him and scorn him. "You'd not dare speak so were Gailard . . ."

He interrupted her. "Alive? But he's not, and you're alone."

He was still laughing as he laced the entry closed. Ellyn began to weep then, and by the time she turned to her dinner it was cold.

They struck camp a little after dawn. The air was chill and the trampled ground frosty. A cold, uncaring sun rose into a steel-blue sky where birds hung, anxious for the pickings the horde would leave behind. Ellyn was allowed to perform her ablutions—watched still—and then lashed once more to her horse, which Rurrid still led. Now, however, Athol rode with them, and his obscene suggestions were added to her torment. She steeled herself against the two, endeavoring to blot out their words as she forced herself to remember and review everything her mother had told her. But she could not help but wonder if Ryadne had been wrong. Did she truly own the magical talent, why could she not summon that power? She had tried hard enough, and found . . . nothing. The morning breeze seemed to freeze the tears on her cheeks, and was the land she traveled magnificent in its rugged beauty, she did not see it, for she could only think that she was alone and Gailard was dead and all hope was lost.

CHAPTER FIFTEEN

The blue of the sky and the white of the billowing clouds shifted into a whirlwind pattern, like colors swirled on a painter's palette, one merging with another until there was no pattern, only movement. I felt a wind pluck at my hair and suddenly knew that I rode the sky. I cried out in unalloyed terror as I realized that I floated above the land, and looked for the comfort of Shara's presence. For a moment I believed she'd betrayed me, and all she'd promised was lies, for I saw only a tawny-eyed eagle, its wings spread wide to catch the air currents, sailing beside me.

Beside me?

I turned my head and saw that I, too, wore wings. I could not understand this at all—until my companion opened her beak and spoke inside my head.

It's the swiftest way, Gailard. Trust me.

I looked down onto a distant landscape. Cloud shadows chased the sun across wide moorland and stands of heather, dark woods and rushing streams. I saw a hare dart from cover and felt an immense urge to plunge after the creature.

No! We've no time to hunt.

I turned my gaze back to my companion, barely wondering how I could see so far, so clearly. The sheer wonder of what I did—what I was become—impinged on my mind.

What have you done to me?

Nothing, save give us a means to catch up with Eryk.

By transforming me? By making me an eagle?

I thought on what she'd told me of Nestor's hunters.

Only until we find Ellyn. Then you'll be yourself again, I promise.

I hawked my fear, then regretted my doubt. Indeed, I began to enjoy this mode of travel, and as I melded better with my strange new form, I found it a wondrous thing to ride the wind and beat my wings and sail over terrain horses would find hard going; river crossings that—afoot or on horse-back—must have left me soaked; cliffs that would take a day to climb; woodlands that should need long, slow traversing. I beat my wings, spread my pinions, and laughed as best an eagle can.

So do you trust me?

Yes.

Then let's find Ellyn.

I screeched approval and bent my wings to catch a faster current.

We sailed above mountains and moorlands, over darkly looming brochs and deep, blue tarns, until we saw the massed forces of the Devyn and the Agador camped in a valley that was separated from the Dur lands by only the narrow ridge between.

Eryk's camp spread along the valley, with watchmen at either end, and more on the ridges above. The Dur's main camp was some distance northward, centered on a tarn around which the horses they'd captured grazed, warded by boys and old men. From our bird's-eye viewpoint, I could see bands strung out across the sweeping moors, some bringing in more horses, others with deer and wild fowls for the cookpots. I felt a great pang of nostalgia, for this was what I remembered from my youth: the high, wild freedom of these lonely moors and mountains, where a man could travel for days alone and see only the horses and the wild animals.

Yes, I had fought then—warfare amongst the clans was surely not unusual—but neither fought as Eryk would have it. Declarations would be issued, challenges; conflict would be discussed in advance, at the Moots, when claims and counterclaims might be issued and rebutted, and always messengers would be sent under peaceful banners to announce impending conflict. What Eryk did was different and wrong. He crept like some skulking wildcat upon his prey, and that was not honorable.

I squawked a protest and Shara told me to land.

We found a rocky outcrop hidden from Eryk's camp and winged down. Again, the world swirled about me and I felt a sudden nausea that ended as I realized I stood on solid stone in human form. I also realized that my arms were thrust out in memory of my recent wings, and began to laugh. Then stopped as I saw Shara kneeling, her head down and her body shaking.

I went to her. "What's amiss?"

She raised a slow hand. "A moment, eh?"

I waited, and after a while she rose. Her face was pale, and she wiped at her mouth. "Ach, but that's a hard spell. Is there water nearby?" Her voice was hoarse and breathless.

I glanced around. Rainwater was pooled in a bowl not far off. I brought her to it, aware of her slender frame as she leaned against me. She seemed weak, and that golden armor she'd worn was gone, replaced with the clothes of a Highlander woman—albeit unmarked by any clan colors. I could feel her shuddering. She crouched above the pool and splashed her face, then drank.

"The transportation spells are difficult," she said when she'd recovered. She leaned against the stone, breathing deeply. I saw that she'd splashed her gown, which clung wetly to her breasts. "I must rest before we go on."

"I thought . . ." I said, and shrugged, not sure just what I thought. "Did you not tell me Nestor created hunters—how is that different?"

"It's very different." She frowned, her mouth down-turned in expression of disgust. "That one changes things forever. What Nestor made shall never again be a man, or a dog—only what Nestor made it. What I did was change us both for a little while; but now we are ourselves again. But by the gods, Gailard, it weakens me. I need to rest awhile now."

And with that she stretched out and went to sleep.

It was a warm enough day and I had nothing save my tunic to cover her with, so I left her where she lay and wandered across the outcrop. On three sides rose high stone, reaching up toward the valley's rimrock; on the fourth, a gentler slope went grassily down to a trail that looked to devolve upon the valley's bed. I could see the camp below, but not what lay beyond. I could see Eryk's grandiose pavilion, and wondered if the smaller tent beside held Ellyn captive. I waited awhile, but saw no sign of her; I returned to Shara, waiting for her to wake.

The sun was moved some distance across the sky before she opened her eyes, and my belly felt hollow.

She sighed and lifted to a sitting position, glancing around, then chuckled as my empty stomach rumbled. "I fear I could not carry provisions."

I shrugged. I was accustomed to hunger, but still preferred by belly filled. So I asked her, "Can we not hunt as eagles?"

"No." She shook her head. "What the bird would eat should not be enough to satisfy us. Besides, as I said, such spells are mightily draining and I'd not deplete my power any further."

I suppose my disappointment must have shown on my face, for she sighed and said, "And even could I, every spell I weave is likely a beacon for Nestor and his hunters—and I'd not alert either him or them to my presence until I must. No, what we do next has to be in human form."

I wondered how we were to reach Eryk's camp and rescue Ellyn. I'd assumed that we should again take the form of eagles, or some other bird, and fly to the camp. But when I said this, Shara smiled and answered me. "It's not so easy, Gailard. Think on it—two eagles landing in the midst of that camp? We'd be easy targets for the bowmen. Besides, that spell's so draining I doubt I can work it again for days."

"Nestor seems able," I said, thinking of all the magic flung against us in the Darach Pass, "and you said he . . ."

"I know what I said." She rose to her feet, wavering a moment so that I gave her my arm. "But Nestor's all the ambition of Danant to strengthen him—all Talan's desires and hatreds, and the force of a belligerent army around him. *That* strengthens him, whilst I've only myself and you."

I frowned, not properly comprehending.

"Magic's a subtle thing," she said, "that depends upon an interplay of forces. The belief and the emotions of those surrounding the sorcerer deliver power. Listen, when you've faced men in battle, when were you stronger—when the men with you believed in you and you knew you could count on them, or when you doubted them?"

"When we fought together," I replied.

"And so it is with magic," she said. "Nestor's all the feelings of Talan's army to draw on, and that makes him *very* strong." She hunched her shoulders an instant and gestured toward the distant camp. "Even here, where your brother plays into Nestor's hands—that strengthens him. It's as if his power extends across the land—and that weakens mine. So I must be careful I do not give us away."

"So what do we do?"

And Shara looked me in the eyes and said, "What we can; but the next moves in this game must depend largely upon you. I'll help you all I can, but Ellyn's rescue shall be mostly your affair."

"And do we rescue her? How shall we escape Eryk?"

"My strength will return in a few days," she said, "and then I'll be better able to assist."

"Then why not rest here?" I asked. "Until your strength's returned?"

"Even Vachyn sorcerers need to eat." Shara laughed and gestured at our surroundings. "And there's nothing here, so we must go down into that valley and rescue Ellyn before this war begins."

I said, "It would surely be easier if they were fighting. There'd be confusion then—the warriors gone from the camp."

"Save you forget two things," she gave me back. "Eryk would use Ellyn as a pawn in his game, and the Dur own the scrying magic."

I cursed myself for the one omission; did not understand the other.

"The Dur know Eryk's coming," Shara explained. "They gird for war."

"Of course!" I slapped my forehead in frustrated anger. "And Eryk will set her in the van. Or send Mattich those pieces of her he threatened. Either way, the Dur must be wary of combat. Shall they flee?"

Shara shrugged—which drew her damp robe tauter over her breasts—and said, "Perhaps; but if they do, I think Eryk will pursue them. One way or another, there *shall* be a war of conquest that can only further Nestor's—all the Vachyns'—aims."

"So we must save her," I said, "as soon as possible."

Shara nodded.

The cloud gathered and hung above the valley, rendering the night dark and the trail we took treacherous. We made our way down the grassy slope—which proved to be a thin layering of sparse verdure over shale—and came slithering and stumbling onto the trail below. I began to find a grim amusement in our progress. By the gods, had we not *flown* here, ridden the sky as majestic eagles? But now we went afoot, falling and tripping, less sure of our way than any beast—and surely noisier. And more: we were two against many. I had thought that Shara's magic must ensure our success. But now . . .

I halted where the trail curved, forming the first of a series of long traverses. It would be close on dawn before we could hope to reach the foot, and the camp would wake with the sunrise. Also, by now we were both very hungry; I could hear Shara's belly emit little ladylike grumblings.

She smiled when I remarked on this and said, "All well, we'll take food from the camp."

I stared at her. "It shall be hard enough to take Ellyn. And we'll need horses if you can't fly us away, or turn us into wolves, or . . ." I shrugged, wondering if I went to my second death.

"We'll find a way," she said, and her face grew grim. "We have to."

It was a long descent, but we reached the foot with dawn still some hours off and halted in the cover of a pine thicket. We could see the camp clearly, sprawling along the valley to either side of a shallow stream that fed into the tarn, and that gurgled as if amused by our presumption. I watched awhile and found what hope I could muster.

"You cannot use your magic yet?" I asked. And when Shara confirmed what I already knew with a shake of her head, "Then do you wait here while I steal us horses?"

"No." She shook her head again, but this time she was smiling. "I'll come with you—I've a way with animals."

And without further ado she set out in the direction of the horse herd.

"By the gods, woman! What do you know of stealing horses?" I forgot for a moment that she was a Vachyn sorcerer. "This is man's work. Just wait, and I'll bring them to you."

She only continued on her way, leaving me to fall into step beside. I had no other choice, save to argue—which would likely alert the camp's dogs and bring men after them. So I went with her, believing that I should soon die again and Ellyn be forever lost.

But she was right; she did have a way with animals.

We approached the herd and a dog came out to inspect

us. It was a typical Highland dog: muscular and long-legged, with shaggy hair and large jaws, its coat brindle. I drew my sword, readying to hack the beast down when it attacked, but Shara stayed my hand and stepped forward. She murmured words too soft for me to discern and knelt, opening her arms. The dog growled a moment, then came into them and she stroked its muzzle, its chest, and the great beast lay down and panted like a puppy eager for attention. She fondled the underside of its jaw and beckoned me on; the dog followed, nuzzling at her legs, and we approached the herd.

The watchmen were asleep—which spoke to me of either massive confidence or the laxity of Eryk's rule; surely our father would never have tolerated sleeping herdsmen—and we wandered in amongst the horses. Some snorted, but Shara spoke to them and they grew quiet as the dogs that gathered about us. I found my bay and Ellyn's chestnut, and looked to Shara to choose her own mount.

She shrugged and whispered that I should choose for her, so I selected a black mare that looked to own both speed and stamina, and we led them away, back to the stand of pines.

"Can you ride bareback?" I asked.

Shara looked up from the dogs she stroked (they'd followed us—or her—like puppies hungry for their mother's teats) and said, "Yes." She went on fondling the dogs as if we had no cares.

"It shall be a hard journey," I said. "We'll need to ride swift to escape Eryk. It would be easier if . . ."

"I cannot use magic," she said, recognizing my thought. "It was all I could do to find you—bring you your gear—and fashion that spell that brought us here. And listen, Gailard—magic leaves a trail. Every spell that's wrought leaves behind traces, like spoor for those with the talent. What I've already done shall leave . . . tracks . . . for Nestor and his hunters. I'd not leave any here, nor to where we go; so best we go mundane."

I grunted, somewhat irritated by her calm demeanor. It seemed to me that I had placed my life in her hands. Surely I had replaced my instinctive mistrust of magic with belief in her abilities, and forgotten—or forgiven—that she was a Vachyn sorcerer. Now it was as she had promised—that Ellyn's rescue lay in my hands. I stared at her and asked, "So what now?"

"We find Ellyn," she said, still stroking the dogs, "and take her away."

I think that it was then that the enormity of what we planned truly sank in. "Away from this camp, across the lines of warring clans, and—do we survive that—to your broch?"

Shara nodded. "Have you a better plan?"

I shook my head.

"Then best we get to it, eh?"

She rose, shedding panting dogs, and smiled at me. "We'll learn to live together, Gailard. Perhaps you'll even learn to trust me—after we've rescued Ellyn."

"If we live," I grumbled.

"There is that," she allowed. "Shall we go?"

"With them?" I stabbed an irritable finger in the direction of the horses and the dogs. "What shall we do—walk into Eryk's camp with three horses and a dog pack?"

"No." She shook her head. "Let's leave the horses here; the dogs might be useful."

I grunted again, and she smiled and chuckled, and asked me: "Are you afraid of dying again?"

"I'd rescue Ellyn," I said. "And for that, I need to live."

"Then come here."

She dabbled fingers in the beck and scooped up mud from the soft bottom. She smeared it over my face and through my hair. I started, backing away from her applications.

"By all the gods, woman, that's how we dress our corpses!"

"And are you not a corpse?" she asked. "Have you not died?"

I nodded, beginning to understand; Shara daubed me thoroughly, but not so much that folk would not recognize my face. Then she smiled and said, "Shall we go, then?"

I looked at the dogs.

"They'll come with us," she said. "Do you Highlanders not believe that dogs carry your souls to the afterlife?"

That was true, so I shrugged and decided to follow her plan, whatever it was. Surely, I had none of my own that was better.

We left the horses amongst the pines and went down toward the camp with all the dogs around us. The clay was wet and sticky on my face, uncomfortable as it began to dry. I scrubbed at my eyes for fear they'd stick and cloud should I need to use my blade. Dogs nipped playfully at my breeches and my hands, as if this were all a great game, but none of them made a sound. I turned toward Shara and saw that she now wore the white robe again, and had daubed clay over her own face, so that she looked like a beautiful ghost.

She smiled a thin smile and murmured, "Trust me," and walked boldly toward the nearest tents.

We walked in the grey hours of the morning, when night contests with the day and all is misty oblivion: the time when ghosts walk and old folk die. The grass beneath our feet was damp, the moon was gone away behind the clouds; it was too early for the birds to sing. We walked through an ethereal oblivion that wreathed us in mist. Before us stood the tents; I saw the clan banners of the Agador on this side of the stream, those of the Devyn limp in the mist to the other. The glow of banked fires cast faint light on the shapes of sleepy sentries, but even were they drowsy I could not believe we could pass unnoticed, and hesitated, motioning that Shara wait. She halted, still surrounded by the dogs, as I studied the panorama before us. The sentries were spaced at wide intervals, but save we crawled worm-like I could see no way we might pass them unobserved— and surely not with all those dogs milling about—but then

Shara touched my elbow and smiled at me and walked confidently forward so that I was left no choice but to follow.

Did magic save us then? Was Shara's power not so depleted as she had suggested? I did not know—only that we passed between the sentries as if we were ghosts. I anticipated a shout, a flung spear, but none spoke or turned or moved to halt us, and we walked on amongst the tents of the Agador to the stream. We splashed through the water and came to the tents of the Devyn.

It was all still and misty, the silence disturbed only by those sounds any sleeping camp makes and the soft padding of our feet, the small noises of the dogs that accompanied us. I let my memory guide me to that small tent I'd seen beside Eryk's pavilion, where two men squatted before the entrance. They did not seem especially alert—I supposed they felt confident, surrounded by so many—but they still held swords rested across their knees, and there was sufficient distance between us that they'd have time to rise and give the alarm before I might reach them. I wished Shara had brought me my bow, and motioned her to the temporary refuge of a nearby tent. Eryk's great billet was separated from the rest by a circle of open ground; only that small bivouac that I prayed held Ellyn was nearby. I studied the distance and put my mouth close to Shara's ear.

"I can't reach them in time—not without they give warning."

She smiled, cracking the clay around her wide mouth, and whispered back, "Trust me, and stay silent. Come."

And set out directly toward the sentries. The dogs went with her and I speeded my pace to catch up, raising my blade as I prepared to die.

Halfway across the open space the sentries saw us and rose, hefting swords and bucklers. Shara continued toward them, and in the mist, white-robed and daubed with clay, with the shapes of the dogs moving around her, she seemed entirely ghostly. The two guards stared at her transfixed. I saw her intent then. It is believed in the Highlands that when we die, our souls are escorted Beyond by the messenger, Helig, and her pack of soul-hunters, and to those two sleepy warriors it must have seemed that Helig came awandering with my shade in tow. Neither spoke—only stared wide-eyed and gape-mouthed—but I saw one's lips move and read my name there. I grinned, and it likely seemed to them that my shade was risen from the tree and come seeking vengeance. One began to shudder, and Shara raised a hand, pointing. The man fell to his knees, letting go his blade that he might clutch his buckler across his chest. The other goggled, then turned his head as if seeking help from the sleeping camp, then took an unsteady pace backward.

I saw that he was about to flee and darted forward, hacking my blade deep into his neck, so that his burgeoning cry was stifled in the flow of blood. I smashed him down and spun to drive my point into the other's back. It was not an honorable blow, and I felt guilty at the shedding of Devyn blood; but these were Eryk's men, and I had sworn to protect Ellyn. I saw no other choice.

I withdrew my blade and turned toward the tent.

The entry was laced from the outside. I cut the strings and pushed the flap aside, ducking into the dark interior. There was no fire and all was shadowy, a single shape stretched on the floor, covered with a blanket. I set my sword down and plucked the blanket aside. Ellyn stirred, waking with an irritable grunt. Then opened her mouth to scream as she saw me.

"Quiet!" I slapped my right hand across her mouth and she bit me, hard. "It's me—Gailard. Do you understand? It's me!"

She stared at me, much as the guards had stared, and slowly nodded. I removed my hand. It hurt where she'd sunk her teeth, and I sucked at the cut.

"But . . ." Her eyes studied my face, filled with hope and disbelief. "Gailard? You're dead. I saw you die—they made me watch." She drew back as if afraid. "Am I dreaming? Are you a ghost?"

"You're awake, and I'm not." I showed my bitten hand; blood oozed across the palm. "See? Ghosts don't bleed, eh? I'll explain later, but hurry now."

She went on studying me as if she could not believe what she saw. I said, "We've an ally, but we must be gone before the camp wakes—so quick now!"

I yanked the blanket away, grateful that she slept full-clothed, and took up my sword. Ellyn rose, shaking her head as if she'd dispel a dream, and touched my face.

"Why are you painted with mud?"

"In the name of all the gods!" I grunted. "I'll tell you later. But for now, hurry!"

Ellyn nodded and at last went to the entry. I checked the tent for supplies, hoping there might be food—my belly now felt hollow—but there was none, only the blanket and a sorry mattress. I followed Ellyn outside.

Shara stood there, still surrounded by the dogs. Ellyn studied her curiously. "I . . . know . . . you."

"You summoned me," Shara said. "I heard you calling."

"How?" Ellyn asked, looking now from Shara to the milling dogs, to me, her face creased in confusion . . .

"We've no time now," Shara replied. "Later—when we're safe—you'll understand."

"Save we stand here debating," I muttered.

The morning was still grey and misted, but that brume was thinner now, and to the east I could discern a brightening glow that heralded the sun's rising. The camp would wake soon, and save we were long gone we'd be recaptured. I doubted I could survive a second execution.

Shara said, "Follow me," and I said, "Stay close," and we started back through the maze of tents.

As we reached the stream I heard a bird burst forth in song, and then the sound of a man coughing; a horse whickered, and I knew that our time ran short. Before us, an entry flap was thrown back and a woman emerged, carrying a bucket. She stretched and looked about—saw us and screamed.

"Run!" I shouted.

The woman went on screaming and a man dressed only in his undergarments came out, holding a sword. He gaped at us, turned toward his wife, and then bellowed in alarm.

We broke into stride as the camp woke behind us.

We raced for the perimeter and I sped my steps to get ahead; surely there could be no chance of passing the sentries unnoticed now. I hefted my sword and held my buckler across my chest, intent on carving a way through so that at least Ellyn and Shara have some chance of escape.

I saw men gathering—four or five sentries, alerted by the shouting behind us—and then heard Shara call out in a strange, high-pitched tone. I glanced back, fearing she was caught, or pricked by an arrow, but saw that she only cried out as she ran. Then all the dogs that had accompanied us raced by me and fell on the sentries, so that they were overwhelmed and fell down screaming as we went by. I heard more shouts, men and women calling to one another. Some screamed that the Dur attacked, others that Helig walked amongst the tents with her pack of soul-hunters; some that dead Gailard was come seeking vengeance.

Even so, I could not see how we might now hope to escape. The camp was awake and warriors came afoot after us. I heard the song of arrows join the chorus of the wakening birds, and javelins whistled through the air. I turned, thinking to buy the two women a little time.

"Take the horses and run! I'll find you if I can."

"No need." Shara called out again and the horses emerged from the trees, trotting toward us.

Shara sprang nimbly astride the black; I hoisted Ellyn onto her chestnut, then slung my shield on my back and leapt onto my bay. We dug in our heels and set off along the valley at a gallop. I felt an arrow thud into my buckler, and looked back to see men flighting shafts at us, more racing bareback in pursuit. I crouched along my horse's neck, holding back behind the two women until I saw a group of warriors come running to block our forward path. Shara turned her mount up the slope, Ellyn following, but I knew that that height could afford us little advantage. It slowed us, and the dozen horsemen chasing us were trailed by more, and closing fast, and those warriors ahead were climbing the slope to cut us off. I cursed, and urged my willing mare onward, charging the climbers.

There were ten or so of them, mostly Agador, but Devyn amongst them, and I recognized Rurrid at the van. It seemed his hurts were mended, for he carried a buckler and a blade and was shouting furiously. I saw Athol at his side, clutching a spear. I had no time to unship my shield—which was by now pricked with several arrows that would other-wise have pierced my back—so I raised my sword and shouted a battle cry and galloped headlong at them.

The slope was grassy, dotted with little pines whose shed needles softened the going. I'd sooner have had firm ground under my horse's hooves for such a charge, but I had no choice in the matter. Indeed, it seemed to me that choices were removed from my hands and I was entirely in the lap of the gods now, so I screamed and attacked.

Rurrid swung his blade as I charged him, and I turned my mare a little aside and cut down at his head. He darted back, lifting his shield. Athol flung his spear, and I leaned sideways, momentarily forgetting that I'd no saddle or stirrups to hold me firm. Almost, I fell; but the spear went harmlessly past me and I swung the bay around and rode him down. I was maddened then—it had been Athol who flayed my back, and even was it on Eryk's command, he'd been overly willing. And were it not for him and Rurrid, Ellyn and I might have gone peacefully into the Highlands.

I became awhile lost in the battle madness, like some berserker.

He fell away from the horse and I spun her around, so that as he rose I brought my sword down onto the dome of his skull. I noticed as the blade fell that he was balding.

Then the circle of shiny pate was lost in a welter of blood as his head split under my blow. If he screamed, I could not hear him for the clamor, but I saw him die, and that gave me much satisfaction.

Then my mare shrilled and bucked, and I was again almost unseated as she kicked out. I turned, seeing Rurrid about to deliver her a second cut, and hauled back on her mane so that she flung her hind hooves at his chest and he was sent tumbling. I spun her around again, so lost in dreams of revenge that I forgot Ellyn and Shara, and the other warriors awhile. I was only intent on slaying him.

I leaned down to cut at him, and he took my blow on his shield, kicking himself backward as he prodded his blade at the mare's belly. I smashed his sword aside and set my angry horse to pirouetting over his body. I heard her hooves clatter against his shield, and then he was scrabbling away like some great insect. I was, then, quite unaware of the thunder of approaching hooves, or the arrows that flew negligent of friend or enemy toward me.

Rurrid backed against a pine and found he could crawl no farther. Only stand up and face me.

His face was pale, and his eyes wide with the knowledge of his impending death. A thread of blood ran from his mouth, and a distant part of me wondered if my mare had broken more ribs or only opened the wounds I'd delivered him. Even so, he faced me as a Highlander, and I allowed him some honor for that. He raised his buckler and his blade, and coughed out a blood-spittled shout as I came at him.

I turned his blow and hacked down against his shield. Then my mare screamed and rose up as if she'd return him hooves against his cut, and he ducked, exposing his naked neck. I slashed him there, and he fell down, and I sprang from the horse to drive my blade across his face. As he fell sideways, I cut again across his belly, so that he squealed and dropped his sword, clamping a hand across the wound. I saw blood squirt from between his fingers. I hacked him again and he was still; I snatched his hair and took off his head in single cut. I threw the head away. It went bouncing down the slope, and I was abruptly aware that I stood afoot, with armed warriors around me and more riding up.

Sanity returned, and with it the realization that I had lost this war for the satisfaction of personal revenge. I was surrounded, and more warriors approached. All they'd need do was flight their arrows, fling their javelins, and I'd be dead.

I raised my sword and prepared to charge; to die like a true Highlander.

The mist was lifting now, the sky no longer grey, but blue, with the sun lofting over the valley wall, and birds singing. A soft wind blew through the trees. I thought that it was not such a bad day to die.

Then I heard that high-pitched calling again, and dogs ran barking amongst the men readying to kill me, others snapping at the heels of the pursuing horses so that the animals kicked and bucked and shed their riders.

And then Shara and Ellyn came down the slope and rode through the men surrounding me. Shara reached out for the bay mare's mane and brought her to me that I might mount.

"That was foolish," she said.

I shrugged. "Perhaps; but I'm not sorry."

"You might be." She indicated the camp, which was now all awake, with more men coming after us. "Are we not gone soon, we'll be caught. Even now . . ."

I mounted the bay. I saw, off in the distance as the sun rose and filled the valley with light, Eryk mounting a horse all trapped with silver; and riders flinging out to either end of the valley, moving to cut off all our avenues of escape.

"We've lost too much time," Shara said. And I did not need her to add: because of you.

I nodded, shamed. I could not see how we might escape

all those riders. They were, for all the attentions of the dogs, too close—too many came toward us, from behind and ahead, that we might escape. I felt a terrible guilt for my betrayal of trust.

Then, from either end of the valley came war shouts, and from the farther rim a volley of arrows.

CHAPTER SIXTEEN

Ellyn could not, even now, quite believe it. She could not comprehend how Gailard still lived, nor properly understand who—or what—Shara was. It seemed, from the few words they'd exchanged as they fled, that Shara had restored Gailard to life, and would take them all to some safe stronghold—which seemed to Ellyn no more likely than Gailard's resurrection. Yet if the one was possible, then perhaps so was the other—and surely the one was true, for she had felt Gailard's hands on her and they were not the hands of a ghost, but fleshed and warm, smelling of leather and sweat and metal. And now he fought their pursuers with a terrible fury. She experienced an almost guilty joy as she saw him take Rurrid's head, and had she been able, she'd have ridden down to spit on the sundered skull. But Shara held her back, and only rode in when it seemed that Gailard must be overwhelmed.

"He's headstrong," the strange woman had said.

Ellyn had spoken without thinking then, concerned only for Gailard's safety. "He's brave!"

Shara had laughed and nodded and loosed that odd, high-pitched call again, that set the camp's dogs to attacking. "So shall we go rescue him from his bravery?"

Ellyn was not sure she liked the woman, for all Shara

obviously played a major part in her rescue. She seemed
overly familiar with Gailard; but his safety was the paramount concern now, so Ellyn went with Shara, down the
slope, knocking men aside with her horse until they reached
her guardian and he was mounted again.

Even so, it seemed impossible they could evade Eryk's
warriors—until the Dur attacked.

"It's Grandfather!" Ellyn shouted as they thundered
along the valley wall. "By the gods, he's brought the Dur!"

Then she wondered how she knew that; and then forgot
the thought as they rode through a stand of pine and she
must duck her head to avoid being swept from the chestnut
mare. She was not accustomed to riding bareback, and it
took all her concentration to stray astride, the desperate ride
made worse by singing arrows and her own tumbled
thoughts.

How could Gailard be alive?

Who was Shara?

Gailard shouted a warning and she saw riders moving
to intercept, a small group of Dur horsemen turning to pursue. Perhaps even now, she thought, they'd not escape.

Nestor stared, frowning, into the flames. The coals in the
brazier were dying and the odor of the entrails grew thick,
filling the chamber with a miasmic stench that began to offend even his nostrils. He rose to open windows that loosed
a fetid stream of smoke and smell into the gardens of the
palace.

Something was wrong; something had happened that
he could not properly understand.

He could not exactly define it, save to know that some
great magic had been worked to disturb his plans. It was as
if he had dreamed, but could not recall the images—only
know that they upset him, leaving a lingering doubt. He
filled a glass with wine and drank it down, pacing the chamber as he pondered the aetheric disturbance. It came from
the east, where his hunters went, but his hunters had not yet

found Ellyn. It was too soon, even for one of those swift-runners, and he'd have known had the chase been already successful. So it was something else—but what, he could not discern.

He cursed, wondering if the Dur magic was stronger than he'd thought, then decided it could not be—the Dur owned only the scrying talent, no more. But what it was, he could not say; nor would, he decided, when Talan asked him how things went. Better that foppish fool continue in his absolute trust and deliver both Danant and Chaldor into the hands of the Vachyn. Soon enough his creatures must find Ellyn and slay her, and then Talan would truly own Chaldor, and rely more on his Vachyn sorcerer—and all that great stretch of the joined lands, and the river between, be under the Vachyn's aegis.

Nestor smiled, dismissing his doubts for the while, smoothed his robes, and went to meet his puppet employer.

Egor Dival scowled at him as he entered the council chamber; Nestor beamed back and said, "It goes well."

Talan said, "Good. Egor's news is equally welcome."

Nestor seated himself, smiling pleasantly at the surly general as Talan motioned that Dival expand.

"We own the heart of Chaldor," Dival said. "We've broken the last remnants of Andur's army, and there's no more resistance. Our troops are on the borders, we own the coast—save against the Hel's Town pirates—and we're secure as far as the Geffyn Pass."

"Beyond which are the Highlands," Nestor said. "What of them?"

Dival's scowl deepened. "Does your magic not tell you?"

Nestor retained a bland visage, aware of the old general's resentment. "I bow to your superior knowledge," he said.

"It's as I've told you—the Highlanders fight a war of their own." Dival addressed himself to Talan. "They're not so concerned with Chaldor, nor likely to rise in its defense.

Even do they, they must come through the Geffyn"—he turned to Nestor—"and we hold that pass firm now."

"Excellent!" Talan clapped his hands joyously. "It all goes well. Save . . ." He looked at Nestor.

The Vachyn smiled and said, "My hunters have not yet found her. But they will, my word on it. She may hide, but they'll find her ere long."

Talan beamed; Nestor smiled; Egor Dival scowled.

"That's nine boats so far—you've done well."

Mother Hel rested back against the stacked pillows, watching Kerid with the languorous interest of a cat as he washed. Midmorning light painted her sleeping chamber with shades of gold that matched her hair and the bangles he'd brought her.

"Against which you'll trade me, what . . . ?"

He had largely given up bargaining with her. The Mother set her own rules, and did he bring her nine or ninety captured boats and all their cargoes, still she'd set her own price, and trade him what she thought fit. He toweled his face and looked at her, wondering if it was worth it, deciding that it was—surely she *was* seductive. And where else could he go to continue his war against Danant?

The Mother shrugged, disturbing a sheet of Serian silk so that she lay half-naked, laughing as Kerid's eyes fastened on her body.

"Six warboats, if you like."

Kerid was surprised by the generosity of her offer.

"Six?" He threw the towel aside. "You've that many to trade?"

"Not yet." She stretched, her toes drawing the sheet farther down her body. "But my shipyards could build them in a year."

"*Build* them?" Kerid halted on his way to the wide bed. "Why must you build them? You've more than that lying idle."

Mother Hel smiled and threw the sheet aside. "Yes," she said, "and largely thanks to you."

Kerid had taken a step forward as he saw the sheet thrown away; now he halted again.

"Thanks to me?"

"Kerid," she said softly, like a cat's purr, "you've become the worst—or best—pirate this river knows. You decimate Talan's navy, and your war halts trade. Come here . . ." She patted the bed: Kerid went to where she indicated.

"The Durrakym is dammed," she said. "Talan's too busy conquering Chaldor to bother much about trade; Chaldor's owned by Danant . . ."

"No!" Kerid barked. "Talan shall never own Chaldor, not while I live."

"He sits in Chorym now," the Mother continued as if he'd not interrupted her, "and he's warriors along all of Chaldor's borders. The river trade's dried up . . ."

"Then give me boats and I'll open it again!"

"You don't understand." She stroked his chest. "Listen to me, eh?" She waited until he nodded his agreement. "Serian and Naban hold boats—trade vessels—to the north, but they're afraid to venture farther south. They fear this war; fear your piracy . . ."

"I've not touched one of their craft!" Kerid protested. "Only Danant's."

"You and I know that," the Mother said gently, stroking him as she might one of her kittens. "But they do not. They only fear they'll be raided. They fear to come farther south than Hel's Town. Remember that Talan set Chaldor's banners on his boats when he attacked them—now they wonder, and will not venture southward."

"Then talk to them," he urged. "Explain."

"There's a better way," she said.

"Yes!" He pushed her hand away. "Give me those warboats and I'll wreck all Talan's navy. I'll open the river . . ."

"No." She touched his lips, stilling his protests. "Listen

to me. You become a trader, or an escort. Offer Naban and Serian safe passage downriver under your protection. Guarantee their boats safe passage, escorted by your vessels. In return, a fee."

"I need my boats to fight Talan's navy," he said.

"This would earn you easier coin," she returned, "and swifter return on your investment. And you'd still have boats to send against Danant. Think on it—you escort the southbound vessels, and then sail north. Northbound, you can attack. It's the best of both worlds, no?"

Kerid thought on it awhile, then ducked his head in agreement, and turned to Mother Hel. "But what's in that for you?"

"A tithe on every boat that docks here," she said, "and another from you for every boat you take south."

Kerid laughed. "By the gods, lady, you still drive a hard bargain."

"Should I not?" she asked. Then: "Do you agree?"

"Yes."

"Then I'll lease you two boats for now; more does this enterprise succeed."

Kerid smiled and began to laugh, and they clinched their bargain.

CHAPTER SEVENTEEN

I recognized the clan colors of the Dur even as Ellyn shouted. I could scarce believe our good fortune, and wondered if Shara's magic played some part in this. Her expression, however, was surprised as mine, and I supposed it was only happenstance or, perhaps, the scrying talent that brought Mattich's warriors at so fortuitous a moment. Even so, we were still a long way from safety—the Dur were heavily outnumbered, and did their bowmen rain havoc on the camp, still their riders were a long way off, and faced at both ends of the valley with far greater forces. I saw the riders on our tail turn back to face the Dur charge, but those ahead divided, the larger band moving out to meet the attack as a smaller group continued toward us. I feared that even now we should be taken, and shouted that the women speed their flight.

I rode a little way ahead, seeing that seven mounted men rode to intercept us and that our paths must meet in moments. The Dur were too far distant to aid us, and I doubted I could overcome seven warriors. The battle madness had left me now and I felt only a cold dread that at this last moment all should still be lost. I hefted my sword and wished my feet were set in stirrups, my buttocks in a saddle; I could fight better then. I shouted that Shara and Ellyn go up the slope and endeavor to skirt around the attackers as I delayed them.

"No!" Shara called back. "There are too many, Gailard."

"What else?" I demanded. "I'll try to hold them long enough you can reach the Dur."

Ellyn stared at me with eyes that seemed dismayed and full of hope at the same time. Shara pointed up the valley wall.

"Climb, as you say—but together! That shall slow them, no?"

I nodded, but I could see little gain in such a maneuver, for the climb would slow us, too.

Then Ellyn cried out, "Look!" and I turned to see a group of Dur break off after our pursuers.

Shara said, "Come, it's our only chance," and when I hesitated, "Do you not, then I shall remain with you."

I saw determination in her grey eyes and knew that I did not want to see her die. I was still, despite all she'd told me, unsure of her motives—why she chose to aid me, or cared for Ellyn's fate—but I wanted her to live. I asked, "Can you not use magic?"

"No." She shook her head. "We can only flee—or fight."

I cursed and motioned her away, up the slope. Ellyn followed, and I went after, aware of the arrows that sang toward us. It is, however, difficult to sight an accurate shot from the back of a running horse, and harder still when the target is above and the ground uneven, and none hit. But I could tell from their sound that our pursuers closed on us, and when I chanced a backward glance, I saw that the distance lessened and the group of Devyn and Agador should reach us before the Dur caught up.

To make matters worse, Ellyn was finding this headlong bareback ride difficult. She clung to the chestnut mare with grim determination, but it was an awkward ride and her clumsiness hampered the horse, slowing the beast as it negotiated the root-strewn slope. I saw that we should be caught, and made a desperate decision.

I swung my buckler from my back and strapped the shield to my left forearm as I heeled my horse around. Then I slammed my heels against her flanks and sent her thundering back down the slope, directly at the seven men riding up. They were spaced out now, two to the fore, then three in line, and the last side by side at the rear. My attack took them by surprise—they'd not anticipated so suicidal a move. I swung my blade into the face of the man to my right and took his companion's blow on my shield. The first went tumbling over his horse's rump, the bow he held cut in two; the other swung at me and spun his mount as I went by, headlong at the next group. I smashed a man to the ground and heeled the bay to a dancing turn that allowed me a blow that took another from his saddle. Then I felt my horse lose her footing and slide, shrilling, from under me. I sprang clear and rolled across ground slickened with the blood of the men I'd cut. I came to my feet as an Agador heeled his mount at me. He swung a blade, but it was clearly his intention to ride me down. I thrust my buckler forward and leapt aside. His mount snorted and reared as my shield slammed against its soft muzzle, and I brought my sword around in a sweeping cut that carved a bloody line across its belly. A part of me asked forgiveness of the animal, but what other choice did I have? And surely my cruel blow was effective; the horse screamed and pitched its rider clear, sending him flying into the path of the remaining three, who trampled him underfoot.

But then I stood alone against three angry men intent on slaying me. I saw that two held swords, the third a bow—that he nocked as he halted his mount, shouting that the others hold back and let him finish me. He was a Devyn, and I recognized him. We'd caught horses together, and fished, and once I'd have named him my friend.

"So, Aeyon, you're Eryk's dog now, eh?"

"He's headman, Gailard, by your father's choice."

"And you obey him. No matter that he obeys Rytha?"

"He'll make us great; he leads us to conquest."

Aeyon drew his string, sighting down the shaft at my chest. I raised my buckler, knowing that at such short range the powerful horse bow would drive the shaft clear through the wood and leather and metal into my body. From somewhere up the slope I heard Ellyn scream; from down the incline I heard hoofbeats. The two Agador circled me, cutting off any chance of retreat.

"He'll lead you to disaster." I forced a careless laugh. "The gods know, he couldn't even slay me. He had me dragged and whipped and hung on the tree. The crows picked out my eyes there, Aeyon, but I'm still alive. Do you truly believe you can slay me?"

My words had the desired effect. I saw doubt in Aeyon's eyes, and the bowstring eased a fraction, the arrowhead trembling.

"I cannot understand that," he said. "How can you live?"

I said, "Perhaps I don't; perhaps I'm a ghost. Perhaps you should put down that bow and come with me."

Aeyon said, "If you are a ghost, then this shaft cannot hurt you."

I said, "No, but I might claim your soul."

"Or I."

Aeyon turned as Shara appeared. She was once again dressed in white, and afoot, and Aeyon stared at her aghast, and I heard him say, "Helig?" an instant before the arrows took him in the chest and throat and he fell from his horse. And then men came running to hack down the two Agador, and I saw that the Dur had caught up. I breathed a great gusty sigh of pure relief.

Shara said, "That was a stupid thing to do, Gailard," as we were surrounded by armed men who stared at us as if they were unsure whether to save us or slay us.

"But it was very brave," Mattich said. "It was the action I'd have taken, were I younger."

He nodded approvingly, his dense beard brushing his shirt. He was old now—older than my dead father—and his hair was all gone grey, but there remained a vitality about him that belied his years and was echoed in the muscling of his body. His eyes twinkled as they studied me.

"He *is* brave," Ellyn said, surprising me. "He's saved my life more than once now."

Mattich smiled fondly at his granddaughter. I said, "I couldn't think of anything else." And shrugged as I found Shara's eyes accusing me of foolhardiness.

"You might have died," she said. "Seven against one?"

"He's a Highlander, Lady," Mattich said, as if that explained it all.

"So's his brother," she answered curtly.

Mattich poured fresh cups of brose before he answered. "Eryk's a different kind of man. He's a weakling who dreams of strength, and his dreams are fed by that Agador bitch, Rytha. They'd turn the Highlands upside down to have their way." He glanced at me, ducking an apology. "Colum was a fool to banish Gailard."

I shrugged, embarrassed. For all my father and I had fallen out, I did not enjoy hearing him denigrated—even must I agree with Mattich's judgment of Eryk. I said, "But how did you come to attack his camp just then?"

"The women told us." Mattich laughed and gestured at his wife. "Always listen to the women, Gailard."

I looked to Clayre. She was a small woman, her hair silver as snow bathed in moonlight, her face as dark and lined as old leather, but her eyes were bright and I could see Ryadne's inheritance in her features. She smiled sadly. "The talent," she said. "You know of that, of course. Ryadne owned it; and this one." She looked fondly at her granddaughter. "Though she's yet to understand it, she'll learn, eh?"

This last was directed at Shara, who nodded solemnly.

"We . . . sensed . . . Eryk's intention," Clayre went on, "and knew that he planned some great move against us. Just what, we were not sure—but we readied. And then"—she looked again at Ellyn and Shara—"there was a . . . *movement* . . . that troubled us, and our dreaming took us to the valley."

"Fortunately for you," Mattich concluded. "The gods know, if we'd come later . . ."

"We'd be dead," I said. "I stand indebted."

"No." Mattich shook his hairy head. "you guard my granddaughter, no? You risk your life for her—it's I owe debt, not you. I stand in your debt; and yours, Lady."

Shara inclined her head graciously, and I wondered what Mattich knew of her—for it surely seemed he knew something. He deferred to her as if she were . . . I was not sure. His attitude reminded me of my own, when first I found favor in Andur's eyes, and how I dealt with Ryadne. It was as if he saw her as some great lady and also a friend, awed but not afraid.

"What shall you do now?" she asked—of Clayre rather than Mattich.

Husband and wife exchanged glances, but it was Mattich who answered. "We've not the numbers to defeat Eryk, so we'll go away awhile until things are settled. Perhaps if he can't find us, he'll give up. We'll go into the Barrens and let him hunt us. With winter coming on, I think he'll tire of that and turn back—it's hard to fight when the snow falls deep. Let him hunt the Quan and the Arran awhile, and perhaps he'll give up his dreams."

I saw Clayre frown at that, exchanging a look with Shara, and knew that Mattich was wrong. But I said nothing, feeling that in this company of talented women Mattich and I were out of our depth, and best advised to keep our mouths shut.

Shara said, "To the Barrens, eh? Then might we come a ways with you, for I'd take these two home."

"But you'll return her?" Clayre asked.

"All well," Shara said, "in glory."

Clayre nodded, as if that settled it. Mattich shrugged; Ellyn and I frowned our confusion.

We talked late into the night, moving from the tent to the ground outside so that all might hear, and Mattich's most trusted folk give their opinions. As many women as men sat in council, and I saw the great advantage the scrying talent gave the Dur. This was the smallest of the Highland clans, but they had never been defeated. When aggressors moved against the Dur, either they were ambushed as Eryk's force had been, or the Dur were simply gone—thanks to that ability to foresee events.

"And what do you see now?" Shara asked Clayre. We had already explained our presence in the hills, and told of events in Chaldor, told them why I brought Ellyn north.

"Little enough," the old woman answered. "It's as if some fog invests our dreams."

"That's Nestor's presence," Shara said, "Vachyn magic at work."

The Dur seemed to have no trouble accepting that, nor that Shara was Vachyn. It was as if the scrying talent made the women kin with the sorceress, colleagues even.

"But what shall you do?" I asked. "Eryk's bent on destroying you, and Shara says that Nestor's set hunters on our trail. Surely Talan will look to conquer you—with his own forces if Eryk cannot do it. Winter might hide you for a while, but come the spring . . ."

"Hide," Clayre said, glancing at Ellyn. "Hide in the Barrens until . . ." She looked to Shara, who nodded as confirming some unspoken communication. She turned back to me. "Our talent's not so dimmed we cannot see immediate danger, so we shall go into the Barrens until . . . matters . . . are sorted."

I frowned, not quite understanding. The new moon shone above us, and the fire flickered, layering faces with patterns of light and shade. I felt I sat amongst some coven, albeit of benign witches, but still mysterious to me, their conversation as much a matter of looks and glances as words. I encountered a strangeness that made me uneasy. I had sooner that Mattich ordered his warriors gird for battle and we ride against Eryk; but so direct a response was not to be, and I recognized that I must accept and go with Shara.

"And us?" I asked.

Clayre and Mattich laughed together, as if I questioned some foregone conclusion. "Why, you shall take our grand-daughter to the Lady's broch," Mattich said.

"And see her safe," Clayre added, "until she comes into her own power."

"Then call on us," Mattich said, "and we're hers to command."

I looked to Ellyn, but she appeared oblivious of our talk. She yawned prodigiously, her lids drooping over her eyes, her head nodding toward her chest. I understood her weariness, for I was mightily tired, too. I had eaten well, and drunk my fill of brose and ale, and the fighting had taken its toll of me. I had as soon found a tent and crawled beneath blankets as sat talking. But the future seemed to me all strange and diffused behind mists of magic, so I rubbed at my weary eyes and forced myself to concentrate.

I had commanded half a thousand men, but I had not planned wars, and it seemed to me that I had become a pawn in some jigsaw of magic and bellicose ambition played out by the Vachyn sorcerers and Talan and Eryk, and that now it was Shara and Clayre and Mattich who designed my future. I felt I did not much care, save for Ellyn's sake, but when I glanced at her, she seemed in far worse state than me. She had demonstrated her fondness for the brose, and now sat heavy-lidded and swaying beside me. Her head rested on my shoulder, and I leaned against her.

I drank more ale and let the fire warm me; I felt wary of my unplanned future, and it seemed that that lack of knowl-edge seeped into my bones, so I fell back on the mercenary's habit—let others decide your destiny, then pick up your sword and fight.

At some point I was aware of hands lifting Ellyn's weight from my shoulder, and of her drunkenly grunted protests, and then of Shara urging me to my feet. I set an arm around her and followed her; I'd have followed her anywhere. Indeed, I remember (vaguely) attempting to loosen her clothing, to kiss her, and she turning away, and stronger hands carrying me to a most comfortable bed, into which I sank and (so Shara advised me) spent the night snoring.

My head ached come the dawn, and I quit the tent to find fresh water. It was a high, bright morning, summer hanging on autumn's cusp, the sky a fine, clear blue straddled with windblown billows of white cloud. Birds darted overhead and waking horses nickered, their sounds met by the barking of the camp's dogs. The air was scented with heather and horses and cookfires, and for a nostalgic moment I thought I was young again, and at home amongst the Devyn. Then I remembered, and sank my aching skull in the bucket and wished I'd not drunk so much the night before.

Shara emerged from the tent and I stood waiting as she bathed. I remembered sufficient of the previous night's events that I felt embarrassment, and offered her an apology.

"It's of no matter," she said. "You were weary and drank a little too much."

The morning sun shone on her hair and droplets of water sparkled on her smooth cheeks. She was very beautiful, and I wondered how old she was. She appeared young, yet clearly owned ancient wisdom. I bowed my thanks for her dismissal of my foolishness and asked after Ellyn.

"Still asleep. I suspect she'll regret the brose when she wakes and finds a long ride ahead. But she's young and she'll recover." She laughed, and it was a sound that seemed to me to echo the birdsong and the dancing sunlight. "Shall we walk awhile—there are things we should discuss."

I nodded and we strolled through the waking camp. Shara was dressed in the clothing of a clanswoman, and I could not tell if this was another aspect of her magic or simply borrowed gear; but when she looped her arm in mine, the sensation was entirely physical, and despite my aching head and the awe I felt, I found myself aroused.

"We'll go with the Dur into the Barrens," she advised me, "and then strike off alone. We must bring Ellyn to my broch and teach her what she needs to know."

"And your broch is where?" I asked.

She said, "In the Styge."

"The Styge?" Arousal—the easiness I had felt in her company—dropped away, replaced with a sensation of cold and horrid dread. No human being went into the Styge by choice, and those who did did not return. That place was worse than the Barrens according to legend; and legend was all we Highlanders knew of the Styge. I stared at her, aghast, and mouthed the words again.

"Where better to hide from the Vachyn?" she returned me. "A place where no man goes. The Barrens to either side, that none care to cross. Then such mountains as none have set eyes on."

"Or not returned from," I muttered, wondering and more than a little afraid. "To cross the Barrens is more than most would dare. The Styge . . ."

"Is a wonderful hiding place." She clutched my arm tight, leading me on—almost unwilling now. "Think on it, Gailard. I fled the temple and would find a place where not even the Vachyn—not even my father—could find me. I found the city in the Styge, and I've been safe there since. Now Ellyn and you shall be safe there—none shall think to find us there, and we can teach Ellyn all she needs to know."

I swallowed hard. I was tempted to withdraw my arm, no longer sure of the woman's motives. She had saved my life. The gods knew, she had given me back my life, and without her I could not have rescued Ellyn. But the Styge? I stared at her, nervous.

She chuckled and drew me on, and there was something in her eyes that I could not deny, but only trust and go with her.

"It shall be no easy journey," she said, "but worth the taking. We shall be safe there, and you can teach her swordplay whilst I shall tutor her in other matters."

"Magic?"

Shara nodded. "She's much power, Gailard. Perhaps even more than I own, but she cannot recognize it yet—so she must learn, is she to reclaim her throne."

"Shall she?"

"If I've aught to do with it." Shara looked up at me, her grey eyes earnest. "Are we to defeat Nestor and Talan, then we must both give Ellyn all our knowledge, and see her safe to maturity."

"And then?"

"We come back—when Ellyn's ready—and we go to war."

"We three?"

"We three," she confirmed, "and the Dur. The gods willing, we shall find more allies—perhaps in this your brother shall prove our tool."

"Eryk?" I gasped. "What help can he be?"

"He looks to conquer, no? He'd make himself headman of all the clans, and have them all bow down to him. Like the Vachyn," she added bitterly. "And how shall the clans take that?"

"Hard," I said. "They'll fight him. But what if it's Nestor's magic influencing him? Shall Nestor not come to his aid? Shall Talan not send an army to help him?"

"Perhaps," she answered, "but you Highlanders are hard foes, no? And does Eryk—with, or without aid—stir up the Highlands, then shall it not be like disturbing some wasp nest?"

I ducked my head, understanding. "He'll turn the clans

against himself," I said, "and make them our allies against his plans."

"Exactly!" She clutched my arm tighter, drawing it against her side so that I felt the swell of her breast. "And Ellyn shall return as the Highlands' savior. Are the gods willing, then we'll win ourselves an army and defeat Eryk."

"And then we've only Talan's army to beat," I said. "And the Vachyn."

"Yes," she answered cheerfully.

"But first we must go into the Styge?"

"To my stronghold," she said. "To my broch there—where we shall be safe."

I stared at her, loosening her grip that we might stand facing one another, eye-to-eye. "Can I trust you?" I asked.

She met my gaze unblinking. "Yes."

I studied her face. I saw no guile in her, but still she was Vachyn-born, and would take my charge and me where none ventured willingly nor returned from alive. But she had raised me from the dead and risked her own life to save Ellyn. For all I was afraid, I could not find reasons to mistrust her, so I ducked my head, accepting.

And she set her hands against my cheeks and brushed her lips on mine. And as I drew her closer and would have kissed her harder, she pulled back, escaping my grip, and said, "No. We've things to do." And smiled and turned away, back toward to the camp.

I think it was then that I chose to trust her and fell in love with her.

We returned to the tent and woke Ellyn. She was in a foul mood, complaining of her aching head and uncomfortable bed. I was mightily tempted to drag her out and douse her in cold water, but Shara was all solicitous, urging the fractious child to rise and perform her ablutions, reminding her gently that we must be soon ahorse and on our way.

"I can't!" Elyn exclaimed. "I cannot possibly ride until

I'm recovered. I need tea and a decent breakfast. And more sleep. Leave me be!"

"We might," I said, "but I suspect Eryk's men are looking for you, and before long must find this camp."

Ellyn glowered at me. "You're my guardian—protect me." She turned her reddened eyes on Shara. "And you can surely weave some spell to hide us."

"No." Shara shook her head. "We must travel without magic's aid, else Nestor's hunters shall locate our trail. Even now, we're in danger of that."

Ellyn grunted and flung herself back onto the bed, tugging the covers up to her chin. "I'm surrounded by savages," she cried. "I forget when last I had a decent night's sleep."

I was about to drag her from her bed, but Shara motioned me back. "Do you see what's to eat?" she asked.

I shrugged and quit the tent. I had thought that Ellyn and I had come to some sort of understanding, but she seemed now to have regressed to her former, petulant self, and I was willing to drag her up and spank her—save that Shara's expression had suggested even more forceful argument. I found us tea and bowls of porridge, honey and warm bread, and brought my bounty back to the tent.

Ellyn squatted outside, her face pale with more than the aftereffects of her drinking. She spoke not at all, but took the provender I offered with a lowered head and only a brief nod of surly gratitude. I looked at Shara, wondering what their conversation had been, but she only smiled and thanked me, and set to eating.

Then Mattich, whose tent stood next to ours, announced that it was time to depart, and we struck camp and set out for the Barrens.

"I hate her!" Ellyn's tone was low as her mood, her face red and contorted into such angles of discontent as I'd not seen before. She glanced at me as she spoke, then returned her narrowed gaze to Shara's back as if she'd bore holes into the woman's soul. "Why do you listen to her?"

"She saved my life," I replied, "and yours. And she promises to help us."

"Do you believe her? She *is*, after all, a Vachyn."

"Yes, I trust her. She risks her life for us."

"Us?" Ellyn's voice was a strident whisper. "I think it's you she'd aid."

"Me?" I stared at her. "What do you mean? She'd teach you to use your talent properly and see you set safe in Chorym, on the throne."

"Could my grandmother not teach me?" Ellyn snapped back. "And do I regain the throne, shall *she* not stand beside, whispering in my ear? Isn't that the Vachyn way?"

"Not hers," I said. "I believe her honest."

"That's because . . ." Ellyn returned me, and fell silent.

"Because?"

"Can you not see it? She wants you; she'd make you her . . . her . . . *consort*. Her paramour."

I laughed so loud Shara turned to look at us, and the folk surounding us chuckled and whispered amongst themselves.

"I've a vague memory," I said, "of attempting to kiss her last night, but she spurned me."

"You don't understand women," Ellyn snarled.

"No." I shook my head. "I don't."

Ellyn glared at me. "She'll ensnare you, and you'll become her plaything."

I looked at the woman riding ahead of us and thought that she could ensnare any man, and that I was a most unlikely candidate for her affections. The gods knew I was aging and no match for Shara's wit, nor had I wealth to offer—indeed, little save my faith and my sword. Which, of course, was sworn to Ellyn.

"I doubt that," I said.

Ellyn snorted and fixed her eyes forward and for the remainder of the day refused to speak to me.

Nor much in the days thereafter, as we traversed the edges of the Highlands toward the Barrens.

The land here was all high valleys and roaring rivers that foamed down out of the plateau that held the Barrens, which in turn bordered the vast mountains of the Styge. Stretches of pine wood dotted the landscape, and sometimes little copses of birch, but mostly it was a place of tussocky grass and great spreads of gorse and heather that rustled in the constant wind and threw up grouse and dunnocks from our path. Overhead, buzzards and goshawks soared, and lonely eagles. There were deer to hunt, and rabbits, and we ate well. Moreover it seemed that we'd left Eryk behind, for Mattich's tailguard reported no pursuit, and we came in peace—save for Ellyn—to the Barrens.

There was a daylong climb up a steep wall where grass and gorse and heather gave way to bare rock that jutted and jagged. Black-faced cliffs spewed red water, and all the trees that grew there were solitary and stunted, like withered fingers clutching at life. It was not yet summer's end, but the wind was chill there and somehow soured, and as we climbed, we left the birds behind—as if nothing could survive in that place.

We reached the rimrock and looked out over a sterile landscape. Rivers ran, but fed little growth. What vegetation there was was poor and stunted and grey as the earth. The streams were dull, their passage seeming flaccid until they reached the edge of the dismal plateau. There, they appeared to find some renewed vigor and hurled themselves eagerly toward the brighter country below. I did not relish the journey ahead; but I felt I had no choice: I was committed now, and when Mattich reined in his horse and announced that he'd take his clan off along the edgeway, I thanked the old man and his kindly wife, and accepted the provisions they offered us and swore (again) that I'd protect Ellyn to the extent of my life.

And then we three stood alone in the Barrens.

"We've a ways to go yet," Shara said, "so shall we go on?"

It was some time after dawn. The sun was up, but it seemed not to light the grey stone or the dull streams. No birds sang, and it appeared that all the light fell on the low-lands behind us. Streamers of grey cloud hung above us, but when I looked back I saw that they ended on the rimrock and gave way to blue sky and white billows, as if we left a world behind.

"To where?" Ellyn demanded. "What is there here?"

Shara pointed toward the Styge. "Safety in my broch, where you can learn to use your talent."

I followed her hand and saw the Styge for the first time. The mountains were a warning spread by the gods across the horizon. They were vast, so big they were a shadow over all the west and north. I could not imagine such size, nor how Shara could choose to live there alone.

"How far are they?" Ellyn asked.

And Shara shrugged and answered, "A month, perhaps less. It's hard to say here, for time changes."

"And there are strange creatures, no?" Ellyn said. She turned her eyes to me and I wondered if she sought trust or excuse to escape.

"None that shall harm us," Shara replied.

"Thanks to your magic?" Ellyn wondered. "Or to Gailard's sword?"

"Perhaps both," Shara said. "But save you trust us both, what other choice have you?"

Ellyn grunted irritably and we set out across the horrid wasteland.

CHAPTER EIGHTEEN

Ellyn followed them, letting the chestnut mare find her own way across the stony ground. The horse needed no directing, but only trailed behind the others as if she were afraid of losing her way in this odd landscape—which suited Ellyn, for she'd much to ponder, and no desire to inspect her surroundings.

The gods knew, they were bleak as her mood. The Barrens seemed to be all grey stone, as if some unimaginably large fire pit had been emptied across the world, leaving in its wake only ashen ground baked hard as ancient clay. Here and there stood stands of stunted trees, like half-grown pines, their limbs contorted by the ever-present wind that seemed cold by day and warm at night, as if it designed itself to disturb. There were streams, but they ran grey as the landscape, turgid and empty of fish; nor did any birds sing, or fly overhead, or game start from the crags and ravines that were the sole disruptions of this miserable landscape.

And to make matters worse, Gailard appeared besotted with the Vachyn sorceress. He danced attendance on her, bringing her water before he delivered it to Ellyn, offering her the first choice of food, gazing at her with calf-dumb eyes and stumbling tongue like some peasant suitor. Ellyn hated her, and knew that was unfair—which only made it worse. She must follow and learn from the woman. It was her only choice now that her mother's clan was gone away, and she recognized that Shara owned magic that could benefit Chaldor. Was Ellyn to regain her father's kingdom she must learn to use her power—but still she resented the way Gailard was entranced. The gods knew, he was only a savage Highlander hire-sword, but he'd surely felt something for her before he encountered the Vachyn woman— and that was gone now, as he smiled and preened and bowed. He was, after all *her* guardian—and surely should pay her more attention than Shara.

I shall learn from her, Ellyn thought as she watched them, *and gain my full power. I shall raise the clans and dispatch Talan and his hired Vachyn and take my throne in Chorym. And then I shall send that woman away and Gailard shall be all mine.*

She liked the thought. Gailard would be her general, set in charge of all her legions, and live in the palace, always at her beck. And did it take awhile, then Ellyn would be old enough to call herself a woman, and as queen of Chaldor Gailard would see her for herself, and . . . She blushed at the notions that entered her mind and cursed Shara for the threat she represented.

Then blushed anew as Gailard turned back and called for her to move up and join them, which meant she must ride between them, with Shara affecting conversation and Ellyn pretending to friendship as the guardian scanned the land ahead and rode in his usual silence.

Ellyn was convinced he spoke more with Shara than he ever had with her.

"These pirates are become a problem. What shall you do about them?"

Talan held out his cup that a servant might fill the vessel, scowling at Egor Dival as wine poured into the goblet.

Egor Dival shrugged and said, "We all believed the

Durrakym secure, and concentrated on the landward conquest. That was your wish, no?"

"The land *is* secure now," Talan answered. "Chorym's ours and all of Chaldor to the borders, but our ships are sunk or stolen, and we lose trade with the northern kingdoms. I did not conquer this land to lose trade. What's the point of gaining a new kingdom if my ships can't even cross the river safely?"

Almost, Dival answered: Very little, and you'd have been better advised to enjoy your inheritance and leave Chaldor alone, but you listened to your hired Vachyn and dreamed of grandeur. But all he did was bow his head and ask, "What would you have me do?"

"Rid me of these pirates," Talan demanded.

"They come from Hel's Town," Dival said.

"Then attack Hel's Town!"

Dival stared aghast at his king. "No one attacks Hel's Town." Uninvited, he seated himself and gestured that a cup be brought him. The waiting servant glanced nervously at Talan before complying. "Take that path, and you'll be embroiled in a war we cannot win."

"Against pirates?"

"Against Mother Hel, who's the ear of Naban and Serian, and can send a fleet against us and close the whole river."

Talan scowled, affecting a dismissive tone. "Even the Sea Kings?"

"Perhaps," Dival said. "No one knows just how much power she controls, or what allies she commands."

"She favors these pirates," Talan said. "So does she ally with Chaldor?"

"I think," the general answered, "that Mother Hel allies with profit, and the pirates bring her bounty."

"By raiding *my* craft," Talan declared irritably. "By escorting those of Naban and Serian downriver, exempting them from my tolls."

"You've all the wealth of Chaldor now," Dival said. "Is

that not enough? Let things settle, and we'll get back our trade."

"No!" Talan hammered a fist against the table, spilling his cup. "I want something done now. See to it, eh?"

"It is not best advised to upset Mother Hel," Dival said.

"The gods damn Mother Hel!" Talan glowered as his cup was righted and refilled. "I want this piracy ended!"

Egor Dival nodded reluctantly. "I'll do what I can."

"Which shall be?"

The old general shrugged. "I'll order our river patrols increased and send an embassy to Hel's Town."

"That is a most excellent idea." Nestor spoke for the first time. "An embassy, yes."

Dival frowned; it was unusual for the Vachyn to agree with him, and he wondered what hidden game the sorcerer played.

It was soon enough revealed, for Nestor ducked his oiled head as if digesting the notion and finding it palatable, then smiled and said, "An embassy, yes . . . But perhaps not the *usual* embassy."

"What do you mean?" Dival asked.

"Do you send an official embassy, all pomp and ceremony"—the Vachyn addressed himself to Talan now, who sat all ears—"then I suspect you'll get back soft words, excuses, and nothing be done."

Talan's eyes narrowed. "What do you suggest?"

"A few trusted men," Nestor expanded. "Let them go unannounced to Hel's Town—not as your representatives, but only as lost men seeking refuge. Let them watch and listen, and before long, I'd wager, they'll know just who these pirates are."

"And then?" Talan demanded.

"Why, then they slay the leader."

"What?" Egor Dival set down his cup with a force that sent wine spilling across the table. "You speak of assassination?"

Nestor waved a languid hand. "I speak of clearing the river of troublesome rabble; of destroying this nuisance that plagues our king."

"*My* king," Dival said, "not yours."

"We both serve Lord Talan." The Vachyn fixed Dival with cold eyes. "Do we not?"

"To my death," the old general avowed. "But assassins?"

"Why not?" asked Talan.

"Because that is not how Danant fights her wars," Dival cried, aghast that his monarch should even consider such a plan. "Your father never used assassins."

"Nor a Vachyn sorcerer," Talan returned. "Nor ever conquered Chaldor; but Nestor's given me this kingdom, and I like his plan."

"There's no honor in it!" Dival protested.

"But much profit," Nestor murmured. "Think on it— we can set our navy to hunting these pirates, but with only poor hope of success, and so many ships tied up in the venture. Or we can send a few men—with far better chance of ending this nuisance."

"Times change, Egor," Talan said. "This is a new world we inhabit, and wars are fought differently now. I like what Nestor tells me."

"And there are spells I can lay," the Vachyn added, "that shall render it impossible for them to reveal who sent them, even under torture."

"Mother Hel's no fool," Dival argued. "Does she support these pirates, then she'll know your killers came from Danant."

"To know," Nestor said calmly, "is not the same as owning proof. Does Mother Hel *know*, still she'll not be able to face the world with firm *proof*. And has she no proof, what can she do? No more than she does now—which would seem to be the gift of refuge to enemies of our king. I'd see all those enemies destroyed, General."

"As would I!" Dival barked. "But honorably." He turned to Talan. "I beg you, my liege—do not agree to this. It shall sully your name."

"I'd have my river safe," Talan replied. "I have decided, Egor. Let there be no more disagreement, eh? Only give Nestor what he wants."

"More honest men to befoul with his magicks?" Dival sighed noisily. "You ask much of me, my king."

"Too much?" Talan leant forward, fixing the older man with questioning eyes. "Had you sooner be relieved of your command? Perhaps you'd like to return to Danant, to tend your estates?"

Egor Dival met his king's gaze awhile, then lowered his head. "I serve you," he said. "And Danant."

"Excellent!" Talan clapped his hands. Like, Dival thought, a child presented with some new and novel toy. "Then we're in agreement."

"I command the *Ryadne*." Nassim turned aside to direct a stream of black liquid into the spittoon, wiped his mouth on his sleeve, and raised his mug. "Kerid helms the *Andur* and commands us all. Why do you ask?"

The man facing him—Tyron, he called himself—shouted for fresh drinks and smiled. "Why, because I'd join you. Word's out along the river that a pirate fleet harries Danant's vessels, and I'd be a part of that." He tossed coin to the servingwoman and tapped earnest fingers against his chest. "Chaldor-born, me."

Unimpressed, Nassim grunted and tasted the ale. "Where in Chaldor?"

"A little place I doubt you've heard of," Tyron answered. "A river town called Fortys—mostly fishing, but I took to the river when I was thirteen. Signed aboard a trader and never went home again."

"And what did you do in the war?"

"I was a deckhand on the *Valiant*. When she went down

I swam to shore and took up a sword against Talan's army. Then I made my way north, and here I am."

"And you want to join us." Nassim cut a fresh plug of tobacco and began to chew.

"Yes!" Tyron nodded eagerly. "I'd see those Danant bastards feed the fishes, and Talan defeated. I'd see Ellyn claim her rightful throne."

"Folk say that Ellyn's dead." Nassim picked tobacco from his lips.

Tyron shrugged. "I'd heard she fled into the Highlands with that traitor Gailard."

Nassim shrugged in turn. "Whichever, she's gone, and Talan rules Chaldor."

"But not the river." Tyron leaned forward, his expression earnest. "You pirates dent Talan's pride. You know there's a bounty on your heads?"

"Enough to set a man up for life," Nassim said. And laughed. "Save are we beaten we'll likely rest on the bottom, and our heads shall be hard to find."

"But you fight on!" Tyron said. "And I'd fight with you."

"We're fully crewed." Nassim spat out more liquid tobacco. "Why not seek a berth on one of Mother Hel's ships?"

"Because I'd sail with you!" Tyron declared. "Must I wait until you've a berth, then I'll wait. But you'll speak with Kerid? You'll introduce me?"

"I'll speak with him," Nassim promised.

Tyron said, "My thanks. Another mug?"

Nassim shrugged. "Why not?"

He drank the ale and quit the tavern, leaving Tyron with the assurance that he'd speak with Kerid and make the stranger known to his captain. Then he made his way to Mother Hel's palace.

Kerid kept him waiting awhile, which was not unusual when they were in harbor. Mother Hel was, Nassim understood, somewhat demanding of Kerid's attentions, and surely Kerid was dishevelled when he appeared, and Nassim smelled perfume on him.

"Your efforts on behalf of Chaldor are admirable."

"I do my best." Kerid grinned. "It's a hard thing, diplomacy."

"No doubt. Can we talk privately?"

Kerid heard the urgency in his friend's voice and gestured toward an oak door carved in bas-relief. A servant dressed in the Mother's scarlet livery swung the portal open and they walked through into a garden scented with late-blooming roses. Paths of pearly marble wound amongst the luxuriant bushes, and little arbors offered benches where they might sit and speak unseen and unheard over the play of the dancing fountains.

"I met a man," Nassim began.

"I'd thought you were happy with Cristobel," Kerid interrupted, then fell silent as Nassim's swarthy features contorted into a disapproving frown. "Forgive me . . . Go on."

"He calls himself Tyron," Nassim said. "He made himself known when we docked after that last voyage. I was waiting in the tavern for Cristobel . . ."

"That was three days ago," Kerid said.

"And he's been there since." Nassim glanced around, seeking a place to spit. Finding none, he directed his tobacco onto the ground. "He's taken a room there."

"So?"

"He wants to join us. He says he's Chaldor-born and served on the *Valiant*."

"The *Valiant* was sunk with all hands."

"Yes, but he claims he swam ashore, and now he'd be a pirate and fight Danant."

"Then sign him up, and when we've a new craft we'll take him with us."

Nassim wondered if Mother Hel's bed addled Kerid's mind. "He's too much coin for a shipless riverman. Listen—

if he *was* on the *Valiant*, then he lost his berth early in the war. He says he comes from Fortys, but he's not been home since he shipped out at thirteen—so where does his money come from? He's no berth now, but he can afford a room, and to ply me with ale and questions."

"What are you saying?" Kerid asked.

"There's more." Nassim motioned that he wait. "Yvor told me that he was approached by another refugee from Chaldor who'd sign on, and Martyn spoke of two more. All claim to have fought for Andur and fled when Talan invaded; all have coin aplenty, and seem to spend it readily."

"Loot?" Kerid asked.

"They have too much," Nassim answered, "if what they say is true."

"So what do you say?"

"That perhaps Talan sends spies."

"That's not so surprising, eh? We must be hurting him somewhat by now."

"Even so." Nassim shrugged. "I don't like it."

Kerid nodded. "I'll speak with the Mother, see what she thinks." He paused, plucking a rose that he twirled a moment between his hands, ignoring the thorns that pricked his palms. "Perhaps we should speak with these would-be allies."

"They all want to meet you," Nassim said.

Kerid grinned and dropped the rose, crushed, to the marble pavement. "Are they spies, what can they learn? That we raid Talan's boats? That's common knowledge in Hel's Town."

"I think there might be more to it," Nassim said.

"I'll speak with the Mother," Kerid promised.

Gulls sat sleeping on the bollards as Nassim walked the harborfront, seemingly oblivious of the cats that prowled the wharves. Sleek shadows under the filled moon transformed the river to a kaleidoscope of flickering patterns.

The Durrakym lapped gently against the stones and the
Ryadne tossed on the slight swell like a beautiful woman
peacefully asleep in her bed. Nassim watched her awhile,
loving her sleek lines, thinking of her speed and maneuver-
ability. She was his first command, and he loved her fiercer
than he'd ever loved a woman. Cristobel was a delightful
distraction, but he'd others along the river, and none so en-
trancing as the *Ryadne*; he swept a protesting gull from a
bollard and sat, staring at her. There were no sailors aboard,
nor any harbor patrols, for Hel's Town was neutral territory
and none offended the Mother on pain of death. But Nassim
wondered about Tyron and the others, and feared that if they
were spies for Talan that they might seek to cripple his wondrous vessel. So he sat and cut a plug of tobacco and began
to chew, thinking that he might spend this night on board . . .
just in case.

He rose, his knife still in his hand as footsteps came soft
across the cobbles. He turned to find Tyron approaching. A
cat mewed, looking up from the fishhead it chewed, and the
stranger kicked it aside.

"That's deemed unlucky here," Nassim warned.

"A cat?" Tyron smiled and shrugged. "A miserable
scavenger—like you."

He closed the short distance between them, moonlight
glinting on naked steel. Nassim thrust his own blade forward even as he saw, from the corner of his eye, three other
men moving from the shadows, all holding knives. He
shouted, hearing his cry echo unanswered off the walls, and
spun, launching himself onto the deck of the *Ryadne*.

Tyron followed, and as he landed, Nassim sprang forward,
driving his tobacco-stained blade deep into the man's throat.
Tyron did his best to scream, but the severed artery choked his
cry in blood. Nassim kicked him and stamped on his wrist,
reaching down to snatch the knife from the assassin's hand. It
was a longer blade than his own, narrow and twin-edged, with
a fuller running down half its length. He slashed it across Tyron's eyes as the other three came leaping down to face him.

Nassim backed away, holding both blades defensively before him. He shouted again, but still no answer came, nor hope of aid, and the three spread out, looking to encircle him.

He moved across the steering deck and a man darted around to deny him access to the short ladder that ran down to the rowing platform. Nassim spun, blades thrust out, moving in threatening circles. He knew that he could slay one, but doubted he could defeat all three, and they blocked his avenues of escape. He knew them then for assassins, well trained and deadly.

But he was no innocent; he'd lived too long on the river, and fought too many battles, to be easy prey. He feinted an attack, pretending panic, and smiled grimly as he heard a man laugh, contemplating easy victory. That one he cut across the belly, spinning even as the man cried out to drive his second blade through the descending hand of the one to his left. There was a grunt of pain and the knife fell from the assassin's fingers. Nassim twisted his own blade, feeling the steel grate on bone as it was torn from his grip as the man stumbled away.

Abruptly he felt fire lance his back and knew that he was stabbed. He flung himself forward, hacking his remaining knife at a cursing face. The man jumped back, and Nassim kicked him, his foot landing hard against a knee so that the man whimpered and fell down.

Nassim felt fresh fire scorch his ribs and turned, barely deflecting a thrust that would have pierced his midriff. He stepped backward and felt a hand clutch at his ankle. He drove his free foot into a yielding belly and stamped over the fallen man. He heard pained cries, and felt a savage enjoyment. He faced two now—one dripping blood over the formerly pristine deck, but still holding a long blade in his good hand; the other unharmed and grinning wickedly as he advanced.

Nassim eased a little way back. He felt a sticky warmth running into his breeches, and a curious exhaustion. His

feet were leaden, and he saw that he left bloody footsteps
across the deck. His eyes were hard to focus—the two men
seemed to shimmer in the moonlight; it danced over their
blades, and he knew that he could not defeat them. He must
escape or die.

He waved a blade that had become suddenly heavy and
mouthed a riverman's foul curse. And summoned all his
waning energy and propelled himself backward to the
taffrail and fell over it into the Durrakym.

The water engulfed him. He could not decide whether it
was warm or cold, for his body experienced both sensations,
feverish as his movements. He felt his limbs chill and his
heart race hot. He let go his weapons and thrust his head
above the surface, gasping in a deep breath before he dived
again, forcing himself to swim. For an instant he heard
shouting, then all was silent as he struck out beneath the
surface, making for what he hoped was the shoreward direction. Hoping he'd not emerge to find Talan's killers waiting. Hoping he could survive to warn Kerid that assassins
were sent.

The hunters paused, staring down the long slope at Cu-
na'Lhair. The creatures did not know the name of the
place, only that it was the first habitation of any size they
had seen in days, and that the town bustled with activity.
They hunkered down amidst a stand of windblown pine
and began to chew the meat they had stolen from the last
farmhouse along their path. The occupants, an elderly
couple, had objected to the creatures' depredations, and
the hunters had slain them. They had been hungry, and the
farmers' shouting had irritated them. Now they felt only a
mild frustration: their psychic senses told them the
quarry had come here, but there were so many life-scents
drifting on the breeze that they knew finding them would
be difficult, and had they taken to the river, perhaps
impossible. They must, they decided, enter the town and

find some human that had spoken with the quarry, but not yet. The sun was still high and mortal men would likely take objection to the hunters' distorted forms. When night fell, they thought, they would enter and see where the trail led.

CHAPTER NINETEEN

I did not like this place. It was aptly named, and its desolation seemed to creep into our souls. Some, I knew, would call the Highlands bleak—and surely they were wild and lonely—but there was a great beauty in the hills and moors, and here there was none that I could see. The land was all stony and empty, as if drained of life. What little vegetation grew was sparse, the grass more grey than green, and the trees no better—all twisted by the constant wind, gnarled as the fingers of old arthritic men whose blood ran dark and sulfurous as the miserable rivers. We rode swathed in the warm gear Mattich had gifted us, thankful for the food he'd supplied—for surely there was none to be found here. Mostly, we rode in silence. Ellyn continued in her dark, morose mood, and Shara seemed contemplative, lost in her own thoughts. For my part, I rode wary, scanning the dismal landscape for sign of danger, recalling the tales of my youth, of the weirdling creatures that were supposed to inhabit this strange and empty place.

That night we sat about a sorry fire that sputtered and sparked in the gusting wind. The tents I'd set up provided some little protection, and I'd tethered the horses on a pitiful sward where they might take what sustenance they could from the grass and the few thorny bushes. Our own provisions were not that much better, but at least we had hot tea, and a flask or two of brose.

"I'd heard the Barrens are filled with strange creatures," I said.

Shara nodded. "So the stories go, but I think there are not so many." She chuckled, gesturing at the vista. "What is there for anything to eat here?"

"Us," Ellyn grunted.

I glanced at her, for her tone was surly, as if she sought argument.

"You've my magic to protect you," Shara said.

"Which you say you cannot use for fear of these hunters," Ellyn returned. "Or was that a lie?"

"No lie," Shara answered equably. "The less magic I employ, the better for now. But is it truly necessary . . ."

Ellyn snorted.

"And my sword is at your command," I said.

"*My* command?" Ellyn pouted, refusing to meet my eyes, hers flickering a moment in Shara's direction.

"I am your appointed guardian," I said, "and while I live, no harm shall come to you."

She snorted again, and tossed her plate aside, drained her cup, and rose. "I shall retire," she announced, with the hurt dignity of a troubled child.

Shara and I sat silent as she entered her tent. Then Shara said, "She's much to learn."

I said, "Not the least, manners."

Shara shrugged. "She's young and afraid. She's lost so much, and faces so much. Would you not be afraid?"

I looked around. Dark clouds sailed the sky, driven streamered on the wind, obscuring the moon. It was so dark I could not see far beyond the fire's glow, and I felt the horrible emptiness of the Barrens deep in my soul. I nodded and answered, "I am. I do not like this place."

"None do," Shara said. "Save those lonely souls that live here."

"Like you?" I asked.

She shook her head. "I've no more liking for this place than you." She shuddered, staring about awhile so that I must resist an impulse to put an arm around her shoulders. "I *feel* what made it . . . Old wars, bloodily fought in ways we cannot imagine. I dream here, Gailard, and they are unpleasant dreams."

"Wars?" I asked, confused. "Who's ever fought a war in the Barrens?"

"The Old Folk," she replied, her voice soft, as if she feared to arouse ancient spirits. "Those who inhabited this world before we came. They owned powers we can only dream of—which I do."

She laughed then, but it was a quiet, nervous laugh, as if she feared to wake sleeping monsters.

"Here." I poured brose into her cup. "This shall help you sleep."

She smiled her thanks and sipped the liquor. I said, "And what lonely souls *do* live here?"

"Ellyn's not entirely wrong to fear them," she answered me, sending a chill up my spine. "I doubt they'll attack us, but even so . . . There *are* creatures in this place that resent humankind. Things made by an older world that know only hatred."

I laughed, seeking to cheer her. "So there's not so much difference between that world and this, eh?"

"Likely not." She sighed. "Perhaps we never learn from our mistakes, but only perpetuate them by different means."

"I don't understand," I said. "Surely each mistake—do we recognize it—is a lesson learned."

She smiled at me then, fondly. "Perhaps for you; perhaps for individuals. But for humankind, for all of us? Listen—the Barrens were created by war, by weapons beyond our imagining. This land is sere because it was scorched, as if the gods poured fire and poison on the earth. Men rode the skies then, and they did not fight with swords or spears or bows, but with the power of the sun itself, and things that might slay a man a mile away."

"No arrow travels that far," I said, softly, awed.

"They did not use arrows," she said. "Their strength was beyond our ken. But is the strength of the Vachyn sorcerers not beyond the ken of ordinary men? Did Chaldor know magefire before Nestor came? Do you not see? Talan would conquer—he'd own Chaldor, and with Nestor whispering in his ear, he'll look to Serian and Naban—and all the old mistakes come again. Does Talan employ more Vachyn, then they might transform your Highlands with their magicks, and make them like the Barrens. Their power is different, but the end might be the same—surely their intent is not so different than the Old Folk's."

"Save we halt them," I said, thinking that I had heard more than my mind could properly encompass.

"Yes: save we halt them." Shara yawned and rose. "And now I'd find my bed."

I watched her go, my mind all atumble. I considered myself only a simple soldier, but it seemed I had become enmeshed in a web of massive intrigue that should take more than plain steel to cut. I drank another cup of brose and went to check the horses.

They were restive—they liked this place no better than I—and I spent awhile gentling them. Then I found my tent and settled into troubled sleep.

The next morning, as we traversed a pan of ground that seemed a combination of sour earth and salt, I saw strange tracks. There were three lines, one smaller than the two that crisscrossed the silvery-grey soil. The first was clawed and went on two legs, the others far larger and running on four. They crossed our path from east to west and there was no dung, so I trusted that they'd passed us and gone on, and offered no threat; but still I strung my bow and rode with an arrow held ready to nock.

Then, around noonday—as the sun shone reluctantly from a louring sky that was a combination of grey and red like blood on old, faded cloth—we came to a wood.

It was no such wood as I'd ever seen. The trees were black and hung with spiked boughs, and none higher than the head of a mounted man. The thorns that stabbed from the thickets were crimson—the brightest color I'd seen in days—and long as my thumb. They rattled in the wind as if they clutched toward us, and I felt a great reluctance to enter. I would have found a way around, but the wood stretched out before us and Shara pointed to a path and bade Ellyn and me follow. So I drew my sword and set my buckler on my left arm and did as I was told.

I swear that the branches parted as Shara rode through, then thrust toward Ellyn and drew back, and clutched at me. I supposed that the women's magic protected them; I had only my sword and shield. And I knew that I felt thorns rattle against my buckler, and that my pretty mare snorted in protest of the pricks that stung her. I felt stings on my flesh, and slashed at limbs that shifted and moved and sought to entwine me before Shara called back, "Offer no offense. Don't hurt them."

Them? Sad, sorry thornbushes were *them*? I rode into mysteries I could not understand.

I felt a spike prick my thigh, another my sword arm, and I felt a great desire to strike out, to cut my way through this mad wood, but I obeyed, and the questing boughs drew back as if leashed by Shara's magic. They granted me passage and we followed a winding trail that delivered us onto a wide plain that ran out all grey as the withered flesh of long-dead corpses to the great cliffs of the Styge.

I thought that it should take us no more than a day to reach those peaks, and could not understand how we had reached our goal so swiftly—save that it was as Shara had said—that time was different in the Barrens. Surely we had crossed them sooner than the time I understood allowed.

And surely our path was barred.

I thought they were likely the creators of the tracks we'd seen. Their paws certainly fit, for they were huge and clawed, descending from massive legs of scabrous flesh that rose to groins kilted with orange hair, so that it was impossible to determine their sex. Their anger, however, was clear, for they waved taloned hands toward us and roared a challenge that overcame the howling of the wind. Their upper bodies were bare as their legs, nor less muscled, nor any less scabrous. Indeed, as I studied them, I saw that their worst deformities lay above. Sores decorated their torsos and faces, which resembled those of the simians I'd seen carried by Nabanese sailors. The jaws thrust forward beneath wide nostrils, the eyes small and red and glaring from under overhanging brows tufted with the same red hair as hid their midriffs. Their arms were long as their legs, and they seemed undecided whether to stand or settle on all fours— save as they beat their clawed fists against their oozing chests to challenge our intrusion.

The wind carried their scent to us, and it was foul. My horse snorted and began to kick. Ellyn cried out, struggling to retain her seat. Shara waved us back.

"I'll deal with these."

I forced my anxious mount past Ellyn's curvetting black.

"How? With magic?"

Shara nodded, staring at the creatures that blocked our way.

"And leave that trail you spoke of? I thought you had better not leave such spoor."

"What other choice have we?"

"Are they mortal or magic?" I asked.

She answered, "Both."

"Are they mortal, they can be slain."

I sheathed my sword and slid my bow from the quiver. Strung the curved wood and nocked a shaft. I took another and set it between my teeth. Then I slammed my heels into the bay's ribs and—willing as she was, for all her fear—we went charging toward the monsters.

I loosed my first arrow as we closed on them. I saw the shaft drive deep into a bare, greyish-red chest, the creature stumbling back, pawing at the fletchings. I snatched the second from my mouth and fired within a few hoofbeats of the other. I was proud of that shot, for it took the thing in the right eye, and it fell down screaming, the bloody arrowhead protruding from the back of its skull.

I was on them then, and I drew my sword and cut down at the first I saw—which was the one pierced through the eye—even as I wondered how either could still fight, still live. I clove its skull and heeled my horse around to swipe a blow across the other's back as it rose, snarling, its paws reaching for my horse's belly. I cut it from massive shoulders to hairy ribs, then took a blow on my shield that near unseated me. Instinctively, I reined back, so that the mare reared and plunged and drove her forehooves down against the creature, which roared and pawed at her even as it was knocked away. I turned her and swung my blade against the monster's face, then cut deep into its neck. It fell onto all fours and I reached from the saddle to stab it in the spine. It slumped, whimpering, onto the bare ground.

Blood red as mine came from its back, and in a while it ceased its twitching and lay still. I waited until I was sure both were truly dead, then beckoned the women on. Shara approached with troubled eyes; Ellyn's contained that mixture I'd seen before, of admiration and resentment. Both skirted around the corpses, which gave off a most foul odor.

"Best we leave these fast behind," Shara said, "for their deaths are likely to call other things."

"I thought there were not so many." I wiped my blade as I spoke; I feared the blood of such beings should corrupt the honest steel.

"There aren't," she replied. "But even so . . ."

I glanced at the bodies—and saw that little tendrils extended from the ground where their blood pooled. Small shoots, like plants rising to the spring sun, but black and withered as mummified flesh until they touched the blood, whereupon they became crimson, thickening and moving with much greater unnatural vigor. I gaped, caught in horrified fascination, and saw thorny leaves sprout even as I watched, reaching toward the sundered flesh, grasping like taloned hands, fresh tendrils growing to drive deep into the wounds. I spat, for it seemed my mouth was filled with the foulness of this land, and heeled my horse away.

Shara lifted her black to a gallop and we set out toward the ravine. I looked back once, and saw that both bodies were hidden beneath a mass of writhing foliage, from which rose prickly bushes akin to that black wood we'd traversed. I mouthed a near-forgotten prayer to those gods I was no longer sure I believed in—and wondered if we had not been wiser to go with the Dur.

But I was committed now, and so I rode northward, trusting in Shara. Even had I not come to believe in her, I had no other choice now.

We came to the ravine and she turned her mount east a ways until we came to a precipitously descending trail. The stone of this deep gully was black, and the trail was smooth as glass, falling sheer away on the open side. Our horses' hooves slithered on the uncertain surface and after a while, Shara reined in and dismounted, proceeding on foot. Ellyn and I followed suit, she cursing and I nervous, fearing that one animal or another might fall and drag its owner over the brink. But we reached the foot safely and found ourselves facing a wide stretch of gritty soil, like dark sand. I wondered if once a river had run here, for things protruded from the bottom that seemed to me like the bones of huge fishes. Indeed, I thought I saw a vast and many-fanged skull thrusting up, but I had no chance to question Shara, for she urged us on and mounted and took her black horse across the shaley bed at a fast canter to the trail that rose on the far side.

There, we dismounted again and climbed a winding traverse no easier than the descent. Ellyn gave up her cursing in favor of a labored panting that was broken only by her requests that we halt and rest. Shara would have none of that, but called back that we must reach the summit before night fell.

Before night fell? It was now only noon—as best I could tell under so grey and featureless a sky—and for all the climb should take us longer than the descent, I could not imagine it lasting out the day.

Save as we climbed, the sky blackened and a bitter wind came yowling down the ravine. What little light there had been faded altogether, and we climbed into night.

"Quick!" Shara called. "We must reach the edge before . . ."

What else she shouted was lost under the screaming of the wind. It buffeted us, and it was horribly chill, but I saw no danger in it. The stone of the ravine protected us from its worst gustings and I thought that we needed only to continue upward to find safety on the rimrock.

Then I looked back and saw what the wind drove.

The ravine filled with foaming black water. It came like a flash flood. In the instant of my looking, the bottom was no longer a grey shale bed, but washed with the torrent. There was no rain to explain this, only a raging tide that swept from the west and filled the bed with a tremendous current that lapped angrily at the walls, rising to send foam splashing at our heels. I saw the bones disturbed and take on flesh, so that vast piscine monsters darted in the current, their skeletal fins rising above the tide, half-fleshed jaws snapping as if they'd leap up and take us like trout rising to snatch flies. I heard Ellyn scream in terror and yelled for her to hurry, my words snatched away by the wind; I saw Shara's face, pale in the dimmed light, mouthing words I could not hear. I felt a great splash of icy water against my back, and fear. My horse screamed and began to buck. I fought her down and slapped her rump, driving her upward so that she collided with Ellyn's mount and both hastened their pace. I heard a sound like a sword striking a shield, and darted a look back in time to see vast jaws closing behind me and sinking back on a fully fleshed body into the raging tide.

Gasping, panting, cursing, we reached the rim of that horrible ravine and halted in wonder.

Or Ellyn and I did; perhaps Shara had known what we might expect.

Below us, the flood raged, filled with massive bodies that tore at one another. Behind us, the Barrens stood limned in darkest night, black cloud sent running by the hammering wind obscuring the moon. Before us spread a verdant meadow lit by a descending sun that seemed oblivious of the darkness behind. Yellow and blue and white flowers decorated the grass that stretched toward a wood of honest pine, and past that the foothills of the Styge, magnificently vast in the setting sun.

I could not help asking her: "Did you know?"

Shara smiled nervously and answered, "Not truly. Sometimes it happens like that. Sometimes nothing at all occurs."

"You should have warned us."

"Perhaps," she allowed. "But had I told you, would you have followed?"

Ellyn gave her answer: "*No!* By the gods, we might have been killed there. We'd have done better to go with my grandfather. That should have been safer!"

Shara caught my eye, and I said, "Save Eryk likely pursues the Dur; and the clans shall likely fight ere long. And you must learn to use your talent—which Shara shall teach you to do, so that you can defeat Talan and get back your parents' throne."

She stamped a heel into the flower-covered grass and scowled furiously. "*Shara* shall teach me? *Shara* shall take me to the Styge and teach me what my grandmother cannot? Shara shall lead you . . . *me* . . . like some . . . some bull with a ring through its nose to wherever *she* wants to go? And all you do is pant and follow?"

I crossed the few paces between us and set my hands on her face. It came only to my chest. "Because I'm sworn to guard you," I said, "and see you safe until you can regain your kingdom."

"You love her!"

I had no answer to that. I did not want to say, No, nor could I say, Yes, so I only stared at her, seeing tears course her cheeks. They wet my hands, and after awhile Ellyn pulled away, rubbing furiously at her eyes, her face flushed. I was unsure whether that redness stemmed from embarrassment or anger, and I did the only thing I could think of.

I drew my sword and went on one knee before her, my blade resting on the palms of my upturned hands. The lowering sun struck bright sparks from the steel, glinting like the tears on her cheeks.

"You are my ward and my queen," I repeated. "I pledge my sword to you, and my life."

"And your heart?"

I stared at her. She was a child, too young to ask such questions, but in her eyes there shone a terrible intensity, so that for a moment I was lost for words. Did she think she loved me? That was insanity: I was old enough to be her father. I wondered how to reply, aware that futures likely hung on my response.

At last I said, carefully, "My heart is my own, Ellyn. You own a part of it, for you *are* my ward; and when you take the throne, you shall own my life to command. But . . ."

She cut me short with an irritable gesture. Her eyes were reddened from her crying, now they glowed with anger and spite.

"And do I command you to forsake *her*? Do I command you to slay her?"

Still kneeling, I said, "That should be an unworthy command. Shara is your friend—your ally—and wise rulers do not order the deaths of allies. Neither Andur or Ryadne would ever issue such a command."

She glowered at me, her hands fisted on her hips. "But if I did?"

I turned my blade so that the point drove into the verdant ground and cupped my hands over the pommel, my chin resting on my knuckles. I stared at her—this child-woman, whose emotions and motivations I found so hard to understand—and found my gaze met with frowning, red-rimmed anger. I could not understand her; I could not understand women.

"No," I said, "for such a command would render you no better than Talan. Do you not understand? I offer you my loyalty, but loyalty is something you earn. It is not a gift, not some pretty present, packaged for your amusement, your whim. It can be given only in honesty, and it is not be played with."

"You choose her."

I shook my head, and rose, sheathing my sword. "I make no choice," I said, "for there's none to be made. My blade is yours; my heart is my own."

She said, "I hate you," and spun on irate heels to stalk off to her horse.

I sighed. I looked to Shara for help, but she only studied me gravely and turned away, going to her own horse. I looked at the sky, but that offered me no better answer, and so I climbed astride my bay, wondering if she, too, would find me annoying. But she only snorted and turned her pretty head that I might stroke her neck. I thought I got on better with animals than with women.

"We'd best be on our way," Shara said, and took us northward, toward the Styge.

That night we camped beside a stream of clear water in which trout basked. I caught us three and cooked them over a fire of hickory. We ate well, if silently, for Ellyn's mood had not changed, and no sooner had she picked the last flesh from the bones than she retired to her tent.

I looked to Shara for help, for explanation. The night was clear and a near-full moon shone from a sky all filled with stars. The night breeze was soft and scented with the aroma of our fire and the wood in which we rested, with the sweet grass and the little flowers. The Barrens seemed far behind; our problems seemed imminent.

"She loves you," Shara said. "Or thinks she does." Then laughed at my expression. "Why not? You're not so bad-looking, and you've proven your worth. The gods know, but you were gallant when you rode out against those creatures, and doubtless you've proved your courage before."

"I could be her father," I protested. "She's a child."

"She's a young woman," Shara returned me. "She's neither child or woman yet, but poised betwixt the two, and thus confused."

I shook my head helplessly. Ellyn was confused? I felt no less certain.

"Listen to me," Shara said. "Her parents are slain and she's alone—save for you . . ."

"And you," I interrupted.

"Her rival now," Shara said, smiling. "Can you not see it, Gailard? Andur set his geas on you and Ryadne charged you with Ellyn's care—you're the only fixed point in her world. What else has she? To ride with the Dur as Mattich hides from Eryk? Then on into clan wars? To go into a world she knows nothing about, knowing Nestor's set his hunters on her trail? No! The only sure, fixed thing she knows is you, so she looks to you for all that certainty she's lost. And she becomes a woman, and so she decides she loves you."

I worried a bone from between my teeth and took our plates to the stream. As I scrubbed them clean I said, over my shoulder, "But she's so young, and I'm so old."

"Not so old," Shara said, "and a great hero."

I shook the plates and turned. She stood behind me, looking down with solemn eyes.

"A great hero?" I must admit that I liked that appellation.

"Yes. I think so."

I rose. Her face was a little way below mine, and we stood very close. I could smell her hair and the musky scent she carried on her skin.

"And all the rest she said?"

Shara shrugged. "The angry voice of a young woman."

I looked into her eyes and said, "Perhaps she spoke the truth."

"Did she?"

I put my hands on her shoulders. "I don't know."

The night was warm, but even so I felt a greater warmth emanating from Shara's body. I felt myself stiffen. I pulled her toward me, and she pulled back.

"No!" She set hands against my chest and pushed me away. "This is complicated enough, no?"

I let her go. But still I must ask: "Why can it not be simple?"

"Because it's not," she said. "Because we must consider Ellyn, and all she means."

I groaned. It had been a long time since I'd had a woman, and in that instant I wanted Shara more than any woman I'd known.

"We must reach my broch," she said, "and see Ellyn safe. I must teach her. You understand that, don't you?"

I nodded.

"And is that not more important?" she asked. "That Ellyn comes into her power and defeats Talan and Nestor?"

I ducked my head again; but I wanted her then, so much.

CHAPTER TWENTY

"We found him crawling away from the harbor," the guardsman said, "and recognized him as one of your captains, so we patched him up as best we could and brought him here."

He indicated Nassim, who stood—barely—dripping water and blood onto the tiles of the palace floor. Kerid sprang forward, putting arms around his friend that Nassim not fall down.

"Come, sit." He brought the staggering man to a wide bench and laid him down. "A healer, for the gods' sakes! Will you send for a healer?"

Mother Hel nodded and barked orders that sent startled servants running.

Nassim said, "Forgive me. They took me by surprise." Pain and river water made his voice harsh.

"There's nothing to forgive," Kerid answered. "What happened?"

"It was Tyron," Nassim explained. He shivered as he spoke, and gritted his teeth against the hurt of the knife wounds. "I killed him, but there were three more. I cut them, but I think they live still."

"Not for long," Mother Hel declared, and turned to the guardsman. "Find them! I want them brought to me. Alive."

The guardsman looked confused and Kerid said, "Speak with my other captains. Ask them who's looked for berths these past days—strangers, likely claiming to be refugees from Chaldor."

"And bring them here, to me," Mother Hel said. "Alive."

The guardsman saluted and ran from the hall: the Mother's tone brooked no delay.

The healer came and servants carried Nassim to a bed, where the healer began to perform her rituals. Nassim fell into a deep sleep.

"Shall he live?" Kerid stared at the supine body.

"Likely." The healer washed blood from her hands. "He's strong, and filled with purpose. But, also, he's bad cut and swallowed much water. I'll tend him again when he wakes."

Mother Hel ordered a second bed brought to the room, where the healer would sleep, and beckoned Kerid to accompany her.

"Your war comes home to me," she said when they were alone, "and I do not like it."

"No more than I." Kerid filled a glass, pacing anxiously. "These must be the assassins Nassim spoke of."

"Perhaps." Mother Hel nodded, her young face stormy. "Or was it just some dockside brawl?"

"I told you what Nassim told me." Kerid spun around, spilling wine that fell unnoticed on the floor. "Who else would attempt this?"

"You command a pirate crew," the Mother said, "and pirate crews are wont to fight."

"Not mine." Kerid set his glass down lest he shatter it in his anger. "And that by your orders. My crews do not fight in Hel's Town."

"No, that's true. So what do you think?"

"That it's as Nassim believed—Talan sends assassins against us."

"We'll find out," she said, "when they're brought in. I'll

have answers of them, then . . ." She left the rest hanging,
full of ominous promise.

It took a day to find them all, but they were dragged to the
palace by Mother Hel's fish-mailed guards and delivered to
a section Kerid had not seen before, nor—save for his
anger—wished to see now.

There was a door of dark wood that opened on a winding stairway, leading down through gloom lit by lonely
lanterns to darker quarters that were surely below the level
of the river. Braziers glowed, heating metal instruments,
and other apparatus stood menacingly about the central
chamber.

The three surviving men were strapped to benches,
naked. Kerid could not tell if they sweated from the heat of
the braziers or from fear, but he shivered. He watched as
Mother Hel approached the closest. She held a cat in her
arms, half-grown, and dropped the animal onto the man's
body. He winced as the claws dug into his flesh, bucking
against the restraining leather. The cat mewed and sprang
away, darting from the dungeon. Its claws left bloody tracks
down the man's belly, and Kerid, for all his desire to punish
them, could not help but wince in sympathy.

He watched as Mother Hel leaned close over the man.
She wore a gown of black that hugged her body tight, and
was cut low across her breasts. In other circumstances it
would have been seductive. She said, "Who sent you?"

"I don't know what you mean."

"Who sent you?"

"What are you talking about?"

"Who sent you?"

"No one! I don't understand." The prisoner stared at her
with wide and fearful eyes. "I came to join Kerid in his fight."

She gestured, and a huge man clad in leather stepped
forward, carrying a metal rod that glowed red at its tip.

"Shall I tell him to put this to your eyes? Or to your
manhood? Tell me who sent you. Tell me that and I'll only

have you branded. Your choice: to go free with the world knowing you wronged Mother Hel, or to die in pain. You'll tell me, either way."

The man said, "No one sent me."

Kerid turned away as the rod was applied to the man's flesh. He could not block out the screams.

"Useless," he heard the Mother say. "Try the next."

There was a rack, and a wheel, a tub of water that might boil lobsters, but all the prisoners did was scream and die.

"They've been magicked," the Mother said when the last man was consigned to the river. "There's a geas on them that only a Vachyn might set. Ordinary men would have spoken."

Kerid wondered how she could talk so calmly. The gods knew, he'd slain men without thought, but in battle, not like that. He stared at this woman he slept with—perhaps loved—and wondered what he did. Then set aside the wonder, for he needed her to defeat Talan and . . . he was not sure.

"Vachyn magic," she said when they reached her chambers. "Only the Vachyn can seal men's tongues like that."

"So?" Kerid filled a glass. He felt a need to wash his mouth clean.

"So?" Mother Hel turned toward him, her face older in its ire. "Do you not understand? Hel's Town stands inviolate of politics or Vachyn magicks—that's the understanding. That's always been the understanding! But now . . ." She took a kitten from her shoulder and tossed it onto the bed. "That agreement has been broken. And who would break it but Talan?"

She stared at Kerid.

"How many boats do you need?"

He stared back at her. "For what?"

"To defeat Talan, you idiot! To invade Danant and destroy this presumptuous upstart who assumes to send assassins into *my* realm."

Kerid topped his glass and began to calculate numbers.

The hunter wiped Jach's blood from its mouth and curled into the straw. The human thing had told it more than it knew, and now there was a clear direction, information confirmed by aetheric instinct: the Highlands. Tomorrow it and its fellows would go there; tonight it would sleep, sated. Come first light, they would continue the hunt.

It felt no doubt that they would find their quarry.

"I am bored." Talan set down his cup. "I have conquered this sorry country, and now I'd go home to Danant." He looked to Egor Dival. "How say you?"

"We own it," Dival replied. "We've our soldiers at all the borders, and there's no more resistance."

"There's still Ellyn," Nestor said.

"I've patrols on all the roads." Dival addressed himself to Talan, not looking at the sorcerer. "And her likeness posted on trees, in taverns—everywhere—with a reward that must tempt the loyalest of Andur's folk."

"And there's still the pirates," Nestor said.

"Are your assassins not dealing with them?" asked Dival.

"Yes." The Vachyn smiled at the general. It was a smile that held no humor or friendship, only the promise of scores to be settled later. He turned toward Talan. "But until they are dealt with, I think it unwise you cross the river. They might, even now, wait for that."

"I can take a fleet," Talan said, "and you. Surely that would be protection enough?"

"Of course," Nestor agreed, "but do you return to Danant, shall folk not say you fled?"

"I flee from nothing!" Talan glared at the sorcerer.

"*I* know that." Nestor's voice was oily, his smile unctuous. "But with Ellyn—Chaldor's heir—abroad, folk might think you fear her."

Talan looked to Dival, who said, "Danant prospers, all

despatches report that the land fares well. The harvest is in, and . . ."

"I know all that!" Talan snapped. "And I'd go home. What do you think, Egor?"

Dival hated to agree with the Vachyn, but in this he felt no choice, so he said: "It might be as he says. I think you should remain here, at least until spring. Rebuild Chorym, and let all Chaldor—all the world—know that you are now the Lord of Chaldor and Danant, both."

Talan grunted irritably. "And Ellyn?"

"I'll send embassies to the Highland clans," Dival said, "offering reward do they bring her to us."

"Save my hunters shall find her first," Nestor said, "and slay her. Her and Gailard."

Egor Dival shrugged. "Either way, I deem it wise you remain. You must let Chaldor know that you rule now, and fear nothing."

"I agree," said Nestor.

"By all the gods!" Talan began to laugh. "I'd never thought to see you two in agreement."

Nestor beamed; Dival scowled.

Talan said, "Very well, I shall remain until winter's ending. But is Ellyn not found by then, or dead, I go home."

Dival said, "She'll be found by then, I'm sure."

Nestor said, "She'll be dead by then, my word on it."

"I am Pawl of Danant, sent by my lord Talan, who now commands all of Chaldor." The emissary bowed deep for all he felt scant respect of this Highlander savage. "My lord holds Chorym and all the lands around, and he would make alliance with you."

Eryk smiled, glancing sidelong at Rytha. "So Talan would make us his friends, eh?"

"He would," Pawl said, taking the chair offered by one of the barbarians who served this overweight lordling. "He would offer you much—in return for . . ."

"Ellyn, no?" It was Rytha who spoke, interrupting her husband and the emissary. "He'd have the child now that he's lost the mother."

"Ryadne is indeed dead," Pawl said evenly, "and my lord Talan would confirm the succession."

"He'd own the throne," Rytha declared. "And to lay claim to Chaldor, he must own the daughter."

"It would," Pawl said carefully, "render the . . . transition . . . easier."

There was a threat in his words that the Highlanders ignored, or failed to comprehend. Rytha snorted laughter and turned to her husband. "You see? They come to us as I promised you. Talan would have Ellyn—and to have Ellyn, he needs us."

Pawl sipped the foul liquor they'd given him. It was fierce as fire and sat uneasy in his belly, but he supposed it was their way and he must accept it as part of their disgusting hospitality. They were undoubtedly savages—the gods knew, they lived in squalid tents and stank as if they'd not bathed in weeks, if ever. But he was charged with this embassy, and it were better for Danant that the Highland clans accepted Talan's rule—else likely another war must be fought—so he must smile and play the diplomat, and bring this petty chieftain to Danant's cause.

"My lord would know where Ellyn is," he said, "and—all well—see her returned to Chorym."

He hesitated as Rytha laughed, joined by her husband. He sniffed, wishing that he might take out his handkerchief—which was scented—and press it to his nostrils. The air seemed filled with the odor of fresh-butchered meat, and dogs and horses, and sweat. He glanced sidelong around. He had only three men with him, and these barbarians could cut them down in moments. He wished Egor Dival had not entrusted him with this mission.

"I'm sure he would," Eryk said. "The one or the other, eh? Or know that she's slain."

Pawl could not resist asking, "Is she? Your message said you held her."

And saw a cloud descend on Eryk's face.

"No. She escaped."

"To where?"

The Highlander gestured to the north. "She went away with the Dur. They went into the Barrens."

"And you did not follow them?"

"No sane man ventures into the Barrens."

Pawl sensed something more here than just clan warfare. There was something hidden behind Eryk's pouchy eyes that the chieftain would prefer remain concealed.

"What else? Are we to be allies, I must know."

"Helig came." It was Rytha who spoke. "She came with Gailard's ghost and her hell-pack, and took Ellyn away."

Pawl wracked his memory for what he knew of Highland lore, and sighed. "So a goddess came with a ghost and stole Ellyn away?"

Eryk nodded. "And then the Dur attacked us, and they escaped."

"And what happened to the Dur?"

"They fled into the Barrens."

"And you've no idea where Ellyn is?"

"No."

"Save she fled with Gailard's ghost, aided by this goddess."

"Yes. But we shall find them!" Eryk slapped the sword buckled on his fat side. "We shall slaughter the Dur when they emerge, and if Ellyn is with them, I'll give her to you."

"I am not sure," Pawl said cautiously, "that I can stay that long."

"Then go back to Chorym," Eryk said, "and tell your master that I'll give him Ellyn—or proof of her death—in return for his support."

"Which should be?" Pawl asked.

"Acknowledgment that I am lord of all the Highlands,"

Eryk said. "And soldiers to aid me, do I need them. No trade from here to there, save I am paid a tithe. I'd see your men and mine in Cu-na´ Lhair, and have the half of all that passes there."

"You ask for much," Pawl said.

Eryk said, "You ask for Ellyn."

The emissary nodded. "I believe my lord Talan might agree."

"Save he does," Eryk said, "he'll not see Ellyn."

"There is that," Pawl allowed.

"There is most definitely that," Rytha said. "And without us, you'll not have her."

"I must report this," Pawl said. "Shall you wait on my king's word?"

"May it not be long in coming." Eryk waved a dismissive hand. "Go back and tell your king that we are in agreement—then deliver me soldiers."

"In return for Ellyn," Pawl said.

"Alive or dead," Eryk promised.

CHAPTER TWENTY-ONE

The pretty plain and little copses gave way to pine-clad foothills that rose like blue-green waves lapping against the vast heights of the Styge. Those mountains loomed above us as if they walled the world; their crests were wreathed in cloud and they stretched imponderable, and seemingly impassable, from horizon to horizon. The air was already chill, and I thought that on the flanks of those summits it should be very cold indeed. I wondered where Shara's broch lay— and how we would reach it, for I could see no trails or passes, nor imagine who would build a broch in so lonely and inaccessible a place. But when I asked her, she only laughed and promised me surprise, and took us onward.

So we climbed through the foothills and left the woods behind where they gave up their hold on the rocky ground, and climbed some more, over bare stone cut through with little rushing torrents that reminded me unpleasantly of that strange riverbed, until we came to a sheer rock face. Shara turned north there, following a narrow path that demanded much concentration, for as it rose higher so it was walled vertically on our left and dropped away sheer on our right. Ellyn squealed when she saw it.

"Another precipice? Shall we ever reach this hold of yours?"

"Soon enough," Shara promised.

"Save we fall off!"

I said, "Are you careful, you'll not."

"A mountain goat might fall off this!"

"Then be *very* careful." For all I cared for her, I grew
weary of her carping. Indeed, I thought that were we alone I
might well set her across my knee and at last deliver that old
promise. I could not understand her irritation. It seemed as
if she resented Shara's aid, and found reasons to complain
her life was saved. I could not understand the workings of a
woman's mind.

"It's not so far now," Shara said.

Ellyn snorted and heeled her chestnut so that the horse
snorted in turn and sent loose stone tumbling over the edge.

"Careful!"

Ellyn turned a moment to glower at me, then gave all
her attention back to the horse. I sighed and followed her
upward, feeling that we climbed into the sky, wondering
where we would camp this night, for I could not imagine
finding any suitable place on this fly's walk.

But we did: a bowl that seemed cut by unnatural means
into the side of the cliff. Thin grass grew there, and little
bushes that sported red berries the horses found edible. A
waterfall cascaded down the inner wall, gathered in a
splashing pool, and ran out through a channel into a hole in
the southern wall. It was a pleasant site, and I erected our
tents and gathered wood for a fire. Shara set a kettle to brew-
ing and, together, we prepared a meal. Ellyn rubbed down
her mare (something I'd taught her along our way) and settled on the grass, a little distance apart. Her face was dark
and she refused to look at either of us. Like, I thought, some
child caught out and unwilling to admit her guilt. Shara
passed her a plate that she took with ill grace. I handed her a
cup—tea laced with brose—that she took with no more admission of gratitude.

It was a pleasant site and a surly evening. Ellyn ate in silence and, when she was done, tossed her plate and cup

aside and rose, announcing that she'd retire. She retreated into her tent like some grumbling bear into its winter hibernation. I watched the entry flaps laced tight and looked to Shara, who shrugged and reached for the discarded utensils.

I stayed her hand and picked them up myself. "I'll do that," I said.

"Why?"

I shrugged. "I'm used to it. I'm a soldier, remember? I'm used to doing things myself."

"You're a strange soldier," she said. "Most would welcome a woman tending them—and leave such chores to her."

"Perhaps." I took the plates to the channel and scrubbed them clean. "But not me."

I looked back and found her studying me; I could not interpret her expression. The moon was risen now, and it seemed that the stars were reflected in her hair. Her eyes were large and lustrous, and I felt desire again. I returned to my scrubbing.

"I think they're likely clean enough by now," she said.

I grinned and set the stuff out to dry.

"We'll reach my broch on the morrow," she said, "do we leave early."

I ducked my head and watched her go to her own tent.

I watched the stars a long time that night, sipping the last of Mattich's brose.

We quit the bowl at dawn. The heights of the Styge hid the sun from our view, but I saw great rays of red and gold strike out across the plain below us, spreading light over the Barrens. Curtains of mist hung about the cliffs as we found the trail again, and it was as if we rode for a while through water, like misty swimming fishes.

I was in a state of some bemusement, for I'd had a most curious breakfast.

I had wakened and found the stream to perform my ablutions, then gone back to blow the fire to fresh life. No

sooner had I done so than both Shara and Ellyn emerged
from their respective tents, busying themselves with the
kettle and the pan, so that I need only sit and wait to be fed.
They worked in unison, but without speaking much beyond
the daily pleasantries, and it seemed to me that they raced to
be the first to finish. So it was Shara who delivered me a
plate of porridge laved with honey, and Ellyn who brought
me tea and a hunk of bread. And I could only sit back and
wonder what prompted such attention.

Then we struck the tents and loaded the horses and
mounted as I wondered what went on.

I cannot understand women.

And gave up the contemplation as we rode ever higher,
the sun emerging over the rimrock to dance bright light
down the cliffs, dispelling the mist so that it seemed as if a
great wave of radiance rolled from the heights of the Styge
to spread across the Barrens, lighting the plain then darkening as it reached that strange riverbed, after which there was
only darkness—roiling clouds and flashes of lightning, then
a hint of light beyond. I chose to look upward, for the brightness there seemed to offer hope, and I was confused and
needed that.

We rode out half the day; slowly for the climbing,
which was now steeper than before, our path winding
around crags and bluffs that thrust like disconcerting fingers from the slippery walls of the Styge. Oft as not, we
must dismount and lead the nervous animals over rockfalls
and gaps in the trail where ancient and recent avalanches
had cut avenues down through the path.

I saw eagles soar past us, and flights of choughs, and
thought their yellow eyes surveyed the prospect of carrion.

Then Shara disappeared.

I was looking up, fearful that Ellyn—who seemed in no
better temper, and had not spoken since we'd eaten—might
fall, and then Ellyn was gone, too.

I urged my bay to a faster pace and saw a thin gap in the
cliffs. It was barely wide enough to accept a horse, but I

heard hoofbeats echoing off the walls. I turned in, and found myself surrounded by vertical darkness. The cliffs were black and hid the sky. The sun did not penetrate there, and I rode awhile quite blind.

Then came out onto a small plateau that hung like some fantastical balcony over the unimaginable.

Shara and Ellyn waited for me. Shara was smiling, girlish as if she introduced her lover to some secret place that was only hers. Ellyn stared in rapt amazement, and I joined her.

Beneath the shelf there spread a canyon. It was kilted in grass, from which sprang such an array of flowers as I'd never seen—all blue and yellow and white and red and gold, and all lit by the sun and brushed by a warm breeze so that it was as if waves rippled there and turned the flowers toward us in welcome. A stream came from the farther end and meandered down the canyon into a cavern below us. Stands of hickory and beech and oak grew there, and deer—which surely could not exist at such altitude—were browsing. And toward the farther end was a broch such as I'd never seen before.

The brochs of the Highlands are all defensive: thin towers that hold men and horses and food against siege. Perhaps—is the clan strong enough—surrounded by an outer wall, where there might be some few, poor buildings. Chorym was all walled and massive and impressive, but not like this.

This was such a place as I'd never seen before, or could imagine. I had thought Chorym the mightiest hold in all the world, but this—for all it was not Chorym's size—seemed somehow greater. In large part because of its curious location, but mostly for its odd design.

It was ringed by a moat tricked out from the stream so as to surround the square walls. The moat was wide and, I suspected, deep. Two small towers, square as the main structure, stood on either side of a fading roadway that ended on the edge of the water. Beyond, there was a short span of

grass that, in turn, ended against the high walls, where I
could see an entrance barred by a great wooden door. From
the corner of each wall there protruded great bastions into
which I guessed, from the portals I saw, were set walkways
from which archers might fire down onto anyone who succeeded in crossing the moat. I could see higher towers beyond the walls, but they were like spectators seated beneath
the highest of all, which, at its topmost level, equaled the
surrounding cliffs, with balconies and portals that might be
defensive or merely designed for the pleasure of the broch's
inhabitants.

I could not imagine anyone attacking such a castle.

"This is my home," Shara said, and turned her horse
down a wide trail that seemed to me to be cut from the raw
rock by skills I could not comprehend.

Ellyn and I followed her down, onto the grass below. I
saw rabbits watching us as we passed, foxes sitting beside
them in harmony, and as we rode through the little hursts I
saw deer browsing unconcerned with our passage. I could
not understand it, but I remembered how Shara had called
the dogs in Eryk's camp to our aid. Then forgot that as I
gazed in closer proximity at the broch.

Shara raised a hand and called out, and the great wood
door trundled down on greased chains to deliver its weight
across the moat. Beyond it I saw a metal curtain rise to grant
ingress to the hold's bailey. I could see no guards, nor soldiers or servants, but the courtyard that faced us past the
walls was well kept, its flags swept clean, and flowers growing in stone trenches and from little metal buckets hung
about the walls.

I heard a clanking sound from behind, and spun my
horse around in time to see the metal curtain falling and the
strange wooden door rising, cutting us off from the outside.
I must admit that I was unnerved by this and touched my
sword's hilt, but not so unnerved as Ellyn.

She dragged her chestnut around in a tight circle, shouting, "We're caught! By the gods, she's trapped us! Now the Vachyn shall slay us!"

I found my blade halfway from the scabbard before Shara spoke.

"There's no harm here. The broch works thus. See?"

I stared about. There were no armed men come to greet us, nor archers on the towering ramparts.

"Who lowered that . . . ?"

"Drawbridge," she supplied, "and the gate's called a portcullis. They're both workings of an older magic than mine; but they answer to my call. And, Ellyn, there are no Vachyn sorcerers here."

I returned my blade to its sheath and looked about. I could still see no retainers, but the broch was in excellent repair. There were smithies inside the walls, and stables, granaries—but none to tend them or keep them in such fine condition. No one to tend the plants or sweep the immaculate flagstones of the courtyard.

Save, from the corners of my eyes, I thought I saw shadows flashing in the sunlight, like those half-understood images you see in dreams and then forget. I felt nervous— Shara was, after all, a Vachyn, and perhaps all this journey had been only some devious entrapment. I dismounted.

I realized that I still touched my sword's hilt, afraid.

Shara saw my perturbation and smiled. "What you see are . . . memories. They last from an older time, when this place was built."

"Ghosts!" Ellyn cried. "By all the gods, she delivers us to Vachyn ghosts!"

"Not Vachyn," Shara said. "Nor ghosts as you understand them. They are not malign—they'd only tend this broch and keep it safe. So *you* can be safe here."

Ellyn scowled, tugging on her reins as if she'd turn her horse and gallop away. I went to her and set a hand on her knee.

"Climb down, eh? Shara's our friend. She's proved that,

no?" I clutched the chestnut's reins. Ellyn loosed a foot from her stirrup and kicked me in the chest. I hung on as she made the horse buck, then got a hold on her belt and dragged her from the saddle.

She landed on her back with a great gasp of exhaled indignation and stared up at me as if I were some horrible, crawling thing she'd found unexpected in her bed.

"Do you see danger?" I asked. I pointed at the empty ramparts, the deserted bailey.

She glared at me and struggled to her feet. "I see a hold we cannot leave, save on *her* permission. I see ghosts, and . . ." She began to weep, and flung herself against me. ". . . I'm afraid."

"You've me," I said, my arms around her, "and know that I'm pledged to defend you."

"Against Vachyn magicks?"

"Even against those—to the ending of my life."

"But," she said, and halted as Shara came to us. We both turned to hear what she'd say.

Which was: "This broch is safe against attack, be it Eryk or Talan or Nestor. They'll none of them find this place, and you *shall* be safe here. Now, shall we see our horses stabled and find something to eat?"

Ellyn wriggled from my protective embrace and looked into my eyes. "Do you truly trust her?"

I nodded.

"Then I suppose I must."

Her tone suggested doubt, but I nodded again and followed Shara to the stables, where stalls were spread with clean straw and mangers filled with oats, buckets of water set ready. It was as if this were some great keep serviced by efficient, but invisible servants.

"I do not understand this," I said.

And she smiled and answered me, "It's magic, Gailard. Have you not learned to trust that yet?"

"Perhaps yours," I answered.

"There's more to come," she said, and beckoned me away. Nor was she wrong.

She brought us to the great tower through halls and corridors that alternated strangely between the immaculate and the decrepit. Some were swept clean, and hung with magnificent tapestries that glowed in the light coming from the tall glassed windows, chairs and tables shining as if recently polished, vases of fresh flowers adding further brightness; others were dank and smelled of mold, weeds creeping from cracked stones, the windows smeared thickly with grime, spiderwebs filling the dusty corners, the angles of ancient, age-damaged furniture. It was as if we walked through a dream, and I felt uncomfortable. But the tower, for all I knew it belonged to an older time, might have been built yesterday. Its stones were pristine, its windows bright and clean, there was an odor of beeswax emanating from the woodwork. No keep could have been better kept, I thought—and as I did, sensed faint and distant laughter, appreciative, and looked about to catch brief glimpses of flickering shadows, as if we were escorted by half-seen servants too modest to reveal themselves. Beside me, Ellyn shivered, glancing nervously around.

"It's like this," Shara said. "They maintain some parts, but leave others as you've seen."

I hiked my shoulders, feeling none too easy in the presence of these ghosts. I glanced at Ellyn, who glared about as if she trusted none of this and had sooner been gone, but when she caught my eye she gave me only a grim smile and followed Shara up a flight of winding stairs that delivered us to a circling corridor where our enigmatic hostess announced we would sleep.

My chamber was the finest I'd seen, surpassing even Chorym's. Thick rugs covered the floor, their intricate weavings glowing in the sunlight that shafted from high windows that opened onto a balcony overlooking the farther part of the canyon. A vast bed laid with clean linen sat like some potentate's catafalque at the center. There was an armoire of some dark and glossy wood, a table set with pitchers of water and wine and ale, a bowl of sweetmeats, three high-backed chairs around it. There was a couch scattered with plump cushions, even a footstool. Shara indicated a door that opened onto a bathing room where a great stone tub was set into the floor, and another that was a marbled and magnificent latrine. I gaped, and she laughed.

"Do you believe in magic, Gailard?"

"How can I not?" I returned. And she said, "I'll show Ellyn to her quarters. Do you bathe, if you want and then we'll eat and speak of the future."

I nodded, dumbstruck by this opulence, and the door closed behind them. I stowed my gear in the armoire and tested the bed, which bounced most satisfyingly under my weight. I went out onto the balcony and inspected the courtyard below, the canyon beyond. When I returned I caught a musky scent in the air. I traced it to the bathing room and flung open the door. The tub steamed, filled with hot water.

I said, "Thank you," to the empty air, and shed my clothes and sank into the tub.

When I was done and all the fatigue of our journey washed away, I dressed and poured a cup of ale. I wondered awhile if it was appropriate to wear my sword here—and decided that there was little point. Whom should I fight, ghosts? I settled at the table until there came a knocking on my door.

I opened it to find Ellyn standing there. She, too, was freshly bathed, and dressed in a long gown of some pale blue material that flattered her figure and complexion. She plucked at it, frowning.

"I understand none of this, nor like it much." Uninvited, she pushed past me into the room and filled a glass with wine. "Are we truly safe here?"

I shrugged. "I've told you—I trust Shara."

Ellyn sipped her wind and grunted at the same time. "But you're besotted."

"Am I?"

She shrugged and rose, restless, crossing to the opened windows, going out onto the balcony. I topped my cup and followed her.

"We're trapped here," she said.

"Or safe," I answered.

"That hurt, you know." She turned to face me. "When you dragged me from my horse."

"You panicked." I gestured an apology. "Not too much, I hope."

"No." She shook her head and assumed a mournful expression. "But it was undignified."

Almost, I laughed.

"You consider me a child." She smoothed her dress. "But I'm not."

"You're Chaldor's heir. And with Shara's help, you'll be Chaldor's queen."

"And you my general," she said. "Is the Vachyn's purpose true."

"I believe it is."

Ellyn pursed her lips. "Perhaps; but she's still a Vachyn." She set her glass down on the balcony's rail and stepped a pace toward me. "I shall be full-grown soon, Gailard. Do you find me . . ."

I was grateful for the knocking. I turned away, crossing to the door. Shara stood there, dressed in a gown of pale green that was somehow both demure and enticing. She smiled and asked, "Shall we eat?"

I nodded enthusiastically and called that Ellyn join us—which she did with poorly concealed irritation.

We followed Shara back down the winding stairway to a door that swung unbidden open on a hall set with a sumptuous table. The smells prompted my mouth to water and my belly to rumble, which prompted a disapproving look from Ellyn, who accompanied us with a haughty dignity that was somewhat undone by her sullen expression. Shara bade us sit and we took our indicated places as she served us. I accepted a silver platter laid thick with roast beef, vegetables, and a rich brown gravy, and could barely wait as Ellyn was served and Shara took her share. The food was excellent—fine as the wine that accompanied it, served from decanters of glittering crystal in goblets that were some intricate combination of glass and silver such as I'd never seen.

"Now," Shara said after a while of silent eating, "shall we speak of the future?" She turned to Ellyn. "You've much to learn."

Ellyn stared at her, dabbed her mouth with a linen napkin, and said, "And you'll teach me?"

"To use your magic, yes." Shara nodded, and looked to me. "And Gailard shall teach you to fight, no?"

"I shall," I promised.

Ellyn stared a long time at Shara. Then: "And shall you swear fealty to me, as Chaldor's heir?"

"I swear," Shara said, "that I shall teach you to use your talent. I swear that I shall fight with you, to drive Talan and Nestor from Chaldor. I swear that I shall do all I can to give you your rightful throne."

I said, as Ellyn continued to stare at Shara, "What more could you ask?"

"Much," she said. "Such as you offer me." She turned again to Shara. "Shall you offer me the same?"

CHAPTER TWENTY-TWO

Ellyn was startled by Shara's refusal. She had thought to entrap the woman, to force her into swearing an oath of fealty that would grant Ellyn undisputed dominance, effectively render Shara her vassal. Then she might, once she'd learned to use her talent, order Shara to some distant part of Chaldor whilst she kept Gailard with her. She had seen how startled he was when she appeared at his door in her gown, and was confident that he found her attractive. Her hair was growing out from its unflattering, boyish cut, and even was she not yet a fully fleshed woman, still her body filled. Soon she *would* be a woman, and she was surprised by her own feelings—she thought that Shara's presence had likely stimulated her to recognize what she felt for Gailard and had long denied. But he, bound by his oath, must stay with her as she grew, and she believed she could make him love her—so long as Shara was not present to distract him.

But Shara only shook her head and said, gently, "I took oaths as a Vachyn that I've reneged. I made myself a promise then—that I'd never again swear fealty to anyone, but make my own choices whom I'd support, and that whosoever that might be must prove himself or herself worthy."

"And have I not?" Ellyn asked, sensing that her trap sprang open, perhaps to snap back on her.

"No." Shara shook her head again. "You have proven yourself brave. But otherwise . . ." She shrugged eloquently.

"What?" Ellyn demanded, trying hard not to scowl and losing the struggle.

"You've proven yourself willful," Shara said. "And often selfish. Certainly stubborn . . ."

Ellyn set down her glass for fear she'd fling the contents into Shara's face and thoroughly disgrace herself as the catalogue of faults went on.

"But even so," Shara concluded. "what I have promised, I shall do. Are you willing, I *shall* teach you to use your talent; and I *shall* support you in your war against Talan. I shall use all my powers to defeat Nestor. But to swear an oath of fealty to you? No, that I cannot do."

Against her will, Ellyn felt her lips purse and her eyes narrow. She clenched her fists and allowed her gaze to wander in Gailard's direction. She could not help herself.

"And then?" she asked. "Shall you take Nestor's place? Shall you be the Vachyns' ambassador to Chaldor?"

"Ellyn!" That was Gailard; she ignored him.

"No, I shall not," Shara replied. "I've no stomach for those games, and once you're enthroned I shall return here. I've no desire to be elsewhere, nor to manipulate monarchs or control countries." She gestured at the hall. "I want no greater kingdom than this, and to be left alone."

Ellyn forced a smile and, carefully, raised her goblet. "So you ally with my cause."

"I've told you that," Shara said.

"But only for your own reasons." Ellyn drank, congratulating herself on a small victory.

"Mine and yours coincide, no?" Shara asked. "Is that not enough?"

"I suppose it must be," Ellyn said. "But how can I trust you, save you swear fealty?"

"As I must trust you," Shara gave back. "Do I teach you to use your talent, am I creating a monster—another Nestor?"

Ellyn choked on her wine, feeling her cheeks redden as she spluttered crimson droplets across the table. "You compare me with Nestor? The god-cursed Vachyn who helped Talan slay my father and mother?"

"You compare me with him," Shara answered.

"With reason!" Ellyn could not help squealing.

"He was a pleasant child," Shara said. "Kindly, even; but when he gained his power . . . he changed. Power corrupts."

"It did not corrupt my father! And my mother had talent and was not corrupt."

"No." Shara agreed. "But what has power done to Nestor? To Talan? To Eryk? Perhaps you're like them."

"I'm not!" Ellyn wiped her wine-stained mouth. "The gods know, I'm not."

"The gods hide their purposes from us," Shara said, "and until you prove yourself worthy, I'll not swear fealty."

"And do I prove myself worthy?"

"Then I'll give you my oath."

Ellyn swallowed. She had thought herself cunning and found her ploy turned around. She felt a terrible embarrassment. How must this look to Gailard? As if she were a willful child, arguing with someone wittier and more sophisticated? She felt her cheeks grow warm, and wished she'd never begun this conversation. With all the dignity she could muster, she set down her napkin and pushed back her chair.

"I am tired. I'll find my bed, do you agree."

Shara nodded, her face calm. "Follow the lit corridors. Or shall I escort you?"

"No! I can find my own way." Ellyn shook her head. Then, an afterthought, small retrieval of lost dignity: "Thank you."

Shara said, "We'll begin your teaching in the morning," but Ellyn did not hear her, for she was making her way from the hall, fighting against the desire to cry.

She found the door—which opened before her seemingly of its own accord—and followed the corridor to the stairs, on to the passageway that led to her chamber. All were lit, as Shara had promised, and it seemed that shadows danced around her, beckoning her onward. Almost, she could discern them, like figures half-seen in a dream. They did not frighten her, but she wondered what they'd do if she sought to leave. The thought crossed her mind: take off this gown that had not impressed Gailard so much as she'd hoped and put on her traveling gear, find her horse, and ride away. Then she thought, to where? Back down that precipitous trail that had frightened her more than she was prepared to admit? Back to the Barrens? She knew she could not cross that wasteland alone, and even did she survive, what then? She had no idea where the Dur had gone, and they were her only other allies. No: she was caught here.

She found her chamber and flung herself on the great bed, letting the tears come now, pounding fists against the pillow, knowing herself caught, unable to leave this strange hold save Gailard came with her. And knowing he would not lest Shara agreed.

It was not fair, she thought. It was not fair at all.

"Willful?" Gailard smiled ruefully. "I'd put it stronger than that."

Shara smiled back, and shrugged. "She's a frightened child on the edge of womanhood. She's lost her parents, and all the comforts of Chorym. She's lost in a land she cannot understand with only you and me to ward her—how else should she feel?"

"Thankful?" he asked. "Grateful that you risk your life to aid her?"

It was a question put so simply, so absent of guile, that Shara could not help laughing—which set Gailard to frowning.

"Have you not done that daily?"

Now he shrugged. "I accepted Andur's geas; made Ryadne a promise. What else could I do other than my duty?"

She studied him, thinking that such honesty—such innocence—was rare. "You might have taken her back to Chorym," she said, testing. "Or left her with Eryk and Rytha. Talan would pay you well for her." She saw his face darken, and she knew that she had offended his sense of honor. "Another man might have done that."

"I am myself."

He scowled as he drained his glass, and Shara watched the candles' light plane his face in patterns of light and shadow. He was a handsome man, and undoubtedly brave. But best of all, he was honorable: whatever guile existed in him was employed in military strategies, the tactics of battle. Face-to-face, he was likely the most honest man she'd known. She felt emotions stir, such as she'd not experienced in more years than she cared to recall. She wondered if those, as much the aetheric plea she'd heard from Ellyn, had brought her to the rescue. She had chosen to live alone, and now she was once more involved in the affairs of men. Another promise reneged? Had, somehow, Gailard's soul called out to her as much as Ellyn's innate talent?

"Forgive me." She lowered her head in apology. "I intended no insult."

He refused to face her for a while, then grinned. "None taken."

The gods knew but he had a pleasant smile. She could understand why Ellyn found him attractive—and the girl did, that was increasingly obvious. Ellyn, she suspected, had sooner been alone with Gailard than share him. But the world turned as it turned, and the three of them were thrown together, and Shara sensed in her bones that Ellyn must learn to use her talent properly and be returned to Chorym's throne. Else Talan would own both Chaldor and Danant, and Nestor would whisper in his ear and further the Vachyn aims of dominance. So Ellyn *must* learn. And were she to come into her full power, then Shara must be her friend. The sorceress stifled a sigh; she could not deny she felt a powerful attraction to Gailard, and it would likely be pleasant if she took him to her bed. But . . . no, she told herself. *I cannot chance making an enemy of Ellyn. Are we to defeat Nestor, then Ellyn must trust me.* So . . . she sighed and made her mouth smile.

"Thank you."

He stared at her, and she saw his feelings writ clear. She knew that if she granted it, he'd follow her to her chamber, and . . . *No!* She threw the thought away.

She said, "Are you done, perhaps we should retire. We've much to teach Ellyn, and we'd best start early."

"You'll teach her magic?" he asked.

"I'll teach her how to use what she already owns," she said. "And, the gods willing, how to use it wisely."

And saw him frown again. "But you told me that Nestor can sense your magic. Do you teach Ellyn, then surely Nestor shall sense it and know where we are. Then he'll find us . . ."

He was quick, this Highlander. She smiled and said, "Not here, not in this valley in the Styge, for there's something about this place that hides it and conceals it from notice. How else do you think I've survived so long without the Vachyn finding me? I can use magic here without Nestor sensing it. This valley is safe, Gailard. Now do we find our beds?"

She watched as his smile transformed from anticipation to acceptance. He rose and bowed, as to some great lady. "My thanks for your hospitality. I shall see you on the morrow, then."

She nodded, watching him leave the dining hall— tempted to follow him. But she sat where she was and waited for the shadows to come from the angles of the hall and clear away the dinner things. She wondered if they laughed at her, or chided her for her reluctance.

"I cannot," she told them. "I must not. Yet, at least."

Amusement echoed against the vaulted ceiling, whispers of laughter and sympathy. Shara rose and turned away, thinking that all the simplicity was gone from her life—and with it all her safety.

She climbed the stairs and made her way along the corridor toward her chamber. She hesitated a moment outside Gailard's door, and heard the whisperings of her invisible servants—some urging her to enter, others prompting caution. She shook her head and went on. But it was hard.

CHAPTER TWENTY-THREE

Ellyn's tuition began the next day.

I woke with unseasonal light on my face, birds singing outside my window, and the air warmer than it had any right to be at this time of year. Curious, I rose and went onto the balcony, from which I saw the canyon bathed in sunlight—even though the sun was not yet risen over the surrounding cliffs. It was as if the glow emanated from some source inside the hold that I could not see or recognize, but must accept as a characteristic of this odd place. I returned inside feeling simultaneously invigorated by what appeared to be a late-summer morning and troubled by this display of magic. There was so much here I did not understand, and whilst I trusted Shara's intentions I could not help feeling somewhat uneasy. I was further disturbed to find a bath prepared and tea steaming on the table by my bed—both poured, I assumed, by the shadows that inhabited this strange place. But I was committed now, so I drank the tea and bathed, then dressed and went down to the hall, where I found Shara ensconced at the table, consuming such a breakfast as I'd not seen since quitting Chorym.

We had agreed the previous night, after Ellyn left us alone, that the child-woman's military training should precede Shara's teachings.

"She needs to learn discipline," Shara had said. "She's headstrong, and do I teach her to use her talent before she's the discipline to use it wisely, she'll likely use it only as a weapon. Like"—she smiled—"a Vachyn."

So we had agreed that I should take Ellyn to practice swordplay for a while, and—hopefully—work off at least some of her frustrated energy.

Which she liked not at all, though I suspect she had anticipated our decision, for she came to breakfast wearing her traveling gear and a grim expression.

She seated herself and ate in silence as we explained. Then looked at Shara and asked, "When shall you begin our lessons?"

"When you are ready," Shara replied. "But meanwhile . . ."

She turned to me and I said, "I'm ready now."

Ellyn scowled and followed us to an armory, where I found her a tunic and leggings and light helmet that fit well enough for practice that she'd not get hurt did I pull my blows, and then a buckler and a light, blunt practice sword. I found myself a heavier blade, of wood sheathed in some metal I did not recognize, and Shara took us through more winding corridors to a cobbled yard filled with fleeting shadows and straw-stuffed dummies.

"I'll leave you now," she said.

"You'll not join us in this practice?" Ellyn asked, her voice scornful.

"Perhaps later," Shara returned her, "when you've learned a little."

And she was gone.

I heard Ellyn mutter, "I'll give you a sound drubbing," and smiled.

"What are you grinning at, hire-sword?"

"Your pride," I said. "I suspect you might find her a more difficult opponent than you think."

"Save she uses magic, no," Ellyn snapped, and raised her buckler. "Now do we begin our lesson?"

I shrugged and raised my own shield to the defense position. "Come at me."

She did—with such a will as expressed her frustration. She swung her weapon in great angry arcs that set the blade to rattling off my buckler and she to panting with the effort of her blows. She was agile, and—I assumed—had taken some lessons in Chorym, but her anger denied what skill she had, prompting her to furious attacks that wasted her energy. I let her go on awhile, then riposted my own blade to send hers tumbling from her hand.

She cursed volubly at that, and went darting after the fallen sword. I poked her in the buttocks, laughing. Then felt the laughter freeze as she swung to face me, her eyes narrowed and furious, her cheeks red with embarrassment and ire.

"It's easy for you! This is all you know, isn't it—to swing a blade and kill folk? How dare you laugh at me!"

I stifled my smile, and bowed an apology as she rubbed at her buttocks. I waited until she had retrieved her blade and went again on guard. "Forgive me," I said, "I shouldn't have laughed at you, but . . ."

"What?" She faced me over her shield.

"You assume so much," I said. "That Shara's your enemy . . . That you can defeat a common hire-sword . . ."

"You're not," she said quickly.

Now it was my turn to ask, "What?"

"A *common* hire-sword," she answered, and had the grace to smile and blush. Then grinned. "So teach me to be an *uncommon* hire-sword."

"First," I said, "you must hold your buckler higher. Use it to protect your body and your face. Use it to deflect my blade—push my sword aside, so that you've room to use your own. And keep your temper! Don't waste your strength in wild swings that I can block. You've a cutting edge and a point—use them wisely. Look . . ."

I brought her to the nearest dummy, which carried a shield on one wooden arm and a blade on the other, its head connected by a chain to the gallowslike upright, so that it would swing with each delivered blow, and showed her the way of it.

She set to with a will, and I watched her for a span, wondering what Shara did the meanwhile in this strange castle. And all the while, from the corners of my eyes, I could see shadows watching us.

We continued at this until the sun stood overhead and sweat ran down Ellyn's face. I thought she might quit, but she did not until I called for her to stop. She was panting now, her shirt dark with perspiration. I found a water bucket I'd not seen before (and that likely had not been there before) and dipped her out a cup. She drank eagerly and stared at me as we found a bench.

"Is battle like this?"

I chuckled—I could not help it—and gestured at the dummy she'd been hacking. "Usually your enemy responds faster."

"Was it like this in Danant? At the Darach Pass?"

"No." I shook my head, laughter suddenly forgotten. "There were arrows flying there, and javelins. Talan sent his chariots against us; and there was Vachyn magic in the sky and men's minds." I filled myself a cup, remembering, thinking of how it had been—how it always was. "Battle is chaos. It's loud, with the drums and the horns blowing, the noise of men shouting, horses—and men—screaming, the sound of the chariots' wheels, and that whistling sound the arrows make as they fall, the rattle of steel on steel. It's . . ." I fell silent, shrugging, not enjoying the memories she'd invoked. "It's noisy, and it smells."

"Smells?" She frowned at me.

"Of blood," I said, "and dung. Of sweat and piss. Of death. Men smell when they die."

Her frown grew deeper and she shuddered. "But I shall have to fight battles, no? If I'm to defeat Talan?"

"Likely." I nodded. "But you'll be the commander, and commanders don't have to join in combat."

"They leave that to such as you?"

"To common hire-swords," I said, grinning. "Some, at least."

"Did my father?"

I shook my head. "Andur fought with his men. He was brave, and always to the fore."

"Then so," she declared stoutly, "shall I be."

"I don't doubt that," I said, which elicited a smile. "Now—shall we continue?"

She said, "I'm hungry."

I must admit I was, but I deemed it best we go on until Shara summoned us, so I said, "Battles don't stop because your belly grumbles," and we took up our swords again and set back to flogging the dummy.

We kept it up as the sun moved across the sky and natural shadows began to fill the yard. I saw Ellyn wearying, her blows growing weaker, her shield arm drooping. I thought to call a halt, but before I could, Shara appeared, cool and smiling.

"Likely you'll want to bathe. Then there'll be a meal ready."

"Not before time," I heard Ellyn mutter.

"And after," Shara said, looking at Ellyn, "we'll speak of sorcery."

Ellyn groaned.

It was a fine dinner, but when it was eaten Shara took Ellyn off and left me alone. I lingered awhile, wondering what shades might emerge to clear away our plates and cups, but none came and I rose and went to the stables to check our horses. They were content, with water and straw in abundance, and I returned inside to find my room. I paced awhile on the balcony, then settled to sleep.

That was the way of it for some weeks. I'd rise and take my breakfast with the two females, then Ellyn and I would go to the yard and practice. What Shara did, I had no idea, save that each evening she'd take Ellyn away and neither one would speak of what they discussed. I sometimes grew bored and wandered the keep, discovering its curious wonders. I found a library—a vast hall stacked from floor to high ceiling with ancient books—and read some of them, learning much of Chaldor's history, of the Sea Kings and suchlike, but nothing at all of the Vachyn. It seemed there was not a single tome that mentioned them. I explored the armory, finding strange weapons whose use I could not comprehend, and armor such as I'd never seen. Sometimes I'd take my horse from the stable and ride her about the canyon; sometimes Ellyn and Shara would accompany me. Strange journeys those, for animals I'd always known as wild would trot calmly from our path and watch us go by—deer, which seemed to find us no threat, and foxes that sat with lolling tongues like friendly dogs. It was as if I had happened on that paradise the priests promise, when the world ends and the gods deliver all to peace—save that daily I trained Ellyn for war.

She was quick to learn. Andur had already taught her somewhat of swordwork, and she was soon adept. I set her exercises to strengthen her, requiring her to hold increasingly heavy stones above her head, or at arm's length; to squat and spring upright; to run with me in endless circles about the yard. Sometimes I'd take food from the breakfast table, sometimes not, explaining that in war a soldier could not expect to eat regularly. I taught her to hold her buckler correctly, and how to fight without that protection. I tutored her in the use of the bow—at which she excelled—and how to use a knife in close-quarters fighting. And she gave herself to the lessons with an enthusiasm that was at first grim, but then increasingly willing as her prowess grew. After a while, we discarded the padded practice tunics (I took to wearing one when she became good enough to deliver me stout blows) and we trained in full armor, or in only shirts and breeches.

In time, I deemed her fit enough that we took to horseback, and set our mounts to charging at one another, trading blows or loosing blunt practice arrows. She no longer lost her temper when she took a tumble, but only cursed like any good soldier and rubbed her bruises and remounted, and returned to our mock combats.

And meanwhile, the year aged. The canyon grew cooler, though the grass remained green and there was no sign of frost, for all I knew it must be deepest winter in the lands we'd left behind. When I studied the surrounding hills, I saw snow on their flanks, and I knew that should I ride clear of this idyllic valley I'd find frozen streams and bleak midwinter. Here, though, I knew mild sunshine and cheerful birdsong. Indeed, it seemed there were more birds, as if they found a refuge here.

It was a curious respite, as if we had taken a step aside from the normal passage of time and now lived in some alternative world. There seemed to be an endless supply of food and wine and ale—and even brose—that came from sources I did not question. We ate meat, but we never hunted, nor did I find any stockyards, or chicken coops for the eggs we ate; nor ever saw the kitchens or who (or what?) prepared our food or made our beds or filled our baths. And when I ventured to question Shara on such mundane wonders, she only smiled and told me it was magic, and sometimes exchanged a glance with Ellyn, who seemed to know more of such matters than I, but would give me no more information than Shara.

I thought they became friends. Surely Ellyn expressed no more resentment of the sorceress, and as she grew stronger and more skilled, they spent more time together. But I was never privy to their lessons. Shara would come watch us practice and then take Ellyn away to some part of the hold I never saw, for I could never find it—though I sometimes tried to follow them. When I did, I'd find myself wandering a lit corridor that gave onto old and empty chambers all filled with dust and spiders, weeds sprouting from the flagstones, or turning in what I was sure was the direction they'd taken only to find myself back where I'd started, or outside my own room. After a while I gave up and left them to whatever arcane studies they pursued and devoted myself to the library. That, I could always find—as if the shadows would teach me, or at least grant me the opportunity to learn. But I never discovered who built the castle (though I learned much of castles' construction and how they might be torn down), or what had become of the builders. I asked Shara, but she told me only that she had found the place through some magical instinct when she fled the Vachyn.

It was hard in many ways, so easy in others. I lived a life of such luxury as I was not accustomed to, and with a woman I desired but could not have. Shara held me at arm's length, whilst Ellyn made it increasingly obvious that I should be welcomed to her bed. I lusted after the one and refused the other, and we came to an awkward compromise that someday we all knew must be resolved. And meanwhile, I felt time passing in a manner I could not comprehend. We seemed to live in an unnaturally long spring that was followed by a high summer that continued far longer than it should. There was no winter here, and I wondered how long we sojourned in this magical valley, beyond the passing years outside.

I questioned Ellyn as we practiced, but she prevaricated and gave me no clearer answers. I assumed she was sworn to some vow of secrecy, and surely she never spoke of her lessons or her knowledge, save with a secretive smile and a display of renewed vigor that took my mind from the topic as I concentrated on defeating her. By all the gods, she was good! She learned apace and I must work ever harder to hold her off. I believed that before long she might well stand her ground against most men, for what she lacked in weight and strength was balanced by speed and agility. Indeed, she learned so fast I wondered if she used magic, but she denied that accusation and swore she only learned from me.

In which Shara supported her, swearing that Ellyn's burgeoning prowess was naught at all to do with her, but only Ellyn.

I had felt them growing closer, but that remark brought a blush of pride to Ellyn's cheeks and I saw her turn to Shara with a genuine smile on her lips.

"And her talent?" I asked. "How does that progress?"

"As well and as swiftly," Shara replied. "She's an excellent study."

They exchanged more looks then, and I felt somewhat of an outsider. They shared knowledge I knew nothing of, nor ever could be a part of, and I felt suddenly lonely. I wondered what transpired in the outside world. How did Chaldor fare under Talan's heel? Were men—or worse—out seeking us? Was Kerid free, awaiting the call to battle? Did Eryk still hunt the Dur?

I asked Shara, but she only told me: "I do not know. I *cannot* know, for this place is . . ." She hesitated. Then: "It's cut off—a refuge and a haven that seems, as best I can understand it, to exist outside of the world's time. I think we might leave here and find only a few days have passed since we crossed the Barrens. Or years. You remember I told you that time was different in the Barrens? It's even more different here. It's . . ."

"Years?" Ellyn interrupted her.

"Or more," Shara said. "Or less."

"Then Talan might have established his rule." Ellyn frowned deeply. "Perhaps there's no more resistance; perhaps Chaldor has forgotten me."

"Perhaps," Shara replied with an equanimity I found no less troubling than Ellyn's, "but remember what we've discussed. Talan is only a tool in Nestor's hands, and Nestor represents the interests of the Vachyn. They're your real enemy."

"I'd still have Talan's head," Ellyn declared.

I nodded my approval.

Ellyn's face was dour, her voice grim. "And I'd avenge my parents."

"The gods willing, you shall." Shara filled a glass with rich, red wine. "But only when you're ready."

Once, Ellyn would have chafed at that, but now she only bowed her head in acceptance. I knew she learned discipline, but I had not until then properly realized how much Shara had taught her. This was no longer the willful princess I'd threatened to spank, but a queen in the making.

Then a little of the child showed through as Ellyn added, "But not too long, eh?"

And so it went as winter—or another year, or for all I knew, a century—passed, and I began to chafe at the long delay. It was like those stories told when I was a child, of the venturer under the hill where the faery folk live, who lingers awhile only to find, on emerging, that lifetimes have gone by and all he knew is dead and the world all changed.

It would have been easier had I a woman. I wanted Shara. She was, after all, beautiful, and I saw her as a trusted companion, but did I hint she only smiled and spoke of duty. I am ashamed to admit that there were nights I contemplated acceptance of that offer Ellyn made, but I am proud to say that I drove such notions away. But by the gods, had those shades who served us been fleshly, I'd have found myself some wench to warm my bed, for old books are no compensation for a woman's body, and there were nights I lay awake thinking of old loves, and slept only to dream of Shara.

And so it went, until . . .

I thought I dreamed. That musky scent was in my nostrils and I felt her hands on me. I could hear her voice, urging me to wake. I pushed the sheets aside and opened my arms, gesturing an invitation. I think I said, "At last."

"Gailard, wake up!"

I opened my eyes and she was standing over me.

I smiled and reached for her.

She stepped a short pace back and fended off my clutching hands.

"Gailard, we've trouble."

Her voice was curt, harsh-edged with urgency. I lost my pleasant, dream-born notions and sat up.

"Nestor's hunters are here."

I swung from the bed, careless of my nudity, and splashed water over my face.

"Where? How?" I tugged on clothes as I spoke. It had been a while since I'd donned that plated tunic Ryadne had gifted me. I belted on my sword and took up my old, familiar buckler.

"They're in the valley."

"How many?"

"Five."

"So few?" Almost, I laughed. I had assumed she spoke of an army—save Shara's expression was urgent and frightened, and I had never seen her frightened before. "The broch's secure, no? Are there only five, we can pick them off with arrows."

"These are worse than any army. They're Nestor's creations, and they'll be hard to kill."

I frowned. "Can you not use your magic to slay them?"

"Not . . ." She shook her head. "Not readily. They'll be linked to Nestor, and do I slay them, he'll know where we are. He'll sense their deaths and know where Ellyn is. I'd sooner . . ."

"They were slain by steel?" I eased my blade from the scabbard, testing the edge. I saw for the first time that she was kilted for battle. She wore breeches and a tunic similar to my own. There was a long sword on her slender waist, and a buckler strapped across her back. Her hair was contained in a filigree helmet.

"It would be . . . safer."

"Then let's go slay them." I moved toward the door. "Where's Ellyn?"

"Asleep, I hope."

I realized for the first time that it was not yet dawn. The sky beyond my windows was a misty grey; the birds were not yet singing. It was the time I'd have chosen for a fast attack: when folk sleep and are easy prey.

"She can fight," I said. "Are these hunters so bad as your eyes tell me, she could use a bow and not come close."

Shara shook her head. "I'd sooner she'd not. I'd sooner she knows nothing of this until it's over." She hesitated. Then, troubled: "I've taught her enough of magic she could use her talent to slay them, and that would reveal her to Nestor—who'd send an army to hunt her down. And I doubt she can hold her temper in check."

"Do you say that their deaths shall alert Nestor to her presence?" I asked, confused. "Or only does she use magic?"

"He'll know they die," came her answer. "But can we slay them with plain steel, he'll not know where."

"I thought," I said, fastening straps, checking my gear, "that this valley was hidden by magic. That we were safe here from Nestor's observation."

"It is," she assured me, "save . . . These hunters are linked to Nestor as is a child to its mother. There's an aetheric cord that binds them to him, and is that sundered by magic, he'll know precisely the where and the how of it. He'll find us, is magic used."

"*Can* honest steel slay them?" I asked.

"Yes," came her hesitant answer. And a moment later: "With difficulty."

"Then how do we face them? On horseback?"

"No. Animals sense what they are and become frightened."

We paced fast along the corridor, down the winding stairs.

"With bows? Kill them at long range?"

"They move fast and are *very* hard to kill. The only sure way is to take off the head."

"So it's swordwork?"

She nodded.

"And your . . . helpers?" I gestured at the shadows that danced in agitation around us, like the colors of flickering candles thrown by flame against recalcitrant walls.

"They cannot. They've no . . . Oh, Gailard, by all the gods, I'm frightened. Do these creatures find Ellyn, then all's lost!"

"They'll not," I said, "while I live. But you stay back. Let me deal with them."

She laughed then: a short, disturbing bark devoid of humor.

"Not even you can defeat five of these things."

I scowled, my pride dented.

She said, "You don't understand. But you will."

And I did as the drawbridge lowered and we went out to face our attackers.

They looked like men, somewhat. They wore the delineaments of men; they stood on two legs and they wore armor. All bore swords and carried bucklers, half helms settled over tangled hair, vambraces and greaves warding their forearms and legs. When I looked closer at them, I saw their faces were a kind of amalgamation of hound and human, with unnaturally long jaws that sprouted unnaturally long teeth, and their eyes were red, and long sticky streamers of saliva hung from their mouths, as if the anticipation of their goal produced the kind of ecstasy I'd seen in rabid hunting dogs.

I was suddenly aware that the birds had stopped singing. I felt afraid, for there was something about these creatures I could not define—save that they seemed to give off a scent of death, as if that was all they knew and nothing would stand in the way of their desire to destroy. I saw that they were hugely muscled, and I doubted, now, that I could defeat them alone. Nor wanted Shara to face them, for I could not believe that, without help of the magic she'd not use, she could face them in honest combat.

But I was a Highlander, and our attack has always been the charge: so I charged.

Shara shouted that I not, but I ignored her. I screamed a battle shout and swung my sword. I came at the midmost of them—and felt my blade deflected as easily as I'd swat aside a fly. I cut at the creature's head—and saw the thing duck and bring its own blade around in a sweeping arc that would have taken my legs away had I not been quick enough to jump and dart back. A thundering blow landed against my buckler and I felt my arm numbed. I backed away, defensive behind my shield. The creatures grinned and closed on me.

I parried and cut, and fought harder than I'd ever done. This was worse than the Darach Pass. I could not believe their strength or speed, and I was driven back. What cuts I delivered were ignored. I saw blood spurt from them, but they paid it no heed—as if pain meant nothing to them—and I found myself entirely on the defensive, seeking only to survive their attack. Thinking that I could not, and that Shara must die and these foul things go on to find Ellyn and slay her.

I found renewed vigor in that fear and fought the harder, but still they forced me back. It was like waving a sword at a thunderstorm, and all I could do was retreat. A blade swept toward my head and I ducked under its swing, slashing my sword at exposed legs that avoided my blow with an agility that belonged more to a dancing dog than any human being. An edge landed against my helm, another against my side, and I was knocked down. I wondered if I was cut; surely I felt a warmth on my ribs and a terrible loss of breath. I curled, raising my buckler.

Then Shara was at my side, her shield raised above me, her sword sweeping defensive arcs over my head. I staggered to my feet and for a while we traded blows. Mostly, we held our bucklers high and retreated.

We were driven back toward the drawbridge, and all we could do was defend ourselves.

My skull ached and I felt a weakness in my legs. There was a wetness puddling in my boots and a sapping pain in my side. I knew then that I was cut deep. I felt my strength deserting me, and a horrid fear crept into my mind.

I heard Shara cry, "Gailard, we must fall back!"

Fall back? What else were we doing? We could do nothing else under this assault. But to where? The broch? Surely they'd conquer that, even was the drawbridge raised they'd find a way over the walls.

I shook my head. Why was my sight so clouded, why did these abominations swing and shudder before my eyes like darting fish seen through murky water? I swung my blade and shouted a useless battle cry. I felt bereft of hope, and all my efforts to keep Ellyn safe lost under the dread assault of Nestor's creatures.

CHAPTER TWENTY-FOUR

S trange dreams woke Ellyn.
Clawed hands tore away her bedding and scrabbled at her body. Hot breath gusted over her face and she felt her flesh torn, heard horrid laughter. She moaned, and tugged the sheets closer, but that did no good and she opened her eyes to a grey early morning that was silent of birdsong and filled with . . . She was not sure. Could not know—save that something was horribly wrong.

She sat up, wondering.

Tea steamed beside her bed—but Shara had explained that. A bath steamed, scented—but Shara had explained that, too.

The shadow-memories of the castle's builders danced silent attendance, agitated . . . frightened, she thought.

She rose, memories of her dreaming urging her to speed—to forget her usual bath, but only dress.

Why in battle kit? She could not say—only trust her instincts, and belt on a real sword and follow the dancing shadows.

Her first thought was to hammer on Gailard's door, but the shadows beckoned her past that, and she trusted them. The gods knew, she'd come to trust the Vachyn sorceress and the ghosts that served her, so she followed them . . . down winding corridors all filled with grey light and panic

to the outer yard, where the drawbridge lay down and a battle went on.

She saw Gailard staggering back, blood on him. She
could smell it, thanks to Shara's tutelage. He was sore hurt,
but he still swung his sword. And Shara—she could sense the
woman's fear that Gailard not die, or she, or Ellyn . . . but . . .

There was no hope; the attack was too strong.

From only five?

Ellyn remembered Gailard slaying bandits . . . Save,
these were something else . . . not human. Too strong, em-
powered by magic. She watched the trading of blows and
saw her protectors driven back in defeat. Soon—Gailard
had taught her the tactics and strategy of battle—the five
must overcome the two, and enter the broch, and . . .

She knew them then for the hunters Shara had warned
of—created by Vachyn magic, powerful beyond belief, and
linked by their foul creation to Nestor. Their sole purpose
was to slay her as Nestor had commanded them, that Talan
own Chaldor complete.

Shara had warned her against using her talent to defeat
them—that such usage must alert the sorcerer to her presence even in this valley and, did she survive the hunters,
send warriors to find her. Warned her that she must wait to
avenge her slain parents and claim their throne. She had accepted the strictures—the gods knew, she'd not spoken of
what Shara taught her even to Gailard.

But now?

Now she saw Gailard and Shara harried back by mon-
strous creatures that emanated a palpable sense of foul mag-
ics. She remembered all Shara had taught her, and forgot all
the strictures, and summoned up that power and sent it
against the creatures.

Shara gasped and fell back as the power struck; Gailard
flinched, sensing the magical storm pass by him.

Suddenly, there was a black cloud above the canyon,
from which bolts of lightning lanced in precise shafts.

The hunters screamed and were crisped like trees struck by lightning, burned and toppled in an instant. Ashes drifted, settling in grim grey patterns, brighter where the metal of swords and shields and armor were melded to the ground.

Behind the thunderclaps, Shara screamed, "No!"

And Ellyn frowned her confusion.

Had she not saved them?

In Chorym, where he sat in the Palace that had once belonged to Andur and Ryadne, Nestor squeezed a glass so hard it broke in his hand.

Talan Kedassian stared in surprise at his hired sorcerer, suddenly afraid.

Nestor glanced at his bleeding palm and forced a smile. "My hunters have found her."

"And?" Talan asked. "Is she dead?"

"No; perhaps." Nestor picked fragments of crystal from his hand. Blood spilled over the table. "I . . ." He winced. "Cannot be sure."

Egor Dival studied the Vachyn's discomfort with obvious satisfaction and asked mildly, "Why not?"

"Because . . ." Nestor grimaced as he plucked more fragments from his sharded palm. "There's . . ." He hesitated. "My hunters are slain."

"And Ellyn?"

"I don't know." The Vachyn picked the final fragment from his hand and sealed the wounds with silent magic. "But I know where she is, if she lives."

Talan asked, "Where?" eagerly.

"In the Styge," Nestor said. "Across the Barrens."

Egor Dival laughed. "And shall she come out from the Styge and raise an army to defeat us? Or is she trapped there?" He turned to Talan. "Shall I send our army there? To the Styge, across the Barrens, across the Highlands?"

Talan looked confused, glancing from one to the other. "I don't know. Should we?"

"It would be a wasted venture," Dival answered. "That would be a war easily lost."

"Save Ellyn's alive," Nestor said.

"You promised your hunters would find her and kill her," Dival said with some satisfaction. "And there'd be no succession."

The Vachyn scowled angrily. "Even so, she's revealed herself now."

"And much good it does us." Dival laughed bitterly and rose, crossing to a table where maps lay. He spread one chart, beckoning the others to his side, stabbing fingers at the parchment. "Chorym, here; the Styge, here. A long way, no?"

Nestor went on scowling. His mind spun with the loss of that aetheric linkage—five lives of his making so abruptly gone.

"Do you send more of your hunters, how long shall it take them?" Dival asked the Vachyn, not waiting on a reply, but addressing himself now to Talan. "And do I send men, how long shall it take them?" He scowled as he answered his own question: "Too long! By the time either can reach the Styge, the quarry shall be gone."

Talan gestured that he explain.

"The hunters found them and are now destroyed. Likely, therefore, Ellyn lives still—and knows that she was found. Even does she not comprehend properly, Gailard will—and he'll be long gone before either hunters or an army can reach the Styge." He swept a hand across the great expanse of the Barrens and the Highlands. "They could be anywhere!"

"I can send out more hunters," Nestor protested.

"Five were enough, you said." Dival's response was harsh. "But those five are dead. How many more shall you send? And how long shall it take them to find her again? Spring's on us—shall we spend another season here, waiting?"

Talan looked from one to the other. "So what shall we do?"

"Seeking her would be like seeking a needle in a haystack, whether Nestor's hunters or a thousand men are sent." Dival turned to his king, which presented his back to the Vachyn. "But there's another way."

"Which is?" Talan pounced on hope like a cat on a mouse.

"The clans are warring," Dival said. "Pawl tells me that Eryk has chased the Dur into the Barrens—"

"Is this of any interest?" Nestor interrupted. "The squabblings of petty clan chiefs? Let Ellyn come out and I'll have her."

Dival moved a little, just enough that his back remained toward the Vachyn as he spoke to Talan.

"I'll send a fast rider to Pawl," Dival said patiently, "and have Eryk patrol our borders. His clansmen are more likely to find both Ellyn and Gailard—and slay them both. That would save the deployment of our army and"— this with a backwards glance at Nestor—"the sending of useless hunters. Think on it—is Ellyn to claim the throne, she must cross the Highlands, so it's more than likely Eryk shall find her. Let him do our work for us, eh?"

Talan smiled. "Yes," he said, "that's a fine plan. But no promises of gold! Men, a place in my court—but no more."

"I'll see it's done," Dival said.

"You're sure you're fit?"

"I'm sure." Nassim favored Kerid with a glare. "I took a few cuts, no more. And see what those cuts have won us."

He gestured at the harbor and Kerid nodded, grinning now. Boats floated there, kitted for war, ten times the number of his original fleet—indeed, almost every boat Mother Hel laid claim to that she did not need for trade. Most were sleek, low-lying warboats; others were merchantmen rebuilt for battle, with catapults and arbalests newly mounted

on their decks; some were little more than cutters. But all
could fight—and should.

"It was worth it."

"Perhaps I should have let them slay me." Nassim directed a stream of liquid tobacco onto the cobbles. "Think
what that might have got you."

Kerid looked a moment thoughtful, as if he seriously
contemplated the notion, then clapped his friend on the
shoulder and shook his head. "No; I think I'd sooner have
you in command of the *Ryadne*."

Nassim winced under the weight of the friendly blow,
and grinned back even as he cut a fresh plug. "So now we
truly go to war."

"Now the Mother's truly on our side," Kerid replied.
"The gods know, my friend, I'd sooner you'd not been hurt,
but . . ."

"It swayed Mother Hel," Nassim finished for him. "You
realize we're making history here? Hel's Town has never
taken sides before, but now . . . By all the gods, I doubt the
river's ever seen such a fleet! We can sweep Talan's navy
aside and bottle him in Chaldor. He'll not be able to cross
the Durrakym . . ."

"Which may not be so good a thing."

Both men started as Mother Hel came up behind them.
She was afoot, her carriage waiting at the perimeter of the
harbour, the bearers crouched panting in the traces. She
raised her skirts, glancing in distaste at the puddles of tobacco spread around Nassim's feet.

Kerid bowed. "Why not?"

"Is all I've heard of Talan Kedassian true, then he's not
one to linger. Is all I've heard true, he might wish to return
to Danant and leave Egor Dival in Chaldor."

"Or Nestor," Kerid said.

"No." Mother Hel shook her blond head. "He'll keep
the Vachyn at his side."

"Then we contain all three," Kerid said, "and Danant
goes kingless."

"And face all three," said Mother Hel, "when it comes to the real war."

"The *real* war?" Kerid stared at her.

"We can block all Danant's trade," she said. "Indeed, there's little enough even now, but we've not enough men to fight a land war—and it's on land that Chaldor shall be won."

"We can starve them out," Kerid said. "We can raid Danant's coast as Talan raided Chaldor's. We can . . ."

A beringed hand silenced him. "Give generations of Talan's folk reason to hate Hel's Town and Chaldor, both? No; I'd not see that. I'd see this war won as swiftly as possible and the river return to normal."

"But as you say—we've not the men to fight a land war. Nor can we delay." Kerid pointed to the men readying the boats. "They'll not wait. The gods know, they want to fight now."

"And so we go to war," Mother Hel surveyed the fleet with eyes older than her youthful face. "And pray the gods are on our side."

"But I *saved* you!" Ellyn supported Gailard on one side, Shara on the other. His blood spilled over them both as they carried him, his feet stumbling, toward the keep. "Those things were killing you!"

"And their destruction shall alert Nestor to your presence." Shara's tone was sharp, as much with concern for Gailard as anger at Ellyn's presumption. "Do you forget all your lessons? Have I not spoken with you of the aetheric links between hunters and their creator?"

"But they were killing him!" Ellyn's voice rose plaintive. "And they'd have killed you. I saw it! You were defeated, and had I not . . ."

Shara found it hard to answer, for Ellyn's protest was true. Even so she felt a terrible fear that the young woman had lit a beacon that must surely bring Nestor hurrying to the valley, likely with half Talan's army at his back.

"Even so, you disobeyed me."

Their feet rang loud on the timbers of the drawbridge, muffling Ellyn's disgruntled response.

"I am queen of Chaldor."

It was the answer of a sulky child and Shara gave it short shrift. "Not save we defeat Talan. Without that, you are nothing."

Agitated shadows danced in the light ahead, milling beneath the portcullis, in the yard beyond. The birds sang again, but their morning music seemed muted. A horse snickered as if inquiring after Gailard's health.

"Listen, child, let us get Gailard to his bed and tend him. Then we'll talk."

Likely, she thought, it was time to quit the valley—no longer safe—and go out into the world to do what they had agreed they'd do. She had taught Ellyn all she could—save, perhaps, patience—and surely the girl was come into her full strength. That demonstration of power was proof of that. Shara sighed, thinking that first they must nurse Gailard back to health, hoping there was enough time before the inevitable reaction.

Ellyn grunted irritably and staggered on. Gailard was heavy, and his blood was damp on her shirt. He left stained footfalls behind him, more streaks than steps, for he could barely keep to his feet, and she wondered how the two of them might carry him up flights of long stairs. *Gailard,* she thought, *don't die. You cannot die, because I need you.* She wondered who spoke then: the would-be queen or a woman in love?

Behind them the drawbridge rumbled upright and the portcullis fell in a great clatter of metal. They entered the castle and manhandled the near-unconscious warrior across the hall, commenced the arduous task of hauling Gailard to his chamber.

It was not easy, but they succeeded, and at last Gailard

was stretched on his bed. The sheets grew dark, and Ellyn stared aghast.

"Quick now." Shara's voice was brusque. "We must get these clothes off him and staunch the wounds."

Ellyn bent to the task, and in a while Gailard lay naked. She blushed even as she winced. She had seen him undressed before, but then she had felt only fear and horror at what Eryk and Rytha did to him. Now she saw a man she believed she desired stretched nude and badly hurt beneath her eyes. Blood seeped from a deep cut on his right side, above the hip; a gash ran from his left shoulder to his belly, lesser cuts on his arms and legs. One half of his face was blackened by a massive bruise, his hair matted from the blood that oozed from his temple. He was sore hurt, and Ellyn stared helplessly at Shara.

The sorceress ripped a sheet and tossed the pieces to Ellyn. "Bathe the wounds. I must fetch herbs."

"You'll not heal him with magic?"

"Not save I must."

"You did before," Ellyn shouted at the older woman's back. "Why not now?"

Shara offered no answer until she returned, carrying a basket laden with jars and vials and carefully wrapped bundles of aromatic herbs. By then, Ellyn had found a bowl of steaming water and cleaned the wounds, attended by caring but helpless shadows.

"I brought him back to life once, and that's enough for any man. Besides, such magic takes its toll, and I may well need all my strength in the days to come." She spilled water into cups as she spoke, mixing busily, filling the room with strange, pungent aromas.

"I don't understand," Ellyn said. "Surely we're safe now?"

"Surely your presence is known," Shara responded as she smeared Gailard's cuts with her preparations, "and now this keep is no longer safe."

"But it would take Talan's army months to reach us."

Ellyn watched aghast as the sorceress produced a needle and set to stitching the worst wounds. Shara offered no immediate response, bending to her task, then beckoned Ellyn closer. Ellyn thought Gailard resembled some raggedly sewn doll, and then a corpse dressed in its cerements as they lifted him and wound bandages about his body.

"And also give him time to seal Chaldor's borders against your return." Shara did not look up from her work. "Perhaps arrange some alliance with Eryk, that he deliver you to Talan."

"I didn't think," Ellyn said.·

"No," Shara agreed. "And thinking's the first thing both a sorcerer and a queen need do. Act without thinking first and you fall into trouble."

Ellyn said, "I'm sorry. I only . . ."

"Saw Gailard in mortal danger," Shara finished for her, her tone softening. "I know, and perhaps I'd have done the same thing. But even so, you've alerted Nestor to our presence sooner than I'd like." She fastened the last knot and stood back. "I'd have spent longer tutoring you—you've much talent, but little discipline; and discipline's a thing you need if you're to wield your magic wisely."

"Yes." Ellyn was crestfallen. "Forgive me."

Shara nodded and gestured at the unconscious man. "Tending him shall help. One of us must stay with him until he's recovered."

"He'll not die then?"

"Not yet." Shara shook her head. "He's too strong; but still, he's sore hurt and it shall take a while before he can sit a horse. Best pray he's able before it's too late, and Nestor and Talan seal us in."

Ellyn swallowed, knuckling tears of shame and regret from her eyes. "Where shall we go?"

"Back," Shara said, "across the Barrens to the Highlands."

"But Eryk and his fat wife are there."

"And so are the Dur." Shara washed her bloodied hands. "And has Eryk not found them and destroyed them, they'll meet us. Remember your mother's talent?"

"For the seeing?" Ellyn frowned, confused. "I've her blood, but I've not that ability. Had I, then surely I'd have seen those creatures coming."

"Your talent's different," Shara said. "Indeed, I wonder if your forebears did not own the Vachyn magic. Perhaps some bloodline that was lost until you came along—but your grandmother and the other wisewomen have the foretelling. So . . ." She shrugged and found a cloth to wipe Gailard's brow. "We must wait until we're able to travel and then go back. And hope we can find the Dur—and the Dur be still alive and on your side."

Ellyn nodded, forlorn now. Then started back as Shara turned to face her with a stern expression and demanding eyes.

"But meanwhile, you do not use your magic save I give you leave. No matter what, eh? We must travel incognito until we find some allies and look to building you an army, and once we quit this valley we shall be open to Nestor's finding. So I'd have your word."

"You have it," Ellyn promised, and looked to Gailard.

He lay still, barely breathing, sweat on his face, his bandages already staining. She thought it must take him a long time to recover, perhaps longer than the gods allowed them, and she knew she had done wrong. But how could she have stood by and watched him die?

Save perhaps now she must, and she did not think she could bear that a second time.

"I'll take the first watch," Shara declared. "You get some sleep."

Ellyn nodded and dutifully quit the room. Shara lingered by the bed, studying Gailard's unconscious form. He was sore hurt, and she hoped he'd heal in time—she felt a terrible certainty that Ellyn had advanced this deadly game too swiftly. That use of such powerful magic had surely alerted Nestor, and ere long something would be sent, be it magic or an army—so they must go out and look to find El-lyn friends in her struggle to regain the throne.

Sooner than I'd have chosen, she thought. Then looked at Gailard's face and wondered if that was the real reason. Or would she only hold this man safe here for herself? She smiled at her own musings. Perhaps outside the valley she'd know.

CHAPTER TWENTY-FIVE

It was a strange sensation, akin to drunkeness or the effects of that Serian tobacco I'd once smoked. I drifted, unsure what was real and what the fantasies produced by my wounding. I did not think I was dead because at times I hurt too much, as if my body was turned on a spit, flames licking over my flesh. I think I cried out then, or at least moaned, and gentle hands would stroke me and set cool cloths against my face or drip some liquid that tasted too bitter to be only water between my lips. Voices I thought I recognized spoke to me, soothingly, and sometimes I'd see Shara or Ellyn bent over me, but when I tried to speak I could only mumble and they'd shake their heads and answer and I'd drift off again into darkness or dreams.

Sometimes I'd open my eyes (or thought I did) and see the castle's shadowfolk fleshed out, no longer flickering phantoms, but solid folk, men and women in strange clothes watching me, stooping close, concern in all their eyes. Sometimes they'd touch me, as if to calm me or reassure me, but I could not feel their fingers, and I thought they seemed afraid. I surely was; I knew I was sore hurt and gripped by fever. I'd taken wounds enough along the road of my life, and seen enough men die, to know that I'd taken bad cuts and lost much blood. Now, in those brief moments of coherency, I knew I was fevered—and more men died of that than of the original blow. I no longer knew if the gods watched me or cared for my fate, but I prayed to them, for I did not want to leave Shara and Ellyn alone to face whatever should come next.

But I also wondered why Shara did not use her magic to revive me. I supposed she had a reason, but I could not fathom it and I became gripped by a terrible dread: that I had failed, and Talan's Vachyn would send more monsters against the women, or an army, and take Ellyn for his bride, and all be lost. I raved then, and struggled to rise, only to be pushed back—the gods knew, I was weak as a newborn babe—by one of the women.

Then one day I woke to the light on my face, and the sound of birdsong outside my window. I opened my eyes and saw Ellyn slumped in a chair beside my bed. Even in sleep her face was haggard, and when I sat up she woke with a start, eyes springing open in alarm. I saw that they were underlined with dark and weary crescents of puffy flesh.

"Gailard!"

She rose stiffly, like a soldier waking to yet another day's battle, flexing her shoulders even as she reached for a cloth, water, coming toward the bed to bathe my forehead. I lifted an arm I saw was swathed in bandages. "No need." I looked down at my chest, which was wrapped like some Nabanese mummy.

Ellyn hesitated, the moistened cloth dripping water onto my bandages. Then she flung it aside and put her arms around me, which hurt until she drew back. I could not tell whether she laughed or cried, perhaps both, but she kissed my cheek and said, "Your fever's broken."

I nodded, which set my head to hurting somewhat, and said, "Yes, I think so." My mouth felt dry and sandy.

"Oh, Gailard! I was so afraid."

She stared at me, her hands touching my face, my hair. I saw that hers was grown out. She looked no longer boyish, but a young woman fast approaching her true beauty.

"How long have I been like this?"

She said, "Weeks. I was so afraid. I feared you'd . . ."

I took her hands. In her excitement, she was none too gentle, and I still hurt. "It takes more than that to kill me," I said. "What happened. No—wait. Is there ale?"

She nodded and filled a mug. I noticed that she sprinkled some herbal concoction into the cup. It gave the ale a certain bitterness, but still I drank it thirstily. It made my teeth ache, but I asked for a second mug.

"Ach, that's better. What happened? The last I remember is . . ." I touched my head and found it turbaned.

Ellyn explained.

"Then you saved my life," I said.

"And set us all in jeopardy," she replied. "Shara was angry with me."

"She's . . . ?" I hesitated.

"Alive." A cloud crossed Ellyn's weary eyes at my question. "I'll bring her."

She flung out of the chamber and I rested back against the pillows, tugging the sheets down that I might examine my wounds. I saw the bandages—around my chest and ribs, my arms, one decorating a leg. Otherwise, I was naked, which was how Shara saw me when she came hurrying in. I pulled up the sheets.

Shara looked weary as Ellyn, and as happy to see me, but where Ellyn was all fussing fondness, she was businesslike. She checked my bandages and ordered me to lie down.

"Are you hungry?" I nodded and she made a gesture at the shadow-filled air, then turned to Ellyn. "Help me, eh? I'd check those cuts."

I felt a great embarrassment then, for the two of them hauled the sheets off me and, all uncaring of my nudity, set to stripping off the bandages and examining what lay beneath. I saw stitched scars across my chest and ribs, an ugly wound along my right side. I remembered the ferocity of the attack and marveled at Shara's skill. And then forgot it as the room filled with such smells as made my mouth

water, for suddenly the table was layered with appetiz-
ing food.

There was fresh-baked bread, and honey cakes; fruits
and cheeses, thin slices of roasted chicken; steaming,
sweet-scented tea. I thought the shadows laughed, and that I
caught the far-off sound of joyous music. I asked if I might
eat, and Shara nodded grave agreement.

I consumed it all; I found myself ravenous.

"You're weak still," Shara warned. "You must build up
your strength before we leave."

"Leave?" I mumbled through a mouthful of chicken.
"Where are we going?"

"Home!" Ellyn cried. "We're going to find the Dur and
raise the clans!"

I choked so hard that Shara must pat me on the back—
which involved an arm around me and her body settled
close to mine, which I found most pleasurable, and therefore took longer to recover than I truly needed—and said,
"You've news?"

"No." Shara shook her head. "But Nestor will know of
Ellyn's whereabouts now, and take measures."

I had hoped for better news—that the clans rose in support of Ellyn, or that Talan had died of the pox, that Chaldor
rebelled and threw out the Danant invaders. I said, "Eryk
might have something to say about that."

Ellyn went on beaming, but Shara nodded. "Likely
we'll have to face him. But we've no other choice, save to
wait for Nestor to find us."

I felt a chill run down my spine. "When do we go?" I
knew I could not face more of the Vachyn's abominations
yet and hoped I never need to again.

Shara looked at me and smiled fondly. "When you're
ready. Not before."

"I'm ready now," I said. "I can heal on horseback."

"You could die on horseback." She pushed me back
against the pillows and for all I felt recovered, I could not re-

sist her gentle strength. "And I'll not have that. I—*we*—need you alive."

I looked into her eyes. They gave me no answers, but I knew then that I loved her. I said, "Then heal me and let's be gone."

"It shall take awhile," she answered. "Are you to be Ellyn's general, you must be strong."

"But when you are," Ellyn announced, coming to join Shara on the bed, "we shall go to find the Dur, and . . ."

Shara silenced her with a raised hand. I saw then that some further understanding had passed between them as I lay fevered. Ellyn deferred to Shara, as if the child had aged and learned her lessons, and now recognized when she must listen and not speak out.

"We've no other choice," Shara said. "Sooner or later, Nestor will find us, so we must quit the castle. The Dur are our best hope. Has Eryk not conquered them, they'll shelter us. Perhaps Mattich—does he live still—will ally with us."

Almost, I laughed at that. The Dur in alliance with us three fugitives? But it was as she said: our only hope. So I said, "I've claim on the Devyn, no matter my banishment. Can I defeat Eryk in combat, I could win the clan to our cause."

"You're not yet well enough to fight," Ellyn declared.

"But I shall be," I said. "Thanks to you two. I owe you both a life now."

Ellyn smiled; Shara frowned and said, "I did what I must."

But when I asked her, "No more than that?" she turned her face away, and I thought I saw her blush.

I lay swaddled and tended like a babe for some longer time. I no longer saw the shadows fleshed, but still they danced attendance on me in their insubstantial forms, and I believe their phantasmagorical attentions healed me swifter. In time I was able to rise and walk the confines of my chamber, then essay the descent to the lower floors. At first, Ellyn or Shara must accompany me, ready with a shoulder or an arm, to support me as I stumbled, but then I was able to walk unaided, and went out to pace the yard and exercise as best I could with such stitchings in me as threatened to tear apart whenever I grew too vigorous.

I chafed at the delay. I feared that Nestor should find us, or Talan send an army, and wondered all the while what transpired in Chaldor. I organized great plans inside my head: we'd find the Dur and persaude Mattich to support us; I'd face Eryk in honest combat and slay him, claiming the Devyn for my own. And then all the clans would ally with us and we'd ride down into Chaldor like the olden days, when the land dreaded the clan raids. Save now we'd ride only against Talan, who would die for what he'd done to Andur and Ryadne—him and his Vachyn, both.

But first—as Shara insisted—I must heal and regain my strength.

I do not know whether it was her ministrations or the magic of this strange valley, but I healed faster than any man had right to do. Within weeks I began to practice with my sword, then took up my buckler, and began to ride again. I still felt pain, and I knew that I could not face real combat yet, but I also knew that we could not linger here. What season it was outside, I did not know, but I sensed a building storm as surely as if I saw clouds gathering over the Highlands, and knew that we must go out or be destroyed. Ellyn spent time with me, honing her battle skills, but more with Shara in what I supposed was the further honing of her magical abilities. I supposed those lessons were shielded by the valley's innate magic, but neither spoke to me of that, and I did not ask what they did, for while I no longer felt that mistrust of magic, it still held no appeal for me. I'd sooner trust my own strength and my blade, and leave the working of magic to those who understood it better.

My old gear was ruined now, but I found armor in the castle's halls that fit me well, and kitted myself with a surcoat and breastplate, greaves and vambraces, a half helm. I kept my shield and buckler—they'd served me well, and I trusted them, even did the buckler carry the marks of the hunters' attack.

And then one sunny day, Shara declared me fit enough to ride, and announced that we should leave on the morrow.

Ellyn whooped with joy, and we went to the armory to kit her out. She looked, when she was done, like some warrior maiden, and swung her sword in great expectant arcs. I thought that she'd not need a blade, given she could summon lightning from the sky, but she insisted that were we to ride to battle, she'd fight beside anyone who'd follow her. I respected her for that, then wondered why Shara did not choose some battle kit. After all, even a sorcerer could be slain by honest steel, or an arrow.

I got my answer the day we left the castle. We ate our breakfast and retired to our chambers to kit ourselves. I found Ellyn eager in the hall, armored, with a bow and quiver slung across her back. I, too, was dressed for battle. And then Shara appeared. She was dressed in dull blue armor—breastplate, greaves, and vambraces, a light helmet covering her bound-up hair; she wore a sword and had a buckler slung across her back. I gasped, for did Ellyn seem like some warrior princess, then Shara appeared to me an empress ready to defend her cause.

"So," she said, "do we go?"

Without waiting on an answer, she strode past us, and we went out into the castle yard, where our horses were waiting, saddled and provisioned, with shadows dancing around them and us.

"This shall not be easy," Shara said. I wondered if she directed her words at me or Ellyn; likely both. Surely there was a great sadness in her eyes. "This shall not be any story out of legend, where the princess rides out to shouts of joy and all her enemies fall at her feet. This shall be bloody and long, and there will be little joy in it."

"This shall be war," I said. "And I know somewhat of that."

Shara nodded solemnly. Ellyn smiled, her eyes alight with anticipation. And, unbidden, the portcullis lifted, the drawbridge lowered, and we rode out.

Shara's valley remained locked in its seemingly eternal summertime; the Barrens seemed winterbound. We came down from the walls of the Styge toward that grey and dismal land with a chilly wind blowing around us, cold enough our breath steamed and the horses huffed their displeasure. When we camped the first night, still on the mountains' flank, the wind set our fire to streaming sparks, and I saw frost on the grass. When I saw the Barrens at close quarters, they were overhung with dark clouds, penumbras building into great thunderheads that sent brilliant shafts of light dancing over the oppressive landscape. There was neither sun nor moon there—only shadow and the threat of lightning—and my spirit dropped at the thought of traversing that horrid place again.

And it was worse when we came out from the foothills and headed south. The land was even more spare than I remembered, as if the Barrens welcomed the bleakness of winter and clung to that season. The earth was grey and frozen hard; streams lay iced, so that they seemed like transparent veins in the body of the world, all dull and turgid, carrying no life. What trees there were were stunted and twisted and entirely empty of leaves, and bushes rattled thorny fingers as we passed. I had grown accustomed to the birds' singing in Shara's valley, but here there were no birds, nor any song save the keening of the wind, which was a dirge.

At least we were not attacked, though several times I saw tracks in the frozen ground and wondered what insensate strength it must take to drive claws into such hard soil. Those nights we built our fire high and took turns on guard, armored and listening for the warning our mounts might give. Once, I saw the ravaged body of some vastly tusked beast that had been pulled down and eaten—the ground was trampled in the struggle, but all that remained of the animal was scattered bones—but we were not attacked. We nervously crossed that dread ravine which, this time, did not flood, though I saw fresh bones there, tumbled and distorted, and in time we found the plateau's edge weary and hungry, but unharmed.

Below us, then, lay the Highlands, and there it was the beginning of summer. Blue skies stood drifted with streamers of windblown cloud like the tails of racing horses, and the heather blossomed all purple and blue, interspersed with stands of yellow gorse. I saw the spartan dots of hawks, and caught the sweet scent of my homeland on the breeze. But I could not see the Dur.

"They'll find us," Shara said, "or not. We can only go on."

"And if they don't?" Ellyn asked.

"Then still we must go on," Shara returned her. "We've no other course now."

We took our horses down the slope and made camp. The gods knew, but I was happy to be out of the Barrens, with a warm wind on my face and some country I understood better around me. I even managed to snare a couple of fat rabbits for our dinner.

And in the morning the Dur found us.

Ellyn was on guard, and I woke to the clatter of her sword on her buckler. I roused from my tent and went out in only my breeches and unlaced shirt, though I carried my sword and shield.

"Riders!" Ellyn pointed north as Shara came to join us. "Three of them."

I peered into the early morning light and saw the clan colors the men wore. "Dur," I said.

We sheathed our blades, but we could not then know if these Dur riders were loyal to Mattich, or minions of Eryk. Not until they came closer.

They halted a little way off. They wore their bucklers ready, and two held swords; the third a nocked bow. Their faces were hard and tired, and one bore a recent scar across his cheek. They studied us awhile, as if not sure of what they had found, then one ducked his head and eased his shaggy mount a little way forward. He carried his blade across his saddle, and I saw that he was ready to swing; I was also aware of the arrow pointed at my chest. I smiled, thinking that they did not know I was the least threat, that either Ellyn or Shara could strike them down with a gesture.

"I am Rob of the Dur," he said. "Who are you?"

"Gailard of the Devyn," I answered. "This is Ellyn, Queen of Chaldor, and Shara."

I did not know how else to describe her, but it mattered not to Rob, who threw back his head and laughed and shouted, "We've found them! Clayre was right."

He sheathed his sword and looked at me, awaiting permission to dismount. I said, "Do you join us? We've not much food left, but there's tea you're welcome to."

Rob dropped gratefully from his horse, followed by the others. "Tea is welcome," he said. "We've been hunting you awhile now. Indeed, the gods know, there are Dur out seeking you everywhere. We'd thought you dead in the Barrens, or . . ." He shrugged, glancing from my face to those of the women. "It's been so long."

"A season or two?" I posed the question warily, sensing that more time had passed.

"Three years, Gailard." Rob stared at me as if I were crazed. "It's been three years since you left us."

It was as simple an explanation as magic can ever provide, which is to say little explanation at all. The Dur wise-women, just as Shara had predicted, had dreamed of our arrival and sent men to meet us. Rob and his companions—Shawn and Maerk—were the lucky ones. Or not, if what I believed must come of this should happen.

But they had food they shared, so that we ate a fine

breakfast as they told us that Eryk had pledged his loyalty to Talan in return for Ellyn and me, and pursued the Dur since we left the clan.

"So we skulked," Rob said, clearly not liking the embarrassment of such an admission, "until Clayre dreamed of your return, and Mattich sent men to find you. And then . . . Ach, no! Let Mattich tell you the story. Come, and I'll take you to him. The gods know, but he's been waiting long enough."

We struck our tents and saddled our horses and went off to find Mattich. I was somewhat confused, for I no longer owned much idea of just how long we had sojourned in Shara's secret valley. It seemed to me not long enough that so much time had passed—but then she *had* told me time was different in the Barrens and the Styge, and I trusted her.

So we mounted and went to find the Dur.

They were camped in a pretty little combe, its walls dotted with blue pines, a narrow stream at its center, and lush grass all around. It was a small site, and I thought there were fewer tents than I'd seen before, and whilst we were greeted well enough, still I thought there some who looked at us askance.

"We lost too many," Mattich said when we were settled and seated before his tent. "Your brother took it hard that we rescued you, and worse that he could not find you or us after. When we came down from the Barrens, he was waiting . . ." He shrugged.

Shara said, "I'm sorry."

Mattich said, "We made a choice, my lady," and turned to me. "He'd have your head, Gailard. And"—he looked to Ellyn—"yours. He's allied with Talan, who offers much for you."

"How much?" Ellyn asked. And before I could stop her: "Enough?"

Mattich studied her awhile in silence. His face was

grave, and disappointed as he shook his head. "I do not trade in children, or queens. Do you understand what honor is?"

"Yes." Ellyn had the grace to blush. "Gailard taught me that."

"Then you should know," Mattich said, "that you insult your mother's clan."

"Forgive me, Grandfather." Ellyn ducked her head so low it touched the floor of the tent. "I am new to this."

Mattich's frown faded into a smile. "And you've fine tutors. So believe them and me, and know that the Dur stand with you."

Ellyn said, "Thank you."

I asked, "What of Eryk and Talan?"

"Your brother's not a man for winter fighting," Mattich said, "so we had a respite. But Talan sent emissaries with fat and fanciful promises. Can Eryk deliver Chaldor's heir to the Danant bastard, he'll have Talan's troops to conquer the Highlands, and a place in Talan's court. All the clans have that message."

"And how," I asked, "do they take it?"

"The ambassadors could not find us," Mattich said, and laughed. "I heard that the Arran sent them back naked, tied backward on their horses." Then his face grew grave again. "But the Quan listened—and the Devyn and the Agador are bonded under command of Eryk and Rytha. So . . ." He shrugged. "I do not know how safe you are. It might be better that you . . ."

"I go to Chaldor," Ellyn said. Her voice was firm. "Talan stole my throne. He slew my father and my mother, and I'd avenge those murders. Must I go alone, I shall. *But I'll go back, even do I die!*"

We all stared at her. Shara was no less shocked than I, and Mattich spluttered tea. Only Clayre seemed calm, as if her talent had foreseen this.

"You'll need an army," Mattich said.

"I have an army," Ellyn returned, "are the clans with me. What better army?"

Mattich looked to me. Doubtless, he wondered what power this girlish woman owned. I said, "What other choice? Save we unite the clans and all ride against Talan, he owns Chaldor. And he'll give Eryk men to conquer all."

Mattich glanced at Shara, who nodded her agreement. Then Clayre spoke for the first time.

"I dream strange things," she said. "I dream of great boats that I've never seen before. I dream of them on a vast river—wider than any we know here—and that they fight with Talan. I think you've friends you do not know." She looked at her husband and asked, "What choice do we have, save to lose our honor?"

Mattich grunted. "The Devyn and the Agador were always the greatest—and Eryk owns them. The Quan listen. So, what have we left? We Dur, and perhaps the Arran? Not enough against allied clans, supported by Talan's army. And his Vachyn."

"Gailard," Ellyn said, taking me by surprise, "will slay Eryk. He shall claim rightful leadership of the Devyn. And as the Agador are sworn to alliance, they must acknowledge him. Then we'll command three clans. Must we conquer the Quan, we shall; and the Arran will follow us."

I stared at her. So simple? All I must do is face my brother in battle, slay him, and give the clans to her? I scratched my healing wounds—they still itched—and wondered at her . . . I was not sure of the word . . . Presumption? Arrogance? Trust?

Shara said, "There's no other way, Gailard. I wish there were, but . . ."

She touched my cheek, like a moth's landing with soft wings, fluttering gently—disturbingly. I wondered if Ellyn scowled.

Mattich said, "Could you . . . then perhaps . . ."

Clayre said, "The clans might unite. The gods know, none like what Eryk intends, or have much love for Talan."

I turned my face around the circle of watching, waiting eyes, and knew that my fate was sealed. Andur had set that geas on me, and I had given my sworn word to Ryadne. I could not deny what those eyes demanded.

So I said, "There are conditions," and turned a finger to Ellyn. "Understand that I do this for Chaldor's heir, and do I win, you follow her where she commands. Even to Chorym's walls; even do you fight alone."

Mattich ducked his head. "To Chorym's walls, even alone, the Dur shall follow."

His voice was hard as his eyes, and I knew that he'd take his clan in support of Ellyn, even did it mean they be annihilated. I could ask no more of any man, nor wished to.

"So be it," I said. "I'll fight my brother."

"And I mine," Shara whispered, which set a chill in my heart.

CHAPTER TWENTY-SIX

"Sail ho!" Kerid shaded his eyes as he followed the lookout's pointing hand, seeing the distant shape of a two-master in the morning's early light. The sun sparkled on the water of the Durrakym, reflected in shimmering patterns of brilliance that dazzled his eyes, and the vessel rode too low, and too far off, that he could see her clearly. But he knew that no boats out of Naban or Serian plied the river without the Mother's permission in the years since Hel's Town went to war, so he assumed it must be an enemy craft.

"What's her flag?" he shouted.

"Danant's," came the answer.

"Battle stations!" Kerid barked the order, then shouted for more canvas, that the oarsmen speed the *Andur*'s passage. He saw the *Ryadne* and the *Ellyn* draw alongside, matching pace.

"She runs," the lookout called.

"Then we catch her," Kerid muttered.

"Catch what?"

Mother Hel joined him on the steering deck. She wore a silk robe over what little she had worn in their pleasantly cramped cabin, and the wind blew it taut over her body. Her hair streamed unfettered about her face, and Kerid felt a flush of excitement as she touched his shoulder. He saw the eyes of those men not yet concerned with the possibility of combat turn toward him, and saw them grin. He was not sure whether he felt proud or embarrassed. "A Danant boat," he said.

The Mother turned from him, raising her own hand to squint into the brightness. "She's far off."

"We can take her." Kerid heard the drum-master speed his beat; felt the *Andur* surge under him like an eager hunting dog. To either side the *Ryadne* and the *Ellyn* took up the beat. "We can run her down and sink her."

Mother Hel glanced back at the flotilla that came behind them. Fat-bellied caravels and wide, three-masted merchantmen, with cutters like patrolling sharks to the flanks, larger vessels with Hel's Town folk aboard secure in the center. "Is that wise?" she asked.

"She's a Danant boat," Kerid said, as if that were all the answer needed.

"It might be better that we let her go."

He stared at her, surprised. "And let them tell Talan of the armada we bring against him?"

"It might well frighten him," she said. "Does he know how large a Hel's Town fleet comes down the river, might he not fear us? He'll know he faces more than mere river raiders. Your friend, Gailard, on the one side—us on the other."

"And then ready his defenses, and we find the shoreline armed against us?"

The Mother laughed. "Do you not understand what you've done?" Kerid shook his head, and she laughed again, her arms around his waist now. "You've done what no other man ever has—you've taken Hel's Town to war. That alone should frighten Talan. Does Gailard raise the Highlanders as you hope, then we shall hold Talan like a nut between our fists."

Her hands descended in explicit demonstration; Kerid blushed.

"Even so, surely it's best we arrive unannounced."

"Can we?" She held him tighter. He heard his men's laughter. "Do you truly believe we can bring so great an armada down the river without we're noticed? Talan will have word of our coming long before we arrive."

"She's a Danant boat," he said, "and I vowed I'd not see any of them sail the river."

"Then take her," she answered, easing her hold. "But let some of them live, so that they take word back to Talan."

Kerid frowned his incomprehension.

"Let him know fear. He's his Vachyn sorcerer, and his army, but now he faces more foes than he anticipated. Let him sweat."

"And ready his defenses? Send his Vachyn to the river-bank to meet us?"

"I doubt," she said, "that he'll do that. I think he'll hold his Vachyn close—against any attack on Chorym. Yes, he might send men to the shoreline, but if he does we can sail past and land elsewhere. So take that boat, but let some of the crew live to frighten Talan."

"I'd thought," Kerid said, "that you were reluctant to face him."

"I was." The Mother loosed her grip and went to stand by the taffrail. She stared awhile across the sparkling water, then her lovely face hardened. "But he sent assassins to Hel's Town—*my* town—and I'd see him pay for that, and now I am committed. So show me how you fight. But let some live to take word back, and fear—and, all well, Talan shall divide his forces betwixt us and Gailard's clansmen."

Kerid chuckled and shouted again for more speed.

They caught the Danant boat as it approached a riverside town named Vashti. It was a fishing village, and a port for river traders, with two moles thrusting into the Durrakym that vessels might find safe anchor. There was a Danant garrison there now, and Talan's soldiers saw the fight.

The Danant boat ran for the cover of the moles, but was

caught before it could reach safety. The wind was in the wrong quarter, favoring the attackers, and it had only sails. The three pursuing warboats were propelled by the blood-lust of their oarsmen, and they caught their quarry as she turned toward the promise of safety.

Catapults flung balls of flaming tar across the Dur-rakym; arbalests hurled massive shafts. The Danant vessel lost her foremast and took water where missiles pierced her starboard flank. She lost speed and the three warboats closed, their crews readying to board.

Kerid was again surprised to find Mother Hel at his side. She wore fish-mail armor that fit as snug as any gown. She carried a viciously bladed sword, as much finned as it was edged; and her lovely face was hidden beneath a helmet that was shaped in the contours of a fish.

"This is man's work," he said, after he recognized her.

And was met with a scornful laugh as she elbowed him aside and took hold of a grappling line to swing herself across to the Danant boat.

Kerid gasped, then followed her, so that they landed to-gether on the deck. He took a blow to his head as he turned, needlessly protective, to see Mother Hel slash her blade across a man's belly, sending him tumbling away with his entrails falling in sticky streamers around his feet. Kerid tumbled, and felt a sword land heavy across his back. He fell onto his face. Scrabbled away, trying to find his feet and de-flect the next blow that he knew must break his spine and kill him. And then the Mother was there, riposting the de-scending blow and thrusting her blade into the riverman's heart.

"Man's work?"

She lent him a hand, and he rose apologetic.

Then they both laughed and set to clearing the deck, aided now by the other boarders from the *Ryadne* and the *Ellyn*.

Only three Danant sailors were left at the end of it. And

Mother Hel sent them ashore, naked and stripped of all they owned.

"Tell your master," she said, "that Kerid brings a fleet against Talan. Tell him that he had better quit Chaldor and run home to Danant, else he dies."

The sailors were grateful for their lives, and swam to the shore, where Talan's men waited and watched their king's boat sunk.

"I shall go back now," Mother Hel said.

"Why?" Kerid frowned. "I thought you'd be with me all the way."

"I'd find you more boats." She smiled at his crestfallen expression. "That we win this war you've talked me into."

"Only that?"

"Hel's Town does not take sides," she said. Then added, "Until now. And even now . . . This worries me, Kerid."

He shrugged. "Do as you will. I go on fighting."

"I know," she said, and beckoned men to take her away. "I'll see you later. Somewhere down the river."

Kerid watched her go, wondering if he'd lost her or if she'd come back. No matter—he was determined to go on.

"I've still none of Talan's soldiers to support me," Eryk said sulkily, and turned to his wife.

Rytha said, "There were promises made."

"Indeed there were," said Pawl, "but those were contingent on your delivering—or destroying—Ellyn, and you've not done that."

"She escaped into the Barrens with the Dur." Eryk scowled. "My brother took her off—with . . ." He hesitated.

"I've heard the stories," Pawl said wearily. The gods knew, he'd spent far longer than he enjoyed in these dismal Highlands. "You crucified Gailard, and he was rescued by some Highlander goddess. They took Ellyn away—with the aid of the Dur—into the Barrens."

"And have not been seen since," Eryk said, scowling.

"Nor have you found them. Nor been able to conquer your fellow tribes."

"Give me men and gold," Eryk said, "and I'll give you everything you want. Give me some squadrons and I'll beat the Quan and the Arran into submission."

"It's not so easy." Pawl smiled: the diplomat—be careful of these uncouth barbarian clansmen. "Gold was spent conquering Chaldor, and on men—my king's not so many soldiers he can afford to waste them on useless ventures."

"Not useless," Eryk argued. "I can give you Ellyn and Gailard. Only give me men, or gold to buy them."

"Surely," Pawl said. "Only first, give me Ellyn. Save for that, you've nothing to bargain with."

Eryk stared at the emissary. "I could take your head," he grumbled. "I could send your body back to your king across your horse in shame."

Pawl smiled, his face implying threat.

Rytha touched her husband's hand. "Wait, eh? That's not perhaps the best way to go."

Pawl said, "You could, for you are surely the mightiest lord in all the Highlands. But . . . were you to behead me, then my king would seek retribution. And then you'd surely see all of Danant's force come against you, and I think that you'd be slain. Better we continue our alliance, no? Better that you deliver Ellyn. Do that, and I can assure you that Talan will gift you with gold and men in such quantity as shall satisfy you."

"He'd best," Eryk said.

"Only give him what he wants," said Pawl, "and it shall all be yours."

"I shall," Eryk said, after glancing at his fat wife. "My word on it."

"But soon, eh?" Pawl smiled. "It's been awhile."

"As soon as I can," said Eryk.

"They cannot find her." Pawl ducked his head in obeisance before Talan. "They make promises, but deliver nothing."

He chanced an upward glance to where Nestor sat beside his king—and frightened him more than Talan's wrath.

"So should we ignore them?" Talan addressed his question as much to Nestor as to Pawl. "Are they of no importance?"

"Ellyn is alive," Nestor said, "and you need her—alive or dead—to claim Chaldor for your own. To that end, and more, you need the Highlanders. You need them all."

"All?" Talan shook his head in bemusement. "How many of them are there? Five clans—some few thousand; are they so great a threat?"

"Perhaps fifteen to twenty thousand in all," Nestor replied. "But fierce fighters—better to have them on our side than find them raiding south against us. Better to persuade them to our cause than fight a war with them."

"I've more men than that." Talan beckoned a servant to fill his cup, frowning. "I could send Egor Dival to face them and defeat them—I've surely the men for that."

"Indeed, but spread across Chaldor," Nestor said. "A holding force in every town, and all along the riverbank. You can hold Chaldor like a nut in your fist—but you need Ellyn to be secure."

"But I don't have her, and it seems our clansmen ally cannot deliver her." Talan angled a finger at Pawl. "Is that not true?"

"Not yet," said the luckless emissary. "Eryk has hunted for her these past years that I've spoken with him, but not yet found her."

"So you've not succeeded," Talan said. "You've failed me, no?"

Pawl said, "Forgive me, my lord. I've done my best. But . . ."

Talan halted his plaint with a raised finger. Turned to Nestor and said, "I am tired of these excuses. I've no time for them."

Nestor smiled and pointed a finger even as he voiced low-spoken words. And flame enveloped Pawl.

The emissary screamed once before the fire took him. Then only ashes remained, falling in slow drifts about the chamber that had once been Ryadne's. Talan watched them descend onto the tiled floor and sighed.

"Were all my minions so loyal as you," he said to Nestor. "Perhaps I should ask you to go to the Highlands."

"I believe," Nestor said, "that I serve you best in close proximity."

Talan nodded. "Likely so. Surely I'd not have you far from me. I think that . . . things . . . come against me."

"Do they," Nestor said, "I shall stand beside you and guard you."

"Then I shall feel safe," Talan said.

"So should you," said Nestor, smiling.

Servants cleared away the ashes, and Talan called Egor Dival to the chamber.

"Where's Pawl?" he asked.

Talan smiled at his aging general and said, "Gone. He failed me."

Dival stared aghast at the servants who still swept away the last remnants of the emissary. His eyes turned to Nestor, then to Talan.

"You slew him?"

"He failed me."

"He did his best." Dival's weather-beaten face creased into a deeper frown than any of his campaigns had delivered. "It is not easy to deal with these Highlanders."

There was criticism implicit in his tone and Talan flushed. "He failed me!"

"So you slew him." Dival addressed this latest accusation to Nestor.

"I obeyed my master," the Vachyn said.

Dival snorted sour laughter and turned his eyes back to Talan. "And do I fail you, shall you deliver me the same fate?"

Talan shrugged, and glanced sidelong at his Vachyn mage.

"Hold my lands secure, eh? Let no Highlanders come south."

"Or?" Dival asked.

Talan looked again at Nestor and chuckled.

Egor Dival scowled. It was hard to hide his feelings, but he ducked his head nonetheless, and said, "I am yours to command, my king."

CHAPTER TWENTY-SEVEN

Mattich had scouts out—Eryk remained intent on conquering the Dur, presumably because Ellyn was bloodlinked to that clan, and they had aided our escape, or because he had become Talan's man—and in time the scouts brought word of my brother's whereabouts. The massed group of Devyn and Agador were not yet joined by any allies, neither the Quan nor Talan's men, and Eryk's force was encamped south and east of our combe.

I had taken advantage of the respite to hone myself further, practicing each day with anyone who'd take me on. Often it was Ellyn, whose own swordskills advanced apace. Indeed, I thought her a good enough swordsman that she might face most warriors and win. Also, she worked with Shara (of which practices I knew no more than before) and spent much time with Clayre and the other wisewomen. Surely she matured. There were fewer displays of temper, and she appeared to have lost her arrogance. I honestly believed that if we succeeded, she would make a fitting heir to her parents' throne.

But could we succeed?

To achieve that aim I must face Eryk in battle and win the allegiance of both the Devyn and the Agador, and I doubted that could be won save Rytha be slain—which I did not think I could do. Eryk, yes. I'd put my sword in his fat gut without compunction. But a woman? Much as I disliked her, I doubted I could bring myself to kill her, or even order her death. I chose to set that aside and see where fate delivered me.

When the scouts brought word we discussed our strategy—Mattich, Clayre, Shara, Ellyn, and I.

"He'll find us soon," Mattich said, "so we'd best not delay. They outnumber us, but a surprise attack . . ."

"No." I shook my head. "Are we to win the loyalty of the Devyn and the Agador, we need to avoid fighting. The fewer slain, the better."

"Then how?" Mattich asked.

"I challenge Eryk," I said. "To single combat."

"He'll order you slain on sight." Mattich shook his grey head. "He'll have arrows in you before you open your mouth."

"What other way is there?" I shrugged. "You've not enough warriors to face the Devyn and the Agador—they'd cut you down. And then, most likely the Quan would listen to Eryk, and all turn on the Arran." I glanced at Ellyn, who sat grim-faced and silent. "And then everything's lost."

Shara asked, "Can you defeat him?"

"Is the fight honest, yes."

Ellyn asked, "Shall it be?"

"I don't know." I chuckled, though were I honest I did not feel at all humorous. "Eryk is devious, but I think there's a way."

I outlined my plan, and they listened and agreed.

That night, as I went to my tent, Ellyn joined me.

"Shall we walk awhile?"

I wondered, nervously, what she had in mind, and she doubtless recognized my wariness, for she looped an arm in mine and chuckled and said, "I'll not attempt to seduce you, Gailard. Only offer help."

"What help?" I asked.

We walked beside the stream then, and it was a soft

summer's night. The brook babbled and insects buzzed in the warm air. The moon we Highlanders call the Planter's hung full-faced in a sky all spread with sparkling stars. I halted and turned to face her.

"Magic," she said. "I can weaken Eryk; I can give you strength."

"No," I said, so fierce she started back. "And do you suggest such a thing again I'll set you across my knee and . . ."

"Forgive me? I only . . . By all the gods, Gailard, I'd not see you die."

"So you'd use magic to aid me? And destroy my honor? Do you not understand, even now? I go to face my brother in combat, and one of us shall die. But it *must* be a fair fight, else it means nothing. Do you use magic to aid me, then it's no more than what Talan delivered your father—a victory won through magic, and you're no better than the Vachyn. Are you to rule Chaldor fairly, then you must let men fight fairly."

"Forgive me," she said again. "But . . . I'm afraid."

"As am I," I said, and we walked awhile in silence.

Then: "Please live, Gailard. Should you die, I don't know what I'll do."

She rose on tiptoes then and brushed my cheek with her lips and ran away into the night. I went slowly to my own tent and set to running a whetstone over my blade.

I was checking my buckler when I heard Shara's voice asking if she might enter.

I agreed and she came in. She was wearing breeches and a tunic, her hair gathered in a long tail, her eyes as troubled as Ellyn's had been. I invited her to sit, and filled two cups with brose.

"This is no easy thing we face." She sipped the liquor, watching me over the cup's rim. "Can you slay your brother?"

I nodded. "Can you slay yours?"

"Easily." Her smile was grim. "This world should be a better place without him, without the Vachyn."

"And a better place without Eryk," I said. "For where's the difference betwixt him and the Vachyn? Are they not both ambitious beyond all decency? The gods know, but does Eryk have his way, he'll rule the Highlands as Talan's puppet—and Talan's Nestor's puppet, no?"

She nodded and emptied her cup. "What did Ellyn want?"

"She offered magic to aid me," I said, "and I refused."

Shara smiled. "For honor's sake." It was not a question.

"Without that," I said, "I am nothing."

Shara said, "No," and rose and touched my cheek again, and said, "Slay him, Gailard, and live. I'd not see you die."

I took her hand and for a moment she clutched me, then broke free and turned away. "When this is done . . . When the fighting's over and—the gods willing—Ellyn's enthroned . . ."

I said, "Yes," and watched her go.

I wished she'd not, for I wanted her then, and felt such desire for her as I'd not experienced for any other woman I had ever known. I wanted her with me, to hold in my arms and love her, and wake up in the morning with her, and all the other mornings of my life. I desired her in ways I could not explain, and knew that I must wait, and hope, and not know the outcome of my desire until she granted me permission, or rejected me. And all I could do was my duty—my geas—and hope.

We rode out into a bright morning. The sun was already high, and birds sang loud and joyous. The sky was blue and cloudless, the air sweet with the scent of the heather. I wore my battle kit. Mattich rode with us, accompanied by a small honor guard led by Rob. Shara and Ellyn came kitted in their armor, and Mattich carried that long pole decked with feathers that denoted a parley, which bound the clans to honorable talk. Save Eryk was prepared to forfeit all tradition, he must listen to us and let us depart unharmed. My hope was hung on that pole.

We found Eryk's camp and faced his outguards. Mattich lofted the pole and the guards parted, escorting us through the great bivouac to the grandiose pavilion at its center. They gaped at me as if I were a ghost—which, likely, in their eyes I was. I was, after all, a dead man returned to life.

Word had spread and Eryk came to meet us, accompanied by Rytha. They stared at us, surprised. For a while his eyes lingered on me, as if he could not truly believe I remained fleshed and solid and human. Rytha only scowled and pursed her lips. Then Eryk laughed and said, "So, Mattich, do you come to submit? I see you've brought the fugitives, and I thank you. I'll deal kinder with you for that."

Mattich lofted his pole and cried, "I come to issue a challenge."

Eryk said, "I see a beaten chieftain, and a dead man with him—and a girl I'd have. No more than that."

Ignoring him, Mattich said, "I come to parley."

Ellyn fidgeted in her saddle as if she'd unleash magic now. Shara touched her hand and murmured too softly for me to catch her words. I stared at my brother, despising him. Rytha fixed me with a gaze full of hatred.

Mattich raised his voice, loud enough all those gathered around us could hear. "I come under truce's banner to issue a challenge. Gailard of the Devyn would claim his rightful command. He challenges you to single combat."

Eryk's puffy face paled. "You claim the right of single combat? You are beaten! I need only give the word, and you are slain."

"And you are bereft of honor," Mattich said, raising the pole in a great flourish. "Have you robbed the Devyn and the Agador of all honor? Do you deny the ancient rights?"

The folk around us muttered. I could not tell whether they acclaimed Mattich or supported Eryk. I was aware of nocked bows angled in my direction, and drawn swords, and knew that in an instant we might all be slain.

I said, "Are you afraid, Eryk? You claim command of two clans, but you'd not fight me? Shall you order your men to loose their shafts and slay me in my saddle? That would be easy—*and devoid of honor!*" I leaned down to face him closer. "I challenge you to single combat, Eryk! Fight me for command of the Devyn."

Eryk licked his fat lips. "Our father banished you. You've no right to claim combat."

I said, raising my voice, "Are you afraid? Does a coward lead our father's clan? Do the Devyn and the Agador follow a weakling who'll not pick up a sword?"

Eryk looked to Rytha, whose eyes were hooded and furious, offering him no escape. I swung from my saddle and passed my chestnut's reins to Mattich. I stepped a little way forward and raised my arms, turning around as I shouted at all the camp.

"Kill me now, eh? Tell your archers to loose their shafts; tell your warriors to come on and slay me. Gain your sad dreams, and give the Highlands to Talan. And live without honor, all men knowing that."

I thought I might die then, but I saw a man lower his bow, and another sheathe his blade, and I heard a great whisper of agreement. And saw Eryk chew his mustache and close his eyes as if he prayed.

And then heard him say, no honest choice left him : "So be it. But you're armored."

"I'll give you time to kit yourself," I said. "Or take off mine."

Rytha spat, clutching at her husband's arm. "Slay him now," she urged. "Tell them!"

Eryk shook his head. "I can't. I have to fight him." He stared at me, and I saw him envisage his fate in his own eyes. Surely his was lit in mine. "I've no other choice. I must . . ." He took Rytha's hand. "Help me gird up, eh?"

I watched them go into their magnificent pavilion and I

felt sorry for my brother. I intended to slay him, but I felt sorry for him. I did not know whether our father had made him what he was, or Rytha, or himself. But I knew that I was going to kill him—or he me—and I felt a dreadful sorrow at that. I looked at Shara and saw compassion in her eyes, but no release, no alternative. I drew my sword and waited.

Eryk emerged clad in armor. He wore a deep helmet and a breastplate, his arms and legs kitted with greaves and vambraces. He carried a buckler and a long sword, a wide knife and a small ax belted to his plump waist. Through the eyeholes of his helm he looked to me very angry, as if I had upset all his plans.

A circle cleared around us. I slung my buckler on my left arm and raised my sword. Eryk drew his dagger and clutched it behind his shield, which had always been a trick of his.

Mattich cried, "This combat shall decide who commands the Devyn. By all the ancient rights, the victor leads. Do you agree?"

There was a loud murmur of acceptance, and before its echoes were faded my brother swung his blade against me.

I took his blow on my shield and cut at his legs. For so fat a man he danced back quickly, directing a cut at my head. I ducked under his attack and struck at his belly. He turned his buckler and took the blow, swinging his own sword at my chest. I parried with my shield and cut again.

He turned my blow and sought to close with me. I knew that he'd try to use that knife, and so I held him off, buckler crashing against buckler, swords swinging and probing. He began to pant and I began to laugh—a soldier's trick, that he should have recognized, but he only panted as if his splendid armor weighted him down and he sought only to slay me. He saw that he'd not get close enough to knife my ribs and began to swipe his blade at me in great scything arcs. And so it went, blow for blow, swords crashing on shields, parrying and riposting, sparks flying from our blades. Eryk began to sweat. I saw the glistening droplets fall from his face, and I pressed harder. My head ached and I could feel my wounds stretching. I feared they'd begin to bleed and weaken me. And Eryk was a harder enemy than I'd anticipated, for he was driven by ambition and desire, and he fought better than I'd believed he could.

But then I cut him, where his greaves ended and the joining of his armor allowed me a deep wound. I took his counterblow on my buckler and pressed in hard, and turned him so that he was exposed. And sliced my blade across his leg. He cried out, as bright blood spurted over his pretty armor, and staggered back—which allowed me another blow that sent him stumbling as my blade rang off his helm.

I felt a madness come on me then, as if the drawing of his blood summoned up all my resentment and granted me an unnatural strength. I rained blows against him until his buckler hung from a weakened arm. I struck against his head and smashed his sword aside and put my point into his throat, and turned the blade as I felt it grate against his neck. I saw a great spurt of crimson erupt, and darted back to avoid its fountain.

Eryk fell down then, blood coming from his mouth and the wound in his throat. And I kicked his shield aside and planted my blade in his belly, and drove it deep and turned it, so that he squealed and twisted like an insect pinned on a needle.

I watched him die and felt a terrible sadness, and a great triumph, and raised my sword and shouted, "Who commands the Devyn now?"

And heard Rytha scream, "Not you!"

She came at me with a drawn dagger, naked bloodlust in her eyes. It was pure instinct to put up my shield, but I could not bring myself to use my sword. I backed away. I felt a curious, cynical amusement. Had I come so far, slain my own brother, only to die at the hands of a spurned woman? I deflected her blows, hiding behind my buckler, and she screeched, "Fight me like a man, Gailard! Or are you afraid?"

I heard Mattich bellow, "A fair combat! Eryk was slain in fair fight and now Gailard commands the Devyn!"

There was a murmur of agreement that got louder, like a wind gathering strength, until it was a roar of assent. I continued to fend off the enraged woman even as I heard individual voices shouting.

"Yes! Gailard leads the Devyn now."

"Gailard is clan chief!"

"Long live our chieftain!"

I thought that did I not strike Rytha down, I might not live long enough to enjoy my new-won position. And that did I strike her, even only to wound, I should likely forfeit the allegiance of the Agador. And I needed both clans to follow Ellyn; I was caught in a quandary. I backed around the circle of onlookers, Rytha's blade clashing against my shield. I heard laughter, and some few voices I took to belong to the Agador saying such things as, "He can't fight a woman."

Then Ellyn sprang down from her horse and slammed her buckler against Rytha's back even as she thrust forward a foot to entangle the older woman and send Rytha sprawling on her face. She waited until Rytha turned, that plumpened face red with outrage, and set her swordpoint against the thickened neck.

"I could kill you now." Her voice was harsh and cold, and deliberately loud, that all should hear. "But there would be no honor in that. So I offer you a challenge." She paused, her sword still at Rytha's throat, and glared around. "I do not properly understand how you Highlanders do these things, but I am Ellyn of Chaldor, and the blood of my mother, who was Dur, and that of my father, Andur of Chaldor, flows in my veins, and I challenge you to fight *me*."

There came a great shouting at this, so loud I think only Rytha and I heard Ellyn's next words, which were calm and chill as ice on a winterbound stream: "And save you slay me, I *shall* kill you." I saw Rytha blanch then, and try to wriggle away, but Ellyn's sword held her down as all around us the babble grew.

There was little precedent for this, save what Eryk and Rytha had established. Women did not lead clans; women might fight, but not in single combat. But Rytha had attacked me, in defiance of the ancient ways, and the clans were confused.

I backed away, sheathing my blade. Shara caught my eye and shrugged; Mattich appeared startled, as if he could understand this no better than any other. Rob stared about, his hand on his sword's hilt, unsure whether to fight or run.

Ellyn said, "Well?" and took her point from Rytha's throat.

Rytha climbed to her feet. She was panting and flush-faced. Her eyes reminded me of a rabid dog I'd once seen cornered. She wiped a hand across her mouth, her nostrils flaring, her teeth set in a vicious snarl.

"You, girl? With whose aid? *I* lead the Agador now, and"—she turned, her furious eyes darting around the circle—"I say that the Agador slay you."

I raised my buckler to protect Ellyn, but there was no need. Shara's voice rose over the dying tumult. "And what then of the Agador's honor?"

Mattich's deep tones joined her. "Aye! Gailard slew Eryk in fair fight, and now leads the Devyn. Who disputes that?"

The only response was a massed shout of: "None!"

"And so, by ancient right, he commands Eryk's wife—who gave the Agador to her husband! So who commands the Agador now?"

There were different answers. Most acclaimed me, others Rytha, some called that Ellyn contest the claim. I looked at Rytha and thought that she and Eryk had turned clan law on its head, and now reaped the outcome of their ambition.

Ellyn said again, "Well?"

And Rytha said, sealing her fate, "You're armored."

Ellyn laughed and sheathed her sword. "You can put on armor, or I can take mine off—your choice."

The muttering began again, growing louder, and mostly what I heard was agreement: "Yes! Let them fight."

Then Rytha said, "I'm not so mannish as you, girl. I'm not used to armor—but I'll face you as a clanswoman, with a knife."

Ellyn said, "So be it," and turned away. "Shall you help me, Gailard?"

I glanced at Rytha. She eyed her fallen knife and clearly contemplated plunging the blade into Ellyn's back. I thought that ambition had driven her mad, and held my buckler betwixt her and Ellyn. But then both Mattich and Shara intervened, moving to stand between us as I helped Ellyn unlace her battle kit.

"Can you do this?" I whispered. "You'll fight with knives."

"You've taught me well, no?" She shrugged out of her breastplate.

"But you've never killed anyone." I helped her strip off her greaves as she unlatched her vambraces.

"I think," she said with disturbing calm, "that I can slay this creature with great pleasure."

Stripped of her armor, she drew her knife and faced Rytha. There was a smile on her lips and a dreadful coldness in her eyes.

"So, do we set to it?"

Rytha spat and ducked her head. I watched them both; they bent their knees and extended their blades. I had taught Ellyn somewhat of knife-fighting, of such close-quarters combat, but Rytha was a clanswoman, and had fought this way before. And I cursed myself as I saw her advantage: she wore the plaid—that she might tug from her shoulder and use to entrap Ellyn's blade, or to cosset her left arm against Ellyn's cuts, whilst Ellyn wore only a shirt and breeches. And Rytha was a grown woman, Ellyn only a girl—as tall, but slighter, lacking Rytha's weight, and perhaps her strength. But it was too late to argue such matters as they circled and snarled and came together.

I felt Shara's hand close on my arm, and heard Mattich grunt, as the blades flashed and crashed in the warm sunlight.

I saw Ellyn's knife cut Rytha's plaid, and Rytha's dart at Ellyn's belly in a slashing cut. Ellyn sprang back, belly sucked in so that the probing blade missed by a whisker. Her own slashed at Rytha's face, and had the woman not been so quick, she'd have lost her upper lip. But, like Eryk, she was fast for all her gained weight—and took her face away even as she sought to hack at Ellyn's underarm. Ellyn was no slower; she made me proud as she avoided the cut and came under it to carve a fraying line across Rytha's skirt. There was no blood shed—not yet—but Rytha gasped and lurched back, clearly surprised by Ellyn's skill.

They feinted awhile longer, testing one another, and then Rytha danced forward with her colors swirling at Ellyn's face. And Ellyn raised an arm to deflect the obscuring plaid and drove her blade at Rytha's armpit. It would have been a crippling blow had it landed, but Rytha laughed and swung her arm around so that the long swath of cloth wrapped around Ellyn's head, blinding her, and drove her knife at Ellyn's ribs. I heard myself gasp as Ellyn fell away, tumbling clear of the swung cloth, a thin line of darkness that I knew was blood showing on her shirt. She let herself fall—as I'd shown her—and rolled, coming to her feet before Rytha had chance to stick her or cut her further.

Rytha almost fell over in her eagerness to end the fight, and as she regained her balance, Ellyn brought her blade across in a wide swing that slashed her opponent's shirt from breast to breast.

Rytha screamed as her shirt fell open to expose two large and bloodied breasts. Ellyn turned her arm and slashed again, and Rytha squealed like a pig at gelding and staggered back. Ellyn came on remorseless, stepping on the trailing plaid so that it was tugged from Rytha's hand and all

the Agador woman could do was retreat in pained panic
from the dancing steel.

Rytha blocked more cuts, desperately, sparks flying
from the blades, and moved back around the unretreating
circle. Neither the Devyn or the Agador allowed her exit,
and Ellyn granted her no respite. The blades clattered and
flashed and sparked, and through my pride in how well I had
taught Ellyn, I felt a horrid distaste. I could not bring myself
to harm a woman, but it seemed I had created a woman who
could, without compunction. I wondered if that was male
pride, or perhaps fear, and watched in trepidation and anticipation of the future.

Which came soon enough, and gave me answers.

Rytha pretended a fall that should have brought Ellyn
onto her blade. But Ellyn stood clear and allowed Rytha to
regain her feet—almost, had she not brought her blade
across the older woman's face as Rytha darted a stab at her
belly. Rytha screamed again as her cheeks and nose were
scored, curtaining her jaw with crimson, and lunged forward, seeking to plant her blade in Ellyn's thigh.

Ellyn pivoted clear, letting the knife go past her as she
kicked Rytha's legs away and sliced her knife down the
Agador woman's back. I saw a long line of crimson slashed
down Rytha's spine, and the tattered remnants of her shirt
fall away, so that she rose naked from the waist up. I felt
sorry for her, and grateful to Ellyn that she ended it quickly.

She hacked Rytha once more across the face, and then
as the woman sought to close and put a blade into her gut,
stepped sideways and tripped Rytha again and brought up
her blade so that it pierced Rytha's mouth.

I heard teeth shatter as Ellyn turned the blade, and saw
blood flood over her hand. Then I saw her snatch it clear and,
as Rytha fell, gagging out a strangled scream, take up the
long hair and yank the head back and cut through the throat.

Rytha fell down in a widening pool of gore that spread
over the warm summer grass and was soon surrounded by flies.
Ellyn flung her knife away and fell to her knees, vomiting.

As I went to her, I heard Mattich shout, "So it's decided, no? Fair fight again, and Ellyn won. Clan law prevails! Ellyn of Chaldor has defeated Rytha of the Agador in single combat."

I was aware of shouting. Mostly, I was aware of Ellyn shuddering in my arms, and the rank odors of spilled blood and vomit. I held her close as she emptied her stomach. Then she wiped her mouth and looked up at me.

"Have we won? I did not think it would be this hard."

I was unsure whether she spoke of clan loyalty or her personal triumph, but I heard swords clattering on shields, and discerned the content. I said, "Yes, I think we've won. And yes—it's always this hard. Until you get used to it."

"I'd not," she mumbled, sleeving her mouth. "I'd not get used to this."

"There'll be worse," I said, "when we take the clans against Talan."

She clung to me and I stroked her hair. "I'd not go through that again, Gailard. The gods know, but it . . ." She chuckled sourly. "It makes me sick. I'd sooner use what magic I have—that seems . . ." She doubled over, more spillage flooding from her gasping mouth.

"Cleaner?" Shara came to us, a water flask and a cloth in her hands. "Magic is easy, have you the talent—you can strike folk down without the need to see their eyes as they die. You can summon lightning to slay them and never need look at what you've done. But this . . ." She gestured at Rytha's body and wiped Ellyn clean, pressed the flask to her lips. "This is a little example of warfare. This is what ordinary folk do. Soldiers like Gailard, who serve folk like you."

Ellyn spat water and reached for the flask. "I'm not Vachyn," she said. "I'd not ask a soldier to do what I'd not."

"No," Shara allowed. "I think you learn."

Ellyn nodded; and all around us the two clans hailed us, and I knew that we'd gained the beginning of our army.

CHAPTER TWENTY-EIGHT

Warm summer light spilled through the windows of Chorym's palace, emphasizing the stark messages contained in the despatches Talan studied. He scattered them with a petulant hand, sending them drifting like autumn's leaves to the floor. He scowled and drained a glass of wine and stood up, running hands through his long, oiled hair as he glared around the chamber.

"So there's a pirate navy come from Hel's Town and none of our boats can cross the river! Our ports are blockaded—in Danant and Chaldor, both—and I cannot return home save at risk of my life. How do you explain this?"

Egor Dival said, "We knew they'd fight. This must be the remnants of Andur's fleet."

"The *remnants*?" Talan's scowl grew deeper. "The gods know, they appear to have more boats than we. They blockade us and deny us trade. They seal us here—is that only *remnants*? It seems to me that Hel's Town takes sides in this affair."

Dival opened his mouth to speak, but Talan silenced him with a gesture, turning angry eyes on Nestor as he continued his complaint. "And this has come about since you sent your assassins there. What happened? This idea of yours seems to have stirred a hornets' nest that threatens to sting us badly."

"I've had no word." Nestor raised placatory hands. "You must remember that politics and magic do not always sit easily together. But I can send more men."

"More?" Talan snorted dismissive laughter. "And shall they do better than the others—the ones you promised must end this threat?"

"I think that would be unwise," Dival said, before the Vachyn sorcerer could speak. "I think that those assassins were found, and recognized—and Mother Hel took offense."

"Mother Hel?" Talan pressed fisted hands against his brow. "Is Mother Hel so powerful that she'd fight *me*?"

"It would appear so," Dival said. "Those last despatches tell of more boats than have ever come down the river, and commanded by this Kerid. My information is that he was a commander in Andur's navy, and he would appear to be supported by the Hel's Town pirates."

"What do you say?" Talan demanded.

"That sides are taken that have never before been chosen." Dival favored Nestor with a smile that contained no humor. "I'd say that the assassins were found and put to the question—"

"They'd admit nothing," Nestor interrupted. "Even under torture, they'd not confess. I set such magicks on them as—"

"But the Mother would know!" Dival cut off the Vachyn in turn. "Men sent to slay one of her captains? Who'd want him dead, save us? He escorts Serian's trade and Naban's down the river—they've no argument; only us. So! Does it take a genius to assume that it was you sent the assassins? The Mother is never a fool, and she's doubtless guessed you sent the killers—and chosen to side with Kerid—which means with Chaldor."

Nestor scowled even darker than Talan. "Let me sail the river awhile," he asked, "and I'll scour it of these pirates."

Talan snatched up a missive. "Whilst the clans rise against us?" He waved the parchment in the sorcerer's face. "I should send you off to wander the Durrakym as the clans rise?"

"They shall be easy to handle," Nestor said confidently, and turned to Dival. "After all, we've won the Devyn and the Agador to our side, no?"

Talan crumpled the paper and flung it across the room. Dival said, "No. Rumor has it that Eryk is slain, and the Devyn, the Agador, and the Dur follow Ellyn—who'd unite with the Quan and the Arran, and bring all the clans against us." He smiled wickedly as he studied the Vachyn's surprised face. "Did you not know? Another design failed, eh?"

Nestor's scowl became a snarl.

"Your hunters failed to kill Ellyn," Dival said. "And your assassins failed to slay Kerid. Now we face attack from east and west, both. The Durrakym's blocked and the clans rise—what's your next plan?"

"Enough!" Talan clapped his hands. "We are in this together, no? So must I listen to you two bicker over who's right and who's wrong? Or shall you work together to keep me my kingdoms?"

"I think that might be hard," Dival said, "for we're now pressed like melting metal betwixt the anvil and the hammer. Look." He rose, taking up a map that he spread across the table. "We hold Chorym, and it should be hard to take this place, save with the aid of magic. But if the Vachyn's hunters were slain, then perhaps there *is* magic coming against us. Meanwhile, the river is denied us, and the clans rise against us, and we are trapped betwixt the fire and a hard place."

"So what do I do?" Talan emptied the wine flask into his cup and drained the glass in a long, desperate gulp.

Nestor said, "I can create more hunters."

Dival said, "And send them out to find Ellyn? As successfully as the last? Save she uses magic you cannot find her; isn't that what you said? The trail's cold." He looked to Talan. "Reinforce the border. Send more men to the Geffyn Pass; we can hold the clans there. Meanwhile, send others to the coast to hold the ports. Bring in our warboats to fight the Hel's Town pirates. Even send the Vachyn to open a way across the river. But you must stay! You cannot flee."

"Why not?" Talan asked. "Can Nestor open me a way across the Durrakym, why should I not go home?"

Dival sighed. "Because that shall brand you a coward, and your army shall see you run away. Do you want to give up Chaldor? After all we fought for, shall you relinquish what we've conquered?"

Nestor said, "Let me go to the Geffyn. I can halt the clans, just as we halted Andur."

Talan asked, "And where shall I be the while?"

"Here in Chorym," said Dival, "where you belong, do you wish to hold Chaldor. Leave this place, and you'll have nothing. Flee, and likely the army will flee with you. Why not, if the men see you run?"

Talan turned away, that neither of them see his eyes. He wanted nothing so much as to be safe—which meant a return to his palace in Danant—but he also wanted Chaldor. To be lord of both lands—the gods knew, but that was everything Nestor had promised him when first he'd listened to the Vachyn, and agreed to pay sacks of gold for the sorcerer's services. Danant and Chaldor, both, Nestor had promised. And then the Highlands. And beyond to . . . the dreams were endless when Nestor spun them out. To conquer Naban and Serian, to create an empire greater than any the world had seen. To conquer one land that he have more gold to buy more Vachyn, who'd help him own both sides of the river, from north to south, from its beginning to its ending. Perhaps even to own the ocean coast. To become even greater than the Sea Kings . . .

Fine dreams, now spoiled by fear that some upstart girl denied him.

He turned to face them, sorrowed by his fate. "I shall remain here, then," he said, and looked to Nestor. "And you shall remain with me."

Egor Dival said, "The sorcerer might be better employed elsewhere."

Talan contemplated invasion, the Highland clans striking against Chorym, a Hel's Town navy sailing down the Durrakym, and shook his head. "No! Nestor shall stay with me. Deploy your men as you see fit. But hold me this land!"

"I'll do my best," Dival promised.

Kerid laughed as the catapults sent fire spraying over the Danant boat. He saw the sails take flame and more spread down the mast to wander across the deck. Men sprang overboard and were mashed down under the *Andur*'s sweeps as he closed on the stricken vessel. More still fell beneath the fire of the *Ryadne* as Nassim brought his boat along the farther side. Then both crews were leaping across, swinging up the lines to clamber onto the deck and strike down the few Danant men who looked to oppose them. Kerid knocked aside a swinging cutlass and slashed his blade across the man's belly, kicking him away as he strode to the forecastle, where the captain faced him with a drawn sword and a frightened expression.

"I am Kerid of Chaldor. Do you surrender?"

For a Danant bastard, the man had honor; he shook his head and shouted, "I am Liam, and I serve Talan of Danant, and you'll kill me before I give you my boat."

"So be it." Kerid raised his blade and thrust it at Liam's face.

Liam sprang back, and found his retreat blocked by Nassim, who drove a sword into his back, and kicked him away so that he fell down surprised, staring at Kerid.

Who said, "That was not very honorable."

Nassim shrugged and spat liquid tobacco over Liam's bleeding body. "Neither were those assassins. We fight a war, and we face Vachyn magic, and we shall win it or lose it as the gods decide. But I'm in it to win."

Kerid nodded. "Then best get this hulk doused and towed away."

He watched as Nassim shouted orders and men set to quenching the flames, lines thrown over from the Chaldor boats that they might tow the captured craft to Gessyng and sink her there, along with the others they'd captured, and seal another harbor.

There were none ashore could deny them, and they sank the vessel across the harbor's mouth—her and seven other smoldering Danant boats—and sailed away, back across the Durrakym. For good measure, and the pleasure of it, Kerid sent a few balls of fire raining onto the wharf—to remind the people of Danant that Chaldor was not defeated.

They owned the river now, and Kerid felt it a heady sensation. Danant's ports were sealed—blocked by sunk craft or denied access by the warboats of Hel's Town—and it could surely be only a matter of time before Talan was beaten and delivered his just reward . . .

. . . Save it was as the Mother had said—that this war would be won on land, and for that there must be an army on the land to match what he put on the river. He had his navy, but he did not know if there was any landward force to match. He did not know if Gailard lived, or Ellyn. There was no word save the rumors, and rumors ran abroad like gossip in a dockside tavern. Kerid wondered which to believe. He found it hard to accept what he heard about Gailard, for he could not believe the man was a coward who ran from the Darrach Pass to seek refuge in the Highlands.

But save an army came from there—and Kerid could not envisage any other force opposing Talan—he doubted, for all his triumph on the Durrakym, that Talan might be defeated. Andur's army was scattered in disarray, and no sound landward soldiers were likely to rise and face the invaders save out of the Highlands.

He drank a glass of wine and stared at Nassim.

"What's wrong?" The swarthy man dug a fingernail between his teeth, extracting shreds of tobbaco that he flicked away over the cabin's floor. The *Andur* rocked gently on the current, and through the opened portholes came the triumphant shouting of the victorious crew. "We just won another fight, no? But you look gloomy as if we'd lost."

"The rumors," Kerid said, toeing a spittoon toward his friend and fellow captain, hoping Nassim would use the receptacle. "What if Gailard and Ellyn are dead, and there's no land army to support us? What then?"

"I say we go on fighting," Nassim declared, "until we know one way or the other."

"And if the gloomy prognostications are true?" Kerid asked.

Nassim chuckled again. "Why, then we've a navy still, and we own the river. Mother Hel stands with us, so we can become Hel's Town pirates. Or sail south." His grin became speculative. "That should be an adventure, no? We could take our fleet to the coast. I've never seen the coast."

"No man I know has seen the coast," Kerid muttered. "And the Durrakym's enough water for me."

"We might have to run," Nassim said, no longer laughing. "If Talan wins . . ."

"He'll send all his force against Hel's Town." Kerid reached across the table, filling their cups. "And I could not desert the Mother. I owe her too much."

"No," Nassim agreed, "so we've no choice—we fight until we win or lose."

Kerid nodded.

"One thing," Nassim asked. "What *is* her real name?"

Kerid looked confused. "I don't know," he said. "She's never told me."

Nassim began to chuckle again, and after a moment Kerid joined him.

Ellyn dipped the cloth in the stream and scrubbed furiously at her soiled shirt, her face flushed with embarrassment and disgust. Rytha's blood and her own vomit stained the garment, and she doubted it would ever be clean. Had she another in her saddlebags, she'd have changed, but all her gear was left in the Dur camp, and that was a day's ride distant. She felt the water against her skin and it reminded her of Rytha's blood spilling out—which induced fresh nausea, so that she tossed the cloth away and doubled over, clutching at her belly.

A hand settled on her shoulder and she turned to find Gailard crouched beside her.

"You get used to it," he said.

"Do you?" She heard her voice come out harsh. "Can you?"

"Yes." He nodded solemnly. "The first time is always the worst. After that . . ."

"It gets easier?"

He nodded again, and she said, "I don't want it to get easier. I hope I never again need kill anyone, ever!"

"Then give up your claim." He took the cloth from her hands and soaked it in fresh water, and wiped her face gently. "Leave Talan in Chorym. Let him have Chaldor, and live with the clans. Or go back to Shara's broch."

"I can't," she said. "That would be . . ."

"A betrayal?"

"Yes! Shall my parents have died for nothing? Shall the Vachyn make another puppet king?"

"Then you've no choice, save to do what you must."

"But it's hard," she said. "I didn't realize it should be so hard."

"Clans and kingdoms are not won by soft people," he said.

"My father was gentle." She looked into his eyes, seeking confirmation.

"Andur was a fine man," he said, "and a fine soldier. He was gentle when the circumstances allowed, but in battle . . ." He smiled fondly, memories in his eyes. "In battle he was the bravest I've seen. He knew when he must be strong.

The gods know, but had he not taken the rear guard, I'd be dead now."

"He was a man," she said.

"And you are a queen," he answered. "Or shall be, have you the courage."

"I'd thought . . ." she hesitated, frowning, gathering confused and tumultous thoughts. "I saw Rytha attack you and I thought it should be easy to kill her."

"You had to," he said. "And I could not. Had she lived, the Agador would not be with us. And are the Agador not with us, then perhaps the Quan and the Arran should not join us, and we would have no army to bring against Talan. You had no choice."

"Shall we truly raise an army?" she asked.

"I think the Arran will accept you," he said. "And then the Quan shall be faced with too great a force to dispute. Save . . ." He shrugged.

"Save what?"

"It might be necessary to fight again. But then . . ." He chuckled. "We shall see fighting enough in the days to come."

"I'd see no more than we must," she said. And was surprised by his approving laughter, the clutch of his hand on her shoulder.

"Spoken like your father!"

"He'd have said that?"

Gailard nodded. "Andur fought only when he must. Not to conquer, not to achieve ambition—not like Talan—but only when he had no other option. As you did, with Rytha."

Ellyn sighed and lowered her head, leaning a moment against his chest. "I once thought you no more than a . . ." She broke off, her cheeks red.

"A common hire-sword?"

"Yes. But you're more than that. You're wise."

He laughed loud. "I'm a soldier, no more than that. Now shall we go on?" He rose to his feet, standing tall above her, his eyes suddenly grim. "The Devyn shall bury

Eryk this night, and the Agador Rytha. And we must bring the Dur to them and bond them to us."

Ellyn wet her face and rose. "And you shall be proclaimed clan chieftain of the Devyn."

"I suppose so," he said.

"But who shall command the Agador?"

"I don't know." He stooped, taking up a twig that he tossed into the stream, watching it float away. "No woman has ever claimed the chieftainship, but you slew Rytha, so . . ." He shrugged. "I don't know. Perhaps they'll acknowledge you. Or . . ." he began to chuckle. "Perhaps I'll find myself lord of two clans. The gods move in mysterious ways, no? A common hire-sword commanding two clans?"

Ellyn hesitated a moment, then began to smile. "A most uncommon hire-sword," she said, "who shall be commander of all Chaldor's forces do we win."

"In that case" Gailard returned her, "I suppose I shall have to learn manners."

Ellyn began to laugh, and they went to join the others.

CHAPTER TWENTY-NINE

We gathered in the Devyn and the Agador after Eryk and Rytha were buried. Some families quit our cause, preferring to follow their own paths, and we let them go without hindrance.

Shara put it the neatest. "We face a war," she said, "and we want only those firm to our purpose. Any who doubt our cause should go."

"And not," Ellyn added with an authority that belied her years, "come seeking our favors after we've won."

I was by no means sure we could win, but we were committed now, and gathering an army of Highlanders that I believed *might* win—could we bring in the Arran and the Quan. We sat in Eryk's broch, which I now supposed was mine. It was built up from what I recalled of my father's— fresh walls and larger outbuildings, a floor added to the central tower. The gods knew but it took me by surprise when we came back to the joined camp and I heard myself hailed chieftain of the Devyn. And I could make little sense of the Agador's allegiance, for I was not certain whether that was to me or to Ellyn, and I do not think the clan itself was sure.

Eryk and Rytha had broken all precedence with their bonding, and now I had slain Eryk, and Ellyn had slain Rytha, and none seemed sure whether I or she led the Agador.

Some assumed we were wed; others were swayed by Shara's presence, for they had heard the stories of the sorceress who dwelled in the Styge, and her presence alone drew many to our support. Also, there were no few who had followed Eryk and his ambitious wife solely out of clan loyalty and welcomed their deaths. More resented Talan's intrusion; others looked joyously toward an invasion of the Lowlands. I chose to ignore the doubts and the questions and accept the clan's allegiance; I needed an army, was I to restore Ellyn to her rightful throne.

"What do you see?" I asked Clayre. "How shall we fare?"

Mattich's wife shrugged and smiled warily. "I see battle," she said. "I see the world changing, but I cannot tell you the outcome."

"But you've the dreaming talent," I said.

And she smiled again and answered me, "We dreamers see only little bits and pieces of the future, Gailard; not the whole of it. And there's such a turning of the world involved here that my dreams are like storm-tossed clouds—changing all the while."

I looked to Shara, who shrugged and said, "We've no choice but to go on, eh?"

Briefly, I wondered what use it was to have sorcerers and dreamers on your side if they could not offer better advice. I said, "On the morrow we send messengers to the Arran and the Quan."

"The Arran will join us," Mattich said. "But the Quan . . . ?"

I thought a moment. "Do they not join us . . ." I looked around the circle of faces seated at Eryk's—now my—table. "We cannot afford to leave them behind us."

"What do you say?" Ellyn asked.

"That we cannot leave enemies at our back," I said bluntly. "We must take the clans down through the Geffyn Pass, and save Talan be a complete fool, he shall send his army there to halt us."

"How he shall know we're coming?" she wondered.

"He's sent ambassadors to the Highlands," I replied, wondering how she could fail to see the danger, "and doubtless he's spies. So he'll know something of what transpires here. I think he'll at least suspect a clan invasion, and were I in his shoes, I'd look to block it at the Geffyn."

"He could hold us there," Mattich said. "And are the Quan hostile, and at our backs . . ."

"Does he send his Vachyn," Clayre said, "he could defeat us there."

"We've our own magicians," I said, glancing at Shara and Ellyn.

Mattich said, "Even so. But the clans would sooner . . ." He shrugged an apology.

"I know," I said, understanding, and giving my own apologetic smile to the two talented women. "And I'd sooner fight honestly. But does Talan employ sorcery, what are we to do? Concede him the victory? I think we must fight fire with fire."

Shara said, "We'll use no magicks save you ask us."

"Or we deem it necessary," Ellyn said.

I stared at her and said, "By your promise, eh? Only by Shara's permission. Remember the last time . . ."

"Yes!" Her pretty face creased into a scowl I remembered. "As you will. But if I see . . ."

"Only by Shara's permission!"

She agreed, albeit reluctantly.

"You'll need all your strength when we face Chorym's walls," Shara said, "for I think we'll find Nestor there, and he shall be a hard foe. Hold yourself for him, and leave the rest to your guardian."

Ellyn nodded.

We met Jaime, who led the Arran, the next day. He was a small man, thin and wiry, with hair grey as Mattich's, and deep scars across his face. He would have been ugly, save for his smile, which split his face in two as we outlined our plan.

"The gods know," he said, "but I sent those Danant ambassadors back to their master with their tails between their legs. Swear fealty to Talan?" He spat a mouthful of good brose over the grass in emphasis. "I'd as soon swear fealty to the dark forces—which, by the way, I think Talan and his Vachyn represent. No, I'm with you. Save"—he looked to Ellyn—"you've similar plans."

"I'd have you as my friend," she said. "Not own you, but work with you."

He looked to me. "And you, Gailard? Are you truly leader of the Devyn or her puppet?"

"I'm her guardian," I said. "Andur and Ryadne set that geas on me."

"You went away," he said.

"I had no choice." I shrugged. "I'd not wed Rytha."

"A wise choice." Jaime began to laugh. "Who'd wed that bitch?" Then his laughter faded and he turned wondering eyes on me. "But after we've driven Talan back to Danant, what then? Shall you be her guardian still, and she look to drive Chaldor's domain into the Highlands?"

Ellyn said, "We can sign treaties."

"I can't write," Jaime said.

I said, "Her word is good."

"And yours." He stared me in the eye. "Do you trust her?"

I ducked my head.

He looked to Mattich, who also nodded.

"Then that's enough for me." He spat on his palm and extended his hand toward Ellyn. "The Arran fight with you, Queen of Chaldor. Until your throne is reclaimed or you betray us."

"I'll not," Ellyn said, and spat on her own palm and took his hand.

Four clans now! By all the gods, but it looked as if we

might succeed. Save at the back of my mind was the sure
knowledge that as we negotiated and won our allies, Talan
must be readying for war. I'd not delay, but strike fast—
which meant bringing the Quan into our alliance.

"What's in it for me?" Hain demanded. "For my clan? Talan offers us trade, and his army to support us, do we side
with him."

"You'd be Danant's puppet?" I asked. "You'd bow your
knee to Danant and jump to Talan's summons?"

Hain scowled. "I'd be on the winning side," he said.
"Not join some futile war. Talan would leave us alone."

I snorted laughter at his foolishness. I studied him
and saw a lazy man, going to fat like Eryk. Not much
older than I—surely grey in his hair, but few battle scars.
He had oddly pale eyes that seemed not to fix for long on
any of us, but shift and dart as if looking for advantages
or weaknesses. I could not like him—but I needed him. Or
his clan.

I was about to speak, but Shara overrode me. "Talan
would not leave you alone," she said, "for he's in Nestor's
pocket, and do you bow to Talan's will, then you climb into
that Vachyn pouch."

Hain sipped brose as he studied her. He seemed to me
like a dog wondering which master to follow. "But you are
Vachyn, no?" he said.

"I was born Vachyn," she answered, "but I quit that clan
when I knew what it would do."

"Which is?" Hain asked.

"Rule all the world," Shara replied. "Sit behind thrones
and whisper, so that kings and queens, emperors and
satraps hear only what the Vachyn say, until all is ruled by
them."

"And should that be so bad a thing?" Hain asked. "I
might be a great chieftain. We all might be."

Mattich spat his disgust. "Would you be free, like a true
Highlander? Or would you bend to the Vachyn's will?"

"You ask me to side with this would-be heir of Chaldor," Hain returned. "Is that so different?"

"To the Vachyn and Talan, yes!" Mattich shouted. "And do you refuse to join us, what think you shall happen? By all the gods, man, we'll fight you and destroy your clan. It's as Gailard says—we cannot leave enemies at our rear."

"So, that's it, eh?" Hain turned his pale eyes on me. "I swear allegiance or I am destroyed. Is that a better choice than Talan offers me?"

"Your choice," I said, hating him, "is between honor and its absence."

"And do I refuse to join you?" he asked.

"We'll slay you," Mattich said.

I set a hand on his arm. "No, we'll not destroy you." I looked Hain straight in his pale eyes. "But we shall drive you away, for we cannot have friends of Talan at our back. And do we win, then the Quan shall be outlawed, and be no friends of Chaldor, or of any other clan."

"You leave me scant choice," Hain said sullenly.

"There's another," Mattich declared before anyone could speak. "Single combat."

"No!" I gripped Mattich's arm harder. "That would make for a blood feud, and we look to make a lasting peace."

Hain glared at the Dur chieftain, a hand clasped ready on his belt knife. Mattich met his glower, one hand on his own knife. I feared all our alliance might fall down in feuding, and Talan send his forces to the Geffyn Pass without opposition. He would come through as the clans fought, and conquer us all in our disarray.

Then Shara spoke.

"I am not of the clans," she said. "I am not a Highlander, and my only allegiance is to the defeat of the Vachyn. I'd see the clans joined to defeat Talan and the ambitions Nestor offers him, to which end I can see no recourse save we set Ellyn safe on Chaldor's throne."

"So?" Hain demanded.

"Fight me," she said. "Do you defeat me, then you take your clan where you will, and none shall oppose you."

Hain stared at her as if she were mad. "And do you win?" He chuckled, clearly doubting that outcome.

"Then you swear fealty to our purpose," she answered.

"Save one of these shall forget that promise." Hain stared around the circle of watching, startled faces. "And put a blade in me after I've slain you."

"No." Shara shook her head. "For these are honorable folk."

"And you're a Vachyn," he said, "and can use magic."

"I'll not," she promised. "Do you defeat me, none shall halt you or oppose you." She looked at us all. "Shall you swear by that?"

I did not like to do it, for I felt that any man who hurt Shara must answer to me, else I not be able to bear her death, but I ducked my head and made the promise. Then heard Ellyn and Mattich do the same.

"Even so," Hain said, "I must think on this. I do not fight women."

"You'd see women slain by Talan," Shara said.

Hain shook his balding head. "That's different."

"How so?"

"Women do not fight in single combat." Hain looked awhile around the circle of our waiting faces. "Single combat is for men."

"Then fight me," I said.

"Or me," said Mattich.

Hain shrugged. "I must think on this. I shall go away and consider what you have suggested. I shall deliver my answer in a few days."

We watched him depart disgruntled and I turned to Shara. "Are you mad?" I asked her.

"We need him," she said. "And he needed to be pushed to decision. Let him sleep on it, and see what happens."

It happened that night, and it earned Hain no respect.

I could not imagine what he thought to gain by it, for it was without honor, or much hope of success, and all I could think was that he had been tainted by contact with Talan and the Vachyn sorcerer. Surely, it was not a thing any Highlander—save perhaps Eryk—would have attempted.

Hain had come to parley and ridden away under banners of truce. By all customs we were at peace, and had he elected to ignore our offer of alliance, or chosen to go to war with us, then still he should have sent word to that effect.

Instead, he attacked by night.

It was an insane attempt. The Devyn, the Dur, and the Agador were camped together, the Arran settled only a little way off, and the Quan was not so great a clan that it might hope to defeat us all. I wondered, after, if it was Hain's intention to slay the leaders and steal Ellyn away—a gift to Talan.

And he had seemingly forgotten the Dur talent for foreseeing.

We had set guards, for none of us entirely trusted Hain; but even so we none of us could truly believe he'd take such a chance. I settled to sleep with my head pleasantly abuzz with the aftereffects of the brose.

And woke to Mattich's booming voice.

"Gird up, Gailard! We're under attack!"

I rose, snatching up my sword and shield, and came out from the tent. Mattich laughed. He was full-dressed, kitted for battle, and I was naked save for my undergarments.

"So eager, eh?" He poked his blade in the direction of my groin. "Or do you boast?"

I squinted at him, torn between irritation and concern.

"Clayre dreamed it," he said, serious now. "Hain brings the Quan against us."

"He's mad," I said.

"Likely. But even so." Mattich shrugged, then chuck-led. "Shall you face them like that, or dress for battle?"

I grunted irritably and ducked back inside the tent, hur-riedly donning my gear.

We were encamped in a wide valley cut through with a broad stream that ran deep at its center, the banks to either side steep and undercut. A wide swath of timber spread along the eastern side, and Hain no doubt thought that would conceal his stealthy approach.

He should have remembered the Dur's talent, for we were in position on the west bank as he brought his warriors out from the trees. We stood afoot, our horses held back and bowmen to the fore. It was a dark night, with clouds blown up from the south, bringing a hint of rain and obscuring the moon and stars. We waited kneeling, hidden by thickets of gorse and heather. The Quan scouts emerged from the tim-ber and saw no opposition. They hooted, and the full force came down to the water.

By some unspoken consensus, I found myself in com-mand. I waited until all the riders were in the stream, then rose to my feet and shouted.

Suddenly the night was filled with arrow-song, and be-neath the clouds' overcast there spread a darker shadow as the barbed war-shafts lofted and fell.

The Quan toppled screaming from their horses; horses shrieked and bucked as they were pricked. I called for an-other volley, then led the charge into the stream. From far-ther along the valley came riders—Devyn and Agador, galloping to cut off the Quan's retreat.

Hain was unseated, his mount screaming and kicking as he sought the saddle. He wore full battle kit, his eyes glow-ering furiously through the helm's slits. He swung his blade at me and I took it on my buckler, smashing him back against his prancing, panicked mount. The horse swung round, kicking, and Hain was flung away. He stumbled, flail-ing wildly, and splashed onto his back. As he fell I hacked down against his head. Then I broke his shield arm and set a foot against his sword arm, and knelt astride his chest, holding him down, under the water.

He struggled awhile, but my first blow had stunned him, and he was no hard opponent. I watched bubbles burst from his mouth and then slow, and then felt him still, and saw the bubbles cease. I rose, dragging him up.

"Hain's dead!" I roared. "Shall the Quan surrender now? Or shall they die?"

In the hubbub no one at first heard me. I shouted again, and around me men stared, lowering their blades. Jaime came to me and helped me lift the body higher, adding his voice to mine.

"Hain's dead. Killed in fair fight. Surrender or die!"

The clamor eased, individual combats ending as our shouts were heard, and then ceased altogether. The Quan began to lay down their swords. Mattich came splashing up the stream, trailing his blade to wash off the blood, adding his voice to ours.

I cried out, "Do we speak of peace now?"

There was a murmur of agreement, and a young man waded toward me. He was dressed in fine armor, and beneath his half helm, I saw that he bore Hain's features. He carried his sword in his left hand, beneath his buckler: indication of surrender.

"I am Roark," he said. "Hain's son. You have beaten us, and I acknowledge our defeat." He offered me his sword. "Slay only me, eh? But let the clan go."

"Why should I slay you?" I asked.

"Because I fought you," he said. "And because I am my father's son."

"Do you share your father's intentions?" I asked him. "Must I fight you, too?"

"I don't understand." He unlatched his helm and stared at me. He looked confused. "My father would have slain you and taken Ellyn to Talan. I fought beside him, so I am no less guilty."

"What *would* you have done?" I asked. "Had you not followed your father?"

He hesitated awhile, then shrugged and said, "I'd fight with you, against the Danant."

"But I slew your father," I said.

He looked at me. He was a handsome youngster, about Ellyn's age I thought, with none of his dead father's fat, nor those shifting eyes. He seemed to me honest, and genuinely regretful.

"Must I," he said, "I'll face you in single combat."

"But?"

"I do not think I could defeat you. I think you should slay me, and claim the Quan for your own."

"And so bind them to our cause."

He nodded. "Then I must fight you?"

I said, "No."

He stared at me. "What then?"

"Swear fealty to Ellyn of Chaldor," I said. "Join this alliance, so that all the clans fight our true enemy—all of us, together."

He watched me awhile longer, then ducked his head and offered me his sword and shield. I saw that his blade was bloodied and his buckler dented: he had fought.

"I swear that the Quan are with you, Gailard. I shall follow you, and my clan with me. You command us now."

I said, "No. You are chieftain of the Quan still, and you follow Ellyn, not me."

"As you wish." He knelt. I feared he'd drown like his father, and took his shoulders, lifting him.

"Stand up." I put an arm around his shoulders and raised my sword, and shouted, "The Quan are with us now!"

There was a great uproar then, swords rattling against shields and men shouting. Warriors who had not long ago traded blows and sought to slay one another embracing. I suppose that we Highlanders are sometimes emotional, and our ways are both quicker and slower than those of other lands. But I knew that Roark was with me, because he had pledged his blade, and I could trust him.

I held him to me, Mattich and Jaime with me, and shouted, "Now the clans are one, and we go to Chaldor!"

There was a great bellowing at that, and I heard men roar my name as if I led them all, as if I were lord of all the Highlands. I felt proud, and embarrassed, and shouted Ellyn's name, gesturing that Mattich and the other chieftains join me, and after a while I heard her name taken up until the valley rang with it, and I knew they'd follow her. Perhaps only because I was with her—but still they'd follow because they were pledged now, by word and blood, and I knew we had the army we needed to overthrow Talan and take Chorym back. It would not be easy, for even with five clans at our command we were still outnumbered. But Talan's forces must be spread across all Chaldor, whilst we were massed in a single force that I planned to bring against Chorym in a preemptive attack. All hinged on that, but I knew now that I could avenge Andur and give Ellyn her rightful throne.

I raised my blade high and bellowed with the rest.

CHAPTER THIRTY

Neither Ellyn nor Shara had taken part in the skirmish. Shara had persuaded her pupil that it were better they leave this fight to the warriors, that there be no possibility of any accusing them of using magic, lest the hoped-for victory be later questioned. They waited nervously until riders came ahead of the main force and the two women went to meet the victors as they returned, both their faces alight with joy that they were safe and the battle won.

"Shall Roark hold to his promise?" Ellyn asked Gailard as they sat celebrating. "Or shall he take the Quan away?"

"He'll hold," Gailard answered. "He gave me his word."

"And you trust him?" She sipped her brose thoughtfully—the gods knew, but she'd found a taste for the liquor—and fixed her guardian with an inquiring stare. "After all, you slew his father."

"He gave his word," Gailard repeated.

"But you slew his *father*," she repeated. "How can he forgive that, or forget it?"

"He's now chieftain of the Quan," Gailard said, and chuckled (perhaps cynically), "and that likely assuages his hurt. But—more important!—he knows I slew his father in fair fight, and by Highlander custom that denies him any right to vengeance or blood feud. And he acknowledged that—and swore to support your claim. I trust his word."

She frowned as he smiled fondly, knowing she had things to learn about the Highlanders. They were both a little drunk on the brose and victory and thoughts of what was surely to come. "And I trust you," she said, "for you're my champion and my guardian." Then frowned anew and said, "What if you're wrong? What if he takes the Quan to Talan, or away into the Highlands?"

"He won't," Gailard said. "Wait and see."

And sure enough, as they traveled westward, Ellyn's head aching from the celebrations, Roark brought the Quan to meet them.

They moved in a great mass now, as if, Gailard told her, in the days of old when the clans came raiding into Chaldor, joining to attack the rich valley lands. In time many would turn back, leaving only the warriors to proceed, but for now women and old men and children came with them, baggage stowed on the sturdy little Highland horses that seemed like ponies beside the mounts Ellyn and Shara and Gailard rode, and the Quan stood across their path.

The scouts had brought word of course, but that was only of a Quan camp where fires burned peacefully and meat roasted as if they readied for a feast—which is exactly what they did. Roark came to meet them, flanked by only two warriors, and none armored, bearing only those weapons every clansman carries out of habit.

He held the peace pole himself, a length of pine wrapped round with white cloth and tufted at its top with white goose feathers. He halted his horse as they approached and bowed from his saddle.

"Well met, Gailard."

"Well met, Roark."

Ellyn saw his eyes shift from her guardian to herself and Shara. Saw them hesitate a moment on Shara and then fix on her, and widen. She gasped involuntarily, amazed at

what that look made her feel. She had thought Gailard
handsome—in a rough way—and felt those confused emotions, unsure whether she loved him or merely depended
on him. But Roark . . . there was something magical in
that look.

"He's beautiful," she murmured, unthinking. Then
blushed as Gailard chuckled and Shara favored her with a
quizzical glance.

And before she had time to gather herself, Roark was
down from his saddle and kneeling before her.

He offered his sword and shield, and said, "Queen of
Chaldor, I pledge you my loyalty and the loyalty of my clan.
The Quan shall follow you to Chorym's walls, and can we
not give you back your rightful throne, then I shall fight unto
my death in that purpose."

Ellyn licked her lips, and felt her cheeks grow warm,
and wondered if her companions saw it. She slid gracefully
from her saddle and set a hand on Roark's proffered shield.
He stared at her across the scarred surface of the buckler,
and for a moment she was tempted to giggle—his gaze reminded her of an adoring dog. Then Gailard cleared his
throat and she realized she stared back, no less entranced.

"I accept your pledge and thank you for it," she said. "I
am glad you are with us, and when we have taken back
Chorym from the invaders I shall feast you."

She was not entirely sure what went on between them.
Only that her knees felt weak and her heart seemed to beat
too fast beneath her ribs.

Shara eased her mount closer to Gailard's and whispered, "I
suspect there's more than pledges of loyalty here."

"What do you mean?" Gailard watched as Roark gazed
at Ellyn. He looked like some dog besotted with its master.
Surely his eyes were wide and somewhat glazed, and he
seemed suddenly at a loss for words. Gailard began to wonder if Roark's tongue should loll and he begin to pant, or roll
onto his back that Ellyn might tickle his belly.

"I think," Shara murmured, "that we see love blossoming."

"Ellyn and Roark?" Gailard shook his head.

"Why not?" she asked. "There are unlikelier matchings."

Gailard looked at her eyes, her face, and Shara saw that he knew it was so.

She heard Ellyn say, "You'd best stand up, no? The chieftain of the Quan should not kneel too long."

Roark stood, still staring at her. Then he smiled and ducked his head, "Shall I feast you first?" he asked. "I've readied for it."

"I should be grateful," Ellyn said.

She turned toward her bay. Roark went with her.

"Let me help you."

She needed no help. The gods knew, but she could ride well enough before she set out on this unlikely adventure, and Gailard had taught her better since. She could certainly mount a horse unaided. But she dimpled a smile and let Roark set her foot in the stirrup and lift her astride, and after she was mounted beamed her thanks.

"A love match, I suspect," Shara whispered.

Gailard nodded, obviously confused by the vagaries of women, or perhaps just by the thought of the war they must soon fight.

"So? Shall we go on?" he said.

Ellyn turned toward them as if his voice interrupted a dream. Roark looked startled—smiled and shrugged and blushed all at the same time—and sprang limber astride his mount. "I welcome you all as my guests," he cried. "Do you follow me?"

They ate well that night. There was fine venison roasting in the Quan camp, and good beef, and fresh-baked bread. Ale and brose were supplied in plenty, and sweet puddings of honey and oatmeal. All ate their fill, thinking that in the days to come there would be scarcer fare, and harder won. And all the time Ellyn and Roark gazed at one another, and

seemed like dumbstruck lovers touched by some godly finger that selected them from amongst all the folk they might
have known and picked them out to find each other. Shara
watched Gailard as Ellyn passed Roark food and he filled
her cup, and they exchanged soft words she could not hear
over the clamor, and wondered at his feelings.

Ellyn was his ward, his geas in human form. Was he
jealous, or only protective? Shara was at his side (careful of
what she drank, and both as close and as distant as those
vague promises she'd made him) but she knew that he must
first see Ellyn set safely on Chaldor's throne.

She watched as Mattich pounded Gailard's shoulder,
chortling.

"The gods know, Gailard, but there's a match, eh? Does
this go on, there'll be only one clan."

"What do you mean?" he asked, his voice thickened by
the brose.

"Think on it," Mattich said with drunken solemnity.
"Ryadne wedded Andur and bound the Dur to Chaldor.
Eryk wed Rytha and bonded the Devyn and the Agador. You
slew Eryk, and that little girl who stares so fondly into
Roark's eyes slew Rytha—the Devyn and the Agador are
thus bonded again—and the Arran are with us." He paused
to slap Jaime so hard on the shoulder that the Arran chieftain spilled brose over his breeches. "And now the Quan—
in a love match, it seems. Does this go on, there'll be only a
single clan—following Ellyn."

Then he fell over, tumbling against Gailard's shoulder
and sliding to the tent's floor. Clayre sighed and smiled, and
rose to lift her husband to his unsteady feet and called for
help to take him away to their tent.

Which left a gap between Gailard and Shara.

He looked at her and she knew he wanted her. She
smiled at him and said, "Shall we find our beds?"

"Yours?" He took her hand. "Or mine?"

"*Ours,*" she replied.

He looked drunkenly at Ellyn and Roark. "Why not together?"

"Not yet," she answered.

"Then when?" he asked. "The gods know, but I want you."

She studied his face, aware that he spoke only the truth—for both of them. But no less aware that did she submit to her own feelings it could only complicate this curious situation. Ellyn had seen her as a rival for Gailard's affections, and even now, for all the younger woman appeared quite smitten with Roark, she might well take offense did Shara allow her own emotions to govern her actions. She'd not make an enemy of Ellyn, and so . . . She stifled a sigh and smiled at Gailard.

"When this is over," she said, her eyes encompassing the adoring couple. "When all's settled—all debts and geases paid off—when Ellyn's on her throne and both Talan and Nestor are slain or banished. Then we can talk of that."

"That," he muttered, "might take awhile. Talan will send an army against us. He'll meet us at the Geffyn Pass, and . . ."

"We'll meet him there," she said. "We've the clans with us now, and the chance to defeat him."

"And then go on to Chorym?" His voice was slurred, and she realized that he was drunker than she'd realized. He took her hands and let her help him to his feet. "And what if we can't? Or if we do, and then we go on to Chorym? What then? Shall you then . . . ?"

They walked through the camp. She could smell his scent—sweat and leather—and it aroused her. But she fought down her desire, and when he sought to touch her, evaded his exploring hands.

"When it's done. Eh, Gailard?"

"Your word?"

He faced her with drunken gravity, setting his hands on her shoulders. She was unsure whether he sought to impress his words on her, or only looked to support himself, but she nodded, and brought him grinning to his tent.

"My word on it."

He beamed as if that were answer enough, and she saw him safely to his bed and left him there, returning to her own bivouac. It felt suddenly lonely.

"This is bad news." Talan flourished the despatches with a scowl. "Our Highlander ally is slain and the clans join. They move toward us—all of them!"

"They must come through the Geffyn Pass." Egor Dival set down his cup, crossing to the table where the great map was spread. "We can halt them there."

"Let me face them," Nestor said. "I can bring the whole pass down on them."

"And if you fail?" Talan shook his head. "No, I want you here with me."

"I'd not fail," Nestor said confidently.

Talan favored the Vachyn with a troubled glare. "You claimed your hunters would slay Ellyn—but she's disappeared. You promised your assassins would end the threat of the Hel's Town pirates—but now a navy comes against me. No, you remain here with me."

"The assassins were mortal men." Nestor's swarthy face darkened angrily. "They failed, yes; but I'll vouch my life they did not say who sent them."

"Does it matter?" Egor Dival enjoyed the sorcerer's discomfort. "Obviously, they were apprehended and Mother Hel has guessed their source." He glanced sidelong at Talan. "I advised against that move, no?"

"You did," grunted the king of Danant and Chaldor irritably, "but what matter now? The Hel's Town pirates are on the river. The gods know, they've put my craft to flight, and they seize town after town. How long before they land at Antium and move inland?"

Dival shrugged, continuing his study of the map.

Talan spun to face Nestor again. "And what of Ellyn? Does she ride with the barbarians?"

"I cannot tell," the Vachyn admitted. "Save she uses magic, I cannot sense her."

"She used magic to destroy your hunters." Talan beckoned a servant to fill his cup. Drained it in one long swallow and added, "*Someone* used magic."

"But not since," Nestor murmured, "and save the talent is employed, I simply cannot find her."

"But you knew where she was!" Talan shouted, prompting the waiting servants to start back. "You sensed magic then, you said. So tell me why she lives still."

"If she does." Nestor affected a calm mien. "Have I not explained this to you? That the magic that destroyed my hunters came from a long way off—likely from the Styge. And that place is masked by the magic inherent in the Barrens. I sensed the hunters' deaths, but I cannot pinpoint the location of the mage who slew them. And save that mage uses magic again, I cannot know where he, or she, is."

"Do you tell me there's more than Ellyn ranged against me?" Talan stared aghast at his hired Vachyn.

"Perhaps." Nestor shrugged. "But save there's some further disruption of the aethyr, I am blind. Any sorcerer would be blind."

"Then what use are you?" Talan snapped.

"I defeated Andur's army, and the bulk of his fleet." Nestor remained irritatingly calm. "I broke Chorym's gates for you. Now, do you send me to the Geffyn Pass I shall destroy whoever comes against you."

"I'd have you here with me. The gods know, do the Hel's Town pirates come up the Great Road . . ." Talan snorted, shaking his head vigorously. "And a clansman army through the pass . . . No, you remain in Chorym. Egor, do you see to the disposition of our forces?"

The old general nodded. "I'll reinforce Antium—I believe our men can stand off a pirate crew. And I'll go to the Geffyn Pass myself. I'll defeat the Highlanders and return here. Then, is it necessary, I'll move against the pirates."

"Excellent." Talan held out his cup that it be refilled. "Give me a victory, eh?"

"I shall do my best," Dival promised.

CHAPTER THIRTY-ONE

W e came to Cu-na'Lhair as the Highlands' summer ended. It was a pretty day, for all the nights now grew chill, and the sky stood blue as polished steel above us, billowed to the north with folds of white and grey that threatened rain. The air was edged with autumn's promise. We had held council the nights before, and decided that this was where the women and children and old folk should leave us. Winter comes swift in the Highlands and the animals left behind would need tending, the brochs and homesteads mending, the crops gathering. I had feared that some warriors would desert us in face of a winter campaign, and spoken long of Chaldor's soft winters, but none did. It seemed as if all were fascinated by this great adventure, nor less that those pledges made to Ellyn were held steadfast. I wondered how many would return here.

We camped outside the town—which had already sealed its gates against us and manned its walls—and I went with Shara and Ellyn, Mattich and Jaime and Roark to persuade the authorities that we intended no harm, but would go by peacefully to the Geffyn Pass.

It seemed the sheriff was appointed spokesman, for it was he answered my shout from the walls, kitted in full armor and escorted by bowmen. I was aware of their unblinking eyes and the barbed arrowheads as we spoke.

"I am Gailard of the Devyn, also guardian of Chaldor's Queen . . ."

"The Queen is dead," he interrupted. "Ryadne slew herself."

"Her daughter is alive." I gestured at Ellyn, resplendent in her armor. "Ellyn is queen now, and would take back her throne."

"That child? I'd heard Talan slew her, and that Gailard betrayed Chaldor."

Ellyn snorted, setting her horse to dancing. I motioned her silent, but I heard Roark mutter a curse and say, "That child? One word and I'll have his head."

"Easy, easy." I rode my bay a little closer to the walls and raised my voice again. Bows were adjusted to sight on my chest. "We come in peace. The clans have no quarrel with Cu-na'Lhair. We'd only trade and go on."

"And shall we let you in, all you clansmen? We've received ambassadors from Chorym . . ."

"Talan's!" Ellyn shouted. "Doubtless with soft words and easy promises. Trade with Chaldor, perhaps? Gold coins to fill your pockets? And in return—what? Danant's soldiers stationed here?"

The sheriff was slow to answer. "There were . . . promises . . . made," he allowed.

"I'd thought," Ellyn replied, "that Cu-na'Lhair was neutral."

Roark said, "We could take this place easily."

I was proud of Ellyn's response. "No! I'd not disrupt old ways, and we cannot afford to destroy this place." Softer, so that only Shara and I might hear, she murmured, "But we could." Then, louder to the sheriff, "I am Ellyn of Chaldor, daughter of Andur and Ryadne, and I go home to reclaim my parents' throne and free Chaldor of Talan's domination. Now shall you open your gates and let us in?"

"And do we not?" came the answer.

"Then we'll go by," Ellyn replied. "But know that if we do, Chaldor shall no longer trade with Cu-na'Lhair. I'll build another town—far greater—and extend the Great Road, that all trade goes past this place, and you'll become a backwater, shamed by your cowardice."

She sounded to me like a true queen then, and I glanced at Shara, thinking that we'd taught her well. Shara met my eyes and smiled, not saying anything. The sheriff huffed and waved that we wait awhile, disappearing behind the ramparts.

He returned with several folk about him—the city fathers and burghers, I supposed. They all stared down at us and went away again, and then came back to announce that we six might enter to discuss our needs.

They were nervous. Danant's ambassadors had assured them that Chaldor was firmly in Talan's hands; that Ellyn was slain; that their best interests lay with Danant.

But all the clans stood camped in sight of the walls, and that army was a more immediate force than anything Talan might send—so they conceded that we might trade with them, and that Cu-na'Lhair would remain neutral. I breathed a sigh of relief when it was done, and was grateful to return to our camp. I'd not have a hostile town at our back as we entered the Geffyn Pass.

We remained six days outside Cu-na'Lhair—it was something of a festival, what with the trading and bartering—and when we left we took numerous folk with us: those who'd join our purpose and see Talan thrown back across the Durrakym.

The women and old folk and children turned back then, and only the army went on, to the Geffyn Pass, where I was sure Talan's forces would meet us.

"We can destroy them," Ellyn said. "Do Shara and I employ our magicks, we can fling them back like . . . like . . ." Her face flushed. "Like Nestor defeated my father."

"And tell Nestor you live?" Shara shook her head. "Use magic now and he can find you."

"So?" Ellyn turned enthusiastic eyes toward her tutor. "Surely we can defeat him do we act in concert."

"Perhaps," Shara said, "but he's strong, and I'd not confront him until we reach Chorym."

"Why not? Can we not defeat him and Talan's army, all together, in the Geffyn Pass?"

"Talan won't send all his army there," I said. "He'll send a part, and hold the rest back to defend Chorym."

"And he might have employed more Vachyn sorcerers," Shara added. "I'd know the odds before we face him—or them. Do we use magic, he'll answer in kind."

"I'd sooner he were bottled up in Chorym," I said. "And I suspect that Talan will keep him there. The Danant usurper is not known for his courage, and I think he'll want his tame mage at his side."

Ellyn scowled.

"We face them blade to blade," I said, "in honest battle. Let the clans push into Chaldor and surround Chorym, then use your magicks against the Vachyn."

Shara voiced her agreement, and all the chieftains, and Ellyn must be satisfied with that.

Save: "I'll fight with you," she said.

At which Roark touched her hand and whispered to her. And she scowled deeper and said, "No! Gailard taught me to fight, and I'll fight with you! I'll not sit back and watch men die for me."

Roark opened his mouth to protest, but I forestalled him. "She's a canny warrior," I said, "and can defeat most men. But even so . . ." I looked at her. "A general commands from safety. And a queen . . ."

"I am not general, nor yet a queen. Put me on my parents' throne and I'll sit back and command. But until then, I fight with you!"

I looked to Shara for support, but she only shrugged

and favored me with an enigmatic smile. So I said, helplessly, "Not to the fore."

"I'll play my part," Ellyn answered.

"And I'll ward her," Roark declared dutifully. "My oath
on it."

Which, for some reason I could not understand, irritated me.

We came to the Geffyn Pass. There was frost on the grass
now, and the sky hung grey above us. Summer's swallows
had gone away, leaving the sky to crows and ravens and
hawks. I thought that Talan's army would face us at the farther end, the ingress to Chaldor, and planned accordingly.

I sent scouts ahead, and they returned with word that
the Danant force waited for us at the southern exit. That it
was a mighty force of chariots and mounted archers supported by hoplites—which was what I'd anticipated.

Danant, like Chaldor, was a flat land ringed by hills,
and the Danant style of warfare was adapted to the terrain.
Danant fought swift, mobile battles, with chariots and
mounted men; the heavy-armored hoplites there mostly to
sweep up and slay what the horsemen left behind. I hoped
they kept it so, and sent men into the hills to study anew
what we faced. Then set out my strategy, which Mattich
and the rest accepted, though it was a new style of fighting
for them.

We cut poles from the pines that grew in abundance
along the pass, and hacked both ends to sharp spikes. Then,
by night, we set the poles firmly in the ground, slanted forward. We could see the fires of Talan's army burning, but his
soldiers never heard us, and come the morning of the battle I
sent Roark and his Quan warriors to clambering up the
south side of the pass, and Jaime and his Arran to the north.
I waited with the Devyn and the Agador and the Dur,
massed to face the main attack. Shara and Ellyn were the
only women with us now, and they both girded for battle.

I rode forward with Mattich and a few others, as if we were the small vanguard of some ragtag clan army. We halted when we saw the force massed before us and pranced our horses as if in consternation. I had climbed the hills the night before and knew exactly what we faced. Talan's general had set his army square across the mouth of the pass—around two thousand warriors, most of them mounted on horses or in chariots. There were perhaps five hundred hoplites, but did all go as I hoped, they'd be of little account. Did it not, they might sway the fight.

We rode on, nocking arrows to our bows as a squadron of mounted archers came to meet us. We loosed shafts at one another, and I shouted in pride as I tumbled a man from his horse. Mattich cursed as his mount was hit, almost bucking him from the saddle. We traded more shots, then turned and ran, pretending fear, pursued by the Danant archers.

Before we reached the wall of spikes—it was most important the Danant force not see that barricade yet—some five hundred men came charging out on foot. The Danant riders halted and turned back. We waited, and I felt my heart pound, for all depended on our luring the greater force to us. It was noonday by then and a warm breeze blew out of Chaldor, redolent of horses and metal and warfare, and in a while the prey came into my trap.

There was a great rumbling echoed from the walls of the pass as the chariots came toward us. Birds rose in confusion and the roadway gave up great clouds of dust from the speeding wheels. They rode four abreast, packed in by the walls, with the mounted archers racing between and behind the charioteers lashing the two-horse teams, each chariot with one or two armored men readying bows or javelins. I was afoot, and I remembered the Darach Pass and the plain beyond, and Chaldor's terrible defeat as I watched the racing chariots bear down.

I raised my buckler and shouted, and we ran back as if terrified by Danant's might.

Back past the wall of sharpened poles that were still hidden by a line of men who waited until the chariots and the archers were almost on them before retreating.

So that the leading horses ran headlong onto the spikes and were stuck and held as I waved to Mattich, and he blew a horn that called Roark and Jaime down even as chariot piled on chariot in terrible disarray, and the warriors to either side of the pass unleashed their bows and sent arrows raining onto the Danant force.

The momentum of their attack was such that none could stop or turn back, but must press on, even as horses climbed over the backs of the chariots and screamed and died, filling the Geffyn Pass with the stink of blood and ordure, and the moans of dying men and animals. I shouted again and led the charge that brought all our Highlander army out from behind the poles, and down from the walls of the pass to fall on Talan's men like ravaging wolves.

It was close quarters then, and the chaos that brings. I lost sight of Ellyn and Shara as blades clashed. Arrows flew; men and horses died. The Quan and the Arran came down to seal the exit, bottling Talan's men. I clambered over the body of a screaming horse to put my sword into the charioteer's belly and smash away a probing javelin. The man I faced was armored in magnificent silver, and when I drove his spear from his hand, he drew a great, wide-bladed sword and slashed at my head. I ducked under his swing and knocked him from his platform with my buckler, and as he fell, I drove my blade into the gap between his breastplate and helmet and opened his throat. I trod on him as I progressed to my next victim, thinking that I'd grind Talan's head thus. I saw an archer—somehow still mounted—aim a shaft in my direction, and raised my shield so that the heavy warhead rattled into the buckler. I slashed my blade across the horse's muzzle and it screamed, rearing, spilling its rider, who died under my blade.

I strode on through the carnage, hacking and cutting, slashing, taking blows on my shield as all around me rang the war shouts of the clans. Then a horn sounded and what few of the Danant force survived turned and ran. I bellowed that the clansmen hold back, and that our archers pick off whom they could, and more Danant men died in the retreat. I clambered a little way up the pass's wall and surveyed the carnage. I calculated that half the enemy force was slain, and when I looked beyond the ingress I saw that what was left was mostly chariots and the hoplites; there were few mounted archers left alive, which suited my purpose well.

I returned to the road and trotted to the mouth of the pass. The air stank of blood and dying, and I rested a moment on my sword. I was getting old, I thought. I was out of breath, and my buckler felt heavy in my hand. I glanced back and saw no enemies left behind me. I looked ahead and saw fleeing chariots and an army in disarray. I panted like a dog on a hot summer day.

Then Mattich was at my side. "By all the gods, we beat them!" His armor was bloody, and he rested, panting like me, on his sword. "We turned them back."

I said, "Yes," as I watched the remnants scurry away down the Great Road. "For now."

He nodded, understanding.

"Victory!" Roark joined us. "We've shown Talan what the clans can do, eh?"

I turned to him. His helm was dented and there was blood on his sword, and his youthful face was flushed with pride despite the cut that dripped blood down his cheek. I said, "A skirmish won. Not victory, yet."

"No." He shook his head. "But the first step, eh? The first step to setting Ellyn on her throne."

"Where is Ellyn?" I asked.

I looked around and saw her coming toward us with Jaime and his Arran. They were laughing together, and she held a bow. The quiver slung across her back was empty of shafts.

"By the gods," Jaime shouted, "but this child can flight an arrow!"

Ellyn blushed with pride. Then gasped as she saw the blood on Roark's face and ran toward him. I felt somewhat hurt as she touched his cheek. Surely I had blood on me, even was it not my own.

"She joined us," Jaime said, "and shot with my best."

I glowered at him and he added, abashed, "I'd not time to send her back—even did she agree to go. But she was safe; I watched her."

I grunted and looked for Shara.

She came through the charnel wreckage like some lady maneuvering her way through the detritus of a ballroom. Or a goddess walking past the foolishness of humanity. She smiled at me and frowned at Ellyn, who—intent on Roark's small wound—did not notice her.

"She would not stay; I could not stop her."

I shrugged. "No matter now. We won the day."

"And tomorrow?"

I glanced at the sky. Twilight fell; swifts and swallows darted over Chaldor, snatching insects from the darkening air, and crows gathered along the Geffyn Pass, waiting for us to leave that they might feast. Talan's men grouped defensively some little distance off. I could see their bright pavilions and the beginnings of fires.

"They'll not attack tonight," I said. "But we'll face them again on the morrow."

Shara nodded. "Nestor's not with them. He'd have used magic, I think."

"Where is he then?" I asked.

"In Chorym, with Talan," she answered. "Save they've both fled."

I shook my head. "Talan will not give up so easily."

"Then it shall be as you say." She smiled at me. "We shall find them both in the city."

"We must go past these first." I gestured at the army before us. It was still large, although we now owned the greater number. "And Chorym shall be hard to take."

"We do what we must, no?"

I smiled and touched her cheek, and nodded.

Mattich said, "Do we attack again, Gailard?" His face was lit with battle joy, and beside him stood Jaime and Roark, like hounds straining at the leash as they scented victory.

"Not yet," I answered. "We rest and face them in the morning. Save . . ."

That night small groups of Highlanders rode out to harry Danant's army. Fire-arrows shafted across the starry sky to ignite tents and wake sleeping men; horses were loosed from the picket lines and sent stampeding away; sentries died with arrows in them, or their throats cut. I gave my enemies a troublesome night as I slept soundly, for all I dreamed of Shara and that unspoken promise: I *needed* to take Chorym.

I rose while the sky was still that opalescent grey that precedes dawn. The air was poised between the Highlands' chill and Chaldor's late summer, and only the earliest-rising birds interrupted the sounds of clinking of armor and nervous horses, of muted conversation and the scrape of whetstones on steel.

I ate a bowl of porridge with the chieftains and set out my strategy.

"We fight on open ground now," I said, "and they'll have the advantage there. Listen . . ."

When I was done, I turned to Ellyn. "You will hold back, eh?"

"I fought well enough yesterday." She glanced at Jaime for confirmation. "Why not today?"

"Because," I said, "if you are slain, all this falls apart."

Roark said, "Gailard's right, my . . ." He caught himself as Ellyn smiled.

I still felt that strange resentment, but I looked to the Quan chieftain and said, "Take her with you, eh?"

Roark nodded, understanding.

I turned toward Shara, who grinned at me and made a small gesture that sealed off any further words.

"So let's to it," I said.

The Danant army set its chariots to the fore, the hoplites gathered behind. Whoever commanded them knew what I knew: that did they not halt us here, we must come down into Chaldor unopposed and lay siege to Chorym, where Talan lurked.

There were perhaps seven hundred chariots facing us now, and I knew they'd deploy on a sweeping line to ride in and crush us—followed by the hoplites. I ordered the bulk of my army to mount, leaving some few hundreds behind afoot. The finest archers from all the clans I set to the fore, and we rode out.

Danant came to meet us. The chariots thundered on the road. I held my cavalry back as the archers behind us fired in volleys. Horses and men fell, and the chariots spread wider, riding off the road onto the fields to either side. The ground was softer there, the grass dew-wet, and the heavy chariots slowed.

I raised a hand and shouted the charge, and all our clansmen came racing to the attack.

I caught a glance of Ellyn, drawing shafts and firing from the saddle of her chestnut mare as if she were born to be a warrior. I was grateful that Roark flanked her, his buckler raised. Then I was too occupied with warfare to think of aught than survival.

We charged the Danant chariots in a mass. Their archers and javelin men were better suited to this kind of fighting, but we held the numbers now, and our mounts were more accustomed to such terrain than theirs. We took them down from their vehicles and slew them.

I tossed my bow aside and drew my sword. A chariot raced toward me and I swerved my bay, bringing my buckler across as a javelin arced toward me. I took it on my shield and sliced down through the traces of the horses, swinging my blade up to stab into the chest of the charioteer. He screamed and fell back against the warrior behind him, whose head I took off with a single sweep.

The shaft in my buckler was heavy, and I could not shake it loose. It weighted my arm, dragging my shield behind me. I hacked at the pole, then cursed as it refused to cut. I flung my buckler away and raised my blade as a sword crashed against my helmet.

The sky was brightening now, but not so much as what I saw. I saw stars spinning randomly, and suns bursting in profusion before my unsighted eyes. Instinct raised my hand against another blow, but then a sword crashed against my back and my mount screamed and began to buck and I fell down as she reared and toppled.

I saw a chariot coming toward me. I saw the hooves of the horses pounding, and knew they must crush me down, and I must die. I saw a javelin arc toward me, and rolled aside—into the path of the charging hooves. I thought that I had died once—on Eryk's tree—and that it was not fair I should die again, not with victory in sight.

Then the chariot was gone in a flash of fire, as if the gods sent down a thunderbolt to save me, and Shara was at my side, urging me to my feet.

I clambered upright, leaning on her. She held me as the battle raged around us.

I shook my aching head and asked, still dazed, "What did you do?"

"I used magic," she said. "You'd be dead, else."

"But Nestor?" I said. "You'd not alert him with magic?"

"I saw a choice," she said. "I could see you die, or use my power. No choice at all."

I put my arms around her and thanked her, and she smiled at me and said, "I'd not see you slain, Gailard. Ellyn needs you to win her this war."

"And was that your only reason?" I could smell her

skin, and even was she armored, still it was good to hold her close.

But then she pushed away, staring into my eyes, and shook her head. "You know it was not."

I smiled and bent to kiss her, but she turned her face aside. "Not yet, eh?" Her voice was soft and I wondered if I heard regret. "As we agreed—we take Chorym first."

Then the fighting raged around us again and we were separated as I found my blade, and she hers, and we swung and hacked and fought to survive.

The sun came up and drove off dawn's grey light. The chariots withdrew and massed for another charge. There were fewer of them now, many bogged down in the soft ground to the sides of the road or standing empty where the clansmen had taken the drivers and the javelin men. What few were left rallied. I heard a horn call and the Danant force grouped and charged for the last time.

The hoplites came on. Their armor was heavier than ours, and with their swords and spears and axes they might have turned the fight to Danant's advantage, save I'd had experience of fighting them and prepared for this. Jaime and Roark called back their men and loosed fresh volleys of arrows that slew the hoplites before they could reach the chariots. It was like the winnowing of wheat—save wheat does not bleed or scream—and when the last shafts were flighted, it was man-to-man combat again.

And when it was done no more than a hundred chariots fled eastward, and there were no more hoplites, and we looted their deserted pavilions, and spoke confidently of taking Chorym. Ellyn gazed fondly at Roark, and I enjoyed Shara's nursing of my wounds and thought of victory and its rewards.

And wondered if we could achieve it.

I thought we might—and surely we had won a great battle—but Chorym's walls were strong and hard, and it had taken Vachyn magic to bring them down, and so I wondered, and thought of Shara, and determined that I would.

CHAPTER THIRTY-TWO

Egor Dival nursed his broken arm as Talan ranted. His head ached beneath the bandages, and even now he could not quite understand how the barbarian clansmen had defeated him. He had been confident of victory—that he'd halt the Highlanders at the Geffyn Pass and throw them back in disarray—but they had broken his men in bloody battle and sent Danant's finest running. It was an embarrassment that Talan could understand even less.

"How?" The Lord of Danant and Chaldor spread his arms wide, as if to encompass the battle Dival had described. "How could they defeat you?"

"They are ferocious warriors," Dival said, "and all the clans were there. Thousands of them."

"Savages!" Talan beckoned a servant to fill his cup; drank it down in a single gulp. "Highland savages!"

"They matched our numbers," Dival said. He studied Talan's face, but from the corner of his eye he could see Nestor watching him like some black crow waiting for him to weaken. "And they were well-ordered. They did not fight like clansmen."

"And how do clansmen fight?" Talan snarled.

"Not so well ordered." Dival shrugged, regretting the movement as his wound sparked pain. "They were organized, and commanded by someone who understands warfare."

Nestor said, "Gailard?"

"I saw a man who might be him," Dival allowed. "But who commands, I cannot say." Almost, he shrugged again—then thought better of it.

"And Ellyn?" Talan snapped.

"I saw a woman with them." Dival licked his lips. A glass of wine would not go amiss, but it seemed unlikely Talan would offer him one, and he would not ask. He was filthy from the road, and weary to his bones. Unused to defeat, the Geffyn Pass had taught him somewhat of the enemy he faced, and he wondered how long it should be before he faced that enemy again. "It might have been her."

"It was." Nestor spoke with supreme confidence. "And save she's learned the art of her own, there's another with her."

"Another what?" Talan demanded.

"A sorcerer," the Vachyn said.

"How do you know?"

"I sensed magic." The Vachyn turned his dark eyes on Dival. "What did you see?"

"My men slaughtered, clansmen fighting in ordered ranks." He was tempted to add, "whilst you sat safe here," but deemed it wiser to hold his own counsel. "I saw the Highlanders fight as they never have before."

"What else?" the Vachyn asked, as if the deaths were nothing. "Think!"

"There was . . ." Dival hesitated. "I'm not sure, but . . . There was a moment when it seemed a thunderbolt struck."

Nestor said, softly, "Shara."

"Shara?" Talan swung to face the Vachyn. "Who, in the name of all the gods, is Shara?"

Nestor rose. His face was set in angry lines, and it seemed to Dival that he was like a black thundercloud drifting across the room. He took up a cup and held it to a servant for filling, carried the goblet to the window and drank before answering.

"Shara was my sister," he said slowly. "She was strong in the talent, but she found fault with our Vachyn ways. She chose to leave us and go away. We did not know where . . . until now."

Talan gaped. "You say we face a Vachyn?"

"I say that my sister lives." Nestor turned from the window. "You remember what our ambassadors brought back—that Gailard was hung on the tree by Eryk, but . . . *something* . . . saved him? And when my hunters were slain? I think that must be Shara's work. I thought her gone eremitic, but . . ." He frowned. "Even does Ellyn possess the talent, still she's too young to use it without aid . . . without tuition. I think . . ." His frown grew deeper, darker. "I think my sister lives and aids these rebels."

"By all the gods!" Talan flung his cup across the room. Gold buckled and jewels burst loose. A frightened servant scurried to retrieve the wreckage. "Are you telling me a Vachyn comes against us? What do we do?"

"I can destroy her," Nestor said. "Let me ride out to face her."

"The clans are coming," Dival said warningly. "They'll be outside Chorym's walls ere long."

"Aided by a Vachyn?" Talan paced the room. "I'd go home to Danant!"

For once both Dival and Nestor shared an emotion: they looked at Talan with contempt in their eyes. Dival said, "That should be admission of defeat. Flee now, and you'd best relinquish all claim on Chaldor, give the throne back to Ellyn."

"It should be difficult," Nestor said. "Remember what word we've had from the coast—that the Hel's Town pirates hold the river and seal us in. It should be hard for you to flee now."

"Then what do I do?" Talan asked, looking from one to the other like a frightened dog unsure which master to obey.

"Ready for siege," Dival said. "Call in all our forces and hold Chorym. No matter how well organized they are, the Highlanders are not used to siege fighting. They'll break against the walls."

"Hire more Vachyn," Nestor said. "Give me two of my kin and I'll break this pitiful army, and my sister with it."

"And how shall I hire them?" Talan asked, scowling. "The Durrakym's sealed, you say—so how shall you send word? And how shall I pay them? The gods know, but I've bled my treasury dry to fight this war, and so far Chaldor's given us nothing save grief. Even had I the funds to hire more of you, I could not raise them here, nor send for them across the river."

"Then you must trust me," Nestor said.

"Trust you?" Talan's scowl grew deeper. "You told me to trust you when you promised your hunters would slay Ellyn. But by all accounts, Ellyn lives—and comes against me with a Highlander army and your Vachyn sister. And *you*!" He swung his frightened, angry eyes toward Egor Dival. "You said you'd hold them and defeat them at the Geffyn Pass—and now you say they come into Chaldor. What next? What else must I suffer?"

"Siege," Dival said bluntly. "Save you'd risk crossing the river."

"Not with Hel's Town pirates abroad!" Talan shook his head. "No, I must . . . I must . . ."

"Act the man?" Dival asked. "Prepare to face your enemies and fight them face-to-face?"

"Do you call me coward?" Talan glared at his general.

"Do you run," Dival said bluntly, "yes."

Talan chewed his lower lip awhile. Then: "Can we defeat them?"

"We stand behind strong walls," Dival said. "The clans are not used to siege fighting. I believe we can break them here."

"And I can hold against whatever magicks Shara commands," Nestor added. "Let her come to us. Her and Ellyn, like birds driven into the net."

"So we'd best remain?" Talan asked.

The Vachyn and the soldier nodded, and once again spoke with one voice: "What other choice do we have?"

Like rats in a trap, Dival thought, *without safe exit, and therefore only the one choice: to fight until we win or die.* He rose, wincing as his wounds sent tendrils of pain lancing through his limbs, and ducked his head barely low enough to acknowledge Talan.

"I'd see to my men. There were too many hurt . . ."

"Go; go." Talan waved a dismissive hand and Dival limped from the chamber. When the commander had gone, Talan turned to Nestor. "You *can* defeat your sister?"

"I can," Nestor promised. His smile was evil. "Let her and the Highlanders come here, and I shall destroy them all."

"You're so confident?" Talan's voice rang hollow with uncertainty.

Nestor said, "How do you kill wasps?" And when Talan shrugged and shook his head in confusion, "You set out a jar filled with honey and water, with only a small entrance, and the wasps cannot resist the temptation, and climb in and drown. It shall be thus when this bobtail army comes to Chorym. We shall gather them all in and slay them."

"And if . . ." Talan hesitated, torn between the desire to believe his hired Vachyn and the very real fear that he might be defeated, "It does not work out as you plan?"

"Even do they take this city," Nestor promised, "I'll spirit you away to safety in Danant—my word on that."

"Then I cannot lose," Talan said.

"Does worse come to worst," Nestor returned, "I'll see us safe away, and leave Egor to face the Highlanders. Let him take the brunt, eh?'

Talan nodded, smiling nervously, and said, "A most excellent plan, my friend. So long as we shall be safe."

"Wake up, damn you!" Nassim shook Kerid hard. "Wake up! You've got a visitor."

"What?" Kerid woke from a pleasant dream of Mother Hel to the waft of tobacco-tainted breath. "What do you say?"

"You've a visitor," Nassim repeated. "Best wash and dress."

"Who?" Kerid rose thickheaded from his bunk. Three Danant vessels sunk was surely reason enough for celebration, and it had been a most pleasant dream. He had not seen the Mother since she aided him in that fight. She had gone, she said, to seek more boats.

"You'll see, are you quick enough."

Nassim grinned wickedly and left the cabin. Kerid groaned, rubbing hands against his itching eyes, and doused his aching head. He splashed water over his body and swiftly toweled himself dry. They could not be under attack—surely not with a score of craft anchored in formation, a flotilla that must deny Danant priority of the river. But what? Nassim had sounded urgent. He dressed and went on deck.

And gasped as he saw the vessels sitting the water to the north, and the golden-painted longboat that swept toward the *Andur*. The woman seated amidships unmistakable. Her hair shone like gold in the sun, and her face set his heart to beating faster. He hurried to the bulwarks that he be the first to hand Mother Hel over the rail.

"I . . ." he said.

"Had not expected me?" She smiled at him, and then took his face in both her hands and kissed him. Which set his head to swimming deeper, so that his already-unsteady legs threatened to give way beneath him. He put his arms around her, as much for support as for want of holding her. "I had not seen you for too long a time. So . . ." She gestured at the river, the craft floating there. "I thought I'd come avisiting."

"And brought . . ." he said, staring at the navy that sat the Durrakym's tide in terrible splendor.

"All my people; all my boats." She pushed away from his arms. "I grew bored with waiting for you, so I thought I might end this affair as early as we can."

"I thought," Kerid said, "that you'd leave this fight to me."

Mother Hel shrugged. "I break precedent, but . . ." For a moment, lashes closed over her eyes and Kerid wondered if she blushed. Then her face was stern again, and also hinting at a smile. "I missed you. I cannot understand it, but . . ."

Kerid drew himself up. "You missed me?"

"Yes."

"I'm flattered."

"You should be. Now show me your cabin."

Kerid hesitated only a moment, that he might survey all the boats. The Durrakym was covered with a mosaic of vessels that set his head to spinning in amazement. Long, low-drafted warboats hung like waiting hounds around fat-bellied traders set with catapults and trebuchets. Three-masters anchored alongside brigs and lateen-rigged single-masters. And on all the decks stood men and women readied for war, armored and eager. It was more, and better, than he'd dared hope for, and he laughed and offered a courtier's bow and took the Mother down to his cabin.

"So you come with me?" His fingers worked on the lacings of her gown; hers on his shirt.

"I shall." Her hands dragged off the garment. "I'll not wait alone, wondering what fate befalls you."

"It will be hard." Her dress fell away and he began to loose her undergarments. "Talan will not give up easily."

"The gods take Talan." Her hands found his breeches and dropped them. "I'll fight Talan myself to keep you alive."

"I thought,' he said, and gasped as she tugged off his boots.

"Don't," she said, hauling him down onto the narrow bunk.

He held her when they were done and wondered. He said, "I never thought . . ."

"Nor I," she said, touching his lips to silence him. "I am Mother Hel, and I never thought . . ."

"That we'd . . . ?"

"Yes. Now be silent and listen to me."

He stroked her hair as she spoke.

"I own Hel's town—I am the Mother—and I have ears beyond the river. Thus I heard that the clans rise against Talan, and . . ."

"Gailard lives?" Kerid rose excitedly. "And Ellyn?"

"Perhaps both. I heard that a battle was fought where Chaldor ends and the Highlands begin."

"The Geffyn Pass?"

She nodded, sending long tendrils of blond hair to stroking across his chest.

"I believe a Highlander army moves against Chorym. So I thought I'd aid you in your fight."

Kerid smiled and kissed her. "If Gailard brings the clans to Chorym, I must help him."

"I know," she said. "That's why I'm here."

Kerid said, "I love you, Mother."

Mother Hel said, "Show me, and then we'll go to war."

Ellyn held her mare to a canter that matched the pace of Roark's little Highlander pony. The long-legged horse fretted somewhat, anxious to run and frustrated by the smaller steps of the lesser animal, but Ellyn would not quit Roark's side. She could not understand it. She had believed she loved Gailard, for all he was her father's age and uncouth; indeed, ofttimes horribly arrogant. But Roark . . . she had felt her heart flutter when first she saw him, and their eyes had met and she had seen the same reaction in him. And he had ridden with her in the fight and taken arrows in her defense, and she loved him. She had not told him yet, but he knew; and she knew that he loved her. Or—perhaps more accurately—adored her. She saw it in his eyes, and the attentions he paid her, and liked it, as if he spread a warm blanket around her on cold nights, or wafted a fan to cool her in summer's heat. When they ate, he offered her the finest cuts, and passed her brose and ale as if he were her servant. Yet he was no more a servant than Gailard. He fought well—she'd seen him in battle—and he was . . . Like Gailard, but younger. And so handsome.

She started as he turned toward her.

"What?"

"Nothing.'

Ellyn blushed, and turned her eyes—reluctantly—from his face.

They rode the Great East Road now, passing farm-houses and fields where cattle lowed. Folk fled before them, frightened by the advent of a Highlander army after Danant's depredations. Those folk she'd had the chance to speak with before they fled had told her of taxes and tithes that bled them dry; of Danant's soldiers taking what they would, as if Chaldor were only some great purse that Talan looted. Some houses were burned down, and there cattle lowed mournfully for want of milking; and sometimes with-ered bodies hung from trees, pecked by crows. More sat on dead animals, and the warm air carried the stench of death.

"They've ravaged your land," Roark said.

"And shall pay for it," Ellyn replied.

"You'll be queen."

She nodded, and almost said, "And you my consort." But that was for later—after Talan was defeated, so she only said aloud, "Yes—do we take Chorym back."

"We shall," Roark said gallantly. "How can we not?"

"Talan sits there," Ellyn said, "with his Vachyn sorcerer. It shall not be easy."

"We shall take the city," he said, "and give you your rightful throne. My word on it, and my life."

"I'd not see you slain," she said.

"I'd die for you," he said. "Do you not understand?"

"Yes." Ellyn nodded. "But I'd sooner you lived."

And stay with me, she thought, *and be consort to my queen, like my mother and my father, and the gods grant it be so.*

And then she sat her horse in silence as the Highlander army continued down the Great East Road toward Chorym and the settling of scores and restitution, and wondered if the battle would be won and she see Talan paid back and suffer her revenge.

Or . . .

She chose not to think about the alternatives. Gailard would take Chorym and she would claim back her parents' throne. She would wed Roark and bind the Highlands to Chaldor. And then . . . She must speak with Shara about this, but why not pursue the war? Into Danant, and take what Talan had stolen from her parents? Go on to destroy the Vachyn? The gods knew, but Shara had explained their intentions, and it would be a gift to the world to end the Vachyn ambitions.

But first, Chorym. One step at a time, as Gailard had taught her. Learn to use the sword first. Learn to hold it and swing it, learn to defend yourself, learn to shield yourself—then attack.

She looked back to where her guardian rode alongside Shara, and felt a pang of . . . regret? Jealousy? She was not sure, save that her feelings changed, and she gave up her dreams of Gailard and loved Roark.

But mostly she dreamed of defeating Talan and taking Chorym from him, and sending him running homeward . . . could she not slay him first.

CHAPTER THIRTY-THREE

We met with little resistance as we rode west, and collected a ragged army of dispossessed folk who joined our cause in hatred and defiance of Danant's rule. Most of Talan's men were already fled, and more scurried like panicked rats at our approach. What few remained to face us, we crushed easily, so that the clansmen spoke of Danant's cowardice and assumed an easy victory. I knew it could not be so, not while Talan still held Chorym. I knew it should be long, and prayed the clans remain. Siege warfare was not their style of fighting, and I feared they might grow bored and desert Ellyn's cause. Mattich and the others assured me they'd not, but I wondered how their men would take the long weeks encamped around the city, with Vachyn magic likely abroad and no swift victory in sight.

And then our goal loomed before us, and I deployed my army. It felt strange to face those walls as an enemy. I remembered Chorym as my home, where Andur had raised a simple clansman, and I had found kindness and learned of the world beyond the Highlands. Now I must attack and wreak destruction on that place that meant so much to me. I supposed it must be worse for Ellyn.

I had prepared for this, remembering those books I'd read in Shara's castle, and I set our men to unusual work. We gathered wood for the construction of ladders and battering rams, siege towers and crude catapults. There was plenty available—the detritus of Danant's siege—and the folk still inhabiting the surrounding farms and villages came out to help us, hailing Ellyn as their rightful queen, so that before long all was in place and we stood ready to commence what I hoped would be the final battle. I was surprised—and therefore worried—that Talan made no attempt to halt us. I had anticipated forays, Vachyn magic—some effort to delay us—but none came. And as I watched the engines built I saw Danant's men observing us from the ramparts. There was a figure I recognized from the Geffyn Pass, and I supposed the man beside him, resplendent in golden armor, was Talan himself. They were joined by another, robed in black, and I knew he must be Nestor, for even at this distance there seemed to be a dark and evil aura about him. I studied the walls, seeing where fresh stone was set like scars on the body of an old friend, and wondered where Ryadne had fallen, and vowed anew to avenge my friends.

Shara and Ellyn stood with me, and I turned to the sorceress I loved.

"Why does he not act?"

As if in answer to my question, I saw the dark-robed mage raise his hands. They pointed toward us.

Shara paled and raised hers, mouthing words I could not understand as lightning flashed across the sky. Not in honest verticality, but slanting horizontal from the city walls. I saw a moment of brilliant light, as if I gazed upon a mirror that reflected back the full brightness of the sun, blinding me. Then there was a clap of thunder that seemed to shake the ground and drum deafeningly against my ears. Light burst all around us, and I smelled scorched grass. I saw Ellyn copying Shara's movements, voicing the same incantations. I felt my sword hilt grow warm against my palm, and my hair prickle as if I stood exposed in the center of a storm. Then silence—perhaps because I was deafened—perhaps because I stood within the aegis of Shara's protective spell. My hearing returned, and I saw men fall to either side in screaming torches.

"He's strong," Shara said softly. "He'll send more such magicks against us."

I had no need to name her brother. She said, "I think perhaps he tests me; perhaps waits on me. He'll sense my presence by now." She hesitated, shuddering. "The gods know, but I sense his, and I suspect he waits to test my strength. Or . . ." She stared at the distant figure, a frown creasing her brow. ". . . he organizes some vaster magic that takes him time."

We watched the shapes quit the ramparts. I felt that the first blow in a long battle had been delivered—that Nestor tested Shara's strength, and Ellyn's. And wondered what should come next.

Ellyn stared at the walls of her home and sighed. "When it begins," she said softly, "it shall hurt Chorym, no?"

"As little as possible," I promised uselessly.

"As little as possible?" She barked a laugh and gestured at the engines we'd built, the piles of stones, the waiting men. "I was born here, Gailard. Save for my time with you, I lived my life here. Now we come to ravage the walls my ancestors built, the place my father built. Doubtless there are still servants there." She flung an accusatory finger in the direction of the walls. "Folk I knew, who served me and helped me. I remember a maid—Tyli—who set a compress on my knee when I fell in the gardens. I was . . . five? . . . and Tyli picked me up and dried my eyes and tended my hurt. Her hair was grey when last I saw her, but likely she's still there. And Daryk, who shod my pretty white mare. Is he still alive behind those walls? And shall our attack kill him? And Tyli, and all the others?"

"We've no other choice," I said. "Save to leave."

"Perhaps we should." She looked away across the fertile plain. "Perhaps we should go back."

"We've come too far," I said. "The gods know, but we've done what none other has achieved—we've united the clans in your cause, and do you now say 'up and go,' all that is lost."

"And more," Shara said. "Do we quit now, then Talan owns your kingdom and will bleed it dry. And Nestor will whisper in his ear and lead him on to greater ambitions. And where would you go?"

I watched as Ellyn's shoulders trembled. I heard her stifle a sob, and would have touched her, held her, had she not needed to make this decision alone.

"This is not easy," she sniffed. "Folk I knew shall likely die because of me."

"War is not easy," I said. "Think you that I shall enjoy sending men to their deaths?"

"You slew your brother," she returned me. "Was that easy?"

"I'd no love for Eryk, and he gave me no choice," I answered her. "But these?" In turn, I indicated the circle of warriors ringing Chorym. "These men follow me in your name, and I shall not enjoy seeing them die."

"Did my father face such decisions?" she asked.

"Yes." I nodded. "And such doubts. But he swerved from them no more than your mother when she faced Talan from those walls. She had a choice then. She might have surrendered and held Chorym intact, save she knew her duty."

Ellyn coughed out a choking sound that might have been another sob. "I do not like this," she said.

"War slays the innocent," I said. "How many died when Talan seized Chorym? How many farmers died? You saw the burned houses, and the bodies on the trees as we came here. Would you allow that to continue?"

"And give the Vachyn another kingdom?" Shara added.

"You are Chaldor's queen," I said. "Not all those folk down there are Highlanders. You've farmers in your army now, and shepherds, and vintners, and traders, all from Chaldor; those folk from Cu-na'Lhair who joined your cause. All those joined us to defeat Talan, and they follow us because they'd see you on the throne, and peace come again."

"I've no choice then," she said.

"I think not." I shook my head. "I think that kings and queens often have no choice, but only the duty to defend their land and seek the greater good."

"Then let it be so," she said, smiling as she saw a rider galloping toward us.

Roark slowed his pony a little as he approached, but still managed to dismount on the run. A flourish designed to impress Ellyn, I thought, but must admit he was a good horseman.

I was surprised when he addressed me.

"There's a force coming up the Coast Road," he announced. "I do not think it's reinforcements from Danant."

"Then who are they?" I asked.

He shrugged. "I don't know. My scouts reported them only just now. I thought it best to advise you. They come in numbers."

Roark's Quan held the western section, which commanded the Great Road out of Antium—which was the port from which Danant would, logically, deliver reinforcements. I wondered what force came from there, if it was not out of Danant.

"What do they look like?" I asked.

It was a moment before he answered, for—having delivered his message—he gazed into Ellyn's eyes like some love-struck puppy. It occurred to me to wonder if I looked at Shara so sickly. I also wondered if I must offend him by bringing him forcibly to the point—that some unknown army marched toward us, and we could not know whether it was friendly or hostile. I could not imagine where a friendly army might come from, and I felt like shaking him, or slapping his face that he wake to the potential danger and take his eyes off Ellyn.

"Odd, so my scouts say," came his answer as he tore his gaze from her face. "Like vagabonds. Surely not clansmen,

nor Chaldor folk. My scouts say they've a woman leading
them. She rides in a carriage drawn by men, as if they were
horses teamed to draw her." He shook his head as if this
were the strangest thing in the world.

"I'd see them," I said. "How far away are they? And
how many?"

"Six leagues," came his answer. "And perhaps a quarter
our numbers."

I calculated distances. Dusk approached. An army
might halt for the night, or march on to attack at dawn; I
needed to know what force came up the Coast Road. Was it
hostile, I'd need warriors to hold it and block the road.

"No chariots?" I asked. Was it a force out of Danant, it
would surely come with vehicles and mounted archers.

"All afoot," Roark answered.

I turned to Shara and Ellyn (whose eyes were still fixed
on Roark) and said, "Do you hold here while I go look?"
And to Roark: "Stay here. Send word to Mattich and Jaime
that a force approaches. Have them send one quarter of our
men to hold the Coast Road until I return."

Then I ran for my horse.

Roark was not so besotted with Ellyn that he forgot his
duty. I mounted my bay with Quan around me, and we galloped westward as the sun went down and bats came out to
fly the summer sky. I wondered what new counters were
thrown into this deadly game.

I halted my mare as fires sparkled ahead, spread across
the Great Road and the countryside beyond. From the quantity of twinkling flames I estimated there were about a thousand men approaching, and circled my escort a little way
southwestward to where a low ridge paralleled the Road.
Were whoever led this force not a fool, there had to be sentries up there. But I had six clansmen with me, and I believed we could approach unheard and unseen—and extract
answers.

We left our mounts in care of young Malcum (who
would have objected were he not in such awe of me) and

worked our way up the ridge. Sure enough, as I came to the rim I saw men waiting amongst the trees there. The moon was up now, the Hunter's Moon, and its light showed them clear. I could not recognize them by their dress, which was most odd—baggy breeches and brightly colored shirts, little armor, and that mostly mail like the scales of fishes, or crude plate, or leathern vests. They carried wide swords and long daggers, two held bows, some long spears with recurved heads. None wore helmets, and I saw that their hair was worn long and gathered in pigtails or braids, and that hoops of gold and silver pierced their ears. I motioned for my men to follow me and worked my way along the ridge until I found two alone. I whispered my intent and we crept toward them.

I took the first from behind with Calum as Otran and Vys seized the other. I clapped a hand over a startled mouth that opened to shout a cut-off warning as I grasped his sword arm. Calum punched him once in the midriff and smiled wickedly as he set a dagger to the man's throat. Otran and Vys were no less efficient, and in moments the sentinels were hauled from the ridgetop into the shadows below.

Calum held his dagger's point to the man's throat as I released my grip.

"Do you cry out," I said, "my friend will stick you. Who are you?"

Dark eyes glowered at me, but he kept his voice low as he answered, "I am Leonardi of Hel's Town. Who are you?"

"Gailard of the Devyn, commander of Chaldor's army and Guardian of Ellyn."

I was surprised by the smile that split his swarthy face as he began to chuckle. Calum pressed his blade closer, as if he thought the man gone mad.

"Poor welcome you offer us, Gailard. We come to aid you and you threaten my life?"

"What?" I demanded, confused. "What are you talking about?"

Leonardi stared at Calum. "Tell this oaf to remove his

blade. I find it hard to speak with a dagger pricking my throat."

I nodded to Calum. He took the dagger away—but held it ready.

Leonardi said, "The Mother can explain it better than I. Her and Kerid."

"Kerid?" That name rang loud bells whose sound I could not quite believe. "The same Kerid as sailed in Chaldor's fleet?"

"The Mother's consort," he answered. "Now, do you leave me go, I'll take you to them."

Calum said, "Don't trust him. This could be a trap, and they on Talan's side."

Leonardi said, "I might have to fight you, fellow. I give my word and you doubt it? I tell you, the Mother took us off the river to aid you. I give you my word you'll be safe with us."

I studied him awhile. I had read somewhat of the Hel's Town pirates, and heard more of them from Andur; he surely fit the descriptions I'd read. I nodded to Calum. "Let him up, eh?"

Leonardi rose, grinning at Calum as if his pride was assuaged. "Come," he said. Then motioned to where Otran and Vys held the other. "But let Cyrus go, too, eh?"

I gave the order and the one called Cyrus rose cursing. Leonardi beckoned him and told him to alert the (ineffective, I thought) sentries of our arrival. Leonardi himself would bring me to Kerid and the Mother.

We went down the slope.

I saw that most of this strange army slept on the ground. There were few tents and no horses, but a phalanx of men armored in fish mail, with spears and swords—faces hidden beneath piscine helms came to block our path. Beyond them I saw a great pavilion that shone like water under the moon's light, with the palanquin Roark had described resting on the ground before.

Spears were leveled in our direction and Leonardi

cried, "Friends! I am Leonardi and I bring Gailard of Chaldor to meet with the Mother."

His voice was loud enough to carry the distance, and I sensed he boasted—as if I were a prize. I eased my sword, ready to draw. *Were* this a trap I'd sell myself dear.

Then a man emerged from the magnificent pavilion and a voice rang out.

"Gailard! Is that truly you? In the names of all the gods, I'd scarce dared hope . . ." He paused to call back toward the pavilion, then came running toward me.

I recognized him: Kerid.

He pushed past the armored guard and embraced me.

"There were so many rumors . . . You fled Chorym, you died . . . By the gods, Gailard, it's good to see you again. You've an army now? The Mother heard it was so . . . Come, you must meet her."

He took my arm and led me to the pavilion. My clansmen followed, like restless hounds on my heels. Kerid shouted that they be fed and wined, and brought me to the woman who stood between two braziers that lit her golden hair with sparks of light. She was very beautiful, and seemed much older than Ellyn, but she held a regal stance and surveyed me with calmly imperious eyes. She wore a silvery gown that seemed to be constructed of mail, and clung to the contours of her body as do a fish's scales. Rings glittered on her fingers, jewels from her ears. Her small waist was encircled by a narrow belt that held a long, thin knife.

"This," Kerid said, "is Mother Hel. She commands this army we've brought to aid you."

It seemed that the girl expected some acknowledgment, and I'd not disappoint any allies I might find, so I offered a Highlander's obeisance to an equal. I bowed my head and lowered a knee.

"Do you come to aid Ellyn of Chaldor in her rightful war, I welcome you and thank you."

"We do," Kerid said.

"Mother Hel?" I stared at this beautiful, imperious woman. She reminded me of both Shara and Ellyn. "Then this army you bring must be the Hel's Town pirates."

"Not all of them." She turned away, beckoning me into the pavilion. "Perhaps one third. The rest hold the Durrakym against Danant, that Talan not bring more soldiers to his cause, or find any trade." She glanced fondly at Kerid. "I was . . . persuaded . . . to support you, and so Hel's Town has taken a side."

She gestured that I sit. There was a table of some dark wood inlaid with silver motifs, matching chairs, silver plates and decanters, goblets of crystal. The one she took was set with jewels. I wondered how so much opulence was transported without horses.

"I break all precedent," she said. "Hel's Town does not take sides in the land wars, but . . ." She glanced again at Kerid, who stared at her much as Roark did at Ellyn. Or perhaps I at Shara. "I was persuaded that it were better Hel's Town aid you than stand neutral. So I offer you an army."

"And they're fine fighters," Kerid said.

"Why?" I asked. I'd know my allies before I trusted them.

Mother Hel blushed, I thought. "I have come to trust Kerid," she said. "And he convinced me of your cause. I'd not see Talan of Danant own the river—nor his Vachyn hireling. Say me nay, and I'll go home. I'll go back to my ships and leave the river clear."

I said, quickly, "I'd not see that, Mother. I'd sooner have you on my side, and see Ellyn on Chaldor's throne. I thank you for your aid, and welcome you to our side."

She nodded imperiously. "And how goes your war?"

I told her, and she said, "Shall we make a difference against a Vachyn sorcerer?"

"Shara's with us," I said. "And Ellyn owns magic now. Can Danant not send more men . . ."

"They'd find it hard," she said coolly. "The Durrakym's held by my—pirates, you call them? No matter—there's not a Danant vessel can cross the river without a bloody fight they'll likely lose. So what do we do here?"

"Talan and his Vachyn sit in Chorym," I said. "They've made no major move against us yet, but Shara wonders if Nestor gathers some great power."

"And what do you do?" she asked.

"I've siege engines ready," I said. "And now you're with us, I think we can attack."

"Even against the Vachyn?"

I shrugged. "I cannot know what Nestor plans, but all the Highlanders are ready. We must begin soon, win or lose."

"How far to Chorym?" she asked.

I said, "Six leagues."

"We'll be there on the morrow," she said. "Close on first light. Do you wait for us to come up before you start your engines?"

I nodded.

"We'll take the city," she said. "I think that not even a Vachyn sorcerer can stand against the combined might of the Highlands and Hel's Town."

I grinned at her. I liked her. I said, "Thank you, Mother."

Kerid said, "You'll stay with us tonight?"

I shook my head, hoping I offended no Hel's Town protocols. "Thank you, but no. I'd bring Ellyn this news as soon as I can."

Mother Hel said, "Then we'll talk more tomorrow. I'd speak with Ellyn and this Shara. Come the dawn we'll be with you."

I smiled and rose and made my farewells, and rode back to Chorym with the good news.

CHAPTER THIRTY-FOUR

The chamber had once been pleasant—a room filled in summer with light from the high windows, warmed in winter by the heat of the great hearth, set round with comfortable chairs in which a visitor might sit and peruse one of the many books or scrolls that filled the shelves along the walls. Now the windows were hidden behind sable drapes, and the books and scrolls and parchments were all given to the fire that blazed under the high arch, giving off a rank odor of putrescence that suggested the pages of the library burned things more mortal than paper.

The chairs were all shoved to the sides of the room, the center of which was occupied by a single table on which Nestor had set the instruments of his magic. Some were inanimate—pieces of bone and stone, crystal vials containing fluids that seethed and bubbled, skulls and the drying wings of dismembered birds—others were living, and moaned as the Vachyn performed his arcane magicks.

Nestor moved around them, mouthing incantations that set little sparklings of dark light to dancing about the chamber, and his living objects to screaming. He seemed not to hear the cries—or did not care. He only went on with his cantrip, taking up a knife when it was needed to carve through flesh, selecting those organs necessary to the spell and casting them into the flames, adding a bone or a wing, or a skull so that the fire sputtered and blazed and gusted foul, stinking smoke that filled the room before the chimney took it and raised it up over Chorym's walls.

Outside, men watched the smoke rise and spread, uncommanded by the wind, obeying only the Vachyn's diktat.

There came a knocking at the door and Nestor hesitated an instant. Heard Talan's voice, and slashed a cut across a woman's eyeball and another over the curve of her throat as he continued to mouth his spell. He dug the eye out and drenched it in the spouting blood, then tossed the horrid burden into the fire. Only then did he open the door.

Talan gagged as he entered the awful chamber. His eyes clenched shut as the foul smoke assaulted, then watered as he forced them open. He swallowed noisily and pressed a scented handkerchief to his mouth.

"What do you do?" His voice was muffled by the 'kerchief.

"Your will," Nestor said. "A glass of wine?"

Talan shook his head. He clearly wanted to swallow nothing that came from this chamber.

"I am sure now that my erstwhile sister stands against me." Nestor smiled confidently. "She and Ellyn. I sensed two magical presences when I sent that bolt against our observers."

"And they deflected it." Talan's voice came thick through the cloth, heavy with the desire to vomit. "They live, and the Highlanders build siege equipment."

"It means nothing." Nestor leaned back against the table. His hands rested in pools of blood that he ignored. "I conjure such a spell now as defeated Andur. It shall succeed again, against these clansmen."

"Why not strike them again with that lightning? Destroy their machinery, their leaders?"

Nestor smiled. "Because my sister can deflect it. She's strong, and she has Ellyn to support her."

"You told me Ellyn was weak in the talent."

"She grows daily stronger," Nestor said. And before Talan could protest, "It's as I told you—let the wasps come to the pot and they're trapped."

"As we are?" Talan gestured at the walls, flinging out both his arms. Then stifled on the stench and began to choke, so that his words came thick and muffled. "We are surrounded. Barbarian clansmen ring our walls, and it seems the Hel's Town pirates command the Durrakym. Tell me who's the pot and who's the wasp, eh?"

"We've all our enemies gathering here," Nestor said, "just as I promised you. Let them all come, and I'll destroy them in one fell swoop."

"Can you? Truly?"

Nestor ducked his head. "Do you not trust me any longer?"

Talan hesitated a moment before answering. Then: "I wonder if more force comes against us than even you can defeat."

The Vachyn barked impatient laughter. "Let them come. I shall defeat them all—on your behalf. I shall destroy my sister and Ellyn, the Highlanders. The Hel's Town pirates, do they dare oppose you. All of them! Just as I promised."

Talan said, "I hope so."

"Believe so." Nestor gestured at the door. "I'll give you such a kingdom as this world has never known. Only trust me, eh? And leave me alone now to defeat your enemies."

Talan smiled—a wan curving of his frightened mouth—and left the stinking chamber.

Talan went to the ramparts, where the air was cleaner, and found Egor Dival.

The old man was still bandaged—there were few healers left in Chorym, and none the invaders trusted save their own who were in short supply—leaning morosely on the battlements and surveying the army that now surrounded Chorym.

"So, does your Vachyn offer answers?"

"He works a cantrip even now," Talan said. "He promises victory."

Dival spat over the new brickwork. "Look at that, eh?" He gestured at the plain below. "Do you see what they do?"

Talan stared at the distant army. "They build siege engines, I suppose. Just as we did."

"Which no Highlander army ever did before. And is all I hear true, they've *two* sorcerers to support them. And likely an army of Hel's Town pirates coming to their aid."

"I've got Nestor," Talan said, defensive. "Not some hedgerow wizardess and her protégé."

"And they've got every god-cursed clansmen the Highlands ever produced. And folk—do I not miss my guess— from Cu-na'Lhair, and farmers and shepherds and just about everyone they've picked up along the way." Dival sighed, easing from the wall to nurse his hurting arm. He stared at his king. "Do you believe we can defeat them?"

"It's as you said—these Highlanders are not accustomed to siege warfare."

"Nor are we—from this side of the walls."

Talan frowned. He longed for a glass of wine, but it would look amiss did the Lord of Danant and Chaldor ask for drink here, so he fought the desire and made his face stern. "Chorym is mine; I'll not give up the city. And we've Nestor . . ."

Dival barked sour laughter. "He sent his magicks against them once before, no? And what did we see?"

Talan closed his eyes a moment, remembering that strange cloud of translucent light that had settled about the three Nestor promised to destroy. The bolt had been deflected like an arrow from a shield. "Nestor promises me victory," he said, praying as he did that it be so. "He conjures a great magic even now."

"But in the end," said Egor Dival, "I think it shall come down to honest swordwork."

"Then you're well fit for the task," Talan snarled, and quit the ramparts.

Dival watched him go, thinking that soon they both must die. He wondered why did he not feel sorry.

The smoke rose from the chimney and streamered against the sky. Then it turned, unbidden by the breeze, and gathered, coalescing into a great mass of darkness that hid the sun and then the moon and the stars, and then grew until there was only drifting shadow. It ran from over Chorym to descend across the surrounding forces like the horridly whispering voice of nightmares, and as it fell men began to shiver, and some to weep, and think of lost hope and lost loves, of betrayals and death.

"This is Vachyn magic, no?" Ellyn asked.

Shara nodded. "The foulest kind, I think."

"What can we do?"

"Nothing as yet."

"There must be something." Ellyn's voice was forlorn.

Shara's was stern with purpose. "Only hold on, and wait for Gailard to return."

"And is this new-come army from out of Danant?"

"Then we've lost. Or we die here."

"Only those choices?"

"Save we've allies." Shara raised her shoulders in a shrug. "Had we the Dur women with us, perhaps we could foretell the outcome. But . . ." She shrugged again and forced a smile. "We've not, so we can only wait."

"Until?" Ellyn asked.

"Gailard returns," said Shara, "with news that's good or ill." She shivered, as if she wondered at his return.

"You love him," Ellyn said.

Shara met the younger woman's gaze. "Don't you?"

Ellyn paused awhile before answering. Then, carefully: "Not as I thought I did." She laughed nervously. "I hated him at first. I thought him an uncouth savage. But then . . . He's not, is he? He's a noble man, and I should have known that. My father named him friend, and my mother trusted him. So I should have. But . . ." She shrugged in turn. "I thought I loved him, and so I hated you—because you stole his heart. I saw the way he looked at you—and you at him—and I knew. I wanted to send you away then. I thought that I'd banish you and have Gailard for myself. Save I needed to learn from you, and so I must suffer your presence."

Her voice trailed off. Her eyes grew moist.

Shara said, "And now?"

"There's Roark," Ellyn answered shyly. "I love him."

"And what of Gailard?" Shara asked.

"He does not love me," Ellyn said. "Not in that way. He loves you as I love Roark."

Shara ducked her head in acknowledgment.

"Are you . . . ?" Ellyn asked. "Have you . . . ?"

"No." Shara shook her head. "Not until Chorym is won and you take your parents' throne."

"Nor we," Ellyn said, smiling.

"Then best we take the city soon, eh?"

Ellyn began to reply, but then Mattich came into their tent. His visage was fearful. "Best you come quickly," he declared. "This god-cursed Vachyn magic frightens our warriors, and your presence can strengthen them."

"Come." Shara rose, holding out a hand to Ellyn. "Come, sister, and let's to our duty."

CHAPTER THIRTY-FIVE

I pushed my bay hard on the return, leaving the smaller, slower Highland ponies behind me. I'd bring word of our newfound allies to Ellyn and Shara as quickly as possible, and it would not be the first night I'd spent sleepless in battle's cause. Did Mother Hel and Kerid bring up their army as they promised, we might commence our attack that day.

By dawn, the Mother had promised—and I thought her a woman who'd keep her word. The Hel's Town pirates would march through the night and be with us early. Then those siege engines my Highlander kin did not properly understand might be brought into play and we assault Chorym's walls without fear of attack from the rear. I laughed into the night.

Then gasped as I saw what lay ahead of me.

Mist drifted across the road like the trailing threads of spinning spiders, insubstantial at first, so that I assumed it no more than the combination of the day's heat with the rain-dampened ground, but then thicker . . . So thick that, within paces, it became a wall of grey that hid the Hunter's Moon and all the stars. I could not understand it. Vapors rising from the fields might account for some part, but this was such a brume as decorated the Highlands' woods in deepest winter. It was clammy and chill at the same time, so that I felt sweat bead my brow even as I shivered at the cold that struck into my bones. I felt my knee begin to ache, where a year and a lifetime ago that pike had struck me, and also the wounds Nestor's hunters had delivered; and my mare began to fret, slowing her pace and turning her head nervously as I urged her on. Soon I must dismount and lead her, else she'd have thrown me and run off. Her eyes rolled and her ears were laid back, and she swung her head from side to side as if she heard, or saw, or sensed, things within the fog that I could not.

I guessed that Nestor had begun his work. I drew my sword and cursed the mare as she began to buck and I let go the reins before she plunge her hooves onto me. She snorted once and turned around to disappear into the mist. I pressed on.

And in time saw somewhat of what I'd witnessed in the Darach Pass and across the Durrakym.

Dawn was gone and the sun shone over Chorym. But from the city's walls, like smoke from the nostrils of a pipe user, there rolled great banks of grey mist. They encompassed the surrounding army and the countryside a league beyond. It was as if clouds fell from the sky to roll across the land, and all was grey and lost save for the thunderbolts that struck from above.

They descended in lancing flashes of brilliant light that crashed against the land beneath and left the heavens ringing. I saw columns of fire, and recognized the shapes of my siege towers and catapults burning. I shouted as despair filled me—another reminder of the Darach Pass—and stumbled forward even as I saw answering flashes rise from the ground to strike against Nestor's magic, so that both the darkened sky above my army and that over Chorym were lit by counterpoised brilliances. I ached and hurt, and felt a terrible desire to throw away my sword and buckler and flee. It was as if the mist whispered that I could not prevail and had better run.

I had experienced this before, so I fought my doubts

and fears and pressed on. Roark came out of the brume. He carried a torch that did little to light his way. Strands of hair hung lank about his face and his eyes were haunted. He held a sword that he pointed toward me, and gasped in relief as he recognized me.

"Thank the gods, Gailard, that you're safe. Thank them more that you're back."

"What happens?" I asked.

"It began awhile ago," he said. "At midnight, I think. This mist came up and then . . ." He ducked his head as a peal of thunder roiled above us and light came down from the sky. I heard a horse scream briefly. "Ellyn and Shara do what they can. But . . ." He shook his head. "Best they explain, for the gods know I cannot."

"Do the clans stand?" I asked.

"So far." He nodded and wiped at his mouth. "But does this go on . . ." He shrugged, glancing nervously around. "My Quan will hold, else I'll have all their heads. But . . . This frightens them, Gailard."

It frightened him, too. I could see that, and must admire him for his steadfast purpose. Perhaps he *was* fit for Ellyn.

"Bring me to them," I said. I could no longer find directions in this fog. "And spread the word that an army of Hel's Town pirates comes to support us. They come up the Coast Road, and they're welcome."

He nodded and shouted orders to his men, which impressed me. And then impressed me more as he asked, "The warriors I sent with you, they're safe?"

"I left them behind," I said, "to bring our allies safely in."

"The gods be thanked for that."

"Thank them when we've won," I grunted. "Now bring me to Shara and Ellyn, and send for Mattich and Jaime."

I found them where we had established our command center. It was no grandiose thing—only a cluster of tents with one large enough that we might confer at the middle of the ring—guarded by nervous clansmen who flinched at each skyborne blast and stared at me like puppies experiencing their first storm. That sense of horrid dread that accompanies Nestor's magicks was less present here, which I supposed was due to the proximity of Shara and Ellyn.

I found them inside the tent. They sat to either side of a small table, their hands stretched out that they might link their fingers, four hammered-tin bowls between them. One held earth, the second water, the third a candle, and the last was empty. Both their faces were pale, and their eyes were hollow. I hesitated, unwilling to break their obvious concentration.

And Shara said, "It's begun. Nestor has summoned all his power. He looks to destroy the siege engines. I . . ."

The tent shook like a rag doll tossed into a gale as light filled the morning. I felt the ground tremble beneath my feet, and for a moment I was blinded even through the canvas. I clutched at a pole and shook my head, rubbing at my eyes.

"We can defend the men," Shara continued out of a dry mouth, "but not the engines. They're mostly gone."

I ducked out of the tent and saw more pyres loft through the mist.

"What next?" I asked. I stared at Ellyn, who seemed oblivious to this conversation. Her eyes were rolled back so that only the whites showed. "Shall more—worse?—magic come against us, or honest battle?"

Shara said, "I don't know—I cannot know! Only that I and Ellyn hold Nestor's magicks off the warriors. For now . . ."

New thunder rolled across the sky. I watched as Shara trembled and shuddered—as if her very bones, the templates of her brain, the blood running through her veins were seared.

Nor was Ellyn better; she clutched at Shara's hands and screwed her eyes tight. I saw tears leaking from the closed lids, and pain that made her face haggard. Her lower lip was bleeding where she'd chewed it.

"Not for much longer," Shara muttered. "He gathers strength, and . . ."

The shock tumbled me off my feet. I rose unsteadily to see the table trembling, water spilling from one bowl, earth from another, the candle's flame wavering. I smelled the roof of the tent scorching.

"He finds us!" Shara's voice was harsh as stones rubbed together. "He's wrecked the engines and now he'd slay us."

"How can he know where you are?" I asked, even as I saw little curls of flame descend from the canvas ceiling.

Shara let go of Ellyn's hands. "When Ellyn slew those hunters, he found her . . . pattern in the aethyr. When I destroyed that chariot, he found mine . . . Now we're so close he can locate us precisely, and direct all his power against us. We . . ."

A bolt of lightning struck the ground directly before the tent, and I felt its heat as I was flung back. I saw the ground scorched and flames run up the guy ropes. The oiled canvas began to burn. I picked myself up and saw Ellyn on her back beside her overturned chair, her eyes wide and blank.

Shara said, not steadily, "We must move away. This drains me and might kill Ellyn. She's strong in the talent, but not so strong she can survive this."

"Where?" I asked as I took Ellyn in my arms. "Where shall be safe?"

"I don't know." Shara turned her head in a helplessly negative gesture. "Beyond the mist? *I don't know!* Only away from here."

I had never seen her frightened before, and that frightened me. I stumbled from the tent. Canvas walls fell around us in lickering tongues of fire as I carried Ellyn out. Shara gathered up the pots, careless of their contents, and I thought the thunder and the lightning and the sense of horrid dread grew stronger as they were emptied.

I held Ellyn and looked about. I could see no farther than a few paces, but I could hear men shouting in fear, and the shrilling of terrified animals. I thought our only chance was to attack—but could not see how we might. Not now, when the siege engines I had relied on to break Chorym's strong walls were all burning. By the gods, I could see them even through this unnatural fog: bonfires rising in hopeless sparks toward a sky that was sometimes late summer's blue, and sometimes dark as winter's night—alternating in an eye's blink between the one and the other, so that my eyes were tricked and confused and I could not tell if Nestor delivered us light or dark. I could only feel the dread that filled me and wonder if the Vachyn owned such power as must defeat us and destroy us at his whim.

Shara emerged from the burning tent with a satchel on her shoulder. I saw that her hair was scorched, her face muddied with ashes. I took her arm and dragged her away before the tent could collapse and engulf her.

It fell down in a great gout of flame that sent us all starting away. I wondered if I heard laughter fill the sky. Then Roark came out of the brume, and Mattich and Jaime were with him.

"I'll take her," Roark said.

I looked to Shara, who nodded. So I handed Ellyn to him, and he cradled her in his arms.

Jaime said, "What is this, Gailard? The gods knew, but there are men of mine who've run. We're not used to fighting such as this."

Mattich said, "Roark told me we've allies coming. But can we hold? Shall they defeat this?"

We all ducked as fresh thunder roiled the sky and lightning stalked like some long and multiply legged insect across the ground. I heard the screams of men join those of the animals. I saw tents burst into fire, cooking pots explode, stacked wood ignite. My head swam. Old wounds ached. I felt afraid—and, as I remembered the Darach Pass, angry. That helped.

"We *shall* defeat it," I said. "We've the Hel's Town pirates coming to our aid. They hold the river against Talan's men, and they bring at least a thousand to our landward forces."

"But shall that be enough?" Mattich asked. "The gods know, I've . . ."

He shivered as light filled the sky and pointing fingers lanced toward us. Fires erupted around us.

Shara screamed, "We must be gone!"

And we ran through the horrid fog until we were clear, and there was an open field. It had once owned a stone wall, but I supposed that had been taken by Talan—or us—to load catapults, and now it stood empty, like an old mouth pulled free of teeth. There was a farmhouse, or its relicts— for that, too, was torn down in war's purpose. But the grass was green, and the fog was ended here, and it was morning and the sun shone bright, and Roark set Ellyn down.

Shara said, "This will do," and began to unpack her satchel.

Mattich said, "I cannot promise the Dur, not against this." He gestured back at the ring of fog we had escaped, where the lightnings still flashed and fires still burned and men and animals still screamed. "My warriors are frightened."

"Nor I the Arran," Jaime said. "The gods know, we're with you in setting Ellyn back on her throne. But this . . ." He shook his scarred head. "This is . . . Gailard, we fight a battle we cannot win. Talan's Vachyn is too strong."

"NO!"

Shara's voice seemed loud as any thunderclap. "Do you not understand? Do you give up now, you hand the world to the Vachyn. Give up the fight now and Talan shall own Chaldor, and soon the Highlands, and you'll be conquered. And do you think that Talan and Nestor shall forgive you? *No!* They'll take your heads and make all your clans their servants as they go on to conquer."

"But we cannot fight magic," Mattich said. "We face walls we cannot break, because the magic has destroyed Gailard's engines."

"And your power cannot defend us," Jaime said. He pointed an accusing finger at the supine Ellyn. "She's strong in the talent, you said, but look at her. What use is she?"

"Hold!" Roark stared angrily at Jaime. "Hold your tongue, eh? The Quan stand with her and I'll not hear her insulted."

Jaime shrugged an apology. "You love her, but I love my clan no less—and I cannot see her use in this war, save as Chaldor's heir."

"She's strong with magic," Shara said, "and in a while she'll wake." She emptied her satchel and began to set her pots on the ground. "And you have no choice betwixt failure and defeat. Shall you run away and be hunted down by Talan's soldiers and Vachyn magicks, or shall you fight like a warrior?"

"Against warriors in honest battle?" Jaime nodded. "That, surely. I'll face any man in honest fight. But this?" He gestured at the disturbed sky. "I'd assumed you'd counter this—Vachyn against the Lady of the Mountains— but I see no hope in this. I see my men dying, and scant hope of victory."

"The Quan shall fight to the end," Roark said, "in support of Ellyn."

Shara used her fingers to dig earth from the ground: one pot filled.

I said, "I trust Shara." I watched her pour water into another; set a candle in a third; set the last, empty, on the ground. "And in Ellyn."

Ellyn stirred. Roark laved her face with a dampened cloth and an adoring look, and Ellyn woke and stared into his eyes.

Shara turned from her pots, speaking urgently to Ellyn. "We're beyond the aegis of Nestor's magicks now, and I need you. Are we to succeed, you must help me."

Ellyn groaned, leaning against Roark. "That hurt," she muttered, for an instant sounding petulant as the child I'd known. "My head aches."

"The Hel's Town pirates come to our aid," Shara said. "We're sore beset, but they might make the difference."

"What difference?" Ellyn rose a little way into Roark's arms. "What difference can I make?"

"Enough," Shara said, "do you work with me."

I ducked as horrid peals of thunder struck the sky over the ring of mist that surrounded Chorym. I watched fresh fingers of light touch the ground. The mist hung still and steady and dismal there. I doubted the clans would hold for long, and feared all our hopes be soon shattered by Nestor's magicks and Ellyn's recalcitrance.

"Listen," Shara said, "for there is a way."

She looked at me and smiled.

"Do you remember when I first came to you, when Eryk hung you on that tree?"

I nodded. From the corner of my eye I saw men come running from out of the fog. They had thrown away their weapons and now fled with the look of panicked animals. Mattich and Jaime shouted at them, for some wore the plaid of the Dur and the Arran. Others bore the Devyn colors.

"I must work that spell again." Shara hesitated. "I must go into Chorym."

"No!" My answer was no less explosive than her earlier negative.

More men stumbled from out of the fog as she said, "Save we find a way in, we've lost. We cannot break the walls now, and soon all our army will run. I doubt the Hel's Town pirates shall fare better. So . . ."

"You cannot! You must not!" I grasped her hand. "You say that Nestor can find you now. Do you use that spell, he'll surely know you're coming, and be waiting for you. If he does not destroy you first!"

"What else is there?" she asked.

"Besides," I said as if she had not spoken, "you don't know the city. You'd not know which gate, or how to open it."

"I can open gates," she said.

"Only do you live. And I doubt you should. The gods know, but you'd face Talan's soldiers and Nestor's magicks, and I doubt even you can defeat both."

"What other choice have we?" She looked me in the eye. "Save we enter the city, we lose everything."

I cursed loudly. That awful sense of dread was gone now that I was clear of the Vachyn fog, but old wounds still ached, and I could imagine how the men still encompassed by the brume felt. I watched Roark smooth Ellyn's hair as she sat up. Mattich and Jaime studied me and Shara with dour faces lined with lost hope, waiting for some miracle they doubted could come. Indeed, I was none too sure myself. Save . . .

"There's another way," I said, and touched Shara's lips as she began to protest. "No, listen—you transformed me then. Can you do that again?"

She nodded, eyeing me warily, clearly ready to argue my plan.

"I know the city," I said, "and folk know me—I might find allies. Also, I am a soldier and can fight better than you."

"Not against Nestor's magicks." She shook her head. "Did I transform you, he'd sense *you* coming."

"He senses you and Ellyn," I said. "He knows there are two with the talent, but not of any other."

"Even so, he'd know."

"Suppose," I said, "that you and Ellyn worked your magicks as I entered? Might that not confuse him long enough that I might enter the city?"

She allowed a cautious, "Perhaps."

I paused. This stratagem sprang suddenly to mind—the gods knew that we needed to act swift!—and I had not fully thought it through. "And the Hel's Town pirates shall arrive soon," I said. "What if . . ."

I outlined my hasty plan.

When I was done, Shara thought a moment, then lowered her head in reluctant acknowledgment. "It might work. But it's dangerous."

"War is dangerous," I said.

She put her hands to my face and drew it down that she might put her lips to mine. "I love you, Gailard."

I gloried in that kiss. It was the promise of all I'd hoped for, the promise of reward to come. In that moment, as she drew me close, I forgot Ellyn, forgot my purpose—and knew only that I'd conquer Chorym to have this woman I loved. I'd conquer the world for her—save she'd not have that. But Chorym—yes. The gods knew, I'd stake my life on that—to have her.

She drew apart, and I wondered if she was embarrassed. I laughed. "So let's to it, eh?"

CHAPTER THIRTY-SIX

"They withdraw?" Talan Kedassian stared at the wall of fog that encircled Chorym's walls. He could see no deeper into that magical brume than any other mortal man, but he wondered at the sounds that came from within its shadow. "You're sure?"

"I'm sure." Nestor ducked his head. "Their siege engines are all destroyed and they fall back."

"To where? They flee? We've beaten them?"

Talan rose on the tips of his armored toes, peering at the mist as if he'd force his eyes to find what they could not. Sunlight glittered on his golden armor and he unlatched his helmet for the sake of better vision. A servant hurried to take the helm from him.

"I can see no farther than you." Nestor's tone was irritable. "But I know they fall back. How far, I cannot say—only that they withdraw beyond the aegis of my magic."

"And Ellyn? Shara?"

"My erstwhile sister?" Nestor shrugged. "She works no magic now; neither Ellyn."

"Then they're dead?" Talan asked hopefully. "You slew them?"

"Perhaps." Nestor frowned. "I cannot say for sure. But I cannot feel their magicks at work, so perhaps . . ."

"How can we be sure?"

"I could lift my spell," Nestor said, a hint of mockery in his voice.

"And leave us defenseless?" Talan shook his head. "No, not until we're certain."

"Let me send out patrols," Egor Dival suggested. He looked to Nestor. "Or shall your filthy fog unnerve them, too?"

"Of course." Nestor studied the older man with undisguised contempt in his dark eyes. "Think you I can conjure such a spell that affects only this man, and not that?"

"I thought you omnipotent," Dival returned with no less contempt.

"Hold, hold." Talan raised a nervous hand as the Vachyn's eyes narrowed and Dival's good hand touched his sword's hilt. "We stand on the brink of victory, eh? This is no time to quarrel."

"Save unless we know whether or not the Highlanders are gone," Dival said, "we are sealed in as much as they are sealed out."

"Do Shara or Ellyn work any further magicks, I shall know," Nestor said. "And find them, are they not already slain."

"Which we cannot know whilst that fog remains," Dival grunted. Then he laughed: "A joke, eh? We are trapped by our own success."

Talan looked from one to the other, but it was Nestor to whom he turned in the end. "What shall we do?"

"I would suggest," the Vachyn said, "that I maintain the spell awhile—a day or two—and then let this soldier send out his patrols."

"Which means you must lift . . ." Talan gestured at the brume. "Which shall leave us without defense."

"You've an army here," Dival said. "And have the Highlanders not attacked by then, it must surely be safe. The gods know, their engines are all destroyed and they've no longer the means to break Chorym's walls. We've all our forces here—and the men to defeat them in honest battle. How can we lose?"

Finally, Talan said, "We shall wait for two days. Then Nestor will lift his spell and you can send men out." He nodded, approving his own decision, finding military pride in the prospect of an easy victory. "Are they fled, we'll harry them back to their dismal Highlands."

"And are they not?" Dival asked.

Talan glanced at Nestor, who said: "I doubt they'll remain."

"But do they," Talan said cautiously, looking now to Egor Dival, "your patrols shall return immediately, and we'll let them break themselves against the walls."

"As my king commands." Dival saluted and turned away. Over his shoulder he called, "I'd now inspect my men."

"When this is ended and you are victorious," Nestor said softly, "I suggest something be done about that old man. He lives past his time."

"Yes," Talan agreed, "but not until we know the clans are gone, eh?"

"Not until all is secure," Nestor whispered. "But then . . ."

Egor Dival slowed his stride. He felt a prickling between his shoulder blades, and when he looked back he saw Nestor studying him with darkly speculative eyes, Talan turning quickly away. The old soldier squared his shoulders, wincing as his broken arm shifted in its sling. Perhaps it was some drifting aftermath of Vachyn magic that made him feel so uncomfortable—indeed, almost afraid—or perhaps it was something in the Vachyn's eyes. He could not trust the sorcerer, and it was Nestor had Talan's ear now.

He muttered a curse and continued on his way.

Kerid halted as he saw the fog. He was accustomed to river mists, but this was something different. It seemed thicker

than a full spread of canvas sails, and somehow malevolent.
Even at a distance, with the sun bright overhead, he felt its
cold, and he heard screaming from inside the brume, saw
men running in obvious terror.

He raised a hand, halting the column of Hel's Town pirates, and turned to Nassim.

"What is this?"

"How should I know?" Nassim spat tobacco and
shrugged. "Vachyn magic? Talan's a sorcerer in his employ, no?"

Kerid nodded and looked to where tents were established beyond the mist, as if ring upon ring were set around
Chorym. The city rose on its hill under a blue, late-summer
sky. There was an area of brightness around the walls—then
thick, dank fog, and another clear patch before the tents and
horses and waiting men began. "Wait here," he said, "I'd
speak with the Mother."

He paced back to the palanquin, where Mother Hel sat
staring at the spectacle before them.

"Vachyn magic?" Her question echoed Nassim's.
"Well, no matter. We're committed now."

"We go on?" Kerid frowned. "I'd not expected this."

"No, but we gave our word." The Mother's lips pursed a
moment and Kerid wondered if she spoke of them both, or
in regal plural. "So we see what's what, eh? Let's find
Gailard."

Riders came toward them, hailing their small escort of
clansmen before offering brief bows to the Mother and
Kerid. Their leader was a young man, handsome for all his
face was drawn and haggard.

"I am Roark of the Quan," he announced, "and I bid you
welcome on behalf of Ellyn of Chaldor."

"Where is Gailard?" the Mother asked.

"With Ellyn," Roark answered, "waiting for you."

"Then bring us to him," she commanded, leaving no
doubt in her tone. "And see to the feeding of my men. We've
marched a long way to aid you, and they are hungry."

Roark said, "Come," and turned his pony, leading the pirates toward the tents that sat outside the fog.

Ellyn stared at the newcomers. She thought that until now she had never seen a woman more lovely than Shara, nor so regal. She gathered herself, surprised as Mother Hel extended a hand as if they were equals.

"I am the Mother of Hel's Town."

Ellyn took her hand and said, "I am Ellyn," thinking only after to add, "of Chaldor."

She felt weak still—it was as if Nestor's magicks had addled her mind worse than any excess of brose—but she had a duty to perform, and these were allies come to her aid. She would treat them well, as befit a queen.

She saw Gailard and Kerid smile at one another like old friends, heard introductions made and said, "This is Shara, who aids me. I . . ."

Her head spun and Mother Hel helped her to a chair. "Sit down, child. I've heard somewhat of what you do, and you're clearly hurt. Vachyn magicks, eh?"

Ellyn felt herself eased to the chair. Mother Hel looked not much older than herself, but she had about her an air of command that was hard to ignore.

"So," she said, "what goes on here?"

Ellyn listened as Gailard explained. Roark filled a cup with wine and set it in her hand. Shara sat beside her, with Mattich and Jaime about the table, and the one called Kerid. And another who chewed foul tobacco that he spat carelessly onto the ground, whose name, she thought, was Nassim.

"So you've no siege engines," Mother Hel said when Gailard was done, "and your warriors flee. Talan sits inside Chorym with his Vachyn sorcerer and most of his army. This does not augur well."

"Save," Gailard said, "does our strategy work."

"It's a long gamble you speak of," Kerid said.

"It's the only one," Gailard replied.

416 ANGUS WELLS

"That could cost us dear," Mother Hel said. "You ask my folk to die in your cause. And if your plan fails . . ."

"You can retreat now," Shara said. "You can go back to your boats and return to Hel's Town. Nestor is not yet aware of your presence."

"Save Talan knows by now that we seal in his ports," the Mother answered, "and in time shall doubtless learn of all our part in your war."

"There's that," Shara allowed.

"And does he conquer here," Kerid said, "then likely he'll look to conquer us in time."

"And is all you tell me true," the Mother said, "then even Hel's Town must fall to the Vachyn." She sighed and smiled. "So be it, we fight with you. Even though"—she eyed Gailard quizzically—"I think you insane."

Ellyn felt Roark's hand clasp tight on hers, but her eyes remained steady on Gailard's face as he nodded, and she felt proud of her guardian. And terribly afraid for him.

Mother Hel said, "When does this begin?"

Ellyn saw Gailard turn to Shara and felt a pang of jealousy for all that Roark's touch was comforting. Then she heard him say, "When Shara deems it right. But soon, eh?"

CHAPTER THIRTY-SEVEN

I was a bird again, and it was exhilarating to spread my wings and soar the heavens, for all I was equally afraid. Not so much for myself (save selfishly for what I might lose) as for Shara, who flew beside me.

I had not been able to dissuade her from accompanying me. She would not be convinced that she might transform me alone, that I go solitary into Chorym, maintaining that were she not with me my shape-shifting might be lost, arguing that did Ellyn only hold steady we should both enter the city—hopefully alive—swiftly enough that Nestor not find us. I had my doubts, for she had surely made it clear that Nestor could discern her presence in what she described as the aethyr, which I understood to be that magical world coexisting with the mundane that allowed such changes in being. I was afraid that Nestor would sense her and strike her down, and that filled me with a far greater dread than any fear of my own falling—which I assumed must come, were she slain. I did not think I could bear her death; but she would not heed my protests, and without her, all our hopes must be dashed.

So it was that I became a swallow. The sky—where it was clear—was full of them *(us!)* and it was Shara's belief that we might find sanctuary in their numbers. And as she would not let me go alone, we flew together as Ellyn worked the magicks Shara had taught her. And the clans and the Hel's Town pirates waited on the culmination of my desperate strategy.

We flew swift and straight over the ring of roiling fog. I anticipated tendrils reaching up to snatch us from the sky, or bolts of lightning flashing from above to strike us down, but none came, and we saw in darting moments the sunshine that glistened on Chorym's walls. Nests of mud were built there and we swooped toward them, then lofted, riding over the outer walls to land in a stable yard beyond, where more nests hung and we were surrounded by screaming birds.

One of my greatest fears—after that of simple entry— was that the spell should weaken Shara, as it had before. But she had promised me she shared her strength with Ellyn in this conjuration, and that she would recover swiftly for that conjoining. Even so, as I fluttered awkwardly to the ground (swallows spend little time afoot) and felt my head spin with the shifting back to my normal guise, I was afraid for her.

I rose to my feet, marveling at the magic that could deliver me armed with blade and buckler into Chorym, and stumbled to where Shara lay. She gasped and took my hand, climbing to her feet. She now wore that dull blue armor again, a buckler strapped to her left arm and a sword belted to her slender waist. I clutched her awhile, and then she shook her head and laughed from behind her helm and stepped clear of my arms.

"I told you, no? We flew too quick for him! He'll be confused now. And has he sensed us, he'll wonder who you are."

I nodded, less confident than she, and drew my sword. I liked the notion of Nestor seeking me no more than his finding her. I glanced around and saw a cobbled yard filled with straw and dung. Horses studied us with incurious eyes from gated stalls, and a lazy ginger cat from atop a bale of hay. The outer walls of the city stood above us, and I could see the glint of sunlight on helmets and spearheads there, but no

faces turned toward us and I dared hope we had entered unnoticed.

But for how long? And should it be long enough we ac-
complish our purpose?

There was a gate in the yard, and I took Shara's hand.

"Can you walk? Are you strong enough?"

She ducked her head. "Lead on, Gailard."

I swung the gate's latch and we stepped out into an
empty street. It was one of those that encircled the lower
part of Chorym's hill. It was mostly tanneries and stables,
warehouses and repositories, but along its path there were
some taverns and a few humble houses. I wondered who
might know me here as we trod the flags. We were not far
from the East Gate, and I thought that did my plan go aright,
it should be the first to open. Perhaps not even with our
aid—to which end I had told the clans to shift to the south
and west. Shara had explained that not even Nestor could
see beyond his magical brume, and so there were tents and
fires and horses left to the east as if the bulk of our army
concentrated there. I had fought Danant before and prayed I
might guess what tactics Talan would employ.

But still so much depended on chance.

We clung to the shadows as we went along the street. I
could see the outlines of mangonels and trebuchets along
the city walls, and the soldiers there. This was a poor quarter, and I guessed that those who resented Talan's rule the
most would be here. I thought that this was where the old
soldiers would reside—those who'd come back to Chorym
after the defeat at the Darach Pass, after Andur's death.
Those who'd survived the first siege.

I heard hooves rattle and dragged Shara into an alley. It
stank of ordure, and a thin-ribbed dog growled feebly from
behind a broken barrel. I risked a glance up the street and
saw a squad of Danant's cavalry come trotting down the
street. They looked from side to side, and the officer pointed
men off to explore the alleys and courtyards. I motioned
Shara back, and we retreated deeper into the stench. The

alley was long and narrow, overhung with sorry buildings
from which folk obviously spilled their night soil. It was
cluttered with detritus: clay bricks too moldy to use, pieces
of discarded wood, an ancient, spiderwebbed cartwheel. I
led Shara deeper into the filth and a dog growled, and a beggar slumped against a doorway looked up.

He—I supposed for some reason it was a man—wore a
greasy robe, the hood shadowing his face. I took a coin from
my purse and drew my dagger. It should be his—or her—
choice.

The beggar calmed the dog and rose. Teeth showed in a
somehow familiar smile and he—no doubt now—elbowed
back a door that creaked on rusty hinges and said, "Quick!
Inside, else you're dead."

I was wary. In Andur's time there had been no beggars
in Chorym, but how much had changed under Talan's rule?
I hesitated, glancing back down the alley, and saw two riders enter, ducking under the low balconies and outjutting
casements.

"Hurry, for the gods' sakes!"

I knew that voice. I took a breath and Shara's hand and
followed the mendicant.

We entered a dismal hall. Dust clung thick as any carpet
to the floor, and there was a sour smell of cabbage and urine.
The beggar eased the door shut and slid the bolts closed.
Then turned toward us. I held my blade to his throat—then
gasped as he slid back his hood.

"Haldur?"

The man I had left to defend Antium grinned at me. "I
thought you a coward when you left us there, Gailard. But I
should have known better—word spreads, eh? And now you
come back to free us. Where's Ellyn? When do you attack?"

He laughed and shuffled down the hall to a cracked
door that he opened on a low-roofed room that smelled of
sweat and liquor and old dogs. One looked at me—a brindle
hound that growled halfheartedly as it bared missing teeth,
those remaining all yellow; the others only looked. Like the

men who sat around the table, who seemed in not much better condition than the dogs.

"You're safe here," Haldur said. "Awhile, at least."

He tossed off his robe and I saw two things that struck me hard as any sword's blow. One was that he wore mail, a knife on his belt and a short sword slung between his shoulders, hidden by his dirty robe. The other was that his right hand was gone. A sewn stump ended his arm, and he chuckled as I stared at it.

"The fate of soldiers under Danant's rule." He barked a bitter laugh. "Swear fealty and live—are you willing to lose your sword arm."

"And if not?" I asked.

"Execution." He motioned with his stump and all the other men held up their losses. "Talan and his accursed Vachyn saw to that."

"I'd wondered," I said, "what happened to the army."

"Hung," Haldur said, "or crucified; or slain where they stood, did they fight." He shrugged. "I was captured after Antium, and I was offered the choice. I chose to live. I thought . . . perhaps . . ."

I said, "Haldur, I'm sorry."

He said, "So am I," and held up his right arm. "For this, and for doubting you." He grinned. "Does Ellyn live?"

"She lives," I said. "She waits now, beyond the Vachyn's fog, with the clans."

Shara set a warning hand upon mine. I said, "He gave his hand in Chaldor's cause."

"And you can trust me," Haldur said. "You can trust us all." He smashed his stump against the table. The sound made the dogs whimper. "We can still fight. Perhaps not so well as before, but even so . . ." He locked me with his eyes. "We've waited for some chance to strike back. And when we heard the rumors of an army coming against the usurper . . ."

I heard hooves clatter past, the muffled voices of Talan's cavalrymen, but the shutters were closed and none came to the door. They passed and went away, and Haldur said, "You can trust us."

There was a murmur of agreement. I looked about the room, which was dank and dirty as the men who sat there, save their eyes burned with enthusiasm, as if I brought them hope. I studied Haldur. He seemed old beyond his years. His face was scarred now and he looked not to have washed in a while. He smiled and rose to bring us each a cup that he filled with thin, sour wine.

"The best we have," he apologized. "We old soldiers live mostly on charity, but there are advantages to being beggars." He chuckled cynically. "We can go unseen where others folk's faces would be recognized, and there are plenty of us."

"And are you all with Ellyn?" I asked.

Haldur nodded. "To the death."

"What of your vow?"

"What vow?"

"You swore fealty to Talan."

Haldur, remember, was Devyn; a vow of fealty was no easy thing to ignore.

He frowned, as if I asked an imponderable question. Then: "You've not lived in Chaldor for a while, Gailard. What other choice had we? We could live—and hope, and lose our right hands—or die. We chose to live. We hoped . . . Oh, the gods know, when the rumors began, we *hoped* . . . and now. And now . . ."

He embraced me, and I felt a terrible guilt.

"Now you've come back, and with an army. And we can help you. We can help you overthrow Talan! Tell us what to do, eh?"

I glanced at Shara, and she nodded. "We can use allies."

I explained our strategy.

"We are with you," Haldur said, when I was done. "You've a small army inside the city."

Sometimes, I thought, the gods, however capricious, *do* favor us.

We were kitted in the robes of mendicants. We rubbed ashes and grease into our hair, and smeared our faces with dirt, and Haldur took us out into the city. Dogs followed us—or, rather, they followed Shara, for she owned that strange communion with animals that had aided us before. Filthy and shambling, we went ignored by the soldiers who filled the streets, and those who'd question us were put off by our appearance and the growling hounds.

We visited numerous hovels where old, one-handed soldiers lived, and it was to our advantage that these poorer quarters were all situated in the lower part of Chorym, where the gates were. Haldur would bring us in and speak at first of two more defeated ones, then sound out the occupants until he was sure of their loyalty—which did not take long. All hated Talan and his Vachyn sorcerer for what they'd done to Andur and Ryadne, and when they learned that Ellyn lived they swore to aid us.

It was clear that Nestor suspected some subterfuge. Likely, even, had sensed the magic that brought us into the city. But he could not find us, for Shara used no magic now, and we passed unnoticed by the patrols and watchmen, and within the space of two days had organized our interior army. It was small—not so many had survived the war—but I hoped it should be enough. And that we had time enough; my strategem depended on coincidences of timing and attack.

"Shall it work?" Shara asked.

Haldur had brought us to what he confidently declared was a safe house. He had consigned us a single room, with but the one bed. He supposed us lovers—and had I my way, we should have been. But there were still those understandings, and so we lay chastely together on a narrow bed in a filthy house. The sheets were not clean and beetles climbed the walls and traversed the floor in busy lines. I had slept in worse places, but I doubted she had. I felt embarrassed that I had brought her to such a location, and scratched at a biting bug.

"I think it can. And what else have we?"

"My magic," she said.

"And let Nestor find you? No!"

"It might be easier. Could I slay him . . ."

"No." I closed her mouth with my lips. For a while she fought me, but then I felt her respond, and drew her close. For an ecstatic moment I held her to me, her mouth eager as mine.

Then she pushed me away, and as I sighed out my frustrated desire said, "Remember our promise, eh? Not until Chorym's taken and Ellyn has back her parents' throne. Then, eh?"

I groaned. This was a geas I found mightily hard to accept, and I wondered how women could be so strong. I said, "You might defeat him, but even then there'd be Talan's army. We *must* open the gates. We must grant the clans entry, and for that . . ."

"Yes," she said, "I know. But when the time comes . . . The gods know, Gailard, but I'm afraid for Ellyn. Is she truly strong enough?"

"You've tutored her," I said. "And she'd avenge her parents."

"But this shall be more than swordwork."

She rose on her elbows that she might look down into my eyes. I stared into hers and thought that I could drown there and not care. It was one of those nights that grow hot and sticky as high summer. Dry lightning flashed across the sky, forks striking the farmlands silent as a knife blade, and we neither of us wore any clothing more than scanty undergarments. I wanted her, and knew that she had set that geas on me that could not be broken until we had won. I felt greatly disturbed, and moved apart that I might sit, head in hands, on the edge of our sorry bed.

"Forgive me," she asked. "But until . . ."

My temper flashed. The gods knew, it was unfair to

share a bed and not grant both our desires. I swear that I cannot—and I suspect never shall—understand women.

"You and Ellyn; the clans," I said into my hands. "The Hel's Town pirates; Haldur and his people—we *can* win!"

"The gods willing."

"Perhaps now," I said, "they are."

"I pray it be so." She put her arms around me and I wondered if I had ever felt so happy; or so frustrated. But I did not turn. "For I doubt I could live without you now."

"You must," I said, "whatever happens."

She smiled at me, and said, "We'll see." And then her smile grew sad, and she said, "But never understimate Vachyn magic."

I wondered at that, and would have spoken, but she turned my head and kissed me again and made me forget my fears for a while, so I said nothing more and only chose to hope.

But I slept alone on the floor, for fear my desire should overcome the geas. And I could, almost, have hated her for that; save I could not: I loved her too well, and must abide with my frustration.

The storm had rolled away across the sky and it was a cool, dry morning. Even the hovel smelled cleaner. Sun filled our room and we rose and dressed and went down to where Haldur and his men waited. It was a little after dawn.

We ate a breakfast of thin porridge washed down with watery tea and donned our armor. I was surprised that Haldur's beggars had been able to retain so much, but every man wore something: mail, like Haldur, or a breastplate; and there were shields and helmets. And none were without those secret swords. Some even had small bucklers somehow affixed to the stumps of their wrists.

"The Vachyn's fog has lifted," Haldur said. "I got word not long ago. And Egor Dival sends out his men."

"Then it's time," I said.

We donned our mendicants' robes and went out into the

alley. The dogs came with us in a great pack, and as we reached the opening of the sorry street, Shara paused and spoke softly, sending the dogs racing before us. Then she halted in the mess of the alley and raised her hands and spoke words I could not understand or hear, save that amongst them was Ellyn's name.

This was the part I was most afraid of, for it must surely alert Nestor to her presence. I waited for lightning to strike. My hair stood on end for all its greases, but for a while no response came and we ran toward the gates.

The salvation of Chorym had begun.

CHAPTER THIRTY-EIGHT

Nestor tensed as he felt the magic in the aethyr. There were two sources, one outside the walls and one within. Shara and Ellyn—he had no doubt of that—but which was where he could not tell as Egor Dival went clattering out toward the clansmen. He felt a sudden doubt, wondering if some trap were sprung. He cursed and spun toward Talan.

"Quick! One of them's inside the city."

Talan started, his face pale. "Which one? What do they do?"

"I don't know." Nestor scowled. "But I'll find her, soon enough. Meanwhile, however, have your men search the streets for strangers."

"Strangers?" Talan husked a dismal laugh. "They're all strangers here. Who do they look for?"

"What they've been seeking!" Nestor turned impatiently, staring across the plain. "I told you, no? One's likely here already, and they've some strategem in mind."

Talan licked his fleshy lips. "Shall I call Dival back?"

"No!" Nestor shook his head irritably. "Let him strike the clans—perhaps he can defeat them. If so, our task is easier."

Talan nodded and watched the chariots roll out. A cool breeze blew over the ramparts, but he felt sweat bead his face and fear curdle in his belly. The gods willing, Dival would break the Highlanders with his charge. But if he failed . . .

"Shara summons us. *Go now!*"

Ellyn smiled at Roark as he lifted his horn and blew the clarion call. He leaned down from his saddle and kissed her, then touched her hair and heeled his pony to a gallop. The Quan followed him, thundering out to meet the chariots and mounted archers emerging from Chorym's East Gate.

All around the city horns blew and clansmen rose to the fight, trusting in Gailard and his Lady of the Mountains to open the way. Mattich brought his Dur against the West Gate; Jaime led the Arran against the North Gate; and Kerid looked to Mother Hel, who nodded, and directed the Hel's Town pirates against the South Gate.

Ellyn, lonely now, and wanting to go with her love, turned back to the pots Shara had left with her. She stirred the earth in the one, and the water in the other; fanned the burning candle in the third, stirring its flame, and blew into the empty fourth. It was hard to stand aside, but Shara had explained what she must do, and she knew now that she must obey and follow the instructions—else all be lost. She prayed that Shara and Gailard survive. And Roark.

Egor Dival held his shield strapped hard against his broken arm, and wondered why the healers had failed to mend his bones. They ached, and he wondered if he grew too old. He wondered how he might cast a javelin or nock an arrow when he must use his one good hand to clutch the rail of the bucking chariot as howling clansmen came toward him.

They were not such soldiers as he'd fought before— save at the Geffyn Pass, and they seemed careless of their lives—intent only on victory. They rode small horses and wore little armor. Mostly he saw bucklers and clan colors that fluttered wildly in the rush of their attack. His force outnumbered them, but they charged as if their lives were nothing, and more came afoot. He saw that not all were clansmen, but Chaldor folk and others, as if all the land rose against him. He let go the rail and cast a useless javelin that went by some handsome young Highlander who laughed as if battle were a great joy and swept his sword up and around to cut the traces of the chariot's team even as his followers hacked at the charioteer and Dival felt the vehicle lurch and swerve, and was swept from the deck and sent tumbling— oh, the gods knew, but he was too old for this—onto the trampled ground.

He rolled, tasting dirt and failure in his mouth, and saw hooves stamp around his head. He tried to turn from them, to pick himself up, but they pressed too close and he could only flinch as men dismounted and a blade pricked against his throat. He saw his chariot overturned, and his charioteer dragged off screaming by the runaway team. He felt like weeping. He forgot his hurt arm and his indignity as someone said, "We'll let you live. Awhile, at least, do you submit. Gailard told us not to kill too many."

Another said, "Look at that armor—he'll fetch a handsome ransom. He must be a chieftain of some kind."

The first—the one, he saw, who'd cut the traces—said, "What's your name?"

"Egor Dival." He rose awkwardly, careful to keep his hands in clear sight. "I am commander of the army of Danant."

The young man laughed. "A fine prize, eh? So, Egor Dival, do you submit?"

The taste of defeat was ashen in his mouth. He nodded—what choice else?—and looked past the stamping ponies to where his force was cut down. Those few who lived ran in panic. The way back was closed by Highlanders who raced toward the gate, and those who sought refuge in the countryside beyond were plucked by clan arrows, or

pursued by groups of yelling Highlanders. This was, he
realized, a carefully planned ambush, and silently cursed
Talan for accepting the Vachyn's advice.

"I submit," he said.

Roark smiled and said, "Hold him. Two men, eh? Take him
back to Ellyn and guard him."

Then he urged his Quan onward. The gate was open and
the Highlander ponies were quick enough to go through and
hold it. And for Ellyn's love he'd do that. He shouted for his
riders to follow him, and waved for those on foot to run after, and raced toward the gate.

Arrows rained from the sky, and Roark lifted his buckler to protect his head. He was the first through. Soldiers
clad in plate armor faced him and he smashed his sword
against the first helm as a blade swung at the pony. The animal screamed as the edge slashed across its neck and began
to buck. It reared, and Roark dropped from the saddle and
hacked again, and saw the man fall even as the Quan, supported by the Devyn, came screaming past the open portal
and set to slaughtering the Danant men.

He took a blow on his shield and cut another man down,
and shouted orders that sent clansmen running to settle
wedges against the gate, blocking it open that the rest might
pour through. Then he looked about. Secure the walls,
Gailard had said, then move into the city, toward the palace.
He saw a flight of steps leading to the ramparts and howled
for his men to follow.

We came to the North Gate as tattered beggars fleeing the
confusion and Shara spoke harsh, grating words and
pointed. Thunder bellowed, and lightning struck, and the
gates exploded outward in shards of scorched timber and
melting metal. And Jaime came rushing forward with his
Arran.

I had no time to watch, for we hurried on around the
city to the next portal. The streets were crowded now with

running soldiers and galloping cavalry, and terrified citizens, and we pushed through them with the ease that beggars have, for none want to touch or come close—especially not when those beggars are preceded by snapping, angry dogs.

I saw a squad of horsemen unseated as the hounds nipped at the horses' legs and set them to prancing, and Haldur's men ran in and drew those hidden blades and used them to deadly effect. I drew my own and joined the slaughter, and soon all the riders lay dead and bloody.

Then through noisy streets and filthy alleys to the West Gate, where one-handed men already fought with Talan's soldiers, and again Shara raised her hands and spoke her spell so that wood burned and metal dripped, and Mattich came in with his Dur. I saw old soldiers from Andur's army on the walls now, striking at the Danant occupiers as if they'd no care for their own lives, but would only see Chorym freed. And from the houses came ordinary citizens armed with kitchen knives and clubs, some even with cooking pots that they used to batter Talan's men.

We raced on. All depended on speed, and Ellyn's support—that Nestor be confused and not locate the source of the magicks that opened Chorym's gates. I prayed that Ellyn survive; that we all survive.

"What do we do?" Talan snatched a cup and drained it, motioning that the servant refill the goblet. "Egor's captured and the Highlanders enter the city. Where's your magic now, Nestor?"

"They move fast," the Vachyn answered, "and they're divided. But even so . . ." He paused, closing his eyes a moment. "It's as I thought: one within and one without. The second is easier to deal with. So, her first."

He ignored Talan's whining as he concentrated. Then he raised his hands and wove patterns in the air and spoke soft words. And Talan stepped back, sinking another cup as he felt the power fill the room.

Ellyn worked desperately over the pots Shara had left with
her, mouthing the spells the sorceress had taught her. She
could feel the Vachyn power fill the air around her and above
her. Even in her, in her blood and her bones. It was as if a
storm gathered, covering her skin with horrid anticipation,
like prickling fingers that tapped out a message of defeat
and destruction. She felt it gather and strike—and as it did,
she voiced the spell and sent out the protective weaving.

Nestor's magic struck like a hammer's blow from the sky.

And was deflected, and dissipated, as if a wind blew
against a strong tent.

Even so, Ellyn was knocked to the ground. And the pots
trembled, water spilling from one, earth from another; the
candle's flame flickered and threatened to die. She picked
herself up and returned to her weaving, and when the lightning struck again and she saw the tent burning, she felt less
afraid. She voiced the spell louder so that it covered her, and
those around her, and in a while she felt the Vachyn's magic
falter and turn away. She smiled and went out from the
burning tent and mounted her chestnut horse and summoned her bodyguard to follow her. It was an afterthought
to order off a handful of wounded men to guard Egor Dival.

"Too strong." Nestor shook his head like a man seeking to
shuck off the effects of excessive wine. "She's too strong."

"What do you say?" Talan demanded. "Who's too
strong? Which one? What happens? Are we defeated?"

Nestor spat, and rubbed at his frowning eyes. "Not yet.
I'll find the other and slay her. Then . . ."

The Hel's Town pirates were already clambering up the
walls as we reached the South Gate. They used grappling
irons, and seemed as careless of their lives as the Highlanders. Talan's men sent arrows against them, and tumbled
broken stones onto them, but they continued their assault as
if their lives meant nothing.

Then Shara wove her magic again and the South Gate burst open in a great ball of flame that was matched by the light that struck from the sky.

And Shara screamed and fell down.

I picked her up. Her eyes hung wide, the pupils rolled back so that only white showed, and as I held her I felt scarcely any pulse. I was afraid she was dead—struck down by Nestor's magic. I carried her away from the fighting around the gate as the Hel's Town pirates flooded in, and set her down on dirty cobbles. I rubbed her cheeks and her hands, and felt her flesh cold under mine. I kissed her and willed her to live; I could no longer imagine life without her. But she remained supine, still as a corpse.

"One's struck," Nestor said. "My erstwhile sister, I think. And the other—does she live—shall not be long after."

Talan drank more wine, staring from the high window. He saw folk in the streets: his own soldiers and Highlanders, Chorym's citizens, all fighting. He saw his men plucked from the battlements by armored beggars and howling clansmen. Smoke rose from the four gates and he could see, far off, the wreckage of Egor Dival's chariots. He turned, extending his hand that the waiting servant refill his cup—but the servant was gone and he realized he was alone with Nestor.

He shouted, but no answer came. He went to the chamber's door and shouted again, and again there was no answer. No waiting servants; indeed, only an empty corridor.

"They've fled." His voice was hollow. "They've deserted me."

"They'll come back," Nestor said. "Now Shara's slain, we can defeat them. They'll not last long now."

"Does she live?" Haldur stared at Shara as the Hel's Town pirates raced yelling past us. His beggar soldiers formed a wall between us and the confusion.

"She must," I said, and took her in my arms. "Where can I bring her?"

Haldur glanced around and pointed to a dismal tavern.
The door was locked, and when he pounded on the wood
there was no response. He shouted at his men and they set to
ripping shutters from their mountings, then smashed the
glass behind so that one might clamber in and open the
door. The man emerged with a bloodied sword, and as I carried Shara to a table, I saw a body on the floor. The beggar
caught my look and shrugged. "The landlord argued our
entry."

I ignored the corpse. If the man was not with us, he was
our enemy, and I had far greater concerns than his miserable
death. I laid Shara down and called for water. As I soaked a
cloth and set it to her forehead, I heard tumult outside. There
was a great clattering of steel, and howling battle shouts, the
screams of hurt and dying men, and no few women. I set a
hand to Shara's slender neck and felt a pulse. For an instant
hope rose, but then I felt the pulse flicker, arrhythmic. I set
my ear to her mouth, but I heard only faint breaths that came
irregular. Her face was deathly pale, her eyes closed, and I
felt all my hope turn to ashes. I swallowed the bile that rose
in my throat and forced myself to think clearly.

"There are healers here still?" I asked. "Find them!
And send men to bring Ellyn."

Is she not also slain, I thought. And then: *if she is, I
shall slay Nestor. Vachyn or no, I'll take his head.*

Haldur bellowed orders and men went running out into
the chaos. I dripped water between Shara's bloodless lips
and prayed to the gods I now hoped existed and listened
to me.

"I cannot find her." Nestor frowned, pacing the chamber
like some restless cat unwilling to let go a mouse. "There's
magic abroad still . . ."

"Then you must know where she is." Talan stroked nervously at his splendid helmet. "Strike there."

"I did!" Nestor snapped. "She was beyond the fog, but

now she's gone. She left some magic there, that I believed
her still in place. But now . . ."

"Now what?"

"She's gone. Likely coming here."

"Then you'll be able to find her, no?" Talan picked up
the helmet, wondering if he should latch it in place. He
could see half his army slain and scattered, and hear the remainder fighting in the streets. It seemed, from the vantage
point of the palace, as if all Chorym rose against him. He
gasped as he saw a cavalryman swing a curved sword
against a woman who held up a brass cookpot in defense.
The blade smashed the pot away and cut into the woman's
shoulder. He could not hear her scream, but from the blood
that gouted, she must be slain. But then three more women
and an old man armed with a kitchen knife clustered around
the rearing horse, all careless of the hooves, and dragged the
rider from his saddle. Talan watched as pots and rolling pins
and knives descended.

"Does she use magic," Nestor said, and smiled.

"You find this amusing?"

"I find it pointless." The Vachyn shrugged. "Shara's
slain. Does Ellyn employ her talent, I can find her and slay
her. How can we lose?"

"How?" Talan gasped. "By all the gods, all Chorym
rises against me! The gates are open, and . . ."

An officer, his armor dented, blood on his face, came in.
He offered a cursory salute. "The South Gate's down, and
Hel's Town pirates enter. There are Highlanders through the
others. They fill the streets."

Talan cursed long and loud.

The officer said, "It shall be hard to hold, my king. This
place is a maze, and with General Dival's force lost, it might
be better we withdraw."

"To where?" Talan clutched his helmet to his armored
chest, wishing there were servants left to pour him wine.
"Back to Danant?"

"To the palace." The officer wiped blood from his cut
face. "This is a citadel, my lord. Do we group here, we can
hold."

"And I can sweep the streets," Nestor said. "Call in your
men and I'll cleanse Chorym of this rabble."

"And can you not," Talan snarled, "I shall be trapped
here. As Ryadne was."

"I gave you this city," the Vachyn returned. "I gave you
Andur's head, and Ryadne's death. I've slain Shara. I gave
you Chorym—and I can give it back to you."

"Your word?" Talan asked.

"My word." Nestor ducked his head. "Call in your men
and I'll send such magicks against these invaders as shall
sweep them away like rats in a flood."

"And the city?" Talan stared at the fighting in the
streets.

"Much will be destroyed." Nestor shrugged carelessly.
"But when I'm done, there shall be none dare argue your
rule, nor any willing left alive, and then you can rebuild."

"Or go home to Danant," Talan sighed. Then turned to
the waiting officer: "Regroup on the citadel." And to Nestor:
"Do as you will to win me this war."

Ellyn rode in through the East Gate to the acclaim of the
clansmen holding the portal. She winced at the signs of carnage. The flagstones were slick with blood, so thick in
places that her horse slipped, and whinnied its distaste.
There were bodies scattered all around, too many wearing
the clan plaids, but more in Danant's armor; and as she progressed inward, she saw Chorym folk—men and women,
both—sprawled over the stained cobbles. But those who
lived hailed her as if she alone were responsible for the
rebellion.

Then Roark was beside her, helping her dismount. His
helm was dented and there was blood splattered across his
breastplate. His buckler carried the stumps of arrows, and
the sword he sheathed as he came to her was encarmined

from tip to cup, but he smiled hugely as he saw her, as if
they were participants in some vast and amusing game. Ellyn decided then that she did not enjoy warfare.

And then he held her shoulders and she looked into his
laughing eyes and ignored the blood that decorated his
hands as he brushed her cheek with his lips and said, "We
hold the gates, and Chorym rises in your support."

"And you're not hurt?"

"No." He chuckled, wiping a smear of blood from his
face that revealed a cut. "Only scratches."

She wondered at that. He seemed to wear, on closer inspection, more blood than suggested by only scratches. But
he lived, and she had greater concerns—now that she knew
he survived. "And Gailard? Shara?"

"I don't know," he said. "I got word the other gates . . .
exploded. Your grandfather's brought the Dur in, and
Jaime's come through the North Gate. The Hel's Town pirates enter the South. But Shara and Gailard . . . ?" He
shrugged. "I've no word of them. It would seem they go
with old soldiers—Chorym folk—but I've not heard in a
while."

"And Vachyn magic?"

"None so far."

"I must find Shara," she said.

Roark said, "I can set men to seeking her, but . . ."

Ellyn turned as he drew his sword, his buckler lofting in
automatic defense as a man ran toward them. He was
dressed in mail, and carried a short sword in his left hand.
Ellyn frowned as she saw that his right ended in a sewn
stump where the hand had been chopped.

"Friend! Put up your blade." He halted, panting noisily.
"I am Haldur—Gailard's friend."

"Then welcome," Ellyn said. "What news?"

"Shara needs you. The Vachyn's magicks have laid her
low; Gailard sent me to find you. She needs you."

"What's happened?" Ellyn felt her skin grow cold.

"I don't know." Haldur sheathed his bloody sword.

"She opened the South Gate and . . . *something*. She fell down, and Gailard fears she's dying. I've sent men to find healers, but . . ."

Ellyn gasped as fear filled her, then she nodded and swung back astride her horse. The chestnut could force a way through better than a woman afoot. Though she was not sure what she could do; Shara had taught her more of defense and attack than healing spells. But even so . . . She motioned for Haldur to mount behind her.

Roark said, "I'll come with you."

And she said, "No, stay here. Do as Gailard told you— hold the gate and sweep the streets clean. I'll find you again when I can."

Then she dug heels into the chestnut's flanks and dared not look back as Haldur shouted directions in her ear and she rode through the clamorous streets to where Shara— No! It could not be; it *must* not be!—lay dying.

I looked up as Ellyn came into the tavern. She pushed past Haldur's men and came to stand beside me. Her face grew pale as Shara's as she stared at my love's body.

I asked, "Can you heal her?"

She did not answer for a while, but only looked and ran her hands in slow movements over the . . . I did not want to acknowledge the word, but it was "corpse" that came to mind.

The healers Haldur's men had found had done what they could and admitted defeat. It was no mortal wound, they said, but magic—and against that, they had no power. Ellyn was my only hope.

"Nestor did this," she murmured. "We'd hoped . . . No matter; what's done is done, and now I must undo it. Save . . ." She looked at me and I saw tears moistening her eyes. "Gailard, I'm not sure I can. I fear . . ."

"Do what you *can*," I groaned. "Anything; only save her, eh?"

"Yes, of course. But . . ." She paused an instant. "Nestor

shall find us then, and surely deliver his magicks against us again."

"Do it!" I clutched her hands. "Save her! *Please?"*

Ellyn nodded.

I gestured at Haldur and the others. "Go! Fight, and win Chorym back. But leave us now!"

They went, and Ellyn bent over Shara, listening to her heart's fluttering beat, her irregular breaths as I waited with no less a fluttering heart. I do not think I had ever been so afraid.

Then Ellyn said. "I shall need blood."

Almost, I laughed. She needed blood? The gods knew, but the streets were awash; there was blood aplenty to be found.

She said, "Yours. You love her, Gailard, and she loves you; and in the castle she taught me that blood calls to blood. Perhaps, with your blood, I can save her."

I drew my knife. "How much? Where shall I make the cut?"

Ellyn passed her hands over Shara's body, speaking softly. Then she said, "Your wrist, do I remember aright. How much I do not know."

"No matter."

It was a suicide's cut; but could it give Shara back her life, I did not care. I slashed the blade over my wrist and saw bright crimson burst forth. Ellyn snatched it and held it so that the pouring splashed over Shara's face, into her mouth. She spoke more soft words and I felt a changing in the air around us. I felt my head spin as my blood ran out. Then Ellyn touched my wrist and the wound healed. I saw the blood run toward Shara's mouth and her drink it in.

Then her eyes opened and she breathed a gusty sigh. Her chest rose. I touched her face, and she smiled at me, albeit faintly.

Ellyn said, wonderingly, "I had not thought I could do that. The gods know, but she taught me better than I'd thought."

And all the windows of the tavern burst inward in great sprays of shattering glass and woodwork, and fire roiled from the chimney breast in searching tongues of horrid flame, and the whole building took fire.

"Quick!"

I lifted Shara and ran to the door. Ellyn followed me as burning roof beams crashed down and jars of liquor exploded in fresh fragments of deadly glass. Fire filled the street outside and smoke clogged my throat. I was never so glad to see a man disobey an order as I was to see Haldur waiting to help me carry Shara away.

Even so, I wondered if we could survive. The tavern burned like some vast funeral pyre, and lightning walked the street like some stalking insect that sought us out and would destroy everything in its path. I saw stone walls explode, and wooden buildings erupt in flame. The air seared my throat and watered my eyes. Men and women screamed as they were torched and fell down like burning rag dolls. The dogs that still escorted Shara barked and died, and those that did not ran away in terror. Ellyn screamed as her tethered horse was reduced to ashes. Shara stirred fitfully in my arms, and had I felt afraid before, now I felt true terror. I doubted I could bear to see her resurrected only to have her die in this awful conflagration.

I followed Haldur as he led us into a narrow alley. Flame followed us in searching tongues. Casements took fire and windows melted behind us. Alley cats squealed as they were consumed, and birds fell from the blazing sky in sad bundles of scorched feathers. Haldur darted into a cross alley and the fire rolled by, then came back and found the entrance.

Haldur ducked into a building I thought must be a bakery, where folk crouched in terror as we passed, and brought us through to the rear door, which opened on a little courtyard where there was a pool in which fishes swam. We dived into it as the building erupted in a great column of flame and ash and bodies.

I thought that we could not survive Nestor's attack—that he must find us, now that Ellyn had worked her magic to revive Shara and thus announced her presence, and that he would strike us all down and all be lost—but then . . .

"Come!" Ellyn rose dripping from the pool. "We must move fast."

She gestured at the gate that sealed the little yard. I thought she'd use magic to open the bolts, but she only waved Haldur on and urged him to kick it free, which he did.

So I lifted Shara and ran after them into a street where Chorym's folk fought alongside Hel's Town pirates and clansmen, and Talan's soldiers fell in bloody rows. Fire burst like some loosened dam and came rolling down the avenue in a great wave that ate up and roasted everything and everyone in its path.

"Back!" Ellyn shouted and we obeyed.

We went into a tanner's yard that stank even over the smell of burning flesh and the awful heat that filled the air. We crouched beneath the malodorous vats as the fire went past, and then again as buildings exploded and fragments of brick and wood rained down, burning, all around us. I saw the hinges of the door melt and run down the torched wood of the gate. I held Shara tight against me, setting my body between hers and the detritus that rained from the sky.

I felt her arms clutch me close and her heart beat stronger, and she looked into my eyes and said, "What did you do? I feel a bonding."

I said, "Nestor struck you down. I feared you were dead, but then Ellyn came and I gave you blood. But, surely, we were bonded before that."

She said, "Yes, but even so I thank you. Now help me up."

I set her on her feet and she leaned unsteadily against me as she stared at Ellyn.

"You're far stronger than I believed, but hold off your magicks now, eh?"

Ellyn was moving her hands and mouthing soft

words—shaping a spell to protect us by my guess, but she halted as Shara spoke.

"Best that Nestor believes us dead, no? Let him think that, and he'll end this destruction. Cease all your magic for now."

"He's killing people!" Ellyn protested. "He slays the clansmen and Chorym's citizens with his fire! He sweeps the streets with flame!"

"And many shall die before we can halt him," Shara said in a voice husky with weakness and regret. "But save we reach him, and slay *him*, there shall be more who die in his search for us. Weave those spells I taught you, and he'll find you—as he found me. And then all's lost."

Ellyn ceased her spellweaving.

Shara said, "This shall not be easy, but we must find Nestor and slay him before he destroys all of Chorym in his search for us."

"And Talan," I said. "I'll not let Talan go unpunished."

"No." Shara ducked her head in agreement. "Best we teach all the rulers of the world a lesson."

"Then what do we do?" Ellyn asked.

"We find Nestor," Shara said. "He'll be with Talan." She looked to me. "Where would the rulers of Chorym hide?"

"They'd no need to hide before Talan came," I said, "but now . . . the citadel. They'll be in the palace."

"Then we'll find them there," she said.

CHAPTER THIRTY-NINE

Chorym burned and the fighting moved inward. It was as if a pool of evil dried in the sun, withdrawing from its edges towards its deep center—which was the citadel of the palace. Talan's men fell back on that bastion—those not slain by Nestor's indiscriminate magic, or in honest battle—and found the gates locked against them. The clans pressed on, scenting victory now, and many of the Danant soldiers, knowing themselves forsaken by their king, threw down their arms and begged for mercy. Many were slaughtered on the spot, for mercy was in short supply after Nestor's depredations, but still others were granted clemency and sent weaponless and guarded to the outer perimeters of Chorym. The main part of the city was ours now—but we must still take the palace.

I came through streets and avenues ravaged by the Vachyn's baleful magicks with Shara pale and coughing in my arms. She was weakened by Nestor's attack, but she'd not rest or seek refuge, and I could not argue with her, for I knew that we must strike now or lose this war. Though with the gates of the palace locked against us, I could not see how we might gain our victory.

A pall of smoke hung over the city, rising from buildings that burned like torches from the Vachyn's foul touch. I saw blazing shopfronts and smoldering mansions; gardens emptied of trees and shrubbery, where only charred stumps remained. I saw bodies crisp as roasted meat littering the streets—as many Danant's men as Chorym's citizens or my clansmen—and terrified folk running in panic, seeking some refuge they doubted they could find. The air stank, the charred smell of burning wood mingling with the horribly sweet odor of burning flesh.

Ellyn stared about with wide, outraged eyes that bled tears born of both the smoke and the chagrin she felt.

"How could he do this? This is . . ."

She shook her head, unable to find the words that could express her outrage. And Shara answered, "He's Vachyn, and Talan listens to him. Nothing matters save winning."

Ellyn coughed and spat, and wiped at her face, where ashes settled, and said, "Is this the price of victory? That Chorym die?"

Haldur said, "Give up now, my queen, and my old soldiers shall have nothing. Talan will hunt us down and slay us for our part in this."

I said, "It's all or nothing now. We've only victory or defeat ahead."

Ellyn turned reddened eyes toward us and ducked her head.

We pressed on through the crowded, burning streets toward the citadel. The waves of fire were ended now. I supposed that Nestor believed both Shara and Ellyn dead, and thus ceased his magicks in reliance on the soldiers within the palace. I could not imagine how we might enter—save we break the gates with magic, which must surely tell the Vachyn that Shara and Ellyn survived, and bring his power against us again. And I wondered if Shara could live through that, or Ellyn; but I saw no other choice than to go on. Nestor and Talan must die.

I saw a horse come toward us. I heard it first, because it screamed as its hide burned. Its mane was blazing and it tossed its head in pain and panic. It wore the livery of Talan's cavalry, and as it passed, Haldur thrust out his sword and chopped its throat. It fell down bloody, tumbling over scorched flagstones, colliding with the corpse of a burned child so that both entwined and went skidding in a welter of falling bones and blackened flesh into the wreckage of a garden where an ornamental fountain lay toppled, dribbling sad tears over dead flowers and blackened soil. Haldur looked at me and we exchanged a glance, and went on.

"The streets are clean now." Nestor filled a goblet and passed it to Talan. "Swept with fire, eh? And the only gate's sealed and held by your men. The walls are manned, and no barbarians shall enter here."

Talan took the cup and settled in a high-backed chair and drained the wine in a thirsty swallow. There were no servants left, so he held out his goblet to Nestor to refill as he asked, "And the clans? And the citizens? And those god-cursed soldiers with only one hand? Don't they still fight?"

"But the important ones are dead." Nestor filled the king's cup—a small obeisance in light of what he'd win. "Shara and Ellyn are slain, so we face no magic. And within this citadel, we're safe. We can hold off the clans, and all the rest of that rabble. Heed me, eh? They'll break against the walls."

"They've not so far," Talan grunted.

"But they will now." Nestor smiled at his protégé: another ambitious kingling ripe for plucking to the Vachyn cause. Indeed, already won. "The clans are gathered against us—and are decimated. . . ."

"They own Chorym!" Talan wailed.

"They entered the city, but save they take the palace they've nothing." Nestor filled his own goblet. "And how shall they take the palace? It's but the one gate, and high walls. And you've enough men behind them to fend them off, even without my help. Listen—we've gathered them all together—the clans and my sister; Ellyn and her guardian; every old soldier who fought for Andur; the Hel's Town pirates . . ." He laughed. "The god's know, even Mother Hel herself—all of them! *Every one who might dispute your rule.* Let them come against us now, and we shall destroy them all—and you'll own Chaldor, and the Highlands and Hel's Town. We cannot lose!"

"You're sure?" Talan asked.

Nestor lowered his head in agreement. "It's what I planned: to slay all your enemies in one fell swoop."

Talan smiled and stroked his golden helmet. "I owe you much, my friend."

Nestor shrugged negligently, thinking: *Your soul, fool.*

We found the clan chieftains at the gate. The smoke was cleared here, the worst of the Vachyn's magicks delivered against the lower tiers of the city. Mattich waited for us, and Jaime and Roark. I was somehow surprised to find Devyn there, for I had forgotten that I was, since slaying my brother, equal to Mattich and the others—a clan chief. It was good to breathe clean air, free of smoke and the stench of burning flesh and buildings.

"We caught Egor Dival," Roark said.

Mattich said, "But the others hide behind those walls."

Jaime said, "How can we cross them?"

I looked at the high gate and the parapets beyond. Danant's men stood there, and were their catapults and tre-buchets useless at such close quarters, still I could see no way we might gain entry.

Kerid said, "We've the grappling irons."

And Mother Hel—who I was surprised to find with us—said, "My pirates can climb those walls. They're not so different from a ship's side."

"Save you've Nestor on the other," I said. "And do we assault the gate or try to climb the walls, he'll deliver more fire and lightning against us."

Mother Hel nodded. "Aye, there's that. But what else?"

Kerid said, "We've come too far now to give up."

I sighed, staring around. The citadel was ringed with

clansmen and Hel's Town pirates and Chaldor's one-handed soldiers and citizens. Not all had fled Nestor's burning. There were enough still loyal to Ellyn's cause that we had an army of disparate purpose, but enough to win.

Save Nestor deliver further Vachyn magicks against us.

Then Shara said, "We attack. What else?"

I looked at her. She could barely hold her feet steady. Her face was pale, and her eyes were narrowed with concern. I thought that if I let her go, she'd fall down, but she pushed clear of my arms and faced us all.

"I'll break the gate and we attack."

I drew her away as arrows flew from the palace. We gathered behind the shelter of a fire-blackened wall and I said, "No! You're too weak, and do you use your talent then Nestor shall find you again."

"He'll be weakened now." She squared her shoulders. "Those magicks he's used must drain him."

"Even so." I shook my head, looking from her weary face to the walls. "There must be another way."

"Then name it." She laughed bitterly. "Sooner or later I must face him, for I'm the only one here can hope to defeat *him*."

I looked into her tired eyes. "I could not bear to lose you now," I said. "I'd sooner die myself."

"Perhaps you shall, Gailard my love. Perhaps we both shall, and Ellyn, too. But what other choice have we? It's as you said—we've only victory or defeat ahead."

I swallowed, wondering if the sour taste came from the ashes I'd inhaled or the fear I felt. Her eyes were fierce for all their weariness, and I could only sigh and shrug, and grant her sway.

It was a suicidal venture, and I could envisage little hope of success. But neither could I suggest any alternative, and I knew that we could not linger. So . . .

Highlanders and citizens gathered timber—doors and shutters, broken fences—anything that might be quickly

fashioned into crude, movable barricades as the Hel's Town
pirates spread around the walls. It took what remained of
the day and most of the night, and our assault was planned
for that hour before dawn when the light is grey and even
watchful soldiers grow sleepy.

I prayed that Nestor needed sleep like any mortal man;
and doubted he should.

Then a horn sounded, answered by the others around
the citadel's walls, and the assault began.

There was a great roar as the rough screens were carried toward the gate. I heard the song of arrows, invisible in
the dim light, and the distant thud of a battering ram against
the portal. Kerid whistled, and the Hel's Town pirates set to
whirling their grappling irons in wide circles before the
barbed hooks went sailing upward, over the ramparts. Highlanders sent arrows flying as the pirates began to climb.

Stones rained down upon them, and great cauldrons of
boiling water and oil. They screamed and fell, and those
who survived the descent were oft as not picked off by the
arrows of the defenders. I could not bare to stand idle now,
and so I had a bow and stared into the opalescent light, and
when a Danant man showed at an embrasure, I sent a shaft
into his eye. He screamed and fell back, and all around him
more shafts lofted, sent by the clansmen. But Talan's folk
were well guarded by the high ramparts, and I could not envisage the Hel's Town pirates succeeding—so it would be as
Shara had said. And that assault I feared far deeper than to
take one of those ropes in my hands and attempt that impossible climb. Kerid barked an order and a horn sounded, and
the pirates left off their hopeless assault.

I glanced at Shara and Ellyn, who both nodded grimly,
and set to their work.

It was a grim business, bloody as any of Nestor's handi-
work, and as it continued I waited in horrid anticipation for
the Vachyn to strike against them. It took little time, but all
the while I felt my heart thud heavy against my ribs as I expected the counterstrike of Talan's mage.

I watched as they angled their hands toward the battle-ments of the citadel. I heard them cry out, but I could not comprehend the words—only observe the effect.

It was as if a great incandescent ball of light burst against the ramparts. As if the sun fell to earth and broke. This was not akin to Nestor's indiscriminate fire, but con-centrated on a single section, that exploded in a mass of sharded stone. I saw blocks melt and run, the wall shattered. The sound of it dinned against my ears, but even so I thought I heard the screaming of the Danant men consumed in that terrible destruction. Then—the gods willing, before Nestor had time to retaliate—we were all charging toward the rubble.

It was difficult going. The stones were jagged and hot under my booted feet, and I supported Shara on one side, Ellyn on her other. A few arrows flew toward us, but most of the defenders were dazed by the explosion, and we gained the parapet.

I stood with the two women, my buckler raised to de-fend them. Kerid stood with me, and his tobacco-chewing cohort, and we were joined by pirates and Highlanders even as the main part of our force spread to either side.

"We'd best not linger." Shara's voice was husky with the effort of her spell. She was panting, sweat beading her face. Nor was Ellyn in much better condition. "Move on swift now, lest Nestor locate us."

I looked about. Pirates and Highlanders drove the de-fenders back toward the two watchtowers set either side of our space of wall. Stairs ran down from those small bastions to the inner yard, where soldiers came running in support of their beleaguered comrades. They fell back as arrows and javelins rained from the occupied parapet, and Kerid shouted for his men to clear the watchtowers.

"You know what to do," I said.

He nodded, still grinning, and clasped my hand a mo-ment. "The gods be with you, Gailard."

"And you."

The gods knew, it was a desperate plan, but it was all we had. I snatched a livery from a fallen soldier and draped it around Ellyn's shoulders, set another about Shara, a third about my own. They were all bloody and rent, and we crouched against the inner wall, amongst the bodies, as Kerid took our invaders away.

The ram struck the gate and Jaime cursed as the shock jarred his arms. He wiped a thread of blood from his face where an arrow had grazed him, and ignored the broken shaft that stuck from his side. It had not gone in too deep and he doubted he lost much blood—and by all the gods, he'd see that gate shattered or die in the attempt.

On the other side of the pole Mattich shouted, and the timber was drawn back to hammer again.

"Soon, eh?" He bellowed loud enough they all hear. "Not long and we're through!"

He turned as his shieldman loosed a liquid sigh and pitched onto his back with a shaft driven clear through his neck. A pity that; Massos was a good friend. But the Dur were committed now, and Ellyn was—the gods willing—inside the citadel, and soon the gate would break. When the fighting was done and the clans went home, he'd see his friend's widow compensated. But now . . . He roared again: "Break it! The gods curse you—break it!"

Roark clenched his teeth and leaned into the effort as arrows flung past him. A man screamed, falling with a shaft sprouting from his chest; another grunted and staggered away as a spear dug into his thigh. He risked a glance around, checking that the rough-made shields took the worst of the defenders' shafts. Ellyn was likely inside now—save she be slain on the wall. In which case, he vowed, he'd have the heads of both Talan of Danant and the Vachyn sorcerer. Or die in the attempt. And did they all survive, he'd ask Ellyn for her hand in marriage—even were she Chaldor's queen.

He lent his voice to Mattich's. "Onward the clans! Break the gate and win!"

The gate shuddered, splinters sharding where the ram pounded, and Mattich bellowed, "Again! We're almost through!"

Mother Hel watched nervously, hiding her discomposure from the few guardsmen she retained. Where was Kerid? Did he live still, in the midst of this insane adventure? Or was he slain? She hoped not, and blushed despite herself as she realized he meant more to her than she cared to admit. The gods knew, but it was not expediency alone that had persuaded her to take sides in this landsman's war. It was equally Kerid, with his love for Chaldor and his smile, and . . .

She set those thoughts aside, and asked the gods to let him live and be victorious. She knew that if they failed, she and her Hel's Town pirates—all who supported Ellyn— would surely become objects of Vachyn revenge, become subjects of Talan Kedassian.

She stared at the wild men pounding their ram against the gate, seemingly oblivious of the missiles that fell on them, and wondered at their bravery and their insanity.

"What is it?"

Talan woke from drunken sleep to find Nestor scowling at his bedside. He heard a distant sound, muffled by the curtains and his aching head. He rose groggy against the pillows as Nestor said, "Do you know what that is?"

Talan shook his head, and wished he'd not. "What?"

"They attack."

"So?"

"They're inside the walls."

Talan sat higher. "What?" He flung the sheets aside and clambered naked and confused from the bed. "You promised me . . ." He crossed to the window and saw chaos on the battlements of the citadel.

"They assault the gate," Nestor said, "and there are too many come over the walls."

"But . . ." Talan stared in amazement at the fighting. "You said . . . You promised . . . This cannot be!"

"I . . ." Nestor hesitated. "I had not known they were so strong."

Talan rounded on him. "Send your magicks against them then! Sweep them clean, as you did the streets of the city!"

"That would be difficult." Nestor smiled obsequiously. "Cleansing the streets drained me, and it shall take awhile before my strength is again gathered. And . . ."

"What?" Talan snarled.

"Do I sweep the walls," Nestor said, "then I must sweep them—clean of attackers and defenders, both. Better to trust in your own men. Else there'll be none left to defend you."

"By all the gods!" Talan fumbled for his clothes; it was hard to dress without the aid of servants. "You promised me victory, and I find all Chorym raised against me." He danced on one foot as he tugged on his undergarments. "Is your cursed sister working her magic better than you? Is Ellyn working against me?"

The Vachyn nodded sullenly.

"What?" Talan stumbled as he tugged on a boot, falling back across the bed. Supine, he glowered at the sorcerer. "You told me they were slain."

"I thought they were." Nestor's voice was a snarl of pure rage. "The gods know they should be."

He flung a linen shirt at Talan. The Lord of Danant and Chaldor pulled the garment on and gaped at the Vachyn. "But?"

"Magic's broken the citadel wall and let in your enemies. And, listen . . ." Talan cocked his head. He heard shouting, the clamor of battle, a steady thumping sound. "They bring a battering ram against the gate," Nestor said.

"Highlanders, and citizens and Hel's Town pirates!" Talan laced his linen and began to struggle into his armor. "Help me, damn you! How can I get this fixed alone?"

Nestor helped him latch up his gear. "You've still men enough to hold the palace," he said.

"With them over the walls?" Talan stabbed a thumb at the window. "With them already inside?"

"Only a handful." Nestor flung the windows open and pointed a finger. A man stood on the battlements, nursing a wound. He wore the accoutrements of a pirate. The Vachyn spoke softly and the man screamed, hurled back by an unseen blast that pitched him over the ramparts as flame burst from his chest. "I can slay them one by one."

"Then do it," Talan snapped.

"But not in numbers, and best you be seen." Nestor latched Talan's breastplate. "You are, after all, the Lord of Chaldor. You should be visible, else you lose your people's trust."

"And I *can* defeat them?"

"With my aid? Of course."

Talan belted on his sword and set his golden helmet in place. "I trust you speak the truth, Nestor."

The Vachyn smiled readily. "What else, my lord?"

Kerid took his pirates along the ramparts, sweeping the battlements clean of Danant men. He'd not seen Highlanders fight before, and he thought they were madmen. They seemed careless of wounds, intent only on victory. Indeed, they vied with his pirates to be first in conflict, as if all that mattered was to reach the gate and open it for their comrades. He swung his own blade well enough, but it was often that he must draw back as some screaming clansmen came past him to thrust one of those long swords into a belly, or charge against a shield and hack into the armor of one of Talan's men. He saw them take arrows in their chests and die charging; or pluck spears from a pierced belly and still run on, some planting the spear in their killer before they submitted to death. He believed them crazed and was glad they fought with him, for else he'd not have reached the gate.

But he did, and Hel's Town pirates and roaring Highlanders fell down on the Danant men behind the portal even as the crossbar and the bolts splintered and the gate fell inward.

I led the way down the narrow stairs to the yard below. Ellyn and Shara were both armored, and I hoped that and our stolen livery would disguise them well enough from the Danant soldiers running in confusion toward the gate that we might enter the main palace building unnoticed. I hoped Talan had despatched all his men to fend off the attack, thus leaving the palace unguarded. I hoped to find him there; he did not seem the kind of man to lead the attack. No less did I hope Shara had regained sufficient strength to face Nestor. I hoped a great deal—so much depended on hope; and was I wrong, then all was lost.

We crossed the yard and Ellyn plucked at my sleeve. "Likely the main doors are guarded; come this way."

I followed her, with Shara grim-faced and weak at my side, to a walled enclosure. Ellyn unlatched a wicket gate that opened on what once had been a pretty garden. Roses still grew there, and fountains played softly, but the roses were crushed now with the bodies of men fallen from the wall, and blood and petals mingled on the colored tiles. I followed Ellyn, my arm supportive about Shara, to an inner door that she opened before I could prevent her, stepping through with drawn sword into a dark, cool gallery. I did not know this part of the palace, and must rely on Ellyn for directions.

She pointed toward three doors at the farther end. "That leads to the servants' quarters; that to the inner palace; that to . . ." She hesitated, her voice faltering. "To my parents' chambers."

Those would, no doubt, be occupied by Talan. But would he be there, or in the main hall? Surely not even such a coward-king would hide in private chambers as his men died. But no less surely would he surround himself with bodyguards. I pointed to the third door. Ellyn nodded and swung it open as I stepped past her with my blade poised.

The chamber beyond was wide and empty, stairs rising to a balcony. I could hear feet pounding, and men shouting. I motioned the two women forward and began to climb the stairs.

Two men in shining armor embossed with the images of snarling lions appeared at the stairs' head. Both carried bared swords, and both glowered at us through the eye slits of their helmets.

"What do you here? Where are you going?"

I had almost forgotten that we wore Danant's livery. "We're hurt," I mumbled, still climbing.

"Then find the main hall. These are our king's chambers."

I grunted and shook my head as if I were befuddled.

"The gods curse you, go back!"

One took a downward step, brandishing his sword as if he'd drive off obstinate swine. I raised my blade and stuck it into his belly, between the jointure of his breastplate and tasset. Behind his helm, his eyes widened in surprise, and he gasped. I turned the blade and saw his fall from nerveless fingers, clattering down the stairs. As I pushed him away, Ellyn ran past me, her blade swinging at the second guardsman. He took her blow on his vambrace and brought his sword around in a sweeping arc that would have severed her head had she not ducked and I continued upward to drive my buckler against his casque and send him staggering back. I swung my sword against his head, and Ellyn moved again, stabbing at his midriff. He deflected her thrust, turning it down between his legs. Ellyn spun, using her blade as a pivot to bring him off-balance, his legs going out from under him so that as he fell I was able to stab him through the back of the neck and kill him before he could cry out.

Ellyn smiled at me. "You taught me well, Guardian."

I nodded and held out a hand to Shara.

She shook her head and found the upper stairs unaided.
"There's enough killing," she said softly. "Do we find my
brother and Talan, and end this slaughter?"

I felt a little guilty. I cannot deny that I felt the battle
madness on me, and should have cheerfully faced all Talan
might send at me, laughing as my sword was blooded. But
she was right; too many died in this venture, and we must
still find and slay our real enemies. I bowed my head and
wiped my blade clean and we went on our way.

I began to recognize it now. A door granted us egress
into a gallery that looked down onto the rose garden. Beyond lay those chambers where Ryadne had spoken to me—
so long ago, it seemed—and past them, the inner sanctums
that had once belonged to Andur and his queen.

We crossed the gallery at a run and halted at a door inlaid with ivory and metalwork in bas-relief.

"Is he here," Ellyn said, "he'll be past this door. And I'll
not face him in his filthy colors."

She tugged off the Danant livery. After a moment, I did
the same, baring my Devyn plaid.

Shara said, "Why not?" And tossed the bloodied cloth
away.

Then Ellyn took the the door latch and flung the portal
open as I charged through.

Talan and Nestor stared in surprise as I entered.

The walls were cleansed of Danant soldiers now, and the gate
open. Highlanders and citizens and Haldur's men came flooding through as the Hel's Town pirates and the clansmen swept
down to catch the defenders between two terrible forces.

The Danant men fell back and were caught like metal
betwixt hammer and anvil. They were beaten back across the
yards of the citadel, and those who did not die under the
suicidal assault threw down their swords and begged for
mercy.

There was little to be found. The Highlanders were

battle-crazed, and did a man hold a sword, he was fair game. Haldur's men had old scores to settle, and were they robbed of their right hands, still they could wield a blade in the other. And the men and women of Chorym, who fought with kitchen knives and pots and pans, had the years of Talan's oppression to avenge, and the deaths of their king and queen. The only ones who held back were the Hel's Town pirates. They were accustomed to taking boats and accepting surrender, and Kerid—who had learned much since Andur died—stood back in horror as the slaughter went on.

"I was lucky," he said to Mother Hel.

"How so?" She placed a lace handkerchief scented with flowers against her nose. Her own guard stood watchful around them: a wall of spears and fish-mail armor. "Do you not approve?"

"Of this?" Kerid gestured at the killing and shook his head. "No."

"But you'd see Ellyn given her throne."

"Yes," he said, tensing as the fighting came closer and the guard leveled their spears. Wincing as a Danant man was skewered and tossed aside; as a clansman staggered past with both hands pressed to where his face had been before a sword carved it away. A woman ran by holding her left ear and shouting for a healer. "But this is . . . slaughter. It's different on the river—that's honest fighting."

"They've debts to pay," the Mother said. "Talan imposed his rule on Chaldor unfairly. He employed the Vachyn sorcerer. He used might that Andur—Chaldor—would not, and now he reaps the harvest of his seeding."

"Even so." Kerid shrugged as a Danant soldier staggered past pursued by three women and an old man who beat his armor with brooms and a sickle. "This is . . . unpleasant. It's not . . ." He stopped speaking as the soldier fell down and screamed as the sickle was drawn across his throat. The sickle was blunt and the soldier took a long time dying.

"It's warfare," the Mother said. "It's win or lose. What other way is there?"

Talan wore wondrous armor. I had not seen such fanciful work, all gold and shining—not plated like that of the guardsmen I'd slain, but solid gold, worked with jewels, and etched with snarling lions' heads on the breastplate and the greaves and the pauldrons. He was helmed, and that casque was a roaring lion, its jaws embracing his face, paws cupping his gaping jaw. It shone in the dawn sun, which now rose and spread its light over Chorym, shining in through the windows so that the gold glittered and the embossed jewels sparkled like rainbows. I thought it armor better fitted for the parade ground than real battle.

He stared at us, a hand on the bejeweled hilt of his long sword.

Beside him stood a man with long, oily hair and nails to match. His face was aquiline and sallow, as if he spent too long a time in communication with darkness. He wore a black robe, and even before I heard Shara say his name, I knew him for the Vachyn sorcerer—Nestor.

I felt no choice. I knew that Nestor's magic could slay me on a heartbeat, so I charged.

I felt that strange difference in the air as I attacked. I knew that magic was summoned up, and that I might well be slain before I took another step. But I had no choice. I was, in my blood and bones, in the last breaths of my dying, a Highlander. Our way in battle was the Highland charge, and I was sworn to deliver Ellyn her throne and pledged by my own desire to save Shara.

I swung my blade at Nestor.

Had he been any ordinary man, I'd have taken his head off with that sweep. But he was not, and so I felt my sword bounce as if from a buckler of impermeable steel.

I saw him smile and begin to mouth words and shape figures in the lightening air.

Then Shara spoke, and his hands faltered, and he said, "So, sister, you'd think to defeat me?"

Shara said, "I'd rid the world of you. Who is the stronger, brother? You with your Vachyn magicks, or I?"

Nestor said, *"Me!"*

Ellyn screamed, "You slew my father! You slew my mother!"

And Nestor laughed and pointed a finger that sent her stumbling back. I watched her tumble away and heard Nestor laugh again.

"An apprentice, sister? A little, weak apprentice to follow your sad betrayal? What talent does she own? Enough to defeat *me*?"

I was stretched on the floor. My bones felt as if horses had ridden over them. Every wound I'd ever taken hurt. My knee ached. I felt as if blood burst afresh from every cut, and I was weak.

I turned my head and saw Ellyn slumped against the far wall. I saw Shara, unsteady on her feet but still defiant, facing Nestor.

"You're beaten, *brother*. Your puppet king is beaten! Chorym and all Chaldor is ours now, and you've lost."

Nestor said, *"No!"* And pointed a dirty-nailed hand at Shara.

I felt that magical power stir again, and forced myself up on hands and knees.

Talan stood staring at Nestor and Shara as I drove my blade into his groin, beneath the tasset. He wore mail under the gold, but I found the strength to thrust through the metal, and he was too fascinated with the magical duet to deflect my blow. He shrieked as my point went in, and again as I turned the steel to carve out his manhood and deliver his entrails to the floor. I withdrew my blade as he fell down. He was all bloody, and screaming, and I stabbed again, into his throat so that his wailing ended and he could not decide which wound to hold. He rolled in agony as his blood spilled out over his golden armor, and he died.

And Nestor cursed and flung his magic against Shara,

who flung her own magic back, so that the air crackled as if two storms confronted one another, lightning against lightning. The chamber filled with thunder and I was deafened. I felt apart, as if the battle I witnessed was a dream. Save it was the woman I loved who fought, and so I struggled to wake, but could not, for all my last energies had been consumed.

Save . . .

I saw Ellyn slumped supine as Shara and Nestor faced one another, the air crackling, sparking, as they matched their magicks. I saw all we'd fought for lost did Shara lose this battle. I tasted blood in my mouth as I fought the power of the Vachyn's foul spell and summoned the waning remnants of my strength to lift my sword and cut at his heel.

It was a sorry stab. A Highlander would have laughed and taken off my hand and slain me. It did little more than prick him, but he shrieked as if it were some great wound, and danced away.

And as he did, Shara smiled and shaped more movements in the air that sent him lurching farther back. I dropped my blade. It felt too heavy, and so I drew my knife and crawled after the Vachyn.

Who scowled and pointed a finger that sent me tumbling across the floor as if a wind caught me up and swept me away even as lightning pierced my chest and should have slain me.

But I had died before, so I lifted my head, for all it ached as if drums beat inside my skull and threatened to burst out my eyes, and laughed at Nestor and said—not believing it—"You cannot kill me. Or her."

And Nestor said, "*No!* This cannot be!"

And as he was distracted, Shara summoned up her magicks and sent a bolt of light into him that sent him staggering, his robe burning, flames curling around his face.

He flung back power that she deflected, returning her own so that the chamber flickered and shone with alternating brilliance, and Nestor retreated.

I could no longer move. I felt as if all the blood were drained from my body, as if fire ran through the hollow parts of my bones and filled my lungs with flame. My muscles were jelly and I gasped for want of cooling breath and struggled helplessly to rise, to go to Shara's aid. I saw tapestries burning, and a window explode in glittering shards as magic was flung against magic. Chairs took flame and filled the room with choking smoke. I saw Nestor glance toward a door that was instantly ablaze as Shara sent a spell against the wood to block his escape. Metal fitments melted and ran; a carpet burned. I dragged my head around to find Ellyn, and saw her rubbing at her eyes, a thin spilling of blood painting her cheek where she'd struck the wall. I concentrated all my will as I crawled toward her.

Then Shara cried out and I gasped as I saw her wreathed in fire. Then gasped again, in relief, as the flames died and she stood, albeit unsteady, as she pointed a finger at Nestor and sent him staggering.

He landed against a wall where a tapestry depicting a hunting scene burned, and yelped like a struck dog as sparks fell on him and his weight brought the hanging down in flaming ruin about his body.

He began to scream, flailing beneath the burning cloth, and Shara sagged back as if all her strength, all her power, were gone. Her face was drained and flushed, feverish, her eyes wide as her jaw tensed over gritted teeth. I reached Ellyn—the gods alone knew how, for I was weaker than a newborn babe—and touched her hand.

"Help her!" Was that my voice, that faint and grating plea? "Help her for the gods' sake. For Chaldor!"

Ellyn groaned and spat blood onto the scorched floor. She braced her legs and pushed upright, leaning against the wall, ignoring the sparks that fell on her. Then she tottered on unsteady legs to Shara's side and put an arm around the older woman. Shara clutched at her, the one leaning against the other. I was not sure who supported whom, but together they stood upright and faced Nestor.

Who flung off the burning tapestry and snarled like a
rabid dog cornered by the catchers.

"You've not won yet, sister!"

He raised hands that were blistered and blackened as over-
roasted meat and thrust them out as he began to voice a spell.

Shara said, "Do as I do. Remember what I've taught you,"
and Ellyn nodded and they spoke together, and thrust out the
hands they did not use to support one another toward Nestor.

It was as if two storms met, all the power of the lightning and the thunder contained within the chamber. What
windows were still left intact exploded in flashes of splinter-
ing, melted glass and fragments of wood and stone. There
was a terrible heat. I felt my hair singed, and saw sections of
wall fall free, plaster and stone tumbling in a blazing rain.
Fire licked across the ceiling and burning dust fell over me
in lung-searing clouds. Chairs and tables were consumed in
an instant, falling in thick waves of ashes as I choked and
believed that I must surely die again. And this time not rise.

My eyes were clogged, thick with ashes, but through
the tears and the pain I saw Nestor falter. I was deafened by
the thunder and dazzled by the light, but I saw Shara and Ellyn speak again, and again extend their hands. And then
Nestor was wreathed in flame, and stumbled screaming
about the chamber.

I believe I heard his last words: "This shall not end it,
sister! You'll answer to our kin for this! The Vachyn shall
have their revenge!"

Then I could hear no more, for the thunder filled up my
ears and spun my head, and the light dazzled me. But I think
I saw Nestor burn, and I was surely grateful for that as I
watched a blaze of pure brilliance envelop him and sheathe
him in white light, and fade to leave only drifting ashes.

I remember thinking that we'd got our victory. That Ellyn
should gain her rightful throne, and Shara lived. But that was
all dim and distant as I gave way to pain and the Vachyn's
magicks and closed my eyes as I sank back into oblivion.

EPILOGUE

Egor Dival said, "So they're both dead?"

I nodded. "I put my blade into Talan and slew him. Shara and Ellyn destroyed Nestor."

"He had no children," Dival said. "He was the last of the Kedassian line." Then: "I never liked the Vachyn. I argued with Talan against employing him. I'd sooner fight honestly."

I shrugged—which pained my aching shoulders—and asked, "So? What shall you do now?"

"What choice have I?" Dival shrugged in turn, but with less hurt. "You took me prisoner—I'm your captive." He chuckled. "You Highlanders fight well. Far better than Talan or Nestor believed. So, now shall you take off my head?"

I shook mine. "I think it were better we leave you live. Danant shall need a ruler, no?"

He stared at me and asked with mouth agape. "Me?"

"As you say, Talan was the last of the Kedassians. He was not wed—he has no children—so: Who better?"

He stared at me with disbelieving eyes. "You'd not come against Danant? Revenge Andur's death, our invasion? There's no blood feud?"

"Shara advises against it," I said, "and Ellyn agrees.

She'd have you swear treaties, and do you agree, you can go home."

"With all my men who survive?" Dival shaped a sad smile.

"All of them," I said. "Swear fealty to Ellyn—that Danant and Chaldor shall not fight again—and we've peace."

"Why?" he asked. "Talan would have slain you. He'd have taken your head as he did Andur's. He'd have made Ellyn his bride—or slain her. So why?"

"Because you're not Talan," I said. "Because you don't listen to Vachyn whisperings. Because you're a warrior, and I can trust that. Trust your word."

"And Ellyn?"

"Do you swear to her," I said, "she'll believe you. Should she not?"

"No." Egor Dival shook his head. "Do I give my word, I keep it."

"And shall you?"

He said, "Yes!"

Nassim spat liquid tobacco over flagstones already stained with blood. Smoke still drifted from the palace, where shattered windows gaped like the eyes of watchful skulls. Bodies littered the yard, joined by those dragged from the halls. Outside the city, funeral pyres spread smoke across the autumn sky. Crows and ravens gathered along the walls, waiting eagerly for the feasting. He wiped his sword clean and looked to Kerid and the Mother.

"Was it worth it? We've given Ellyn back her throne and slain a Vachyn sorcerer. But what shall the Vachyn do now?"

"We had no other choice," Kerid said. "I gave Gailard my word."

Mother Hel said, "The Vachyn would have looked to conquer Hel's Town in time. Perhaps now they've learned a lesson."

Nassim cut a fresh plug and set it in his mouth. Then through his chewing asked, "Think you so? Or have we only annoyed them? So that they'll come harder against Hel's Town?"

"We won a great victory," Kerid said. "The gods know, Danant retreats, and Chaldor's safe. Talan's dead, and his Vachyn with him. What more could you ask?"

Nassim shrugged and spat out more tobacco, eliciting a frown from the Mother.

She said, "There's talk of peace now. Gailard persuades Egor Dival to swear loyalty to Chaldor, and I believe the old man will agree."

"Then we'll not be able to take Danant's vessels." Nassim sighed. "I was enjoying this war."

"There shall be others," Kerid said. "Who knows what the Vachyn sorcerers will do?"

"There's that," Nassim allowed.

"I hope not," the Mother said. "War with the Vachyn? Best hope we become . . ." She lost her words, staring at Kerid. "That would be a terrible war, no?"

Kerid glanced at Nassim and grinned.

"Surely terrible, Mother."

Ellyn accepted the chieftains in the throne room of the palace. Her grandfather ducked his knee and swore the fealty of the Dur. Jaime promised the loyalty of the Arran. I swore that the Devyn would always support her. Then Roark pledged the Quan and asked, in front of us all, that she marry him.

She blushed and hesitated a moment before she said, "Yes," and the chamber rang with cheers, and young Roark blushed red as his bride-to-be.

Then Ellyn looked to me and asked, "Shall you command my army, Gailard? Shall you still be my guardian?"

I smiled and took Shara's hand as I shook my head. "I shall always be your guardian, do you ask me. But com-

mand of the army . . . no. I've a bellyful of fighting, and I'd
go with Shara back to her broch." I thought to add, "With
your leave, my queen."

"You shall go where you will." She frowned a moment,
but Roark was at her side and the frown did not last long.
"But might I . . . *we* . . . visit you there?"

"Of course," Shara said. "And we'll not leave for a
while. There's much I'd still teach you."

"My thanks." Ellyn smiled and nodded. "For everything. But"—she looked to me—"if not you, then who shall
command my army? Under my husband, of course?"

"Haldur." I pushed him forward. "He's loyal and brave,
and the soldiers know him."

"Shall you?" she asked.

Haldur bent his knee. "I am at my queen's command."

"Then that's settled." She beamed. "And Kerid—shall
you lead my navy?"

"By your leave, no." Kerid shook his head. At his side,
Mother Hel smiled calmly. "I'd go back to Hel's Town."

"But know," the Mother said, "that so long as my pirates sail the river, Chaldor's shores and ships are safe. And
do you need us again, we are at your beck."

"And my newfound allies?" Ellyn looked to where
Egor Dival stood. "Shall they be safe?" By the gods, she
learned statecraft readily as she had swordwork.

"Your friends are mine," the Mother said.

"Excellent. But who shall command my boats? I doubt
the Vachyn will leave us alone for long, and whilst we feel
secure on land, there's the question of the river."

"Might I suggest a name?" Kerid asked. "He's a fine
sailor, and brave. And he's proven his worth."

Ellyn nodded regally. Was this the petulant child I'd
taken out from Chorym?

"I would suggest," Kerid said, "that you make Nassim
commander of your fleet."

There came a choking sound then, and Nassim's face

went pale as he swallowed his plug. He began to back away, but Mother Hel gestured and four of her fish-mailed guardsmen surrounded Nassim and herded him forward.

"Shall you accept this commission?" Ellyn asked. "Be my commander on the Durrakym?"

Nassim belched, wiping at his stained mouth. Kerid nudged him in the ribs; the Mother studied him with speculative eyes. He looked from one to the other, then at Ellyn.

"Me? Command your navy?"

"Yes," Ellyn said. "You. Do my loyal allies name you, then I'd have you lead my navy."

Nassim pursed his lips, ready to spit, then thought better of it and ducked his head. "I am honored, my queen."

Ellyn smiled. "Then we need to discuss the substance of our fleet."

I saw Mother Hel frown and Kerid begin to grin. I found it hard to stifle my own laughter—the gods knew, but this child learned fast.

"How do you mean?" Nassim asked.

"There are, I believe, numerous craft amongst your fleet that were originally Chaldor's." Ellyn favored the Mother with a beam. "Indeed, I understand that Kerid first came to you with Chaldor vessels. Shall you give those back?"

I watched the Mother's lovely face darken. Kerid whispered in her ear, and her expression grew bright as she laughed. "Those and more," she promised. "Enough you'll own a real navy for Nassim to command."

"My thanks," Ellyn said graciously. "Now shall we celebrate our victory?"

"It were best," Shara said, "that you see to your city first."

I said, "Chorym's been sore hurt, and her citizens with her. See to them, eh? Then we'll celebrate."

Ellyn nodded, taking Roark's hand. "You're right. My joy makes me forgetful. Let's to it then."

So we did not celebrate our victory until some measure of order was restored to Chorym. We saw Egor Dival gone with all that was left of Danant's army, shipped across the Durrakym in Nassim's boats after the treaty was signed. Then we set to housing all those left homeless by Talan and Nestor, and set to rebuilding the ravaged city. It was only when that work was begun, and we knew none would starve, that we had our victory feast.

Ellyn took the head of the table as befit her new-won status. Roark sat puppy-eyed on her right hand, I to her left. An honorable position that—the place of the shield-bearer, the Guardian—and Shara was to my left. Kerid and Mother Hel, Nassim, Mattich, and the rest sat down the length of the long table. We ate well, and drank better, and I knew that I sat amongst true friends.

Even so it was a night not empty of sadness. Come the morning, the Highlanders would depart—go back to their wives and children, and I knew I'd not see them in a while. Kerid and the Mother would set sail for Hel's Town, and Ellyn was preoccupied with her queenly duties and Roark. I felt that a chapter of my life had ended, and even as I celebrated that ending, I felt a regret that I must bid these friends farewell.

And, also, a great anticipation. After all, Talan was defeated and slain, Chorym retaken and Ellyn on her throne. I had fulfilled all my promises—served out Andur's geas, and Ryadne's. It seemed to me a time when I might look forward to the settling of those other promises exchanged with Shara.

I took her hand, and she smiled at me.

I was about to speak when Ellyn said, "Do you forgive me, but I am mightily tired. I'd find my bed, lest I be asleep when our Highlander allies depart."

She smiled at Roark as she finished, and I thought that it had been better put "our bed."

Mattich roared laughter, lofting a goblet that splashed

wine over his shirtfront, and rose to toast his granddaughter and her consort.

"Shall I lead the Quan home, Roark? For I suspect you'll be otherwise occupied."

Roark blushed. Ellyn said with massive grace. "My husband shall decide that, Grandfather. But it might well be awhile before he leaves."

I felt Shara's hand close tight on mine as they quit the room.

"I'd also to bed." Then she added, "Ours."

We lay together under silk sheets. The moon shone in through the window of our chamber and lit the room with silver light that set sparks to dancing in Shara's raven hair, outlined the wondrous planes of her beautiful face. From outside came the sounds of celebration—the laughter of folk freed from oppression echoing from Chorym's streets. I was weary with our lovemaking. It had been even better than I had dared hope, and I was drained, and happy and fulfilled.

She rose above me, leaning on an elbow as she touched my face.

"Was it worth it, Gailard? Was it worth all the suffering?"

I paused a moment. Then said, "The war? The killing? Yes, surely it was. Else Talan would rule here, and heed the Vachyn. And had they won I'd not have you."

She laughed and fell against me, and her mouth was on mine, and my lips replied, and . . .

We woke barely in time to bid our friends farewell.

"We must be gone," Kerid said. He smiled awkwardly. "Neither the Mother or I feel happy on land."

"We'd go back to the river," Mother Hel said. "Back to Hel's Town."

They waved their farewells and set out down the Coast Road to Antium, where the boats waited.

Along the way Kerid asked her, for the first time, for it was the first he dared, "What *is* your real name?"

She smiled and said, "Does it matter?"

He shrugged. "I suppose not. But . . ."

She said, "Miranda." Then she drew the curtains of her palanquin closed, and him closer.

The Hel's Town pirates marched away to the river; the clans rode westward. From the walls and streets of Chorym there came the healthy sounds of rebuilding as the walls and the houses were raised again. The sun shone bright and a cool breeze blew, lofting swallows not yet gone south over the city.

I rested against a parapet not shattered by Vachyn fire or our attack and stared at the farmlands beyond. I felt exalted and weary. Passionate and young and old, all at the same time. I felt that the world had shifted, and I had played some part in that. And I had no idea what the future might hold.

Ellyn was with me. Shara was occupied below, and Roark was gone to see his clansmen off, so we were alone— there was no longer any need for the queen of Chaldor to walk abroad with a guard.

"It was no easy thing," she said.

I looked at her, and shook my head. I was unsure of what she spoke.

"I did not like you," she said. "Not at first. But then I learned that I must look beyond the obvious. Look at the truth. Do you forgive me, Gailard?"

"For what?" I asked.

"For all the insults I gave you," she said.

I felt the wind on my face and chuckled. "You've learned since then to be a queen. And I believe you shall be a very great queen. You'll serve Chaldor well."

"I hope so," she said.

"And if you do not," I said, "I shall set you over my knee and deliver you the spanking you deserve."

She stared at me awhile. "You would, too."

I said, "Yes."

And we both laughed, and she took my hand and we walked away.

And so it was settled, and what the writers of the history books chose to call the First Vachyn War was ended, and for Chaldor there began a time of peace and plenty that surpassed even Andur's reign.

Egor Dival was installed on Danant's throne and the two realms swore treaties of lasting peace that endure to this day. Ellyn wed Roark and bound the Highlands to Chaldor, and there were always clansmen amongst Ellyn's honor guard from that day on. Kerid and Mother Hel returned to the islands, but no Hel's Town pirate ever again preyed on the boats of Chaldor or Danant.

And Shara and I commenced that journey that lasted the rest of our lives. But that is another story.

ABOUT THE AUTHOR

ANGUS WELLS was born in a small village in Kent, England. He has worked as a publicist and as a science fiction and fantasy editor. He now writes full time, and is the author of The Books of the Kingdoms (*Wrath of Ashar*, *The Usurper*, *The Way Beneath*) and The Godwars (*Forbidden Magic*, *Dark Magic*, *Wild Magic*). *Lords of the Sky,* his first stand-alone novel, debuted in trade paperback in October of 1994, and was followed by the two-book Exiles Saga: *Exile's Children* and *Exile's Challenge*. He lives in Nottingham with his dog, Elmore.